School Scandalle

By

Marla Weiss

authorHOUSE™

1663 LIBERTY DRIVE, SUITE 200
BLOOMINGTON, INDIANA 47403
(800) 839-8640
WWW.AUTHORHOUSE.COM

This novel is dedicated to all seeking truth about education.

First published by AuthorHouse 11/30/04

ISBN: 1-4208-0153-8 (sc)

Library of Congress Control Number: 2004097225

Printed in the United States of America
Bloomington, Indiana

This book is printed on acid-free paper.

Royalties from this novel go to the nonprofit Jack Shapiro Mathematics Education Foundation, Inc. to improve math education. Queries should be e-mailed to jshapmathed@comcast.net.

Epigraph quotation reprinted by permission

Cover art and design by Valerie Weiss, valmedart@earthlink.net

"I gave a speech tonight and they called me *the dean of American editors*," he explained. "When they call you the dean, that means you're through."

"Oh, Daddy, that doesn't mean you're through," she objected. "It just means you've reached the top."

"No," Perkins said flatly. "It means you're through."

Max Perkins: Editor of Genius
A. Scott Berg
E. P. Dutton, 1978

1. First Betrayal

I have often thought that I enjoy the perfect employer. For two years I have taught math and computer science at Merritt Country Day School in Palm Beach, Florida—a small, private institution for academically talented students. The headmaster, Charles Long, could be called the ultimate personification of charisma. As a prospective female parent said, "I don't know if this school will work for my son, but the interview I had with the headmaster was one of the best hours of my life." Conceptually, he could portray an ethereal vision of John Harvard in a dedicated teacher's dream. Practically, he has given me both full reign over rigorous curriculum and total support for high standards. So, I was stunned when Charlotte Merritt, young, beautiful, second, and current wife of the founder and board chairman of the school, warned, "Molly, don't trust Charles. Some day he will betray you."

I had heard the story of how Charles had *betrayed* Charlotte during the summer. In fact, the bizarre tale was the buzz at most establishments frequented by South Ocean Boulevard residents. She was away visiting family when her husband, handsomely gray and richly green Parke Merritt, dined one night with Charles Long— something the two men had done frequently for the past several years. Parke apparently felt that treating Charles to fine food, in a man-to-man situation, was a more subtle way to wield influence than making demands in Charles's office. Because Charles lacked cooking concepts but relished gourmet fare and because Mrs. Long's best creation would lose in a contest to a sandwich of orange, plastic-wrapped sliced cheese with iceberg lettuce and yellow mustard on packaged white bread, Parke thought he had the right approach.

Still, the private settings purported by many Worth Avenue bistros were more image than substance, making the Merritt-Long tête-à-têtes commonly known.

Conversation at that fateful dinner, rather than focusing on academics, revolved around a particular annoyance of private school education—fundraising. And the more difficult the prospects became, the more alcohol Parke Merritt consumed. The evening, however, was not the typical board-chairman-has-too-much-wine-and-complains-about-his-volunteering type of event. No, the situation was much worse and considerably more dramatic. The nightcap occurred at the Merritt Trump Tower penthouse where Charles had to haul Parke home. After reaching into Parke's pocket for the keys and opening the impressive door, Charles used all his strength to drag his boss into the bedroom and onto the bed. There, Mr. Merritt passed out.

Relieved of Parke's weight, Charles noticed the extreme clutter. He proceeded to the kitchen for water but stopped, eyes popping, when he saw a similar state of disarray throughout the apartment. Numerous household items, a wide range of clothes, and goods still possessing the original tickets abounded, covering furniture, floors, and shelves—stacked over, under, and around. Drunk Mr. Merritt could not protect his dear wife from embarrassment. Needing to sleep off his state, he was unaware of Charles's detailed inspection of Charlotte's belongings.

The misfortune was compounded because Charles did not keep this horrific evening a secret. In fact, I later learned, he had told almost everyone he saw over the summer. I had been teaching at Johns Hopkins University in its gifted education program—Center for Talented Youth—as well as visiting my sister Grace in D.C. When I returned to school for some preliminary work, Charles recounted the story to me with considerable zest.

"Ticketed dresses were strewn across the sofa in size four. Similar dresses lay over a chair in size eight. And again in size twelve on a table," Charles described.

"Well, at least she bought multiples of four and not two," I offered.

"The apartment was a mammoth mess, and you are making math jokes, Molly," Charles protested.

"I'm sorry," I stated quietly, reflecting that Charles represented Charlotte not merely as one who engaged in excessive shopping. More significantly and tragically, Charles's words suggested a spoiled, manic woman. Yet, this depiction was definitely not the stylish, dynamic, intelligent, sensitive Charlotte Merritt I knew. Was the discrepancy an example of a man misunderstanding a woman or an intruder misrepresenting a scene?

"And one apartment wall was covered with framed photographs of the three of them—Charlotte, Parke, and Stephanie. Pictures in front of their building. Pictures at the pool. Pictures on Worth Avenue. Pictures on vacation. Pictures in formal attire. . . ."

"Well, they are a family." Tired of hearing the word *pictures*, I cut Charles off. Was Charles perhaps envious of Charlotte?

At that moment, I thought I was among a few exclusive recipients of this scandalous news because Charles often confided to me the school's most intimate tales. Indeed, Charles fancied pronouncing *scandal* with the second syllable having both an open letter *a* and the accent as if the word were French and incorrectly spelled *scandalle*. However, not long after, I received a call from the victim herself, telling me of her humiliation and assessment that, based on all the meddlesome calls and suspicious looks she had received, Charles had told many in the school community. From them, the tale spread to the golf, tennis, dining, and yachting club crowds.

Why does gossip attract even the most professional of people? In the case of Charles's tattling on this couple, regardless of their generosity of time and money in founding the school, they had pushed Charles too frequently with their advice and demands couched in gifts and dinners. Charles had told me confidentially that despite the appearance of great friendship, Mr. and Mrs. Merritt were actually often an annoyance to him.

I was certainly moved by Charlotte's story. Though my mind whirled with worries, especially over a strained Merritt-Long relationship, Charlotte had a credible explanation. Many of the possessions, she said, were an accumulation of Christmas gifts over the years from her very large family. She neither wanted the items nor knew what to do with them. As she said, "How do you incorporate fifty new things into an already full household each year?" Her traditional relatives were not willing to adopt a planned, single-gift exchange policy. She was also of the mindset that being prepared by having the right dress or gift at home ahead of time for future occasions was far superior to the pressure of last minute shopping. As a working mother, I certainly engaged in the same efficiency. And, finally, the variety of clothing sizes resulted from frustrating but common female weight gain and purchases to motivate successful diets. She could hardly be ruled guilty on that charge without incriminating thousands of other women. In sum, due to the combination of her bestowals, inclinations, and aspirations, she had amassed an overwhelming quantity of belongings—not, however, singly or collectively beyond the scope of her wealth. Unfortunately, while cleaning and organizing these countless items, including bundling many for charity, she was suddenly called away to a family emergency, leaving the staggering disarray in full sight— unpredictably for Charles Long to discover.

Clearly, Charles had betrayed her, but the matter was unrelated to me. This contretemps should have been a private incident for the Merritts. Thus, I was totally unprepared for Charlotte's frightening, unassociated admonition that Charles would betray me also.

My thoughts immediately shifted to contemplating her caution. Surely, Charlotte had known Charles for more years than I had. Was she aware of something in his character that I had missed? She was definitely insightful. If she were correct, then how would he betray me? An academic betrayal was out of the question—Charles shared my passion for excellence in education, my vision for the school, and my determination for success.

Sexual harassment was the only plausible option, I concluded. In the 1970s at Harvard I acquired almost equal education in that particular political predicament as in mathematics. Male professors were empowered by an abundance of desire while female graduate students were engulfed by an absence of recourse. I could prevent a major incident with Charles Long, I judged, by being alert. I certainly knew the warning signs of sexual harassment well. On the other hand, maybe Charlotte Merritt was wrong.

Charles not only was my employer but also in many ways had become my best friend. I talked to him daily or weekly more than I did any other person except for my husband and children. School was intense, and conversations with him were vitally important for confirming the management of situations and advancing the delivery of knowledge. I thought that our friendship based on professional respect, personal integrity, and prolific effort was solid.

So, somewhat nervous and watchful, I began my third year at the school trying to repress the warning attached to Charles's first betrayal. But then I recalled how I had met Charles.

2. First Interview

Several years ago, my husband Vernon Melrose, a financial specialist, and I decided to leave Manhattan—its cold, crime, and crowds—for a warmer, cleaner, smaller city. We relocated when the offer arrived for Vernon to manage the Palm Beach office of Grey Parent Eastern Trust, a century old, nationally established private bank. Having worked intensely as a computer programmer, I was also ready for a change. We thought that growing up in the sunshine would be good for our toddler son, Blane, and our infant daughter, Mimi. Yet, the move meant fewer career opportunities for me. At first I had been happy caring for our children, remodeling a house, teaching math and computer science part-time at Palm Beach Community College, volunteering for the city's plethora of nonprofit organizations, and taking occasional courses of interest. While these activities seemed substantial in turn, after time they were either routine or complete. My life became quiet, and I wanted more—not leisure and recreation but productivity and intellectualism.

One fateful summer day I tackled the *Palm Beach Post* classified section—starvation thin compared with that of *The New York Times*. My eye caught one ad: *Computer teacher wanted at Merritt Country Day*. I hesitated immediately. *Computer* teacher was incorrect terminology—*computer science* would have been proper. A person does not teach *computer*, a physical object—a person teaches *computer science*, an academic subject. Though this misuse of terminology was common, I wondered whether MCD's careless text was a result of shortening the ad to save money, a sign of sloppiness among those in command, or a lack of computer science knowledge.

Still, I called for an interview appointment. "Four o'clock tomorrow," the receptionist said aloofly.

The next afternoon I dressed in a purple linen skirt and white cotton sweater similar to what I had worn at my dissertation defense about a decade ago. The outfit was casual, but I was comfortable in it. As I drove to MCD, I watched the odometer increase steadily—twelve miles was the final outcome. I contemplated whether the job would be worth the trip because I enjoyed driving as little as possible. We hadn't even owned a car until our move.

Although I had heard considerable tales about Merritt Country Day, I had never visited before. The school was small, only offering grades pre-kindergarten through eight. The campus, dozens of acres in size, looked like a rural convention center with sparse, modest buildings. Each was one or two stories, covered with white stucco, and roofed in thick, gray shingle. First-floor classrooms opened directly to the landscaped outside, while second-floor doors faced stylishly on balustraded balconies. Windows were plentiful, bringing natural light into the classrooms. Thick hibiscus bushes with yellow blooms adorned areas of well-groomed grass.

The buildings were connected by covered walkways in a rectangular grid. However, one diagonal path led from the parking lot to the office. Beginning this distinctive approach was a large, stone statue of the school's mascot—a majestic fish, painted silver and yellow, perched atop a mottled gray, granite rectangular prism. A plaque stated: *Merritt Country Day School, Home of the Snooks*.

I forced my mid-heeled feet to tread quietly as I made my way up the oblique walk. I looked into the windows of the classroom next to MCD's front door. The computer lab, I noticed—with unique tables and a peculiar arrangement of hardware.

Then, my mind asked one question: Was this school the place for me? Now, my mind pounded with similar intensity: Will Charles betray me?

The elderly receptionist, who would have been attractive had she smiled, greeted me even more reservedly than on the phone. "Hello, Dr. Kelman. I'm Priscilla," she stated. "Sorry, but your appointment is postponed. Mr. Long has been called into an emergency board meeting. Would you like to wait or come back tomorrow?"

I was not happy about driving a twenty-four-mile round trip for nothing. "How long would I have to wait?" I asked, staring at her full head of short, gray curls while averting her stern gaze.

"At least an hour," she replied.

"Please inform Mr. Long that I will be back in one hour." I followed the same diagonal path back, this time with a distasteful question in my mind: Did the headmaster commonly disregard appointments? I left for the closest Publix supermarket in search of one hour's worth of non-perishables. The chain's slogan, *Where shopping is a pleasure*, did not befit the moment.

Upon returning to school, again passing the snook and marching diagonally, I entered the office and found the receptionist gone for the day. Unintelligible voices came from beyond. As I waited, I glanced at the material on the coffee table—school yearbooks, brochures, and the like. I wondered if the material contained other errors similar to the missing word *science* in the newspaper ad. My experience as a computer programmer had trained me to read everything as the toughest editor, as if in James Bond style I could eject two red pens from my eyes. Indeed, even a comma missing from a computer program would prevent the entire program from executing. Sure enough, a line thanking the PTO for *their* help instead of *its* help was on the last page of the directory. At least finding mistakes kept me entertained while I waited impatiently.

Finally, yet another half-hour later, I heard a loud, distinctive laugh—natural and hearty, as if the respective person enjoyed the act of laughing as much as that which generated the amusement. A tall, striking man walked forward to the reception area—over six feet, I thought. As he moved, his thin yet muscular frame pressed against his clothing, with his long legs appearing particularly gangling. I mused over his last name fitting his body type. When nearer, I guessed that he was in his mid-thirties, close to my age. I noticed his dirty blond, side-parted hair fell into boyish bangs, creating a preppy look. His features were pronounced yet attractive, his appearance groomed yet casual. Astonishingly, his clothes—gray slacks, white shirt, and yellow flowered tie—matched the school colors!

Just then the phone rang. After glancing quickly at the clock, his blue-black eyes stared at me as he spoke into the receiver:

"Yes . . . yeah . . . okay. Well, I really can't talk now. My four o'clock appointment is sitting here, and she doesn't look too happy." I knew for sure then that he was Mr. Long. His unique hair and eye color combination portended a man like no other. Though I was angry at his making me wait, I liked the humor of his third-person remark— referring to me as if I couldn't hear, despite my being right there.

Terminating the phone conversation as quickly as possible, he offered me his hand. "Hello, I'm Charles Long. You must be Molly Kelman. So sorry to keep you waiting." Despite some apprehension on my part, I had no choice but to place my right hand in his and shake politely. I noticed his distinctly broad hand, especially compared to mine, with his fingers as spindly and disjointed as his legs. I also wondered whether he really was sorry.

Mr. Long escorted me a few steps down the main hall into his small, windowless office with a richly framed skylight, very grand compared to the modesty of the room. Two armchairs for guests faced his desk that was covered with numerous, scattered papers. A silk tree was so close to one chair that dense, cascading foliage would certainly drape the occupant's head. Similarly dangerous, the door was so close to the other chair that any swinging motion would undoubtedly hit the occupant's arm. I opted for the latter chair as green had never been my color, safely leaving the door open.

"So, let me give you some background on Merritt Country Day," Mr. Long began, as he settled into his desk chair. I was glad that he began the interview speaking first. "This school was founded by Mr. and Mrs. Parke Merritt. I have been the school's only headmonster." He doesn't even know me, and he's making such a silly joke, I thought. "MCD has had some bumps along the way, but we service our students well, and they are headed for great results. Last year's computer teacher did a fine job, but her husband's company suddenly transferred him out-of-state. Here it is summer, and I am without a teacher. Some of the board members feel that computers should be the hallmark of the school." He paused for just a second, perhaps sensing that his last remark was somewhat detached.

"Do you have a résumé with you?" he asked, again disconnectedly. I handed Mr. Long my papers and watched his intent expression as he

9

scanned. "Well!" was all he said, seemingly moved, without knowing how to comment on my Seven Sister and Harvard credentials.

I seized the opportunity by asking, "Could you describe MCD's computer *science* curriculum to me?"

"We haven't one," Mr. Long remarked, followed by that same laugh I had heard initially. He was oblivious to my correction.

Now I really was baffled. First, he kept me waiting as if he and his board were so highly important. Next, he volunteered that the school had a rocky start. Then, he failed to ask any questions about me. And, finally, he laughed about a lack of curriculum. At least he was up-front, I thought, but strangely unprofessional.

So Mr. Long's candid comment was a chance to sway him by offering my beliefs about computer science education. "The first personal computer debuted in 1977—only ten years ago," I said. "It's still in a problematic position. Schools either have no computers or they don't know what to do with them. Some principals enjoy showing off their hardware as if the computers are museum sculptures—something to be admired but not touched. Schools want to be progressive, yet the computers aren't good for a whole lot now because they come equipped with little except BASIC. The programming language is very important for gifted children—using the hardware to teach thinking, with students taking command of the computer by writing programs. The connection among programming, logic, and mathematics is significant. But even this programming is a stretch compared to larger computers. Apple's first BASIC interpreter actually had bugs in it—a real frustration."

I refastened my gaze on Mr. Long and continued with hardly a breath. "For other students, the key to the computer will be word processing—using the computer to write better. That software also is so underdeveloped right now. Computer assisted instruction? I'm not sure what its future will be either. Children respond better to a person who smiles than to a box that beeps. Plus the technology isn't advanced enough. Have you ever seen a geography program? The graphics are so bad that the New England states are hardly discernible. Children would learn their states better by putting together a puzzle. And, of course, both at school and in the home, whenever that really takes off, we run the risk of the computer turning into a glorified television, with children sitting passively at the machine, learning and accomplishing little to nothing."

Mr. Long cut me off. "Do you always teach this way?" he asked.

"Oh, I'm sorry. I just have definite opinions about computer science education," I replied.

"Yes, enthusiastic ones. But do you?"

"Do I what?" I asked, apologetically.

"Do you teach with long, passionate monologues?" he asked again.

His face showed that although we were strangers, we had connected. He questioned to tease, not to mock. "I teach with a variety of methods—whatever the students need to understand."

"So what kind of curriculum would you propose?"

"Right now, given the current state of hardware and software, I would teach programming at Merritt Country Day. You say that you have all above average to gifted students. Then let them try. I'm not a babysitter. If you want to use the computers for computer-assisted instruction or games, I'm not your candidate. My résumé indicates that I've brought my programming ideas down to as low as third grade successfully. The children programmed static color images and melodies to well-known songs—a slide show effect. The project combined math and logic with art and music. The final presentation was wonderfully received by students, parents, and teachers."

Mr. Long was impressed. He led me to believe that I had the job. He asked me for salary requirements, classroom needs, and time constraints, anticipating fitting my plans into the daily schedule already created. Copying some papers for me to take home generated more characteristic laughing by Mr. Long as he fumbled, trying to use the new copy machine. *Is he fun or crazy?* I mused so intently that for a moment I feared I had spoken the words.

"I'll call you within the week," were his parting words to me.

"Great. Thank you so much," I said, waving good-bye before he could extend his imposing hand. As I walked down the diagonal path for the fourth time that day, numerous, pointed questions hammered in my mind. Why did Mr. Long laugh so markedly? Why did the board need an emergency meeting? Why did no one proof publications better? Why did I seem to control the interview? Why did MCD have no computer science curriculum?

Again, I noted the twelve-mile drive home. The opportunity wasn't perfect, but I decided to accept the job—except the offer never occurred. I waited for a call or letter from Mr. Long, but neither came. The next week, I phoned him—several times, in fact. But, with surprising rudeness, he never returned my calls. Then one day I received a note thanking me for my intellectual insights into *computer* education, sans *science*, and informing me that he could not work the schedule around my needs—certainly a creative way of stating he had hired someone else for the job. I was stunned. Had I not heard or remembered our conversation correctly? I hardly knew how to assess the situation. The rejection troubled me at first, but eventually I dismissed it because I had no attachments to the school.

I interviewed at a few more jobs, but none was right. I didn't want to spend fifty weeks a year programming in a windowless room, dealing with the procrastinations and inefficiencies of others masquerading as crises. As I continued to search for a career direction, unexpectedly, the day at MCD became just my first interview with Charles Long.

3. First Smile

Although Blane and Mimi attended public school, some of the private school gossip reached me in those days prior to my employment at MCD. I had heard that the new *computer* teacher was, in a word, terrible. She was thirty-something, single, and lacked teaching experience as well as childhood knowledge. Her sole qualification, in the loosest sense of the word, was that she was a computer-user—a middle-tier employee from the airline industry. As one mother said, "Miss D. Dottie Jones didn't even know that pre-kindergarten students on the first day of school can't read the software instructions on the monitor." My information source was unaware that I had applied for the same job.

Although I wondered why Mr. Long had hired Miss Jones, I couldn't reach any definite conclusion based on my brief, first-hand experience with the school. Perhaps the headmaster was just inept at hiring. I did realize, though, not to take the institution's self-declared, high academic reputation too seriously if this incident were indicative.

Unexpectedly, in the school year following my interview, I encountered Mr. Long twice. The first time was in the fall at a dinner sponsored by the Harvard Club of Palm Beach County. The group had engineered a coup in getting the university's president, Derek Bok, as the guest speaker. Mr. Long attended as a member's guest and I as an alumna and club officer. Furthermore, I had volunteered to greet and register guests.

The event occurred at the charming Colony Hotel, perfectly located between Worth Avenue and the ocean. The hotel's stately octagonal foyer, complete with black-and-white checked marble floor and Corinthian columns outlining the perimeter, held the reception table. Though I busied myself focused down in search of people's nametags, I curiously looked up just as Mr. Long stood before me. Because I had not noticed his nametag on the table, seeing him was a complete surprise. I said hello and smiled cordially. He replied the same, with only a nod—not a smile.

Fortuitously, just before dinner the club president asked me to substitute for his wife who, assigned to sit next to President Bok at the head table, had become ill. This serendipity granted me a most stimulating evening. Strangely, while dining I felt Mr. Long staring at me rather than at my neighboring dignitary. During the president's speech at the podium, I positively confirmed my intuition by sneaking a few glances at Charles and meeting his eyes before he quickly reverted his gaze. While thinking that Mr. Long and I might speak later, event-end confusion reigned until I noticed he was gone.

The second accidental meeting was many months later, in the early spring of the same school year. While both at a large educational conference at Palm Beach Community College, we encountered each other in a hallway.

"Dr. Kelman, what a nice surprise." Mr. Long showed pleasure addressing me with a capricious use of my formal title. "How are you?" he asked amiably.

"Fine," I answered cautiously. "How are you?"

"Well," he replied. His choice of word seemed non-colloquial, but I subsequently learned of his insistence that *well* was the only correct response to that standard question. "I'd enjoy having you stop by school some time to chat," he continued.

Shock was hardly enough to describe my reaction. "Fine," I repeated. The word was all I could manage to say.

"Until then," he replied, before walking down the hall.

Mr. Long did not know that I would be attending the conference. Moreover, we both could have been present and easily never have met. The building was expansive and the talks plentiful. Immediately, my mind throbbed again with questions. Why was he so casual? If he truly wanted to speak to me, then why hadn't he phoned? Was he a certified procrastinator, did he have an aversion to the telephone, or had something happened recently that he needed my services? What did he wish to discuss?

Getting answers to these questions demanded responding to his offer, but first I felt the need to test him. I waited a few days, but again, he never called. So I phoned the school to make an appointment, despite the icy-voiced receptionist. "Four o'clock tomorrow," Priscilla stated. Feelings of déjà vu were overwhelming. I was tempted to reply, "Are you sure he'll be free?" Politeness made me refrain from asking.

I certainly did not arrive early at MCD the next day. After the receptionist buzzed Mr. Long, she asked me to wait briefly and then politely offered me coffee. I declined because I didn't want to fumble with the cup when Mr. Long offered me his hand. As I sat in the reception area, I partook in some interesting people-watching. All of the students and teachers who passed by looked friendly, studious, and professional.

Within a few minutes, Mr. Long ushered me into his office. Nothing had changed. Again, I opted for the chair away from the tree. Mr. Long closed the door as I raised my arm out of harm's way. Because this visit was at a much earlier time in the day with so many people walking by, I thought about the office's soundproofing, or lack thereof. At least the skylight provided light without losing privacy.

As the three previous times I had seen him, Mr. Long was wearing the same outfit—gray slacks, white shirt, and yellow patterned tie. I noticed that the neckties were different, but I wasn't sure about the other garments. Perhaps he owned multiples of this school uniform.

Mr. Long explained to me that due to his math teacher, Keith Clark, the school attracted many students with exceptional math talent. I had heard of Mr. Clark's fine reputation. In particular, Mr. Long continued saying that the eighth grade contained a group of boys exceptionally brilliant in math. While MCD was a pre-kindergarten through grade eight school, the parents of these boys had asked for a ninth grade as an attempt to keep them with Mr. Clark one more year. The MCD Board of Trustees, viewing this opportunity as a way to advance the school, approved the request, Mr. Long further explained. As he spoke, I again noticed his large hands.

"So you see, Dr. Kelman, . . ."

"You may call me Molly," I interjected.

He smiled at me for the first time, a crooked but kind smile. Instantly, Mr. Long was not only handsome but also engaging. I thought that I was right, that we had somehow connected at the initial interview. But then I reconsidered—that perhaps he related to any woman he chose—though I hardly suspected the power of his magnetism.

"So you see, Molly, I am in need of more faculty for next year. These boys came to me, requesting to learn computer programming. They said that they like Miss Jones, but that they are tired of working with databases about state capitals. They really want to program."

I had learned my lesson from our first chat. I still had not heard a specific job offer, so I countered with, "What exactly are you asking me?"

"I'm asking you to teach programming to the new ninth grade," he explained.

"All of them or just these boys?" I asked.

"All of them. The class will only have twelve students, and they're all capable. As I'm formulating their curriculum, I'd like to pencil in your course as a major subject," Mr. Long commented.

"Driving twenty-four miles each day for one course might not be worth my time, especially if the course happens to be scheduled right in the middle of the day," I replied.

"Keith is going to need some help in the math department as well. The ninth grade geometry gives him a one-course overload plus he wants to split the sixth grade into two sections—advanced and regular. That would make three courses for you at this point— perhaps more as we start to flesh out the exact schedule. I'm sure I can position all of your classes in the morning or in the afternoon," he guaranteed.

Flesh jumped out at me, but I was more wary of his bare promises than his bodily words. "Is this offer definite?" I inquired. I also wanted to ask why he had hired Miss Jones, but the time was not appropriate. I would uncover the reason eventually.

He smiled askew at me again. I focused on his penetrating, midnight blue eyes contrasted by his typically male eyebrows progressing into middle age with coarse, long, curling hairs, noticeable in shades darker than his blond hair and needing trimming to avoid a nefarious look.

"Well, what I'm proposing is that you do some guest teaching here next month—sort of a special computer seminar for these boys on the math team. That way you can check us out to be sure you really want the job," he suggested. And you can check me out as well, I thought.

I accepted the offer for the special seminar—the only way I could positively rule MCD in or out of my career plans. Having Keith Clark as a colleague could be a valuable experience, I felt.

"By the way," Mr. Long closed. "Are you interested in sending your children here next year?"

"Definitely not," I snapped. I was truly taken aback, with the irksome memory of the dropped job offer still lingering in my mind. Then, feeling I had been too abrupt, I added, "My husband and I are very happy with their current schools." I wasn't sure that the statement was true, but it sounded convincing anyway.

After shaking hands and indeed his hand was king-sized, I tried to leave alone, but he accompanied me to my car. Gentlemanliness was not his motive. I suspected that he wanted to see the car I drove. I wondered what kind of information my steel blue Toyota station wagon would provide about me. His escorting me left no chance for questions to consume my head while walking down the diagonal path. But had I been alone, I would have pondered the meaning of that twisted first smile.

4. First Decision

"You want to go to the Diamond Gala?" Vernon asked incredulously when I arrived home from my second interview at Merritt Country Day. Although Vernon was working at his desk, he was eager to talk about this matter. The Diamond Gala, a black-tie annual bash, was MCD's largest fundraiser. The event was known not only for its glitz but also for its decadence. Although we had received an invitation many times, we never chose to attend.

By necessity we had been to numerous other charity balls, though that kind of evening just wasn't our preference. Of course, I ignored the women wearing dresses, more like costumes, specifically purchased to display ample portions of their silicone breasts. Still, we had to deal with music so loud that keeping cough drops in the glove compartment for the ride home was essential, centerpieces so large that seeing who was sitting across the table was impossible, a dance floor so small that getting elbowed was a minor injury, and food so skimpy that going out for a hamburger was on the mind of many at the close of the evening. Vernon especially enjoyed criticizing the food. Because the only vegetables served at this type of meal were baby ones used as garnishes, he loved saying that the midget vegetables were grown on midget farms by midget farmers with midget tools. Yet the Diamond Gala exceeded all others in Palm Beach—and perhaps the world—in lavishness, featuring special indulgences as Las Vegas-style, female dancers, imported from New York to wear skimpy, feathery outfits, jump into men's laps, and caress their faces.

I sat down in one of the twin, plum-colored leather armchairs in our study. "I didn't say that I wanted to go to the Diamond Gala," I replied firmly. "I just said that I accepted an invitation to guest teach next month at Merritt Country Day."

"And . . . ," added Vernon, moving to the matching chair.

"And, if the experience is positive, I may join the faculty to teach the new high school computer programming course," I said quickly, slurring my words.

"That's a big *and*. Not too long ago you said that the headmaster was outlandish. Now all of a sudden you're thinking of working for him, and we'll never get out of going to the Diamond Gala." Vernon did not look pleased as he crossed his arms.

"You must have many clients who attend," I argued.

"I see them at the other balls."

"Vernon, be fair. He might have had a good reason for hiring that other teacher last year. This city just has too few career opportunities for me to be overly discriminating," I countered.

"Maybe. But the next thing you know, he'll be trying to grab Blane and Mimi as well," Vernon jested, not knowing how truthfully he spoke.

"Well, actually, the matter did come up," I stated coyly.

"What? It's out of the question!" Vernon exclaimed. "Think of whose kids go there." Vernon named dozens of people in town, all known for being jet-setting, absentee parents. "You can't be serious about wanting Blane and Mimi to associate with their overindulged kids. We've worked so hard at not spoiling our children."

"First of all, the school probably has many very nice children whom we don't know. I saw some in the office while I was waiting for my appointment. But you would be happy to know that when Mr. Long broached the subject, I cut him off immediately," I remarked proudly.

"That's a relief," Vernon retorted.

"But, Vernon, at least we ought to discuss the situation. We're not being honest. We never thought that a viable option to the public schools existed, so we overlooked their problems and inadequacies," I pleaded.

Blane was finishing seventh grade and Mimi fifth. Our children had received an excellent foundation at a Montessori pre-school and kindergarten. Both started at two years old and were reading well by four. Fortunately, due to the location of our home, the neighborhood public elementary school was outstanding for grades one through five. Of course, being a school volunteer helped, because, covertly, I always had my choice of teachers. The middle school, though, was problematic. Blane's English and social studies teachers were exceptionally strong for sixth and seventh grades, but the math and science teachers had little knowledge of their subjects. I always felt that Blane could recover in high school science, but math was a worry. Because he did his homework carefully, he learned the basic skills. However, problem solving and logical reasoning were missing in the curriculum, causing a lack of true understanding. The issue was especially acute with Mimi, showing exceptional math ability for years and now ready for middle school.

"I'm thinking that Blane should stay put because he only has one more year before high school. Why risk an unknown? But having Mr. Clark as a math teacher may be a tremendous opportunity for Mimi. The English should at least be adequate at MCD. I can supplement at home if need be." I thought that I had made a pretty reasonable argument as I sunk into the comfort of my chair.

"Let's not decide anything now," Vernon remarked wisely. "See what you think once your seminar is over. Then, after we talk, we'll hear what Blane and Mimi have to say." Vernon returned to his desk to work, and I started mine.

Preparing for my singular course was very time consuming. I wanted to use a computer game that I had created for the microcomputers at Palm Beach Community College, but MCD's machines ran a different version of the language. So I spent many hours at MCD, after school when I had access to the computer lab, rewriting my program.

The first time I arrived at MCD to work, I decided to play Mr. Long's own game, guessing which car belonged to him. I imagined that a sharp, white sports car parked in a dominant spot was his, but I should have realized that his long legs would not fit comfortably in such a model. Charles Long, I learned shortly thereafter, was known for always driving a used Lincoln Continental. His current one was, of course, yellow with a gray interior to match MCD's colors.

Once when Mr. Long saw me through a window, he entered the lab to chat. "Dr. Kelman, what are you so busy with these days?" he asked, seemingly impressed with the way I worked and still clearly delighted with the tease of my formal title.

"I'm recoding one of my games to be compatible with your hardware," I replied matter-of-factly, concentrating on the statement I was typing.

"Is this the same Dr. Kelman who said that she would never baby-sit students by having them play computer games?" His mouth slowly assumed that same askew smile which, combined with his question and tone, assumed a flirtatious manner.

I stopped my work to respond to his gambit. "After letting the students play the game a few times, I arouse their interest by asking them how such a game is created. I assure them that if they follow my instruction day by day, they will be able to program games of similar sophistication. First, I teach language fundamentals and standard algorithms as basic tools. Then, I explain the coding of my game in discrete modules. Before too long, capable students are programming their own games. Bright students thrive on such activities. They take command of the computer rather than vice versa."

I noticed Mr. Long's warm expression as I talked at length. Suddenly, I realized his ploy. He was not interviewing me again—he just wanted to watch me as I spoke. He had not crossed the personal-professional line but was dangerously close.

"Well, I guess I've told you all of that already. That's why you hired me to teach this seminar," I said and shrugged.

He nodded. "I'm looking forward to the results," he commented, definitively tapping a tabletop before departing.

Another day he came and went just as bafflingly but caused more damage. I was out with Blane and Mimi when we stopped at MCD for them to see my program. As soon as we entered the lab, my children noticed the unusual furniture. *Early Thrift* was my description. Actually, the tables and chairs were acquired from a bankrupt barbecue restaurant. Apparently, MCD took donations of any kind. Mr. Long saw us in the lab and walked in.

"These must be your lovely children," he remarked flippantly.

I could tell from his expression that he was scheming. "Yes, Blane and Mimi," I replied, as I indicated each.

"Nice to meet you. I hope I'll be seeing both of you here in the fall," Charles glibly pronounced and left.

"Mom, are we going here?" they shrieked simultaneously.

"Well, I suppose we should consider it," I suggested, but they were speechless. Their quietness continued during the ride home—I knew the familiar silence of serious thinking. In the solitude one blazing question ignited in my head. Why was I even considering a job at a suspect school run by a quirky headmaster with a computer lab that, with a few menus, could pass for a Moo-Oink-Peep Restaurant?

At dinner that evening, Blane and Mimi brought up the subject of changing schools. Mimi had firmly decided that she was enrolling at MCD. She had heard about the smart math students there and was tired of spending all of fifth grade redoing fourth grade math, as she described the situation. Blane's comment, though, surprised us.

"Mom, you and Mimi are going to come home happy and excited every day, while I'll plod along with the same old boring routine. Plus the English teacher for next year is a battle-ax. Pass the rice, please," he said.

Vernon's look implied that reprimanding Blane for his word choice would not further the discussion. "Let's keep an open mind," Vernon suggested, as he handed Blane the bowl. "Let your mother teach her course before we decide anything. Then, if we're leaning that way, you'll both need to spend a day there." Vernon, conditioned to eat fast in his earlier, hectic days on the stock exchange trading floor, had barely started his meal.

"Dad, I don't need to visit," Mimi responded. "I know that I want to go to MCD. I'm not putting up with those idiot math teachers Blane had and the math books with nothing in them except what I already know, and that's final. Mom, I love this squash."

Although Mimi did know her mind from the day she was born, I wondered whether she was so sure or just didn't want to jeopardize her award for perfect attendance at the fifth grade graduation.

Vernon, knowing I was troubled, hugged me especially tightly that night in bed, though he fell right to sleep, as usual. I slipped from beneath his arm and tossed repeatedly until in one frozen position I struggled with the ugly truth: the reality of the terrible math instruction at Blane's middle school.

The typical day was a scene Blane had described to me many times with a child's anger and frustration as strong as an adult's. The students reluctantly but obediently took their assigned seats. On command from the teacher, they passed their homework papers to the students sitting in front of them. The students in the first row walked their papers to the students in the back row. Trading papers comprised the daily routine.

The teacher asked each student in turn to give an answer. Students marked the paper belonging to the neighboring student right or wrong. Not knowing if they, themselves, had gotten a problem correct, because they could not see their own work, made asking questions an unfulfilling exercise. The only discussion resulted from: "Could you repeat the answer to number five?" or "Did you say hundred or hundredth?" When all problems had been marked in this manner, each student called out the score of the neighbor's paper for recording in the grade book—a ritual that violated both teacher professionalism and pupil privacy. Then, the students returned the completely graded papers to the rightful owners. If additional minutes remained and the teacher did any original talking, the topic was her family's recent vacation, her husband's past illness, or her grandchild's current activity. The bell rang, and the students filed out the door. They never looked forward to the next math class— they knew exactly what to expect. The teacher breathed a sigh of relief as she crossed off one more day on her retirement countdown calendar.

Complaining to the school administrators accomplished nothing. Because fixing educational problems was too onerous a task, keeping the status quo became their jobs. Meanwhile, they bragged that the school system was doing a fine job. In reality, the defensive teachers held the children hostages while the children did the teachers' work.

On one occasion, Blane had found the *challenge problem* at the end of the assignment difficult and had asked me for help. I said that the best solution called for proportions. But since Blane hadn't learned about them yet, he decided to leave the problem blank. The next day he heard a few scores of one hundred called out and wondered how those students had done the problem. Curiously, when he asked, no one could supply an answer. Furthermore, when Blane questioned his teacher about proportions, her reply was that such a solution was impossible because the previous page strictly demonstrated long division examples. Deprivation of teaching, affirmation of cheating, or depletion of mathematics—which was the most frustrating aspect of the miserable situation?

I rolled onto my back and focused on a pinpoint light coming from the clock in the otherwise black room. What else was bothering me—that students learned not to value school, with the insightful ones understanding why? Ultimately, I hated that children's one chance at an education was wasted.

Despite continual cries from politicians to improve public education, no one seemed to notice the bane of American math education, the poisonous insult to teaching: trading papers. Was I the only one who considered how students could learn anything by trading papers if they didn't also trade brains? The jarring question reverberated in my head as I fell asleep that night.

For the next four weeks, I not only had teaching the seminar on my mind, but also wondering whether I would be happy professionally at Merritt Country Day and whether the school would be right for either Blane or Mimi or both. The days were intense.

Fortunately, my course went extremely well. The math team boys were as bright as they had been described—perhaps even more so. One, whom Keith Clark had coached into a national award winner, could answer my questions even before I had finished asking them. Though we were all frustrated for the first few days because of my cramming so much background into the short class periods, by the end of the seminar, the students were hooked on programming—the ultimate success.

Mr. Long waited for me outside the lab on the last day of the course. As the boys opened the door, we both heard one call out, "Come to my house tonight to fix the last bug." Another said, "I've got a cool idea for a new program."

Mr. Long walked in and smiled appreciatively. "You've had such an impact on them already, Molly."

"I tried," I replied. "They're great kids. Thanks for coming by."

I was impressed that despite his busy schedule and scattered manner, he knew when my class met and that the day was the last. Flattered, I didn't consider that his main goal was my future commitment.

He ignored my comment but continued with what was on his mind. "Look at this place." He stretched his long arms wide. "Why do we do all of this? Why do we work so hard? Why do we keep growing and improving? We do it for the kids, for the future. But, bright students need bright teachers. I'm so glad I found you. They need you—I need you," he said movingly.

"Thanks," I answered softly. I was inspired but also a little overwhelmed.

"Have you met other faculty members? How has everyone been treating you?" he asked.

"Oh, everyone is so nice. Dottie has made me feel welcome in her lab."

"So, you'll accept the position for next year, Dr. Kelman?"

"Does that mean you would call me Dr. Kelman and not Molly?" I questioned.

"Oh, I'll use both depending on the occasion, but I want the students to use your official title. I'm proud of your doctorate degree."

"I need to talk things over at home one more time," I said. "I'll call you soon."

Mr. Long nodded. He shook my hand, covered it with his commanding left hand as well, and squeezed firmly, pressing my ring into my skin. My mind along with my hand was completely occupied until we parted.

Later that week, after Blane and Mimi spent a day at the school, I informed Charles Long that all three of us would be at Merritt Country Day in the fall. With Vernon's approval, I had made my first decision regarding MCD, and I hoped it was the right one. Admittedly, I wasn't sure.

5. First Graduation

Because, at the time of my programming seminar, a student's education at Merritt Country Day School ended with eighth grade, graduation from middle school was significant. The middle school academic awards also occurred at the event, insuring a large attendance. Mr. Long kindly invited me to attend. I arrived wearing a navy blue, coat-style, thin raw silk dress and a long, single strand of pearls, feeling very good both about my new job and myself. Fully expecting to sit in the audience with the parents and other guests, I was surprised when Mr. Long asked me to be part of the faculty procession. I was not only pleased but also honored. The other teachers could have resented my participation without a year of effort and emotion. Instead, they all seemed to welcome me.

As I walked down the aisle, I saw some familiar faces. Quizzical expressions emerged since word of my employment had not spread yet. Many people knew that I had Ivy League degrees, that I had taught at Palm Beach Community College, that my children were very bright, and specifically, that they were *not* enrolled at MCD. I sensed the fertile gossip.

Graduation, for the most part, was nicely conducted—just the right touch of flowers, music, and formality to make the occasion official yet tasteful. However, two proceedings seemed inconsistent.

The first contradictory event was an invocation by a minister. Nothing religious happened at MCD all year according to its charter, so why should the year-end, grand ceremony begin with something foreign to the ethos of the school? The logic was troublesome. The faculty or students could have thought of a creative, intellectual opening—perhaps a series of quotes from great literature or science.

The other deficient activity was the distribution of awards. Mrs. Long, a history teacher at the school, had rolled the certificates, tied each with a pretty ribbon, and placed them in a carrying basket. Then, at the ceremony, she randomly selected one and handed it to her husband for announcing. So, for example, the first one was for the best sixth grade science student while the second was for the most improved eighth grade music student. Minutes later, oops, the tenth one was a tie for the best sixth grade science student—oh, well. Was only I troubled by this lack of order? At that moment I realized how much Merritt Country Day was a Mom and Pop operation.

Charles made a point of finding me after the ceremony. "Molly, I hope you'll join us for lunch," he offered.

"I . . . ," I stalled. I felt marching with the faculty was imposition enough.

"I want you there," he said, putting his arm around me and pronouncing *Chesterfield Hotel Restaurant* with its totally American name intentionally distorted to French in jest—*Shesterrefeeld Hutelle Resstaurante.* "Do you want to ride with me?"

"Thanks, but I'll take my car so I can go directly home," I answered. His sizable hands and long arms were enough—the big, yellow Lincoln Continental scared me. "You are being too kind," I added, removing myself from his grasp. "Well, I'll see you there, I guess. I'm going to call my husband quickly."

The luncheon was a magnificent buffet. I discovered then that all MCD events were accompanied by delectable eatables, a longing of, befittingly named, Mr. Long. When I arrived, most of the guests were already at tables, happily dining and talking. I hesitated, trying to decide where to go. Momentarily, Charles Long was upon me.

"I saved you a seat next to me," he stated graciously.

"Oh, thank you," I said, following him to the table. His plate was covered with the remains of scrambled eggs, fried potatoes, creamed spinach, and glazed tomatoes. "Looks good, very colorful," I said.

"Help yourself, and then we can talk," he answered.

While I was at the food station, Charles circulated the room. Then I made myself comfortable, eating and chatting with the others at our table. By Mrs. Long's absence, I learned that Charles and his wife rarely attended social events together. Externally, she did not play the corporate spouse role, while internally, she helped whenever needed. Shortly, Mr. Long returned, pushed his chair close to mine, and turned to face me directly. His behavior appeared to trigger the departure of the remaining guests at our table.

"So, how do you like living in Palm Beach?" Charles asked abruptly.

"If we didn't like it, we would return to New York," I replied.

"Yes, you are pragmatic. I've noticed that," he stated.

"In a larger, older city one typically joins established organizations. Here one can be a builder," I said philosophically, not expecting that I had given him the setup for a perfect retort.

With that same crooked smile, he regarded me and emphasized tenderly, "Together we will build a great school." I was overjoyed at how serendipity had worked magic—how the day had progressed to allow this private moment to happen.

Touching my innermost feelings, Charles's special sentence has stayed with me during these past two years at MCD through the good and the bad—justifying work, glorifying achievements, ameliorating problems, and assuaging crises. To me his words were as momentous as a new President's proclaiming, "I solemnly swear," or as meaningful as Elizabeth Barrett Browning's writing, "How do I love thee? Let me count the ways."

I felt as if Charles and I were in complete academic unison. I had experienced years of education—kindergarten through twelfth in a nationally rated public school system, multiple university degrees, summer programs, and more. I had encountered a wide range of teachers, courses, students, and methodologies. And while I didn't start as an educator, I treasured learning. My wanting excellence for my own children directed me to the field. I delighted in finding a headmaster who seemed to share my ideals. His rare remark was an invitation to be a partner in striving to create a remarkable school. My first graduation concluded with an unparalleled opportunity.

Together we will build a great school. Together we will build a great school. Together we will build a great school. I heard his words repeatedly, exactly as he had spoken them.

6. First Caution

As soon as Vernon arrived home one evening, only a week after graduation, I saw on his face that something was wrong.

"Where are Mimi and Blane?" he asked.

"They're both at friends' houses—and invited to stay for dinner," I replied. "We need to get them in a few hours."

"Perfect. Let's go for a walk on the beach."

I suspected that Vernon wanted to talk more than walk—and talk in an idyllic setting. But I changed my clothes quickly and asked nothing, for I knew that he would have told me anything truly serious right away. A few minutes later, we crossed South Ocean Boulevard and walked hand-in-hand along the damp, firm sand.

"My colleagues at the bank have mixed feelings about your new job," Vernon began.

"But graduation just happened. News travels that fast in Palm Beach?"

"That fast," Vernon answered.

"Where I work should not be the concern of anyone at G-PET," I stated sharply.

"Well, it is," Vernon said.

"I'm confused. This issue never came up when I taught at the community college."

"Palm Beach Community College is a state institution. It doesn't bank at G-PET, nor do the majority of its students and parents. Besides, people are virtually anonymous there. You've even said that you never met a parent of any of your teenage students," Vernon commented.

"So?"

"So MCD is totally different. Parke Merritt is one of the leading clients at Grey Parent Eastern Trust, and many of the parents invest with us as well."

"So? You've never told me any bank business. Your colleagues are completely aware of our professionalism in that regard."

"True. But you've also never wanted to know any bank business. Now some of the information may be valuable to you."

"What are you saying?"

"Well, the ultimate news would involve Parke Merritt himself. But picture this scenario. Charles Long promises you a freestanding computer lab because a donor has stepped forward for that very purpose. But I know that the donor actually does not have that kind of money. Should I stop you from spending countless hours with the architect because I know that the building will never happen?"

"I never knew you were so imaginative," I teased, trying to push Vernon into the water.

"Or what if the school itself is in financial trouble because the majority of pledges are from totally leveraged donors?"

"That news would leak anyway, without you," I countered.

"Or you might become upset when a star student is asked to leave the school. You are not told the reason, yet I know that the parents cannot pay the tuition. Or a family makes a large pledge to buy admission, but I know they have no resources."

"Could you please provide an example other than a Palm Beach financial fraud? Next you're not going to warn me that a parent belongs to the Mafia."

"Molly, be serious. Perhaps one of your students starts misbehaving in class. You are puzzled by the change in behavior, but I know that the parents are trying to work out the financial details of a divorce."

"I've heard enough and have a simple solution. You need to come home every evening totally poker-faced. If you have a telltale smirk—a look that says, *I know something you don't know but want to*—then we're in trouble. So the burden is on you. Tell that to your meddlesome colleagues."

"They're not meddlesome," Vernon explained. "They're being proactive. They foresee that I might want to violate the bank's privacy code to save you emotional wear-and-tear as well as time."

I stopped walking, faced Vernon, and dug my heels into the sand. "Fine, I understand. I've heard your first caution. But, they know you and you know me. Integrity is foremost." We walked back home with our arms around each other, enjoying the salt air and saying nothing.

7. First Visit

That summer, anticipating huge work for many future years, I visited my sister Grace at her home in D.C. for a month. Her husband had a corporate job that kept him overseas for extended periods, so she welcomed our company. Originally, she, her daughter Brenna, Vernon, Blane, Mimi, and I were all together. But then the three children left for overnight programs, while Vernon returned to Palm Beach to handle bank business.

Grace worked in the daytime, while I enjoyed the many sights and museums. In the evening, she and I had wonderful talks about a wide variety of topics.

One evening, she relayed a story told to her by an attorney colleague. The woman's capable son, a high school junior the previous year, took the College Board PSAT/NMSQT at his school in October. However, for some unknown, unannounced reason, the school officials moved the exam from the cafeteria, where students sat comfortably at broad tables, to the auditorium, where students sat precariously on narrow flip-up seats with even narrower flip-over desks, requiring flipping back and forth between the test booklet and the bubble sheet. Needless to say, the attorney's son also flipped at the conditions, but the test had started. Compounding his particular situation was the student immediately behind him who was able to reach this boy's chair back, given a tight aisle and long legs. The neighboring student's periodic kicks and frustrated mutterings were further distractions. Clearly, proctors had little control over an auditorium style setting.

"My friend was so angry that she told the principal that airline flights were more comfortable than this test environment," Grace explained.

"What else did she do?" I asked.

"As a lawyer, she thought about suing the school board. But ultimately she decided that such an action would hurt her son's college application. So she organized a large group of parents to pressure the administration, forcing the exam back to the cafeteria, at least to protect future students."

"Why are some educators so stupid?" I questioned.

"That's exactly what I want to ask you. Education is your field," Grace stated.

Suddenly, I had a troubling, overwhelming vision of school administration incompetence—not a premonition of Merritt Country Day, I hoped. In response to Grace, I could only sigh and ask, "Well, what were this boy's scores?"

"On the PSAT, he only made commendation and not semi-finalist. But on the SAT in May, he scored over 1500. So, he's set for college, but still the experience was ghastly," Grace reported.

Just then the phone rang, and Grace answered. "It's Vernon," she said, not surprised because he called frequently. But that night Grace had a funny expression on her face just from hearing Vernon's brief hello. Indeed, his voice sounded a bit hesitant.

"The word's out that Charles is *high on Molly*. I heard it from a few different people," Vernon said.

"Vernon, you and I both know the assertion means that Charles is looking forward to a new, well-educated colleague with some fresh ideas," I clarified.

"Yes, but do the gossips know that?" he asked. "You have to consider the double-entendre of the expression. I just think you should be careful—especially with Blane and Mimi enrolling at the school."

"I can handle things," I assured him, not convinced myself.

"I can hardly wait to meet this odd character," Vernon said.

"I can arrange that at the Diamond Gala," I teased.

"Oh, great," Vernon snapped.

After I finished the call, Grace asked, "Anything wrong?"

"Vernon says the Palm Beach gossips believe Charles Long has a non-academic fixation on me."

"Do you think so?"

"Charles Long is just bizarre and complicated—charismatic, eccentric, flirtatious—even sometimes comical."

"Odd," Grace commented.

"Yes, odd," I repeated, thinking Grace had used the same adjective as Vernon. But I was not going to let anything spoil my first extended visit with Grace.

8. First Schedule

Upon returning from Washington, I immediately checked all three schedules—Blane's, Mimi's, and mine. High school level foreign language began in sixth grade for MCD students, and Vernon and I had unequivocally selected Spanish for both Blane and Mimi. So I was quite surprised to learn that both of my children were placed in French. Additionally, my one course, or probably three as Charles had said, had grown to six—actually a one-course overload. I planned to accept my work graciously as a trade for steadfastness concerning Spanish.

My visit to school began with a firm conversation with Charles. "Charles, how are you?" I asked. He was reading some papers at his desk with the office door open. I remained standing as I entered.

"Well." His reply was consistent. He continued, "How was your summer?"

"Wonderful," I responded. "My family and I visited my sister and her daughter in D.C."

"Does your sister work in education also?" Charles asked intently.

"No, Grace is an attorney for the government," I answered. Curiously, Charles looked relieved. "I'm glad to be back and excited about getting started, but I have a few questions about our schedules. I see that I have six courses. Shouldn't someone have asked me if I were willing to go on overload, especially my first year?"

"Well, you see how it is around here. We all get so busy. Dottie came in last week and pointed out that she had too few prep periods during the day, so I transferred one of her classes to you—the fifth grade computer class." As he finished his last sentence, Mr. Long laughed, his same notable laugh, as if laughing would lighten the gravity of the situation. He failed to mention the materialization of the other two courses, but I decided that checking with Keith Clark would be more informative.

"A phone call or a note in my mailbox would have been nice," I replied. I hoped that this lack of communication was not the usual mode of operation, though I had already experienced Charles's paucity of phone calls. "I'm willing to do the extra course, but the curriculum is the issue. I don't know what Dottie did with the fifth grade last year, and my interest is programming," I explained.

"Can you take programming down to the fifth grade level?" Charles asked.

"Absolutely. I explained that to you exactly during my initial interview," I bandied. Although Charles did not like being reminded of not hiring me originally, he did respect an appropriate spar.

"Then it's settled. We just have to discuss your salary because our last discussion was based on three courses." He had no idea that more was on my mind.

"There is one additional matter. I specifically requested Spanish for my children, but they both got French," I stated factually.

"Did they?" he questioned. "Let me see," he said as he fumbled through the myriad of papers on his desk. Not finding what he wanted, he buzzed the receptionist. I sat down in the chair by the open door. "Priscilla, could you bring me the middle school schedule?" Priscilla appeared within seconds, clearly in command of her multiple tasks. Organization was one of her strong points, complementary to Charles's dearth.

After looking at the schedule, Charles explained, "Oh, I remember what happened. Blane didn't fit into Spanish because he is the only new eighth grader taking algebra. And one of Mimi's courses, I think chorus, conflicted with Spanish. The kids will love our French teacher, Emma Marisienne. She is highly spirited." Ironically, Emma, with whom Blane and Mimi never studied, became my closest friend at MCD.

I continued, "Charles, the teacher is not the issue. My husband and I are firm in our position. I don't think I need to review for you the influx of Spanish-speaking people into this country, especially into Florida, and the resulting professional advantages that exist for those who are fluent in Spanish. I would assume that Merritt Country Day should be able to provide at least what public schools are offering." I tried to speak especially formally when I wanted to win my point. My last line was the one that struck at the heart of the matter for Charles—competing with other schools. I'm glad that I didn't have to threaten that only one member of the Kelman/Melrose family would be starting at MCD that fall.

"I'll see what I can do. I need to speak with Cecily—she does the scheduling," he countered.

"Fine. I look forward to hearing from you," I stated and worried that Charles did not make a notation. Cecily was Charles's wife. Strike two for the Mom and Pop management style.

Within a few days, I received new schedules for Blane and Mimi. They were not only both in Spanish, but also in the same class. Being together in a course—the first time ever and in a new subject—would be fun for them. However, the scheduling issue imprinted on my mind. Shouldn't every effort be made to honor the wishes of parents and students without their having to complain?

Preparing for the coming school year, I pondered the errors of my first schedule. Happily, Charles had averted a controversy. Of course, I told only Vernon and my sister Grace about my thoughts. I wondered how many other matters I would notice that could use improvement. Regarding MCD, my red-pen eyes had started extending beyond the written word to the prevailing practice.

Observing was only the first step—fixing was the necessary second. I could be called a perfectionist, but not an unwavering one. Certainly time constraints and financial considerations did not permit total perfection. Still, for the steep tuition and purported reputation, the parents and their children deserved the best possible. Many nights as I fell asleep, I wondered when I would be secure enough in my position at MCD to speak up about all matters, not just those regarding my children. Didn't Charles say that he wanted my input in seeking excellence? Hadn't Charles spoken unforgettable words? *Together we will build a great school.*

9. First Day

Blane, Mimi, and I arrived for our first day of school at Merritt Country Day on time, but not early. We needed practice getting ready to leave the house together. To look cheerful for the occasion, I wore a matching cotton skirt and blouse in colorful stripes. I pulled my long, dark, straight hair back in a ponytail, reliably a fast style. As we walked up that distinctive diagonal path to the main building, the yearbook photographer took our picture. After all, we were big news on the small campus.

Though I wasn't impressed with our opening faculty meetings, Mr. Long made one meaningful point: we should start teaching immediately from the first minute of each class and assign homework for that night. I agreed with his philosophy. Blane had complained for the past two years that nothing ever happened on the first day of school—just recitation of the school and classroom rules by each successive teacher. He came home from the opening of public middle school enervated.

Merritt Country Day offered an ideal teaching environment with bright, motivated students. The school was small enough for Mr. Long to build a family atmosphere with all customary civil values, especially honesty and respect. Charles set an excellent example in those regards. Discipline problems at MCD were few. If a student didn't behave appropriately, Mr. Long dealt with the matter himself.

Some of my students were a little startled by my teaching manner, but they seemed to enjoy it. Having had a variety of teachers, I fashioned myself after the best—but not a model commonly known. I had definite ideas about the qualities of a true math teacher: knows math well beyond the level of the course to properly address the concerns of the brightest; listens carefully to understand students' questions and answers even when not well expressed; uses non-standard pedagogy to make students remember a concept; possesses high standards to bring out the fullest in each student; stresses individuality to compensate for different learning styles and levels of development; moves at a fast pace to keep excitement in the classroom; imparts enthusiasm to teach a love of math as well as math itself; shows meaning and elegance in problems to reflect the beauty of math; and works in a style that is humorous, inventive, and dramatic to make each class memorable.

In planning for the year, Keith Clark had assigned me to the new sixth grade advanced math course that was Mimi's class and to the algebra course, Blane's class. He didn't purposely have me teach my own children. Rather, because he taught the advanced seventh grade class, he felt that I should have the sixth. Similarly, because he had the high school geometry class, he felt that I should teach the algebra. Keith was fair beyond expectations. When I questioned him about teaching my own children, he merely commented, "You'll be fine." I didn't know then how much I would enjoy teaching Blane and Mimi, acquiring insight into their personalities and learning styles that other parents could never experience.

Remarkable children comprised the fifth grade computer science class. As early as the first day I noticed a student, Noah Sanford, who was so exceptionally brilliant that I wondered whether the bequeath of Dottie's class was further serendipity.

In algebra class one well-meaning but rather saucy-mouthed girl decided to play *telephone*, pointing to Blane and commenting to her neighbor, "He's her son. Pass it on." Although their whispering was audible, I indulged them in their fun. The quality of my presentation and seriousness toward the math won them over, and Blane didn't seem flustered.

The students in my seventh grade math class were delightful except for one girl who kept mentioning Mr. Clark's name, as if no one else were capable of teaching math. I controlled her as well as possible but made a mental note to discuss the situation later with Charles.

The ninth grade boys who had been in my special seminar the previous spring were happy to see me, but the other ninth graders were scared. The difference in math ability combined with my prior instruction created a gap between the two groups that was immediately noticeable.

Of all my courses, though, a distinctive delight was my sixth grade advanced math class—the new course that Keith asked me to develop. Mimi and a few other bright, energetic girls formed this class along with one boy, Daniel, having the same description: intelligent, inquisitive, clever, and enthusiastic. Their excitement of discovering that math was so much more than arithmetic was uncontainable. They exploded even on the first day. These girls and Daniel, I thought, would eventually replace last year's boys as the new MCD math minds.

I taught my computer programming classes in D. Dottie's room and my math classes in two other rooms. The inefficiency of not having my own classroom bothered me later, but on that first day I was so happy that nothing could spoil the thrill. My day went extremely well, and I found myself smiling continuously.

I had requested an area to work during my free periods. In turn, Charles asked the custodian, Joe, to clear a small, inner room acting as a storage closet. The space was a mess at the time of the faculty meetings, so I was surprised on the first day of school that the room was so nicely prepared with a large desk. Part of the room still contained metal shelving storing the music teacher's props and costumes as well as boxes of Charles and Cecily's personal belongings that didn't fit in their studio apartment. Joe's cleaning the room yielded a few square feet of floor space quickly usurped for the folding cot. Thus, my office was the school infirmary as well as the Longs' cedar chest, but I didn't care.

I was working at my desk when Charles suddenly entered without knocking. "What do you think of the desk?" he questioned with a big grin on his face.

"It's great. It has two file drawers, and the floral, carved handles are beautiful," I replied enthusiastically, having no idea what could be so funny about a desk.

He chuckled. I was determined to uncover the mystery, but the time did not seem proper. "How has your day been so far?" he asked.

"Wonderful. My sixth . . ."

"We'll talk later," Charles interrupted. "I was just on my way to a meeting." He tapped on the desktop, leaving as furtively as he had entered.

After my last class, I looked for Charles in his office. I had an inner need for his affirmation of a good first day. Luckily, he was there with the door open.

"Oh, Molly, come in," he said cheerfully. "Close the door and sit down."

I obeyed.

"So?" he asked eagerly, leaning over his desk to pose the question directly in my face.

"Well, my sixth graders are a dream come true, and Noah in fifth grade is amazing. But there is one girl, Greta Greig, in seventh grade who has her heart set on having Keith again," I explained.

Charles smiled astutely, knowing exactly whom I meant and why.

I added, "She keeps commenting that she'll ask Mr. Clark. I can't decide whether she is just naturally difficult or her parents undermined me at home even before the start of school—or both."

Charles sighed before replying. "You know that Mr. Greig is one of our board members. He was not happy when he learned right before school started that Greta would be in your math class. He just assumed his daughter would always have Keith as her math teacher. He said he didn't care how many degrees you had or where you earned them. You were not Mr. Clark—that is all he cared about. And Greta must have heard her parents talking at home. Sadly, she's the kind of child to use, or rather to abuse, information," Charles disclosed wistfully. After the slightest pause he continued. "I didn't tell you because I didn't want to hurt you by putting a huge stumbling block in front of a great start."

"I appreciate your concern, but what did you say to Mr. Greig?" I asked.

"I tried to pacify him by instilling a sense of natural school development. I told him that growth meant new teachers and that I had hired the best," Charles said. His line was a compliment, but it also burnished a spot in my mind. "Then I told him about Mrs. Fiske who was delighted when she heard that her daughter was scheduled to be in your algebra class. Apparently, she knew you from the community college."

"Yes, I taught Mrs. Fiske three computer science courses. The first went so well that she enrolled for the second and then the third. She's very capable, and her daughter was wonderful today. But what did Mr. Greig say about Mrs. Fiske's comment?"

"It didn't matter to him. Molly, handling the students is the easy part of independent school teaching. Handling the parents is often the real challenge. This episode won't be your worst, I'm sorry to say," Charles predicted.

"I guess I do have a lot to learn," I agreed. "At Palm Beach Community, I never even saw a parent. I'm grateful for your support."

"Molly, you have it always. That's my job, especially for teachers like you," Charles said earnestly, focusing his dark blue eyes at mine and reaching across his desk to take my hand that I wish had been hidden in my lap. Though I questioned the sincerity of his gesture, I had every reason to believe his words.

Just then his phone rang. "We'll talk more later. Just do your best," he advised, motioning to me that he needed to take the call. While I moved my chair so that I could open the door to leave, he added with a laugh, "I'm glad you like the desk. Enjoy."

I went home happy—all three of us had a good first day. We enjoyed a nice dinner, talked about our experiences, did our homework, and went to sleep feeling very tired but satisfied. I also was pleased with my personal organization, accommodating my demanding new job by planning whenever possible—from pre-cooking dinners to pre-buying gifts. Ironically, a part of Charlotte Merritt's *scandalle*—shopping ahead—was present in my own design two years before the incident.

This first day was very atypical for life at MCD. As I became part of the establishment, each successive day was filled with issues and exhaustion.

10. First Gala

Vernon was right—in November we were snared into attending the Diamond Gala.

Each year the gala had a different theme displayed in the invitation, décor, menu, and music. More secret than the disclosure of a vice-presidential candidate, that year's theme was especially tightly concealed. Charles chided one teacher who merely asked at the August faculty meetings. Of course, nine months prior like an announcement of conception, invitees had received a *Save the Date* notice that rivaled the stationery of the fanciest parties but intentionally revealed no clue.

Then seven weeks ahead, the long-awaited mailing arrived. The theme was Carlsbad Caverns, with the invitation in the shape of New Mexico. The paper was crayon-colored burnt sienna—for dirt I supposed. Rice paper stalactites were glued to the top of the card.

One key part of the invitation was the listing of *The Committee*, presented with as much pomp as the announcement of a new President's Cabinet. The members of *The Committee*, all women and many mothers at MCD, were listed by *Mrs.* followed by their husbands' names, as if men were beluga caviar and women were chopped liver. Each member was supposed to guarantee the filling of one table to insure a sold-out ballroom. Additionally, *The Committee* was responsible for selecting the theme, securing the necessary services, and soliciting the silent auction items.

School had been in a tizzy for weeks before. Even though *The Committee* was supposed to run everything, the women always needed help from Priscilla, Joe, Cecily, Caroline Jackson who was MCD's business manager, and others at school as well as Charlotte

Merritt. Mothers, not trusting the mail, dashed into the front office with their reply cards and checks before a sell-out. The faculty learned not to bring up a new issue just before the gala—unless it was an absolute emergency, something like a fire or a biting.

Of course, *The Committee* wanted a formal-attired Charles in full attendance like Prince Charles incarnate. Charles, however, as a matter of principle, refused a table assignment unless all faculty members were invited to dine as well. His gesture was the only one regarding the whole event that brought the craziness back into perspective: the gala's purpose was to raise money for the school, but the school was nothing without the teachers. *The Committee* was not willing to treat the faculty because the success of the gala was judged on the *stone* as Charles called the bottom line—the grand sum collected. A competition had developed with *The Committee* each year determined to outdo the *stone* of the preceding year. Thus, complimentary tables for the faculty were beyond consideration. So, a massive breath-holding occurred until a major benefactor eventually stepped forward to underwrite the cost of the faculty.

Vernon and I paid for ourselves. While four hundred dollars a couple was a hefty amount for a philanthropic event, Vernon did not want to be treated. As a result, we had the choice of sitting with other guests or at a faculty table. I chose the latter, also as a matter of principle—not that my decision really mattered. The rounds were so large and the music so deafening that one could only interact with those immediately to one's left or right, and even that was a strain. The other people at the table were invisible by the centerpieces, inaudible by the cacophony, or irrelevant by the circumstances.

Vernon's main complaint was that the gala was on a Friday night, and I agreed. I arrived home from school after five o'clock having had an exhausting day. Vernon, too, had been very busy concluding the week's work at the bank. I surmised that the big hotels wouldn't guarantee a Saturday night a year ahead, but I learned that *The Committee* preferred Friday so that its members could supervise the professional decorator while their children were in school. The logic seemed twisted to me, placing their comforts ahead of the guests'. After a quick nap for me and helping Blane and Mimi organize dinner, Vernon and I dressed in our finery. I chose a dress that I had

44

previously purchased for a cousin's formal wedding. The material was pink, purple, and gold silk brocade, appliqued with small, gold beads—sari fabric but sewn into a gown with cap sleeves, stand-up collar, and empire waist. As I came out of the bedroom to say good-bye, Mimi exclaimed with great thrill, "Mom, you look like an Indian princess."

The gala began promptly at seven o'clock. Entering the imposing lobby at The Breakers Hotel, we saw its usual splendid décor and refined activity—until reaching the foyer of the ballroom. There, the visual and visceral transformation began. We shook hands with the dignitaries in the receiving line—Mr. Parke Merritt, Mrs. Committee Chair, and Prince Charles. I introduced Charles and Vernon as I had promised. Charles gave me a huge smile and an even bigger hug. Happily, I turned back to see him greet the next woman in the same manner.

Immediately, Charlotte Merritt approached. She, Mr. Committee Chair, and Cecily were noticeably not in line.

"Molly, you look stunning," she exclaimed.

"Thank you. So do you, Charlotte—truly elegant," I replied. Charlotte is always so gracious, I thought.

A cocktail hour was first, the time when *The Committee* hoped that guests would bid on the silent auction items. The gala was known equally well for its bounty as for its opulence. *The Committee* had spent a full year collecting hundreds of fantastic items—haute couture, tummy tucks, gourmet gorgings, Baltic cruises, and more. These women had raised begging to such an art that little girls could add the occupation to their list of what to be when they grew up: astronaut, beautician, doctor, lawyer, teacher, silent auction solicitor.

The auction, or course, incorporated the Carlsbad Caverns theme and thus appeared like a major tourist attraction. So guests received not only a glass of champagne but also an acoustic guide. The device's tape described the items at the auction from the first table to the last. Instead of asking patrons to pause the machine while walking between tables, as between paintings in an actual museum tape, the narrator provided anecdotes about Carlsbad.

What *The Committee* hadn't anticipated, though, was that most women refused to wear both the machine strap for fear of displacing their jewelry as well as the headset for fear of messing their hair. So the sound from hundreds of tapes, all started at different times, traveled into the ballroom foyer air adding to the reigning confusion. Women became tipsy, refusing hors d'oeuvres because one hand held the recorder while the other held the champagne.

Exactly at eight o'clock the hotel waiters, indistinguishable in dress from the male guests, rung multiple bells to attract everyone's attention for the grand overture. A symphonic recording of Beethoven's *Moonlight Sonata* drowned the noise of the guides when, suddenly, the many sets of double doors into the ballroom opened. Even through the crowd, I could see the vast chamber, darkly and mysteriously lit. White puffs escaped from a dense fog created by a vapor machine that must have been working for hours.

After waiting our turn in line at the entry, I finally peeked into the ballroom and immediately grabbed Vernon's hand. "Hold me," I said. "I don't want to be the one who falls."

Walking into the mist, we ducked under numerous stalactites. Fortunately, they were not made out of ice, or again women would have complained about their hair. The floor of the ballroom was segmented into ramps of different levels, bordered with stainless steel railings like at the actual Carlsbad Caverns. Guests followed the various walkways in search of their table numbers, all the while dodging the numerous stalagmites rising out of the floor—a particular challenge in high heels.

"What number are we?" Vernon asked.

"Nine," I answered. "Are the numbers consecutive, or evens on one side and odds on the other?"

"I don't know," Vernon whispered. "I can't see a thing." Suddenly, we bumped head-on into another couple having the same problem. The two men started laughing uncontrollably when they realized they were friends from G-PET.

"I'll bet the person with the stalagmite on his seat wins the centerpiece," Vernon snorted.

"Vernon, not now," I pleaded.

The fellow banker, frustrated and stymied, remarked, "Molly, you should be able to figure out these table numbers."

"What's your number?" Vernon asked him while I said nothing.

"Thirty-six," he replied.

"Well, they're both perfect squares. Maybe that's a clue," Vernon said, imitating me by talking math. Vernon's mood indicated a long, portentous evening.

"Excuse us, please," I said, pulling Vernon away from the other couple. When we were alone, I added sarcastically, "No, they're arranged by factor pairs of thirty-six hundred. That would put us right next to *Table 400* and them next to *Table 100*. Have you seen either one?"

We wound up and down the ramps, eventually finding our place. Fortunately, the platforms on which the tables and chairs sat were flat. Each table was decorated with an ice sculpture, again in the shape of stalagmites. The surrounding bowl to catch dripping water held small rocks in shades of brown and gray.

"Whoever wins the centerpiece will need a trash bag to carry it home," Vernon commented. I shook my head almost grateful, for once, that the background noise was significant.

"Just remember that some guests want to be here," I cautioned.

Then I looked around, content while firmly grounded in my chair. Immediately, I understood why most of the four hundred dollars a couple went to pay for the gala, leaving only the auction as profit—the decorations were costly beyond imagination. No one could complain that the theme was superficial.

Dinner began with a tiny cup of soup—a spicy, Santa Fe style, thick tomato broth. The main platter featured a filet cooked in a pseudo fancy Tex-Mex manner, decorated with tiny, yet whole vegetables—carrot fingers, corn ears, and squash heads.

"Oh, look!" Vernon proclaimed. "The midget farmers with midget tools have been busy again."

I sighed, happily knowing that those at our table hadn't heard. Yet, ironically, indulging Vernon in his joke-making became the only safe activity. I had already learned that table-hopping was treacherous, while conversing with the other guests was impossible—one's throat could only endure so much shouting. I asked Vernon,

"Am I imagining this, or is my filet cut square, in the shape of New Mexico?"

He nodded. "There," Vernon said, cutting two diagonals and a rectangle from his steak. "I'm your neighbor, Texas." And so the dinner lapsed.

After the main course, Vernon said, "Let's dance." I must have frowned because he added, "Don't worry, the dance floor is flat."

I turned to look. "Okay," I answered. "But help me get there."

When we arrived on the dance floor, the music had changed from rhythmic rumba to thumping turmoil. The women of *The Committee* and their husbands descended, doing something fresh and frenetic.

"What do you call this?" I asked Vernon while we were trying to fit familiar steps to the music.

"The Caveman Shake," he replied. Just then he got trampled and whacked simultaneously by two different people. "Let's go look at the auction tables," he suggested wisely, taking the assaults surprisingly calmly.

I followed Vernon out of the ballroom, holding his warm jacket sleeve with my left hand and the cold railing with my right. In the lobby we walked from table to table, looking at the treasures and chatting with other guests.

"Molly, after three months of working at MCD, this is exactly what you need," Vernon said smiling, pointing to an item, knowing I never used or wanted the service. A photo from a spa described the complete body massage donation.

"Oh, right," I answered sarcastically. "I hardly need that character telling me my muscles are tense."

"Look," quipped Vernon. "The masseuse has stalagmite finger nails!"

"Maybe dessert is being served," I proposed, realizing that this shopping was futile.

We took a more direct ramp back to the table. "Oops," Vernon uttered, seeing the final course at our places. Dessert, a serious creation, again reinforced the theme—individual chocolate caves filled with hanging and standing ice cream icicles. However, the ice cream had melted into a blob with the lacs and lags hardly visible.

"Molly, at the next faculty meeting, report to Mr. Long the flaw in serving ice cream at a gala with a silent auction," Vernon said.

"Sure, lengthened class periods and baked gala desserts. Oh sorry, the order of importance is reversed," I answered sarcastically.

The evening proceeded until midnight when we were again in the ballroom lobby. I saw Charles surveying the bidding cards. He predicted a huge *stone*. Patrons, mainly parents at MCD, had overbid fantastically on the items. At first, I didn't know whether to attribute their generosity to plentiful alcohol, Breakers ambience, or school affection. Later, I realized that the financially comfortable parents would be manipulated to donate during the school year anyway, so they were smart to acquire something luxurious for their money. The other guests didn't care about the school or the scholarship fund. Some searched for bargains such as a half-price trip to Europe, while *see and be seen* was the reason to attend for most.

Vernon continued spouting endless, nasty wit on the way home. Suddenly, he interrupted himself and asked, "Molly, do you smell something funny?"

"I think it is mildew on our clothes from the heavy moisture in the ballroom," I offered.

"The Diamond Gala just plain smells," Vernon concluded.

"Be nice. Please be nice," I said and sighed.

The next morning as I described the grand event to Mimi over breakfast, a game evolved—voting on the ugliest gown. After I depicted six choices for Mimi, she selected the winner. Mimi's zeal for this fictitious game rivaled Vernon's apathy for the actual event.

The contestants that year, in symbolic terms, wore: a bumble bee frock, a tulip dress, Scarlett O'Hara's ball gown, Wilma Flintstone's rags, Carlsbad Cavern garb, and a slip. Black and yellow dots covered Contestant One with a collar that had not only gathered tulle but also darting antennae. Contestant Two's dress, in shades of pink and red, had a short tulip skirt—a style with fabric wrapping from both sides, meeting in the front center as two overlapping, curved panels. Additionally, the top of this dress consisted of multiple petals, originating at the waistline and culminating at the open bust line. Contestant Three looked as close to Scarlett O'Hara descending the steps at Tara as anyone could. Her advantage was that she couldn't be crowded on the dance floor. Because Contestants Four and Five were members of *The Committee*, they knew the theme well ahead, in time to have outfits custom made. Contestant Four's gown resembled Wilma's cartoon cave-woman image, though in rich, thick, brown silk, with a wide gold belt and matching gold sandals. Contestant Five's ensemble attempted to recreate stalactites and stalagmites out of lightly stiffened gauze in shades of gray, descending from just below the open shoulders and ascending from the ankle length hem. And, finally, Vernon's comment upon seeing Contestant Six was the best way to describe the thin, white creation: "She forgot to put on her dress." After considerable thought, and almost with as much flourish as announcing the fashion designer for the First Lady's Inaugural Ball gown, Mimi declared Mrs. Bumble Bee the victor of the 1988 Diamond Gala Worst Gown Contest.

"Mom, I can't wait to play again next year!" Mimi shrieked with great enthusiasm.

I didn't have the heart to tell Mimi that her father's parting words to me, as we fell asleep that night of our first gala, were, "Do you think we could arrange a conflict for next year?"

11. First Book

Teaching in the same computer lab as D. Dottie was a challenge because she was completely selfish in not sharing the blackboard. On more days than not, I entered the room only to find *SAVE* written on the board—multiple times on every available square inch just in case I might have missed the warning. Initially, I thought nothing of her covetousness—I was busy smiling. However, as demands on my time increased, I became annoyed with Dottie. She certainly was not a team player as Charles fondly described his faculty members. Continually forced to do on-the-spot alterations of my lesson plans, I worried about reduced effectiveness. Eventually, after unsuccessful small requests, I told her that we were sharing the room and that I would be using the full board for my classes, no matter what. I reprimanded her so strongly that I think I actually frightened her.

D. Dottie's second year was dubious. In fact, Charles had misrepresented her initial, professed success with his mild-mannered comment about students' tiring over working with state capital databases. Lacking respect for her, many of the older students sabotaged the hardware by changing the settings of switches as they were leaving class. Consequently, after Dottie was two sentences into her lesson with the next class, a little voice would say, "Miss Jones, my *E* key doesn't work." Or, rushed at the end of the period, a chorus would echo, "Miss Jones, my printer is printing junk." Dottie became so exasperated that Priscilla's bodily trying to keep her from storming into Charles's office became a familiar scene.

One of my ninth grade boys, though he disliked Dottie, kindly went into the lab between classes to reset switches. His pet peeve, however, was her calling the newly released, plastic encased, three and one-half inch floppy disk a *hard disk*. Dottie's ignorance rivaled her incompetence.

I didn't take much pity on her, though. Hogging the blackboard alone didn't solely shape my opinion. I received feedback about her from my children as well. Mimi was in her *Grade Six Computer Class*—Dottie's curriculum had those brilliant course titles. Mimi said that D. Dottie typically got terribly confused while teaching. Daniel, who loved computers, read ahead in the workbook, and experimented on his own, often clarified and finished the lesson. Knowing that Dottie would not freely accept help, Daniel devised a scheme whereby he would ask such a complicated question that he would need to explain his question on the board. Then, he just stayed there and answered it as well, filling in all of the necessary lessons from the text. Mimi preferred Daniel's teaching to Dottie's, and at least Dottie permitted Daniel to assist under this guise.

Dottie was Blane's teacher in *Grade Eight Computer Class*—better known as the school newspaper course, one of her few that had an objective. Blane grumbled about her rampant disorganization, and I deduced the same from the quality of her students' product. She permitted stories about insipid topics such as shopping at the mall. Spelling, punctuation, and grammatical errors were plentiful. Reading the newspapers was quite difficult because supposed sentences were not actual sentences. Many articles were physically crooked because the students did the layout with cutting and pasting. Dottie also engaged parent volunteers to assist whenever possible. That kind of laziness and irresponsibility was not the MCD way.

One telling episode concerned the typing of a dash. I had endured teachers not teaching, but I had no tolerance for those who taught something wrong as if it were right. Blane submitted a word-processed article with a dash in one paragraph. He had typed it correctly as I had previously taught him—with two hyphens and no spaces. Miss Jones changed his paper to space, one hyphen, space.

Blane showed me his paper. "Mom, what should I do?" he asked.

I thought of all her completed newspapers laden with errors, and replied, "Just tell Miss Jones politely that your first version was correct."

He did, and she retorted with no, she was right. So I sent Blane to school the next day with Baker's *The Practical Stylist*, Turabian's *A Manual for Writers*, and Parker's *The* MLA *Style Sheet*—all with bookmarks at the reference for the typing of a dash. These books came from my personal library. I took pride in exactness in English, not only as if every word were part of a computer program, but also more importantly because of the supremacy of accuracy and precision. I could not knowingly have a teacher teach my child anything incorrectly, especially at a school that bragged about excellence. Happily, Blane agreed to this showdown, egged on by a few classmates whom he had told.

My first year at MCD I also became the local representative of the International Computer Problem Solving Contest, never thinking that this event would widen my differences with Dottie. Students in three different age groups formed teams of one to three members. Teams, each with one computer, worked on five challenging problems for two hours. Printouts from teams solving all problems went to contest headquarters for verification and an international ranking. Noah and Daniel as a team solved four problems at the elementary level, while three of my ninth grade boys as a team also correctly coded four problems at the intermediate level.

On the Monday after the Saturday competition in April, I saw Charles at the mailboxes. The mailboxes were in the tiny faculty room that also contained the copy machine, a sink, a microwave oven, one chair, and a table with coffee and Charles's endless supply of cookies. Parents had no respect for the privacy of this room— they helped themselves to the refreshments and the copier as well as whatever snatches of private teacher conversations they could hear.

"How was your big contest?" he asked immediately. "Do you have a minute?"

"Sure," I replied.

"Come to my office, and we can sit down while you tell me." As I awkwardly followed him down the main corridor, I was glad that he had remembered about the contest. He closed the door behind me. I took the seat by the door and he the one under the tree.

Still emotionally exhausted from the whole event, I hardly knew how to answer. "Well, the kids were wonderful, and they enjoyed the experience," I began. "But there were lots of details—inviting other schools in the area, setting up their computers quickly on Saturday morning, moving our teams' computers to separate rooms after school Friday, and getting proctors on a weekend. Some MCD teachers volunteered, but not Dottie. She was upset by everything."

"And the results . . . ," he said.

"Two of our teams scored four out of five."

"That's wonderful, Molly!" Charles exclaimed animatedly, a leaf swishing his forehead. "Think of how much they've learned."

"Well, I'm extremely proud of Noah and Daniel. Noah is only in fifth grade after all, and Daniel has taught himself to program." I refrained from saying that Dottie had taught Daniel little useful.

"And aren't you proud of the ninth graders also?" Charles asked.

"Oh, yes. The problems were really tough. The kids were brilliant. But they could have had all five if I had taught them one certain technique," I replied.

"And what is that?" Charles asked.

"Well, it's a clever use of base two to check all combinations of two options—in this case of inserting a plus or minus between terms in a series, if that means anything to you," I answered.

"Molly, you are too hard on yourself," Charles stated sensitively.

"But they are such wonderful students. They deserve the absolute best," I responded. "I feel as if I let them down."

"You are the *absolute best*," Charles countered. "What was the next highest score regionally?"

"Two out of five," I said.

"And was this technique in any textbook you've seen?"

"No," I said.

"Well, then stop beating yourself up," Charles demanded.

"But that's exactly the point," I explained. "The textbooks on the market are so totally inadequate. They're aimed at the general high school population, so they're insipid. And I'm not being a snob. Not everyone can program—just like not everyone can play the violin. Programming is a very specialized subject. The books should be full of substance, written for gifted students with the prerequisite talent."

"How do you learn these techniques then?" Charles asked with genuine curiosity.

"By studying code of clever programmers—when one can gain access to such material," I answered. "For example, I learned a lot from reading the published contest solutions."

"You look as if you have more to say," Charles asserted.

"Well, I'm worried. I feel as if I need to write textbooks for some of my courses to truly teach the students what I want. But the teaching alone is way more than a full time job. How am I going to accomplish both?"

"If you worry too much, you'll cut down on your productivity. Just take one day at a time," Charles advised.

"I suppose, but there's another problem. Don't misunderstand my tone, please. Dottie is going to have to teach them more before eighth grade. The kids need some background for my courses," I said, trying to be tactful. "You would certainly never drop a student into algebra without arithmetic first."

"What is Dottie doing?" Charles questioned.

"Wasting time, according to Daniel, Mimi, and my other sixth graders," I stated.

Charles nodded and then asked, "Were our kids at all disappointed by the contest?"

"No, not this time," I replied. "They never expected to answer as many problems as they did. But I can tell—now that they've had a taste, their expectations will be higher. What we do in the classroom will have to match."

Charles smiled at me. "Looking back on your opening year," he said, "I don't know anyone who could have accomplished so much in such a short time—and in two subjects. Most importantly, you've earned respect from the students and made them so excited about learning. And you've raised the academic bar here."

"MCD's students are sophisticated consumers. That's what makes this place special," I commented, trying to shift the emphasis from me to the school.

"You can't accomplish everything at the outset. Next year you'll build on this start," Charles offered.

"But I have to write my first programming textbook. I have to compile all of the skills and concepts and algorithms and examples that students need to study—ready to use in one place. I don't have time to scramble each week once school begins. I guess that's my summer project," I said and sighed.

"Your book will raise standards beyond MCD," Charles stated encouragingly.

"Don't jump too far ahead," I warned. "But thank you so much for talking."

As I stood, Charles did the same. Covering my right hand with both his hands, he stated warmly, "Molly, thank you." Then, after an awkward pause, Charles released my hand and asked while opening the door for me, "So are you winding down for the school year?"

"Not yet," I answered. "Spring Festival is next." We smiled at each other. The twist in his grin showed puzzlement, while the spirit in his eyes showed approval.

12. First Clash

Research shows that what adults remember about their long-past middle school days are special events. Granting this thesis, Merritt Country Day alumni will have overflowing memories. Along with all of the other activities, each May the school sponsored a large event called Spring Festival. Students demonstrated creative, original endeavors: music students sang songs, drama students performed skits, art students displayed work, and science students explained projects. But in Dottie's first year her students mindlessly exhibited word processing, spreadsheet, and database programs—and she planned on doing the same again.

My students, however, had other ideas. The ninth graders wanted guests to play their original computer games. The eighth graders had developed exciting, color, motion graphics with kaleidoscopic effects, all hand-coded, using multiple variables within nested loops to create the movement. The fifth grade students had created color images of flags from around the world, also all individually programmed.

D. Dottie, in a fit of envy, refused to share any of the computers. "Talk to Mr. Long," many of my students told me. "If you don't, we will."

I snagged Charles in his office late one afternoon in the middle of all this planning. He said hastily, "Molly, I have ten minutes before the board meeting. What's on your mind?"

I closed the door but did not sit down. "Do you remember when we discussed the results of the programming contest that I hinted at something big for Spring Festival?" I asked.

"Yes," he replied.

"Well, Dottie is interfering. She wants all of the computers for her students to display application software. She won't let us move any of the computers to other rooms," I explained.

"Just let her be," he said thoughtfully. "How many students have the same computer at home?"

"Three," I answered.

"Check if those parents will bring the computers to school for the evening. I can probably borrow two more. Will five do?"

"That would be fabulous," I said gratefully. "Thank you."

As I started to leave, Charles added, "And Molly, I'm going to deal with Dottie after the event." I nodded although I did not know exactly what he meant. Was he referring solely to cooperation or was curriculum improvement included as well?

Some of my students stayed after school several hours each day during the week before Spring Festival. They helped prepare by checking for software bugs, doing all the imaginable and especially unimaginable keystrokes that the guests might. When Charles walked by the lab one afternoon and saw flashing colors on the monitors, he came in to see what was happening.

"Mr. Long, look, this is so great!" Noah exclaimed.

"That's very impressive, but I could make it even more impressive," Charles retorted.

"You know how to program?" Noah questioned.

"Good grief, no! I can't do any of this, but just wait here. I'll be back soon," Charles said mysteriously.

"What does he have in mind?" asked Daniel who, although was not my computer science student, always spent extra time with me.

"I have no idea," I replied with a shrug and kept on working.

Ten minutes later Charles returned with Joe, both pushing a large, floor-model television on a dolly with cables trailing. "Turn off one computer, please," Charles requested.

Daniel could barely contain his anticipation. He readied the hardware for Charles who, with manifest exuberance, disconnected it from its monitor and reattached it to the television. "Now load the graphics, Daniel," Charles instructed. Before our eyes appeared all of the students' fabulous work on a screen four times a monitor's size.

"Wow," shrieked one student.

"Oh, Mr. Long!" yelled another.

"Joe, look at the neat stuff we've learned," commented a third. All MCD students were fond of Joe and eagerly involved him in their activities.

"Can we have this T.V. for Spring Festival—in our own room?" asked Noah.

"Of course," replied Charles. "Joe will be here early to help you set up, right?"

"For sure," answered Joe, beaming at the students.

"Meanwhile, it's getting late. I think I see some parents in the parking lot," Charles stated, looking out the window. The students, still chattering about the television, gathered their book bags, and Joe walked them down the diagonal path.

"Mr. Long, I didn't know you're a techie," I quipped.

"There's more about me that you don't know," Charles smirked.

"Probably true," I said simply, dropping the tease before it led to trouble. "Thank you so much. The kids are ecstatic."

"No, Molly. Once again, it's I who needs to thank you." Then, looking somewhat emotional, he added, "Let's call it a day. I'll wait for you while you turn off the computers." He watched me, perhaps too intently, as I quickly moved around the room, exiting from the programs and shutting down the power. Then he opened the lab door for me.

"Goodnight," I said as Charles turned the other way toward his office. Heading down the diagonal path, I was glad that Vernon had picked up Blane and Mimi right at the close of school that day. While Charles's contribution was marvelous, something about his praise was unsettling.

The success of my students' Spring Festival presentations seemed to be Dottie's final unnerving. At the faculty lunch table on the day after the event, Emma Marisienne exclaimed continual kudos about the games and the graphics. *Très bon! C'est magnifique! Un grand succès!* While Dottie had been busy with her own students in the lab, she knew from one quick look at the large T.V. that Emma was right.

59

After school that day Charles found me grading papers in my closet-office. Although I braced myself for more jokes about the desk, Charles seemed rather serious.

"Your performance was fantastic last night," he began.

"Well, the large television was the big hit. And thanks for borrowing the computers," I replied.

"Look, Molly. Dottie came to me this morning requesting that the school add a computer lab, so you would each have your own," Charles explained.

"Can the school afford it?" I asked, somewhat surprised by Dottie's boldness.

"No, but we're ready for it," he answered.

"Charles, you know I have tried very hard to coexist with Dottie in the one lab. But I refuse to lower my standards because she hogs the blackboard or lessen my curriculum because she won't share computers. The students come first," I argued.

"Molly, you don't have to make your case with me. You have added a whole new dimension to the computer curriculum. You've truly challenged our brightest kids. And you've made computers the hallmark of the school in actual practice rather than figurative speech," Charles responded.

"So what's the plan?" I asked, wanting to correct *computer* curriculum to *computer science* curriculum.

"Well, the board will only approve the purchase based on a full report—classroom needs, curriculum descriptions, hardware suggestions, long-range planning, and so on. I need you and Dottie to write the report," he said.

"Wait a minute!" I exclaimed, shocked. "You told me that after Spring Festival you were going to deal with Dottie—I think those were your exact words. So, dealing with her means more work for me? This year has been packed. Do you know how much work goes into a good report?"

Though some employers might have taken my retort as rudeness or insubordination, Charles smiled at me. His face told me that our professional relationship had reached a special, higher plane—one in which mutual respect breathed freely in an open atmosphere of frankness and honesty.

"I'll ask Keith to coordinate the report. You know he's very detailed, and that way the work will be shared three ways," Charles offered.

Thinking that Keith could act as a mediator, I replied, "Fine."

"Then it's settled," Charles said, tapping the desktop with an affirmative gesture. "Great desk," he added and left.

Dottie and I wrote separate pieces of the report the next week. They were so different in concept that Keith submitted both as two divisions of computer science—applications and programming. Then, curiously, Dottie had a substitute teacher for the entire following week. What had my first clash with D. Dottie done to her? She returned for the final stretch with a very cryptic look on her face.

13. First Party

May provided an occasion for the teachers to interact socially. The faculty gathering that year was held at Elizabeth McFadden's house. Though I had no professional contact with Elizabeth, head of the elementary grades, she seemed friendly and competent. I thought nothing of Charles and Cecily's not hosting the party because they lived in a studio apartment.

Dinner was potluck. I made a rich creation featured in *Gourmet Magazine*. The large cake, with its layers of crisp, cocoa meringues and dark chocolate, whipped cream mousse was, as some like to say about chocolate, sinful.

Unfortunately, at an ill-fated moment, Charles, Vernon, and I were together at the buffet table getting dessert. Charles took one bite of my fattening confection and grinned as it slid down his throat. After a second, particularly large forkful, Charles declared to Vernon, "Molly's cake is better than sex." Had the betrayal warning predated this remark, I might have left at that instant.

"I wouldn't say that near your wife," Vernon replied, not knowing that Cecily had approached the table as well and had heard the entire exchange.

Cecily's eyes darted anger. She was a beautiful woman who emitted mixed signals. She showed off her tall, tanned, toned legs in short skirts, while at faculty lunches she prudishly declared that she never watched any movies containing even a hint of intimacy. Charles didn't appear drunk, so I couldn't blame his comment on alcohol. I encouraged others to take the last few pieces to quickly end the cake, Charles's assertion, and my first MCD faculty party.

14. First Year

Just after the faculty party, my sister Grace and her daughter Brenna arrived for Blane's graduation from middle school. Grace's reaction was unequivocal—she did not like Charles. She based her opinion on his unexplainable unfriendliness toward her, his noticeably under-prepared speech, and his unprofessional reliance on his wife to run the ceremony. After the event Grace and I settled into the plum leather chairs in the study at home.

"Is shyness hiding behind his public persona?" Grace asked.

"Not that I had ever noticed," I replied.

"I don't want to dampen the thrill of Blane's special day, but I worry about your enthusiasm for the job," Grace said. "If shyness is not Mr. Long's problem, then oddness is the only explanation. And oddness can lead to all kinds of trouble."

Odd was the very word Vernon and Grace had both used before meeting Charles, I recalled.

"Did anything particularly strange happen this year?" Grace asked in her attorney manner.

"Well, my desk at school had a bizarre story," I replied.

"Oh?"

"Charles had asked Joe, the head of maintenance, to empty a large closet for me as an office and to buy a desk on sale. Joe shopped at the many charity resale stores. Periodically, Charles teased me about the desk, and I couldn't understand why because the desk was beautiful. Finally, Joe told me that a man had been murdered sitting at it prior to his purchasing it. After the police solved the horrid crime, concluded the trial, and released the desk, the family of the victim gave the item to thrift. With uncanny timing, Joe innocently bought it. Charles, however, recognized the desk from its frequent description in the *Palm Beach Post*: distinctive, hand-carved, floral wooden handles. Joe offered to return the piece when Charles identified it, but Charles told him that it was a great buy and went well with the school's other furniture."

"And Charles thought the story was funny?" Grace asked.

"Yes, he laughed about the desk quite often," I answered.

"That's not normal," Grace stated, matter-of-factly.

Instead of arguing, I tried to explain my feelings about my first year. I gave my sister a panoramic view filled with excitement and achievement. I had worked virtually nonstop, but the remarkable results were worth the time, effort, and risk. Not only did I teach my students an enormous amount of math and programming, but also they taught me an equal measure of what eager students can and want to learn. I received as much as I gave, and what I captured made me an expert on talented children in a way that could never be learned in any special education class for teachers. My education was first-hand—gifted children themselves taught me about gifted children—and what they taught me did not always match what schools of education dictated.

"Well, just be careful," Grace concluded.

"I will be," I answered, again thinking she had just spoken Vernon's identical words almost a year ago when he called me at her home, though she had not heard the conversation.

15. First Reflection

Vernon drove Grace and Brenna to the Palm Beach airport. I was content knowing that I would see them later in the summer. I settled into the sofa in the sunroom for some serious, detailed reflection. While teaching at Merritt Country Day was never totally smooth, overall my maiden year was spectacularly successful.

Charles's plan to keep the ninth grade together in computer programming class did not work. Mid-year we rescheduled those who had not taken my seminar to a new class where the atmosphere was much better suited to their comfort level. Splitting that class was an early, first-hand experience with a crucial doctrine—performance grouping. Mathematically precocious students are capable of so much at a young age and are frustrated by not moving at their own rapid pace. The other students tend to develop math anxiety by having math prodigies in their classes. Neither is happy grouped together or progresses appropriately, and the teacher's job turns from rapture to anguish. Fortunately, Charles not only shared my same predilection but also garnered emphatic confirmation from my work.

My ninth grade boys were wonderful in programming class. One had an older sister taking the supposedly comparable course at the public high school. He frequently criticized his sister's boring work. I started the year using the same textbook, feeling the decision was safe for a new course at MCD. However, within a month I shed the book because its fragmented, simplistic approach was frustrating. By the spring my students had learned enough to program their own games. Most were dozens of pages of code and looked professional visually. The students loved showing off their work at the festival. Teaching this class sharpened my insight into what mathematically talented students could accomplish with first-year programming and affirmed students' writing games as an integral part of a curriculum, exactly as I had anticipated at my initial MCD seminar.

My sixth grade advanced math course was special, and having Mimi in the class was ecstasy. I was thrilled to shape the mind of my own child. While the mother-daughter/teacher-pupil relationship didn't work at home, other than informally at dinner discussions or reading together when she was younger, our bond became magic in the classroom. She was like a high-tech sponge, absorbing at microsecond speed all emitted. The other girls and Daniel, also extremely bright, expressed abundant fondness for math that freely formed into genuine rapture. They became excited, day by day, as I revealed to them that math was a system of logic, a study of patterns, a body of language, and an object of beauty. Together—Daniel, the girls, and I—created a curriculum with boundless potential.

A new sixth grade girl, Bethany, who had been in elementary school with Mimi, entered this advanced math class early in November. Her parents were disappointed with public middle school by the end of the first quarter because they saw their daughter earning all *A* grades with easy effort and little learning, but with a definite emphasis on carrying the right designer purse. Of course, I had to spend many private hours for weeks teaching her what she had missed. I thought nothing of the extra work. MCD's teachers received no monetary compensation for anything of this nature— we were expected to be magnanimous for the good of the school. Bethany's becoming one of my best students was payment enough.

An accelerated seventh grade boy in my algebra class took the College Board SAT to qualify for the summer program at Johns Hopkins or Duke—two of the national centers for gifted students. I encouraged him to try based on his considerable amount of math learned from Keith and me and a few practice SAT exams. During my doctorate degree program, I had read extensively the original work on mathematically precocious youth done at Johns Hopkins University. But when my student's score came back six weeks later— 720 in math—the fascination for me became personal, leading to my teaching there. Though beginning as a whim, the experience whacked my mind into a whirl with the possible widespread implications for middle school math education.

More entries into competitions followed in March with my prize girls and Daniel entering the first contest of their math careers. While their result was lower than expected, sixth in the state, I knew that their math power had been rooted for a successful future.

Also, one Saturday in March Keith asked me to take the ninth grade boys to a Mu Alpha Theta math competition because he was already committed to the state MATHCOUNTS contest the same day with middle schoolers. I agreed for the sake of the students, although I was not happy about driving them an hour on the highway each way. Their adolescent bodies occupied my entire car, and their youthful conversations dizzied me. After the three-hour morning competition, we ate lunch at a nearby pizza restaurant. While my boys played the dot-to-dot games on the paper place mats, we overheard students from a competing school stressfully rehashing math questions. I marveled at how the MCD students took the math seriously at the contest but did not take themselves pretentiously during their meal. Still, like a neurotic mother hen, I nervously worried whether that school at the next table had beaten us. Then, back for the award ceremony, my apprehension quickly changed to applause as the MCD students garnered one trophy after another. The excitement was more contagious than the worst plague, and I knew that with these aggregate competitive experiences, I was undeniably infected.

What were the downside risks in this high-stakes education circuit? One slip from total professionalism could open the floodgates as an incident with Catherine West, a science teacher, revealed. One day in the spring, my sixth grade students arrived for math class uncontrollably angry with Catherine. Apparently, she had misgraded some tests, marking an answer correct on one test and the same answer incorrect on another student's test. But the students' fury was over her refusing to admit her mistake and correct the error. Settling the girls into math was difficult and so unlike them.

I mentioned this matter to Charles later that same morning, as I did with every potential problem, trying to avert a crisis. He dismissed it routinely. However, by the next morning, many sixth grade parents had called Charles, demanding a meeting. They wanted Catherine held accountable for lack of fairness. After some deliberation about whether parents could issue such an order, Charles granted their wish. The parents tried to hang Catherine—though what she had done was hardly a hanging offense. But Charles begged for forgiveness, blaming the incident on exhaustion and stress. Both as a new parent and teacher at MCD, I said nothing. Vernon, however, was very supportive of Catherine. Perhaps he worried about my own vulnerability. The incident certainly revealed the potential power and unpredictability of parents at MCD.

Looking around, I realized that my first reflection had been long enough. I needed to clean a school year's amount of mess at home.

16. First Dismissal

Charles Long dismissed ineffective teachers at the end of a school year. I admired him for doing what the public schools could not—maintaining the strongest faculty possible. In the public schools an administrator fired only a child molester, convicted felon, or someone worse. Not staying current in a subject and not teaching well never interfered with a teacher's accumulating pension years. Still, while politicians annually debated how to improve public schools, few acknowledged this rather simple flaw—the inability to fire under-performing teachers.

The first teacher I saw depart was my languishing colleague, D. Dottie Jones. Technically, she resigned—how Charles preferred the matter to appear. D. Dottie had a push and a pull, according to the expression. The pull was that she longed for more personal excitement. Her love life had gone nowhere in two years in Palm Beach. The push was that she knew Charles, many of the students, and I all viewed her as incompetent.

I learned about her plans on a quiet day at school during the first week after the official closing. Priscilla and I were alone in the reception area. She was organizing the report card mailing while I handed her mine, one by one, for insertion. Despising trite, vacuous superlatives, I wrote a lot about each student. Thus, I was typically the last to finish. Priscilla, in a yellow dress and with her silver hair, was unintentionally outfitted in the school colors. She worked with remarkable efficiency.

"Did you hear that Dottie is going to Germany next year?" Priscilla asked.

"What?" I shrieked in astonishment.

"It's true," replied Priscilla. "That's where she was during her missing week—interviewing in Europe at American schools. She apparently decided that she needed a true adventure."

"So she chose Germany?" I inquired.

"Well, that's where she got an offer. You know job hunting in May is very last-minute," Priscilla said.

"What is she going to teach?" I asked curiously.

"High school computer programming, including advanced placement," Priscilla answered.

"That's absurd," I responded. "She can't even teach sixth grade programming."

"Well, she was here yesterday researching names of teachers and making phone calls. She was looking for two summer tutors before she leaves—German and Pascal," Priscilla disclosed.

"She probably knows the same amount of both languages," I said sarcastically, though actually pleased with the news. Just then Charles entered the front door, seemingly back from a luncheon appointment.

"Oh, Dr. Kelman," said Charles, who, after one year, still enjoyed being playfully formal with me, even in front of Priscilla. "I'm glad you're here. Do you have a minute?"

"Sure," I answered, eager to confirm Dottie's leaving. Priscilla nodded knowingly at me.

As I followed Charles into his office, his exact five words—*do you have a minute*—echoed in my head. He had used those words before, though I had trailed him oppositely, from the mailboxes. He closed the door behind me and then took a paper off his desk while I sat in the chair by the door. He chose the chair under the tree rather than at his desk but quickly pushed the chair forward, ostensibly disentangling from the leaves, but effectively nestling close to me.

"Read this," he said, laughing as he handed me the paper. The letter was a recommendation for Dottie written by Charles. The more I read, the more the words glowed and praised.

"Are you kidding?" I asked.

"I needed to get rid of her," he replied. "She would never have gotten a job if I had told the whole truth." He laughed again.

"That's not really ethical," I commented.

"I'm just doing my job—I need to uphold an excellent faculty at MCD," he countered. "Dottie was okay, and she'll be okay at her new school. But she wasn't great. And we need greatness here."

I thought about how Vernon and I used to play Hearts with our children when they were younger. Before playing the first card, we all passed three cards left, then three across and three right. We called this opening *Pass the Trash*. Now Charles was playing a game with Dottie as the trash.

"You shouldn't have hired her in the first place," I reprimanded. "She had no teaching experience and knew nothing about a computer, except for how to turn it on and off—oh yes, I almost forgot—and also how to book a plane reservation. So how did you ever expect her to be great? You weren't being fair to her."

Charles smiled. He appreciated my lightening the plight with a little humor when, in fact, he knew I was actually annoyed about all my time-wasting, energy-depleting encounters with Dottie.

"She wanted a career change. She applied for the job. So I was *fair* to her—I gave her a chance. She had two years to make the jump—to wow the kids—but she couldn't do it," he said.

I was amazed at how well Charles could change a situation from his being wrong to his being right. How did he learn that maneuver? I didn't consider that he would ever use his special skill against me. Rather, I looked at Charles sheepishly, as if to say, *But you could have hired me*. He must have read my thoughts.

"I hired her because she was willing to take the described job," he continued. "You wanted to change the curriculum, the schedule, and the hours. There was nothing about the computer offerings that you didn't want to change."

"Computer *science* offerings," I interjected.

Charles continued without any discernible acknowledgment of the correction. "And, furthermore, you were only willing to do part of the job. In trying to make budget I couldn't risk the financial strain of increasing from one to two computer teachers—remember without the ninth grade."

"Weren't computers supposed to be the hallmark of the school?" I questioned. "I wanted to make something out of your nothing that you advertised as something. You even admitted to me at my first interview that your computer science curriculum was nothing." Although rather agitated as I repeated words, I continued. "I would never do a poor-to-average job just to keep the status quo. I'm only interested in excellence, and I thought you were, too." Suddenly, I realized that I should have stopped sentences before. After all, D. Dottie was leaving—the perfect outcome.

"Molly, you're so cute when you're angry," Charles teased.

Then I knew for sure that I shouldn't have said so much. "Mr. Long, don't ever patronize me," I said sternly.

"I'm sorry, but you were defending yourself needlessly," Charles said. His words were apologetic, but his tone wasn't.

Charles's chauvinistic non sequitur made me punctuate my mini tirade with, "Then you shouldn't have hired either one of us that year. Now we are all in an unpleasant situation."

"Not so," he replied. "Dottie has gained two years teaching experience here, and she is looking forward to the excitement of teaching abroad. I gave her a letter of reference without compromising myself any more than someone else in my position. That American School is delighted to have her."

I shuddered again at his remarkable rationalization. "But she doesn't know the subject she's supposed to teach there," I said, looking questioningly.

"I know your standards are extremely high, but finding good teachers is very difficult. By the time school starts, every school head has to make a decision from among the candidates at hand— myself included," Charles explained. "Dottie is a good person."

"Something is very wrong with what's happening," I said, clearly concerned with Charles's whitewash. "Being a good person and knowing a subject are two entirely different matters," I added. But then I had another thought. "Wait—did I spend countless hours on the report about the second lab for nothing?"

"No," Charles answered. "We're ready for two labs anyway, and the Board will ask for specifics."

"But I could have written one report. I don't agree with her part."

"Occasionally, we all do some work that is appropriate at the time, but then circumstances change," Charles stated, again glossing over my valid concern.

"I hope it's only occasionally," I argued.

"Let's just focus on Merritt Country Day. You have to understand the magnitude of demands made on me concurrently from so many directions. Not everyone sees the school moving as you and I do. I must educate some of our families and board members first. All of this takes time. I need you on my side, Molly." Charles spoke passionately, seething with charisma.

He reached across, taking both my hands, parallel in his, as if his touching me would confirm my support. I was thankful for the space occupied by Charles's long legs as we sat facing each other so that our joined hands were neither in his lap nor mine. Considering the inappropriateness of his action, I again noticed his large hands as they enveloped my small ones. I nervously retracted, pretending quickly to need my hands to doff hair that had fallen on my face.

"So should I rewrite the report?" I asked, standing to leave.

"No. It'll be fine. We can work around it. The main thing is that it makes a case for two labs," Charles answered, standing and opening the door for me. "Have a wonderful summer."

"You, too," I said, bewildered that he was willing to send an incorrect report to the board.

My head was spinning upon exiting Charles's office. I had only wanted to verify Dottie's leaving, not engage Charles's affections. Why did he feel he had the right to take my hands? At least I had learned why he had hired D. Dottie over me. Despite Charles's strength of personality, he feared excessive change. However, that apprehension was behind us now. I wanted to believe that he would never again hire unsoundly or waver unwisely. His goal was solely excellence, I told myself. *Together we will build a great school.*

I entered the computer lab and looked from wall to wall. Shaking my head at the mess, I hoped that Dottie would save time for cleaning and organizing. Then I sat in the desk chair and pondered.

Why is *Buyer Beware* a well-known phrase in purchasing a car but not in selecting a school? I worried about schools desperate for teachers in certain subjects and felt particularly sorry for the

American parents at Dottie's new school. They probably assumed that the advanced placement computer science course, because offered in the catalogue, would be proper.

Whether D. Dottie had told her new headmaster that she understood the subject or that she would learn it, the truth was that she didn't even know how little she knew. She thought that the syntax of a language like BASIC for the sixth graders or Pascal for her new job solely comprised programming. She had no idea that mastering a large body of standard techniques, developing the art of creating algorithms, and understanding the necessary background in logic and mathematics were also required. I was glad that she would be preparing over the summer when I wouldn't have to watch.

Focusing on poor D. Dottie's struggle to teach computer science in Germany, though, was in the larger picture of education, microscopic. She was merely one more grain of sand on a beach of teachers out of field. And Charles Long, the man who inspired me so deeply, was, in effect, responsible for spattering this speck. Our conversation had revealed a facet of his personality that could cause a tumultuous journey to excellence—a masterful flair for justifying his errors. Unsettled by witnessing my first dismissal, I left the computer lab determined to have a productive summer, but unclear about what the next school year would bring.

17. First Sweeping

A second firing that summer—Elizabeth McFadden, Lower Division Head—was a huge surprise. Besides the business manager, admission officer, and Charles, she was the only other administrator at the school. Again, Priscilla told me, this time one day late in June when I stopped by school to check on Dottie's status of vacating the computer lab.

"How did Elizabeth feel?" I asked Priscilla after hearing the news.

"First very angry and then, believe it or not, relieved," she replied. "Elizabeth worked extremely hard. Now she can breathe again."

Relieved—the word echoed in my mind. For a moment I tried to picture myself as Elizabeth. I imagined my job becoming so intense and frustrating that leaving it, whether voluntarily or by force, was actually welcome. The image, though ill defined, was plausible because after one year the volume and degree of work, whether mandatory or self-imposed, already consumed me.

"Parents and teachers are shocked when they hear," Priscilla added.

"What? You're telling people?" I asked.

"I'm telling everyone who calls and asks for Elizabeth," Priscilla explained. "Those were Charles's instructions. Well, not that she was fired, but that she decided to move near her ailing parents. I think Charles arranged things this way on purpose—he's on vacation, leaving me here to get the word out. He'll have fewer questions to answer when he gets back." Then, abruptly changing the subject she added, "Oh, and Charles called in a message for you this morning. The new computer lab is a go. He said to research new hardware and be ready to present a proposal when he returns—by August first."

"Have you seen the lab?" I asked Priscilla. "It's worse than a month ago. Dottie left everything everywhere."

"She left as well," Priscilla said and shrugged.

I remained in the chair by Priscilla's desk for a few more moments contemplating what had just happened. Priscilla had clearly already digested the retching news because she was busy working, seemingly not troubled by Elizabeth's departure or Dottie's mess.

Proceeding with my work was exactly what I needed to do as well because planning a new computer lab was a sizable task. So, I traveled to Washington in July to visit my sister exactly when NECC, the National Educational Computer Conference, was held there. Seeing Grace and Brenna was always such a treat. Moreover, I was able to shop hardware and software comprehensively and efficiently in the convention's exhibit hall.

Suspecting that Charles would neither call me upon his return nor find a note in his packed mailbox, and with Priscilla on vacation, I called MCD steadily when I returned from D.C. until Charles was back as well. He told me to stop by without giving me an exact appointment. Had he no respect for others' time?

Fortunately, he was in his office when I arrived later that afternoon. I knew to avoid lunchtime.

"Dr. Kelman!" he blared as he stood, hugged me, and closed the door. "You look great."

"It's only been two months," I responded somewhat flustered, sitting in my usual seat. "You look rested."

He nodded, returned to his desk chair, and then asked, "Are you ready for a second, big year?"

"Definitely not. We need to finalize this new computer lab," I answered.

Intentionally changing the subject, he replied, "You didn't ask me about Elizabeth's leaving."

"Was I supposed to?" I asked.

"Don't you want to know?" he questioned, as if playing a guessing game.

"Are you trying to tell me that you want to tell me? If that's your wish, then go ahead." I responded to his gambit, though really wanting to discuss new hardware.

Charles smiled. "Elizabeth was undermining both the school and me. She wasn't being loyal," he explained.

"In what way?" I asked. As long as he started the conversation, I indulged my curiosity.

"In her dealings with parents, students, and board members. I would tell her one thing, and she would say or do the opposite. The situation became intolerable. I had to take out the iron broom again," he said.

I cringed at his metaphor and then focused on his word *again*. I had heard that he had fired several teachers before my starting at MCD. "That's a shame," was all I cared to comment because I had no dealings with Elizabeth or the elementary grades. But then I asked, "Who is her replacement?"

"I'm taking this opportunity to restructure the administration. I've appointed Rhonda Seddon to Lower Division Head and Catherine West to a new position—Upper Division Head. That will free my time," Charles explained. He pronounced *Seddon* in his fake-French joking manner, the same as he did with the word *scandal*, moving the accent from the correct first syllable to the incorrect second and making Rhonda especially French by nasally punctuating the *don*. Rhonda, in fact, in her ever-present silver and turquoise jewelry, was as southwest as one could be. "I'm also forming academic departments," he added. "I would like Keith to be Math Department Chair and you to be Computer Department Chair."

"Computer science," I corrected. "Do I have the option of declining?" I dared asking, knowing the answer.

"Absolutely not," he jested in return. While I enjoyed the humor in our conversations, I had the sense of uncertain destiny in this appointment—and we still hadn't planned the new computer lab.

"What does the job entail?" I questioned.

"Well," he said, trying to be extra charming. "I would like you to help me formulate a job description for the department chairs." Charles looked at me warmly with his head intentionally tilted to one side. Was that a new, coquettish mannerism or had I never noticed it before? It matched his crooked smile, I thought.

Refusing would have been pointless. "Sure," I replied, unintentionally sighing, causing Charles to redouble his head tilt and eye focus. "When do you need it by?"

"Yesterday, of course," was his answer. He laughed heartily.

"Of course," I said. "That's the MCD way." Charles laughed again. I added, "I am concerned about one thing, though."

"Just one?" Charles gibed.

I sat up straight. "Given the sixth grade parents' insurgency over Catherine last year, do you think that charging her with the Upper Division is wise?"

"The parents are very forgiving. They know that she was just stressed. They also know that she's a good person and a great teacher. Besides, she's the only one who can handle the discipline issues. I don't have time any more to sit on the kids myself when they need guidance."

"I'll get back to you as soon as I can about the department chair duties, but may we please talk about the new computer lab now?" I asked.

"I need to check on one thing. I'll meet you back here in ten minutes. You can wait if you like," he said, almost striking my arm with the door as he dashed out.

Leaning back, I noticed for the first time a door behind the silk tree. Why block a closet with such a large item of décor?

Then I gazed into the skylight. I viewed my writing the department chair job description as getting the matter correct. If someone else wrote it, I would probably give Charles edits anyway. I was flattered that Charles asked for my collaboration, for my direct assistance with an academic issue.

Perhaps Dottie's departure had been by mutual consent. But concerning Elizabeth, I had experienced my first sweeping, Charles Long style. While I praised Charles for his strength of personality in dismissing ineffective teachers, I hoped, though, that he would be more careful and thorough before hiring. The painful hurt that was generated seemed so avoidable.

When I had just finished these thoughts, amazingly, Charles returned to his office.

18. First Chair

"Meet anyone interesting in D.C.?" Charles asked curiously, while shuffling papers he brought back from wherever he had been.

"Grace's government friends," I replied.

"So what did you learn about computers?"

"Well, do you remember when word got out about the new lab, how we were getting conflicting advice on IBM versus Apple?"

"Do I remember?" he emphasized. "Kids, parents, teachers— I've never heard from so many opinionated people. Just like with cars, only worse than Mercedes versus BMW."

"Worse than American versus Japanese cars," I added, continuing the metaphor.

"Worse than Volvo versus every-other-car-in-the-universe," Charles rejoined comically.

"Well, I'm prepared to settle the dispute," I stated firmly.

"Do tell," he demanded.

"I pick neither," I said.

"What?" Charles asked.

"I pick the Commodore Amiga. Charles, wait until you see this machine. It's totally user-friendly. Its operating system is window-based instead of command-based. And it operates with so little memory. It has adorable icons that represent disks and files and also has drawers—like a bureau—to keep them in. Its mouse has two buttons instead the Apple IIGS's one—the left for pointing, clicking, and dragging, and the right for menu selection. But, here's the clincher for the kids—it has four thousand ninety-six colors and makes the sounds of a full orchestra," I explained excitedly.

"I think you like it," Charles joshed.

"I love it! It's perfect," I replied.

"You're positive?" he asked.

"I am truly positive. It's such a dream to use compared to those temperamental Apples and DOS-driven IBMs. It will let the kids be so creative," I said.

"How's the price?" Charles asked.

"That's the amazing part—it's actually less for a more powerful product," I commented.

"And software is available?"

"The Logo, BASIC, word processing, and desktop publishing are all superb," I boasted.

"Okay, we'll form a mini-committee that will vote unanimously— you, me, Keith, and two board members I have in mind. And what's the sell to our clientele?"

"That we selected a computer for middle school, not Harvard Business School," I answered.

"Perfect," Charles responded.

"Well, it's true," I protested.

"Not for one moment do I doubt the wonderful things you'll accomplish with the students on these new computers," Charles said affectionately.

Quickly changing the subject, I commented lamentably, "So, Dottie's wish for a second lab is coming true, except that she's not here to see it."

"No, but Renuka Mohmadd accepted the computer position for the lower grades. I'll have Dottie's computers moved into a room for her, and you can keep the current lab," Charles said.

"Computer *science* position," I amended. I was pleased with Charles's plan but confused as to why he decided on staffing without consulting me, his newly appointed department chair. Nevertheless, Renuka, who was teaching fourth grade at MCD, was not only computer-literate but also resourceful and inventive. "Renuka is a great choice—she's a real self-starter."

"So, it's done," Charles said, tapping his desk.

The global *it* was far from done—the new lab would surely generate dozens of issues. However, I redirected the conversation, surprising Charles with an offer.

"Vernon and I will pay for the computers. He's very excited that I'm so excited."

"That's extremely generous of you," Charles said.

"We would like to have the amount deducted from my salary, right up front," I explained.

"Fine," Charles replied.

"And also—this donation is anonymous, please," I requested. Charles looked at me as if he understood. Of time and money, many parents generously gave both, while teachers donated solely the former. Both parent and teacher, I wanted to be comfortable among my colleagues.

"For now," Charles stated.

"For the indefinite future," I retorted. "Well, I have tons of work to do."

"Just two more questions," Charles said, feigning seriousness. "Can the human eye really detect four thousand ninety-six different colors?"

"Of course, not. But it's sixteen cubed—that's the way the machine is built. And your second question . . . ," I remarked, now prepared for another gibe.

"Shall I have Joe move your desk to the computer lab?"

"No, I think I'll leave it behind in the closet for the next roomless, freshman teacher. I'll use the one already in the lab. But thanks anyway," I answered and left.

I immediately went to the computer lab to imagine the new hardware there when Emma tapped on the window.

"*Mon amie*," said Emma as she entered the lab briskly. "Tell me, tell me right now. Is it true that Dottie left for France?"

"Germany," I replied.

"Oh, thank goodness! She has no French accent at all," Emma exclaimed. Then, quickly looking around, she added, "Look at this mess. Tell me that you're not going to clean it."

"Who else? It's going to be my room," I answered.

Emma walked here and there, lifting, examining, and returning small items. "I feel as if I'm in her private, bedroom-bureau junk-drawer. How could she have left all of this? Look! It's a little animal pin—oh, a computer bug. That's so sad. It must have been a gift from a student. Wait! You're not doing the newspaper class—tell me that you're not," Emma begged, seemingly horrified at the thought.

"I appreciate your concern, but I am," I said.

"It's endless, thankless work," Emma cautioned.

"Look who is talking about endless, thankless work. What don't you do for this school? You teach students with scheduling conflicts during lunch and do homework with foreign students even if their native language is not French."

"But the newspaper is different," Emma replied.

"I have no choice. It's part of the job," I said.

"Well, change the job. March into Charles's office right now," Emma ordered.

"I can't. I just came from Charles's office," I accounted.

"Oh, the new department chair thing—he got me, too." Emma sighed and shrugged. "But whom has he made first chair?" she asked, teasingly referring to the MCD faculty as an orchestra.

"Rhonda and Catherine, apparently."

"Aha," Emma said.

"The newspaper class will be fine. Charles is letting me reshape the entire computer science curriculum, and I'm getting new computers. Besides, I enjoy writing, and I'm interested in graphic design. I'll learn something, too, which always makes a new course interesting for me," I explained.

"I'm taking you to Sunday brunch on Worth Avenue to celebrate—right after the first issue is finished," Emma offered.

"Thanks, I accept," I said gratefully.

"*À votre santé*! You'll need it this year," Emma called as she left.

19. First Lab

Faculty meetings were more frustrating than the previous August's. Charles, giving his new administrators some responsibility and freeing his own time, had appointed Rhonda Seddon and Catherine West to organize the sessions. Meanwhile, Charles had found help for me in the form of a carpenter who donated the construction of perimeter tables to hold the new computers and a student who painted the walls a lovely, fresh peach—my choice—over the dirty, institutional beige. The barbecue restaurant furniture remained in the center of the room for math lessons.

However, I still had considerable work—annoying, such as cleaning Dottie's motley mishmash; routine, such as settling into her desk; and serious, such as running diagnostics on the new hardware. So, when I entered the opening faculty meeting greeted by Rhonda saying, "We're going to start off with some Mousercise," I fumed and left, stunned at Rhonda and Catherine's actual choice of activity for their notice to dress comfortably.

I really didn't care that Jane Fonda's *Workout* had been a top-selling video for the past few years or that Disney had capitalized on the trend as well. With everything on my mind, I hardly had the patience to do a Minnie imitation. And Rhonda looked more like a model for a Santé Fe jewelry store than an exercise wear shop. Charles followed me out.

"Molly, wait," he said, running after me.

"Are they kidding?" I asked as he came near.

"I guess what we have here is the Lower Division approach to faculty meetings," he explained in an attempt to make the gathering right.

"It's not a Lower Division approach—it's an Idiot Division approach. Who has time for that nonsense? Didn't you okay their plans?" Obviously, he hadn't, and my asking stung somewhat. "When I get home, when my work is done for the day, I'll get some real exercise, not wasting time when I'm supposed to be getting ready for the school year. Tell Rhonda and Catherine to buzz me if they want to talk about the computer science curriculum," I added sarcastically as I opened the door to my remodeled lab. There I found the carpenter making another mess after I had already vacuumed what I thought was his last batch of sawdust. I shuddered at the disarray. Charles just nodded at me—he knew that I was right. As he opened the office door, I considered that he ran after me not out of concern but as his excuse to forgo the bouncing and gyrating. I was too harried to think about whether Charles had selected the wrong administrators.

The academic preparation was no less daunting than the physical. Logo programming, a language with both geometric and list processing environments, became the sixth grade computer science course. Computer literacy—the history and vocabulary of computer science—along with application software—spreadsheets, word processing, databases, and presentation graphics—was perfect for the seventh grade. For the eighth graders, desktop publishing—a new, promising type of software—complemented the newspaper publication as an integral component. Learning the new software myself, reviewing possible textbooks, and planning lessons and assignments for all three grades was a huge undertaking. Meanwhile, by my helping Cecily and Catherine with the scheduling, I found the periods to continue more advanced programming instruction for the mathematically talented students.

When school officially began, all of the sabotaging of hardware ended. After all, the students knew that I would retaliate severely if they tried anything subversive—not that I had to do anything ruthless to make students behave. With small classes I could see most activity. Furthermore, I set an example the very first time someone misbehaved. All I needed to say was, "Excuse me. Is that how you behave in my classroom? Is that how you behave in this school?" To a more serious offense, I added, "Are you trying to get expelled from computer science class for the rest of the year? Mr. Long and I can easily help you arrange that." Then I stared at the student for a few seconds, and the questionable behavior was over. Though my petite stature hardly made me frightening-looking, somehow the students saw terror in my eyes. Of course, that's my explanation. Charles' opinion was that my students behaved, as opposed to Dottie's, out of respect. Along with daily delivery, consistent fairness and befitting fun were crucial.

Predictably, the worst comments about the new computers came from Mr. Greig, the father and board member who had repeatedly cried, "But she's not Mr. Clark." But the abundant controversies over the hardware selection ameliorated quickly as the students became evermore engaged. In fact, questioning the hardware selection morphed into a different, unanticipated clash as the students became over-enamored with the new computers. Enthralled with the Amiga's spectacular sound and graphics, middle schoolers soon began purchasing computer games and bringing them to school to play during that awful MCD institution called *Activity Period*—the frivolous last class of the day. Whether fighting drooling monsters in mazes, ducking swarming bats in caves, or killing opponent's life-like pieces in chess, the characters came alive on the screen with motion and music. While students delighted in these games, I began to see the evil in the computer more clearly.

With Charles's full support, I waged my own war like one of the software characters—only mine was against all the damage Dottie had done by allowing computer frivolities at school. I resented being a peacekeeper in a room while children actively, vocally, played computer games. Parents could permit their children to play computer games at home instead of reading, exercising, or studying, but I was certainly not going to sanction the activity during school hours. This battle took some time, and often I felt bloodier than the animated, combatant personae on the screen—but in the end I won.

Controversies aside, the joy of having my own classroom was like the delight of a teenager having private space after sharing a room with a sibling or like the thrill of a college senior finally having a single after three years of roommates. The happiness sprang from having everything in the right place, having any mess be one's own, having quiet with the door closed to think or organize, having an item left at day's end be exactly there upon return the next morning, having everything handy to maximize instruction, having free desk space to place one's lesson papers while teaching, and having full access to the board rather than maneuvering around *SAVE* warnings. The ecstasy emanated from efficiency in work and pride in ownership.

Blane had elected to attend the public high school for all four years, but Mimi assisted me in straightening the computers every afternoon and cleaning the countertops when needed. She said she helped to get us home earlier, but Mimi had an attachment to the lab as well. I loved that first lab as I had loved my first apartment with Vernon. That first lab was like a second home.

20. First Father

Even after my lab was functional, frustrations started as early as the third week of school on Parent Back-to-School Night. The annual September event held across the country at public and private schools alike generally welcomed happy, polite parents—but not this time.

One father lambasted my ninth-grade programming course. What particularly annoyed me was that he wasn't a stranger. "What if a student is absent? How does he make up the instruction?" my supposed friend asked aggressively. "He has no textbook to read, and he definitely can't get help from his parents in this subject."

I thought quickly. Was his concern that his son wouldn't be as strong as the previous year's math whiz boys who had shaped the course's curriculum? Or did his last comment reflect a threatened feeling that the student was learning something beyond the father's own comprehension?

I replied confidently, "You know Mr. Long has a policy that students may call teachers at home concerning academic matters, especially during or following an absence. That would be a first step. I would explain what he or she had missed and make an appointment for a make-up lesson. MCD teachers are always giving extra help. And this is not the first class without a textbook—the situation was the same for these students in seventh grade math with Mr. Clark."

My answer, however, did not satisfy this man, ironically a public school teacher. He harped repeatedly on the same themes without variation.

I needed to quiet him, so I interrupted somewhat boldly. "I certainly hope you are not implying that I shouldn't teach substantially each day. I am not going to waste time while one student has a fever or another has

87

a grandparent visiting. Mr. Long has a very clear faculty rule: something significant happens in every class every day. And I am certainly not going to remove computer programming from the curriculum because of a dearth of quality textbooks or parental knowledge."

The tension was evident in the room. Fortunately, another parent quickly asked a totally different, friendly question, and then the bell rang for the change of classes.

At the end of the evening, I told Charles about the incident. He was near the parking lot, saying good-bye to as many parents as possible. "I'm sorry," he said kindly. "You're now fully inducted into the independent school teaching profession."

"Great," I replied sarcastically.

"Next time—and there will be a next time—say to the parent, 'I suggest we finish the conversation in Mr. Long's office.' That will shut him up fast—at least temporarily," he advised.

"Oh, I wish I had thought of that," I said.

"It all comes with experience, Molly," Charles responded, putting his arm around me. The hug was comforting at the time, prior to the betrayal warning.

"I'm going home. It's been a tiring, fourteen hour day, and I teach first period tomorrow."

Charles released me from his embrace, nodding. "Tomorrow— more challenges, no doubt."

Another parent conflict occurred shortly thereafter. One of the sixth graders transferred from Merritt Country Day to public school after the first three weeks in September but then surprisingly returned to MCD at the end of the first quarter. The family's muddle was astounding. While the boy resumed his original schedule at MCD, making up six weeks of Logo instruction was a serious undertaking for both him and me. Charles entered the lab after school one day when I was alone working. He carried a chair over to my computer.

"Dr. Kelman," Charles said. "Always working."

"Something must be serious," I replied.

Charles smiled and asked, "Why do you say that?"

"Because you always either wait until I bump into you at the mailboxes or until I come to you on my own. Your visiting me means a critical concern," I answered.

"Sometimes you are too perceptive for your own good," he commented.

"Well, tell me. I can take it," I rejoined.

"Mr. Doggett called this morning, very upset that his son is not doing well in your course," Charles explained.

"No kidding," I said to Charles incredulously. "Could you do well in a new subject if you missed weeks four through nine of school? This father has nerve."

"I agree completely," Charles responded. "That's not the issue. What are we going to do about the boy?"

"That's easy. Take him out of the class," I answered.

"I was hoping you would say that," Charles replied. "But I was afraid that you would take it personally and be upset."

"Me? Upset?" I asked in a most agitated voice. Charles laughed. "I won't miss either one of them," I added with a smile. Charles tapped the tabletop in his characteristic manner, indicating that the matter was finished. He seemed content as he left.

Soon I clashed with yet a third father. With his days and nights reversed, he was eccentricity exemplified. His oldest of four sons, my student in two classes, cried out for his father's attention, reflecting this need in bizarre classroom behavior. One day he saved his programming exam on an old floppy disk with the metal plate missing, oblivious to creating a damaged file. Another time, after hastily finishing a math test, he marched back and forth from his seat to my desk to the wastebasket, getting tissues, blowing his noise loudly, discarding the wadded trash as if he were shooting baskets, and universally disturbing the other students—until I abruptly threw him out of the room.

Charles arranged for sessions with the faculty, the parents, and a counselor. After seeing no progress, I suggested that we cancel the meetings until the father agreed to eat dinner with his family instead of at three o'clock in the morning. The other teachers, ecstatic over my brazen proposal, readily agreed.

One late afternoon the next week, I saw Charles at the mailboxes. The room smelled of food recently warmed in the microwave—someone's delayed lunch or early dinner.

"Dr. Kelman," he said. "You look worn. Did you have a bad-hair day?"

"No worse than others," I jested with a forced smile, implying that the charm of working at MCD had diminished.

"Come into my office, and we'll chat a little," he suggested. Blane, now a ninth grader at the public high school, was on his own schedule, while Mimi was at the musical rehearsal, so I had time. I followed Charles down the hallway. He took my usual seat, so I was left to sit under the tree. We both pushed our chairs forward—he to close the door and I to disentangle silk leaves from my hair.

"Guess what our friend did today," I began. Charles immediately knew I was talking about the boy with the day-night reversed father.

"Do I want to know?" he asked.

"No, but I'll tell you anyway. He flunked the math test because he left most of it blank. He said that he didn't see the questions. Now he's blind, too, in addition to everything else," I grumbled.

Charles laughed at my line and then became quite serious. "Molly, I need you more than you know. Don't wear yourself out worrying about these kids. Some day they will grow up to be productive citizens. Meanwhile, their parents must take charge," he advised.

"But Charles, some of these kids and parents are totally out of touch with the reality of the school. I have so many wonderful students showing amazing growth. But other families are draining me," I complained. "Vernon always says that at home I talk more about the few troublesome students than the many great ones."

"That's normal. But don't let a few characters sap your energy or divert your attention. I play a little game to help me keep my sanity." Charles chuckled as he completed the sentence.

I braced myself. "A game?" I asked timidly.

"I give secret codes names to the most annoying adults. When they transgress acceptable behavior, thinking of their code names saves me," he disclosed.

Who did he think he was—a Secret Service agent guarding first ladies *Springtime* Mamie, *Starlight* Pat, or *Pinafore* Betty? "You must be kidding. Give me some examples," I urged.

"Well, I've created secret code names for years. Some in my compendium are food-based: *Creep Suzette* was squirmy, *Hannah Banana* slippery, and *Brown Betty* somber," Charles explained. "Some are history-based: *Maid Marion* was innocent, *Robin Hood* stole from the strong students and gave to the weak, and *Amelia Ear-Nose-Throat* always called in sick with a respiratory virus. Then there are others—the current ones."

"The current ones?"

"Sure," Charles said, "I call our little friend's nocturnal father *Batman*. And you know Mr. Zahn on the board? I dubbed him *Comet*."

"I'm afraid to ask why—something about a shooting star?"

"No, because he's so abrasive." Clearly enjoying his own joke, Charles laughed.

"What about Mr. Doggett?"

"Who, *Snoopy*?"

"Do you have a code name for me?" I asked fearfully. I couldn't think of a food with my name. But I quickly decided that if Charles said *Molly Flanders*, I would resign instantly.

"Molly, of course not. You're one of my prize teachers and favorite people," Charles answered as he reached forward and clasped my hands in his. I felt as awkward as always when he took my hands, but I appreciated his sincerity.

"Just checking," I mocked, as I stood and waved good-bye. "Thanks for the encouragement." I carefully maneuvered around his chair, which was partially blocking the door.

That evening sitting at my desk at home grading papers, I smiled while thinking about Charles's fatuous code names. I decided to start my own jolly diversion—awarding one father each year the *Shmuck of the Year* award. Having had several unpleasant encounters, I had a hard time bestowing the initial title. But I decided on honoring the first father who annoyed me—the one at Back-to-School Night.

"What's so amusing?" Vernon asked.

"Just more MCD lunacy," I answered, so engrossed, that I didn't realize I had laughed aloud or that Vernon was nearby. I told neither my husband nor my boss about my secret game.

21. First Dean

Parents of one middle schooler at MCD opened a restaurant just a mile from school. They offered to prepare gourmet sandwiches for lunch one day a week at a discount, with the profit going to the school. Since MCD had no cafeteria or food service, parents and students welcomed convenient lunch options. Charles presented this opportunity to the faculty, suggesting that the teacher who undertook the task could name the project on which the funds raised would be spent. Of course, considerable work was involved—organizing the homerooms to collect the money, collating the orders, phoning the total purchase to the restaurant, picking up the food, and distributing the lunch to the students correctly.

Still energized by my first successful year at MCD, I accepted this offer. Was I crazy or was I the only teacher free the period before lunch? I announced that the profit would buy a laser printer for the new computer lab for more professional printing of the school newspaper.

I even added ice cream to my peddling repertoire. I purchased bars, cones, ices, and other pre-packaged novelties and sold them for a half dollar each—ten to thirty cents profit an item depending upon whether a national or Publix brand. The ice cream flowed steadily from the supermarket to my home freezer to the school freezer to the eager students.

One tiring afternoon I sat at a school picnic table and indulged in a frozen strawberry juice bar while breathing in some fresh fall, non-chalky air. Charles passed by and eyed me enjoying the snack.

"I'm glad to see you taking a little break," Charles commented.

"Would you like one? I'll treat you," I said.

"Sure, but I'm paying," Charles replied, reaching into his pocket. He handed me two quarters.

"Wholesome or decadent?" I asked.

"Oh, definitely decadent. As decadent as possible," he answered.

"Wait right here. I'll just be a second," I stated. I dashed to the stash, made my selection, and hurried back, knowing that Charles could be pulled away at any minute.

Fortunately, he was still sitting at the table when I returned. He was viewing the campus critically in all directions from his position, looking as if he enjoyed the contemplative moment. The nearby yellow hibiscuses were in beautiful bloom.

"A vanilla ice cream bar filled with fudge and peanuts and coated with dark chocolate. It's the best I could do," I offered modestly.

"Molly, you've convinced me—first that unforgettable chocolate mousse cake, then the lunch sandwiches, and now the ice cream. I'm declaring you *Dean of Cuisine*."

"I know you're happy with naming Rhonda and Catherine as Heads, but don't get carried away with titles," I cautioned.

"But you're my first dean," he boasted.

"Are you making fun of me?" I asked.

"Molly, I would never, ever make fun of you. I take you very seriously, plus you keep me honest," he said.

"I suppose this title is like Department Chair—I don't have the option of refusing," I responded.

"You're right," Charles confirmed. "But this time, no written job description is needed. See you tomorrow." He ate his last bite, smiled askance, tapped the tabletop, and walked toward his office.

With astounding irony—because of selling food in order to buy a printer to improve Dottie's legacy for ungrateful students—I had the dubious honor of becoming Charles's first dean. Was my title only a passing amusement for Charles in his job that was becoming increasingly more stressful?

Together we will build a great school. Together we will build a great school. Charles's memorable sentence echoed in my head. Somehow becoming *Dean of Cuisine* was not what I had imagined when Charles spoke those words to me.

22. First Rule

The newspaper class did not deserve the new printer. I foolishly thought that I could accomplish an ambitious project with any type of student. However, as I learned, those particular students were very spoiled, some as members of MCD's founding class and some with parents on the board. Their habits were so foreign to my way of thinking that too much damage had already been done for me to break them. Over the years the majority of maiden students poisoned new ones joining the cohort.

When I tried to enforce high standards, their typical response was, "But the students didn't have to do that last year." I usually replied, "Do I look like Miss Jones?" The students found that line particularly amusing, not just because Dottie was a large woman and I small. No, Dottie changed her hair color almost every month. If color 3B did not find a man for her, then she tried number 4A. The preteen students had enough savvy to know her modus operandi. Unfortunately, my humor did not sway them. They stuck to their lethargy with an ironic vengeance, rebuffing my instruction as an infliction.

Lorna, a girl who should have been the best of the group, was continually late with all types of deadlines. One day she left class leaving hundreds of papers—responses to a student/teacher poll, long sprocket-fed drafts of articles, and personal items as well—scattered around the lab—on the computer countertops, the restaurant tables, and even on the floor. Perhaps the tornado décor worked in her room at home, but I had another class coming into the lab immediately. I gathered her papers and sundries, walked to her next class, and pitched the litter at her. Everyone stared in amazement. Then I left without a word, thinking over and over that I should have listened to Emma and refused the newspaper class. Quickly, I decided that I needed to tell Charles about the incident before he heard from someone else.

Luckily, he was in his office with the door open following my next class. After knocking lightly to get his attention, I asked, "May I bother you for a moment?"

"My dear *Dean of Cuisine*, you are never a bother," he replied.

"Please be serious, Charles. Don't laugh," I pleaded.

Charles immediately laughed—until he detected from my demeanor that I was truly resolute in my request.

"You may not like what I'm going to tell you," I explained. Charles's face became worried. "Lorna, who as you know is so capable, has been impossibly sloppy with her work for too long. Today she left a huge mess in the lab right when another class was coming in. So I scooped it up and tossed the junk at her in her next room—but she had a study hall, so I didn't bother another teacher."

"Well, the last part at least was very considerate," Charles replied gravely. Then he burst into a monstrous laugh.

"There is nothing funny about this," I stated indignantly.

"I already knew."

"You already knew?"

"I already knew."

"Who told you?"

"You don't need to know."

"Only forty-five minutes have passed and somebody at this school has run in here to tell you? Teacher or student?"

"Molly, enough. If someone coughed across campus, I'd hear about it in my office."

"What do you do—breed busy-bodies at MCD?"

Ignoring my question, Charles sighed and now looked very thoughtful. "Actually, I've had a similar experience. Once I was very disgusted with the repeatedly low quality of a student's writing and his unwillingness to try to improve. At a meeting with his parents, I said, 'See this?' as I held up one composition from his folder. Then I crumbled it right before the parents' eyes and tossed it into the wastebasket. And then to make matters worse, since I didn't get a remorseful response, I kept doing it, one composition after the next. So we all reach a breaking point at one time or another."

"You did that?" I asked in amazement.

"I did," Charles confirmed.

"Well, I certainly won't tell anyone. Thank you so much for understanding."

"Is Lorna okay?" he asked.

"She's fine. Hopefully, she'll settle down now and produce some good work. She's so talented," I answered.

"Then the incident wasn't for nothing," he added, tapping his desk, then standing.

Charles could be so insightful and empathetic. I was grateful for my conversations with him.

Before long, however, another unfortunate situation occurred with the newspaper class because of a bug in the word processing program—new software we were using on the new computers. Curiously, files could be saved but not reopened—an extremely frustrating problem. The students suggested using the old computers in Renuka Mohmadd's room and physically cutting and pasting the newspaper. My reply to them was simply an enormous exhalation of exasperation. After consulting with the software company, I learned that the strange problem happened if a computer's internal clock had not been set to the correct date. And I hadn't had time to set the clocks because of all the work getting the lab ready. In fact, dissecting this problem was a superb lesson in software bugs, but the students had difficulty understanding anything that sophisticated.

The matter became dreadful when I found myself arguing with the students constantly. On one particularly horrific day, I stormed into Charles's office, kicked the chair away, slammed the door shut, stared straight into his eyes, and firmly offered, "You may have twice my proportional salary for the newspaper course if you find another teacher."

"Molly, calm down. What happened now?"

"Anything and everything—you pick. Look at me—look at how these kids bring out the worst in me," I expressed agitatedly.

"They need you. This bunch of students is atypically spoiled. And because you're the one teacher who has attempted to do the newspaper class properly, they feel put upon. Of course, there's going to be an adjustment," Charles said.

"We're well beyond an adjustment. They have zero regard for creative ideas, accurate interviewing, solid writing, attractive layout, and timely deadlines. My other students crave learning. They shun it. Charles, they're killing me," I pleaded.

"The problem is that arguing with them only exacerbates the situation. They may be lazy, but they're not placid. They enjoy bickering with you, so let's not give them a chance," Charles stated.

"What do you mean?" I asked.

"Here's a solution. Prepare a list of classroom rules that you will distribute and post. If they break a rule, I want you only to say to them 'Rule Broken.' That will mean that they earned one offense. If they start to debate, you say 'Rule Broken' again. That will mean that they earned a second offense. It's important that you say nothing else," Charles explained. "Since they can't argue, they have no choice but to work. Slowly, they'll come around. If not, after three offenses, they'll stay after school on Friday and do chores for Joe."

"Are you sure this plan will work?" I questioned.

"I'm sure. I've known these kids longer than you," he offered.

"You're so wise."

"Don't confuse experience for wisdom. Anyway, draft your list of rules tonight and put it in my mailbox in the morning. Let's get the system in effect as soon as possible," Charles replied.

"Thanks for your help," I added. As I repositioned the chair, Charles grinned.

"That's what I'm here for, Molly. I don't like to see you this way, but you're so cute when you're upset."

I had heard that remark from Charles once before and did not appreciate it either time. However, the discussion was over, I was exhausted, I had already opened his door, and Charles had been very supportive. I left the comment unanswered.

In the end, Charles's scheme worked. At least the students and I tolerated each other without carnage. However, a father who complained about this first rule earned my second annual *Shmuck of the Year* award. Fortunately for the secret title, MCD had an abundant supply of deserving dads.

23. First Champion

"Dr. Molly Kelman?" a female voice asked on the other end of the phone line. The day was a quiet afternoon in April of what had been a busy second year for me at MCD. Fortunately, I was free, working in the lab when Priscilla forwarded the contact.

"Yes," I replied with a questioning tone because I rarely received personal calls at school.

"Hello, this is the administrative office of the International Computer Problem Solving Contest calling. Congratulations! Your student, Noah Sanford, has won first place in the elementary division," the voice at the other end said.

"Are you serious?" was what came out of my mouth.

"Absolutely. His programs were clearly the best. We will be sending you two plaques shortly—one for the school and one for Noah. Could you please send us a photo of Noah for the press release?" the woman asked.

"Sure," I replied.

"And I would appreciate your making a statement about Noah now," she added.

I paused and said, "If every student were like Noah, every adult would want to teach." Where did that thought come from? I was stunned but pleased since I was generally not a quick thinker under pressure.

"How lovely. Don't hesitate to call the contest headquarters if you have any questions," she added, giving me her name.

"Thank you very much," I said, still shaking while I hung up the phone.

I ran into the main office where Emma was talking to Priscilla. They both looked up because I entered with considerable commotion.

"Molly, what's the matter?" Priscilla asked with a mature tone reflecting her official capacity as the school's front-line defense.

"Remember the programming contest?" I was breathing heavily as I spoke.

"I most certainly do," Emma said. "I was here that Saturday proctoring for you."

"Oh, yes. The afternoon before you broke not one, but four nails carrying the hardware to various rooms," Priscilla commented.

"Yes, that event. The phone call you just forwarded was from the contest office. Noah won first place in the elementary level!"

"Molly!" Priscilla screamed as she got up from behind her desk to hug me.

"Wait—this is an international contest! Tell me Noah won first place in the world," Emma shouted.

"First place in the world—at the elementary level," I confirmed.

"*Succès d'estime!*" Emma declared, waving her arms wildly before embracing Priscilla and me together in one bundle.

"That's it—I'm quitting," I told them teasingly. "I'll never top this award."

Within a few minutes, Charles entered from outside. He saw the excitement but barely responded—presumably too preoccupied with the issue of a long luncheon meeting. As he walked past our joyous demonstration, Priscilla shouted, "Molly, tell him."

Looking at Charles, I knew that the timing was not good. "Noah won first place in the world in the elementary level at the programming competition this month," I said with my voice dropping in tone and zeal with each word.

"Molly, elaborate," Priscilla interjected. Priscilla might have been icy to strangers, but she was loyal to MCD's teachers.

"The woman who called said that Noah's programs were clearly the best," I added.

"*Clearly*, Charles. Did you hear? *Clearly*," Priscilla repeated.

"Congratulations, Molly," Charles replied perfunctorily and excused himself.

"Where has he been?" Emma asked Priscilla.

"I don't know," Priscilla answered. "He's been keeping his own calendar recently."

I didn't let Charles's behavior spoil my excitement. I had sown special seeds in Noah in the fifth grade computer science class that originally I wasn't even supposed to teach, allowing him to blossom in sixth grade. I had learned from my older students to discard the published programming book and write my own materials. Everything worked in unison—professional freedom, hard work, excellent hardware, advanced software, and a remarkable student. I had thought that Noah had a chance of scoring well having solved four of the five problems the previous year with so much less nurturing, but I never expected a first place title.

As I pondered the budding of my first champion, I wondered whether my future students could ever have comparable success. Concurrently, I thought about Charles's reaction. Were his minimal congratulations due to absorption with a serious issue or resentment over a remarkable feat? Charles conscientiously empowered his teachers—he needed to expect noticeable results. Envy on his part would be counterproductive to the entire process. I resolved to speak to Charles about this concern.

I attributed Noah's victory in part to the Amiga computer. Its version of BASIC was far superior to any other on the market. While in some ways Amiga BASIC was similar to Pascal with a wide range of structured elements, the language was also user-efficient with an internal word processor for editing programs.

I attempted to call Commodore to entice the company into using Noah and his international victory in its advertising. My motives were to begin building a stellar college résumé for Noah as well as a distinguished national reputation for MCD. Unfortunately, calling Commodore was almost as difficult as reaching the White House. One person said to call the next in a hopeless chain.

Foolishly, I mentioned my idea to Charles in passing. A few days later, by chance, I noticed Parke Merritt, Mr. Greig, and Mr. Zahn with Charles packed into his tiny office and huddled around the phone with the door left open for air. I thought some emergency had happened but then caught the word "Commodore" in their conversation. I was flabbergasted—they were pursuing my idea, without telling me and without inviting me to participate.

I shoved in. Charles and I exchanged anger in our eyes—Charles at me for interrupting a board activity and I at Charles for double-crossing me. Charles clearly wished me to leave, as if I had walked into a male-only cigar room, or worse yet, a men's restroom. MCD board members behaved as if their activities were sacred. I accommodated Charles and his cronies because if I couldn't get through by phone to the right person at Commodore, they surely wouldn't succeed either. Later that day I learned I was right.

I found Charles at the mailboxes, and this time I asked him, "Do you have a minute?"

"Yes," he replied.

I started walking down the hallway, checking that he followed me. I knew the routine well—the seemingly impromptu setting at the mailboxes, Charles's identical five words, and the procession to his office. I had witnessed this custom with other teachers and had experienced it myself. Now with Charles's living the situation reversed, I wondered whether he empathized with teachers' probable curiosity and possible nervousness as they filed behind him.

I maneuvered my position, forcing Charles to sit under the tree while I stood. Then I closed the door.

"So, Charles, what's the deal? Who's the male chauvinist pig in the crowd? You? Mr. Merritt? Both of you? Oh, maybe it was Mr. Greig—first he didn't want the computers, and now he wants to take credit for them," I said disgustedly. I never stopped to think that no other teacher would address the headmaster in this manner. Candor always came first in my relationship with Charles.

"Molly, you know how men get," Charles replied.

"Yes, unfortunately, I do know how men get, and I don't work with or for pigs," I stated firmly. "May I remind you that I took the heat for selecting those computers, despite the fact that I paid for them myself? May I also remind you that I introduced programming into your abomination of a curriculum and that I am the one who taught Noah everything he needed to win that contest?"

"Okay, Molly, you're right," Charles murmured. "Why don't you sit down?"

"That's it? *Okay, Molly, you're right* is supposed to make everything all better like a bandage with a happy face? And when is the next time your male board members plan to steal my projects?"

Still standing, I stopped firing questions and waited for Charles to reply. The brief pause seemed infinite.

"Molly, you know that your successes are my successes," Charles said earnestly.

"No, I don't know that from your minimal congratulations," I countered, not overly thrilled with his cliché.

"I am very proud of you. You, more than anyone else, are advancing the name of the school. You've established that our mathematically gifted students love programming, and you've shown that a comprehensive computer curriculum is needed for all of the students. But I am often put in a difficult position dealing with the board members. They wanted to make the call." He oozed charm to lubricate his wiggle out of the uncomfortable predicament, but charm did not shield him from the demeaning silk leaves covering his head. And in my anger I wanted to remedy *computer* to *computer science* for the umpteenth time.

My love-hate relationship with Charles started developing at that moment. Few other headmasters, if any, would have given me the essential ingredients for unfettered creativity—the professional freedom to turn Noah into a champion. Yet, one lesson I learned in Harvard's math department was not to allow men to tread on me.

Charles's love-hate feelings for me also began then, I suspected. While I brought excellence and success to MCD, I demanded honesty and integrity from Charles. And though he encouraged me to believe that he was a moral person by nature and upbringing, steering MCD's growth brought trying demands on his character.

I decided to let Charles off easy. "Well, just as long as you understand my point," I said calmly.

"I do," he replied. We smiled awkwardly at each other, and I left.

What kept me going was that joy typically followed frustration at MCD. Not long after the surreptitious phone meeting, my hard work in computer science was not alone in reaping rewards. The results arrived in the mail from the Florida Math League competition. The seventh grade girls, those quintessential delights from last year— Mimi and her friends minus Daniel who had moved away—placed first in the state. I knew that despite their modest finish as sixth graders, they were primed for success.

This top victory was more than an ordinary triumph. The girls had retained the material from my course, allowing Keith to carry them to the next higher level. They had assimilated the way of thinking that both Keith and I had taught them—methods of approaching problems out of context. More importantly, the results established Keith and me as a team—and not just any team. Keith and I were as powerful in the classroom as Reagan and Thatcher at a summit, as dynamic at a math competition as Superman and Lois in a pursuit, as creative in our curriculum as George and Gracie in their comedy, as colorful in teaching as Sonny and Cher in a performance, and as devoted to our students as Ozzie and Harriet to their children.

Yes, Noah was my first champion, but now not my only one.

24. First Magazine

Though the English Department proposed initiating the first student literary magazine, no teacher stepped forward to coordinate the effort. Finally, Alexa Smyth, a history teacher who gave generously of her time and valued creativity in all students, crossed fields to undertake the project.

Problems stemmed from the fact that Alexa Smyth was not simply computer illiterate—she feared and detested computers. Unfortunately, over a period of a few months, Alexa had amassed a large collection of handwritten work, mostly poetry with a few short stories, on pieces of paper of various size, shape, color, and style. Without notifying me, Alexa gave the paper scraps to a parent to type on a typewriter. When I suggested politely to Alexa—for future reference—that edited, spell-checked, word-processed submissions would be a better approach, she replied that she preferred including the typing step for better readability. Her uninformed comment and colossal inefficiency propelled me into Charles's office.

"Charles, I don't know if I can work with Alexa. Look at the time she has already wasted. She has no regard for her volunteer mom," I explained to him one afternoon in early May.

"Molly, just do your best with her. She has much to learn."

"That's an understatement," I emphasized, not satisfied with his reply. "She has no concept of electronic files in a standard format. You've both sought my advice about the magazine too late."

"I have faith that you'll work things out," Charles added, almost indifferently.

"I didn't know that the literary magazine was going to be my project, too. Don't I have enough going on? Can't someone else learn how to desktop publish?"

"But you would supervise so much better," Charles answered, dallyingly.

I simply stared at Charles and left, knowing that the conversation was dead-ended.

Shortly thereafter, the parent volunteer worked in the lab during my free periods typing the full set of creations again—this time using a word processor, including saving them in ASCII format for importing into the desktop publisher, according to my instructions. I attempted to grade papers while she labored, but her questions were continual. "Shall I fix this spelling? Do you think the misspelling is intentional—you know, poetic license? Shall I correct this punctuation? Do you think the mispunctuation is intentional—you know, poetic license? Shall I fix this grammar? Do you think the grammar errors are intentional—you know, poetic license?"

I thought I would scream if I heard *poetic license* one more time. "Just do your best," I stated. After I spoke, I realized that I had unintentionally quoted Charles. My words were as little comfort to her as his identical words were to me because shortly thereafter her questions began again. "Shall I fix this meaning? Shall I include all of these similar poems?"

While I realized the folly of Alexa's undertaking, I was bound by Charles's rule that one faculty member should never speak ill of another outside the privacy of his office. "Type away," I advised simply and sighed.

"I should be able to finish in another three hours if I just word process exactly as is. I'll force myself not to question anything. Is that okay?"

"Perfect. The students are away at a field trip all afternoon," I answered.

After the woman completed her work, my turn was next. No student could have handled the massive desktop publishing demand. The layout for the project required my spending plentiful, uninterrupted hours in the lab.

The next Saturday morning quite early, I drove to MCD by myself. A residential development was under construction along one side of the road. The builder had created a long, curved, artificial lake, beautifully landscaped, acting as a buffer between the street and the residences while providing both for aesthetics and water retention. That morning a lovely, fine mist rose over the lake in an intricate, woven pattern. Normally, I never took enough time to view the environment. I was too busy talking to Blane or Mimi, concentrating on traffic, or contemplating some incident from school. The scene, though, was so picturesque that it gave me a few moments of inner tranquility before facing Alexa's reckless project.

As I worked, trying to place the poems artistically on pages and adding graphic design elements as well, the huge collection exceeded the capacity of the desktop publishing software—a first. I boiled with exasperation. I didn't know what was worst—the poor reflection that the magazine would have on the school if it were ever printed in Alexa's state, the students' loss by not learning proper writing techniques, or the valuable time I expended fixing an ill-prepared person's work.

On Monday I tried to discuss the fiasco with Charles, but he had taken a trip with an MCD Spanish-speaking mother to observe foreign language instruction at a school in Miami. The matter kept until Tuesday. Fortunately, I found Charles in his office during one of my free periods.

"Good morning. How was your visit yesterday?" I asked calmly.

Charles replied, "Oh, Molly, come in and close the door. Interesting—this school has some great language programs. I'm sorry that Emma wasn't along. What's on your mind?"

"Guess," I said negatively.

"The literary magazine?" Charles queried.

"Correct! How did you ever know?"

"I think I like you better when you're angry than sarcastic," Charles said, feigning deliberation.

"Why did you ever allow a computer illiterate history teacher to be in charge of a literary magazine? All she did was collect pieces in random format, waste time by having them typed on a typewriter, and then arrange them all, none rejected, unedited and unmarked, in broad categories—nature, humor, and friendship. How exciting!"

"I don't know what to say. The English teachers were swamped, and the project didn't seem that difficult," Charles replied.

"It shouldn't have been—but it is now," I stated.

"How's the prose?" Charles asked.

"The writing shows no concept of parallel construction. Boring sentences starting with 'there' and 'it' are plentiful. And the spelling, grammar, and punctuation have significant errors," I answered. "So how would you say it is based on that description?"

"An embarrassment to Merritt Country Day. How's the poetry?"

"Weak. The kids think that any piece of free-form rubbish constitutes an acceptable poem, unless you want to use poetic license as an excuse. Furthermore, Alexa wasn't selective at all. She's too nice. Some students have seven poems included when two good ones would have been better."

"Molly, you would make an excellent English teacher," Charles replied, trying to charm his way out of an uncomfortable situation.

"Oh, sure, on top of everything else. You're changing the subject," I reminded him.

"You know, you're always blue when you wear that blue outfit," Charles commented offhandedly.

My "blue" outfit was a three-piece silk knit—skirt, shirt, and cardigan—in a Wedgwood blue and cream stripe. The colors, subdued and perhaps somber, were irrelevant. I hated how Charles commented on what I wore during important conversations.

"First you call me sarcastic, now blue. Stick to the topic, please," I countered again.

"Yes, the topic is Molly's Magical Press. Honor roll certificates, graduation awards, diplomas, musical tickets, playbills, brochures, fliers—what else are you doing?" Charles asked teasingly.

"A literary magazine, remember—the reason I'm here now."

"Sorry, I didn't mean to make light of your time or generosity—or skill for that matter," Charles stated sincerely.

"This trend that is developing nationwide is serious," I explained. "Computer science teachers should not be running print shops on the side just because we are the ones who could work through this new software."

"So what's the solution?" Charles asked.

"You could hire someone to do all of the desktop publishing work," I suggested. "Computer phobes cannot do this work, and I, as your computer science teacher among other jobs, do not have time for it. I don't think my request is unreasonable."

"So, what do I do to fix this specific problem?" Charles asked, not commenting on my idea.

"Be prepared to deal with Alexa. She probably will not be very happy with my changes," I answered.

"She had only good intentions. And she didn't want to bother you unnecessarily," Charles offered, trying to placate my concern.

"I'm not questioning Alexa's intentions. After all, she did the English department a favor. And she's very talented—in other areas. But, not bother me! That's a laugh. By not telling me from the beginning, look at how she has bothered me," I insisted.

"Feel free to take charge," Charles proposed.

"I have no choice but to take charge—just to get done. I'm going to edit, and I'm going to cut. I'm not pleased about doing her work. But I said I would produce this work, and I will. I can tell you one thing, though—this is my first magazine and my last," I declared.

"But, Molly, I'm naming you *Dean of Printing*. Don't you want the title?" Charles teased.

"You're naming me *Dean of Printing*," I repeated with battered declaration. "You're naming me *Dean of Printing*," I said again with rancorous indignation. "You're naming me *Dean of Printing*?" I asked this time with incredulous interrogation. "You're naming me *Dean of Printing*!" I reiterated with wild exclamation. "That really excites me. Now I have two deanships. Wow! Or does this new one rescind *Dean of Cuisine*?" I paused for a moment, standing to leave, but then continued. "You like to call MCD a family, but I'm not accustomed to dysfunctional members created when teachers work out of field. You need to put an end to the practice."

"You are being too hard," Charles admonished.

"*Hardly*," I said as I closed his door firmly behind me.

25. First Show

I expanded the programmed, static and motion, color graphics concept from the previous year's Spring Festival into a full, computer-driven, theatrical production with a story line. I called the show *The Enchanted Amiga Room*, a take-off on Disney World's Enchanted Tiki Room in which robotic parrots hanging from the ceiling talked, sang, and entertained. While I certainly did not string any computers from above, they did perform—telling jokes, playing music, and displaying synchronized, intricate, swirling graphics—all programmed in BASIC by the students. The May event was a spectacular success.

Charles suggested that I present my students' show at the annual meeting of the Florida Council of Independent Schools. I replied that moving six of MCD's computers to a convention hundreds of miles away would be a nightmare—plus I didn't like to drive. Moreover, I had sent a description of the show as an entry to the National Educational Computer Conference—the same convention where the year before I had seen the Amiga on display. To my delight my proposal was accepted. Thus, I was content that my first show would receive enough exposure. But Charles offered to take me to FCIS, almost insisting. Suddenly, the next day he changed his mind, saying that our going away together would cause a scandal, French pronunciation, of course. Why was the trip he had taken with the MCD mother a few months prior to observe foreign language instruction not a *scandalle* in his mind, but a trip with me would be? Regardless, I was pleased to avert a junket in Charles's ominous, yellow Lincoln Continental.

I had no time for post-school-year reflection in the sunroom as I had done twelve months ago because I had to prepare immediately for NECC. Vernon scheduled a rafting trip at the Grand Canyon for Blane, Mimi, and himself while I attended the meeting in Phoenix. He carefully arranged for us to start and end the vacation together.

I believed that the hardware specifications for my show, clearly indicated on the application form, would be met. However, when I arrived, not one computer was present for me. I kept asking myself why I even bothered with programming. Math was so manageable, only needing a board and chalk or paper and pencil. After I made several phone calls, a sympathetic local dealer agreed to deliver hardware for the presentation. After I spouted endless thanks, the dealer gave me some wise advice: assume nothing.

As at all conferences, multiple events were scheduled for identical time slots. Unfortunately, a famous MIT professor was opposite me, but still my show drew reasonable attendance. Those there, including a publisher of computer science textbooks, were fascinated by the visions. Kismet was at work because the publisher and I immediately connected. Curious about the curriculum that would generate such creative work by students, he spoke to me while I repacked the hardware. I told him about my programming textbook, and he was definitely interested.

I spent the rest of the summer writing detailed proposals for him, interrupted only by teaching three weeks at CTY with weekends at Grace's home. I satisfied all of his requests—until the final one. As school was about to begin, the publisher informed me that my book must meet the guidelines mandated by the legislatures of Texas, California, and Florida—the three largest markets. The regulations demanded including virtually all material for a computer literacy course. My publisher absurdly told me not to worry—that the extra text could be placed in an appendix or in *info boxes* at the end of each chapter. I viewed this requirement as ruining my book because programming and computer literacy were two different subjects, deserving two separate textbooks. Stupidly, I realized why algebra texts had scattered biographies of mathematicians or lessons in BASIC—pages that teachers uniformly skipped but that made the books unreasonably heavy for students to carry.

I was astonished and disgusted at how legislators who knew nothing about education could tell an experienced teacher what to write and in the process quash a publishing deal. I added this defacement to my growing list of ills in education.

The experience reconfirmed why I taught not only at a private school but also at one run by a headmaster like Charles Long who granted professional freedom. I certainly wouldn't want to teach out of a poorly designed book again—I had done that enough at Palm Beach Community College where I was simply handed a textbook and ordered to use it. Still, I wondered whether I would regret the decision to terminate my relationship with this publisher. My first show might now only lead to a second show and not a book.

26. First Commitment

Then, ending the summer, the betrayal warning occurred—that ghostly signal of unfaithfulness shrouding my work at Merritt Country Day School. Charlotte Merritt and I had been discussing Charles's unfortunate invasion of the privacy of her home. Suddenly and abruptly, she stated emphatically, "Molly, don't trust Charles. Some day he will betray you."

In the backdrop of my mind, is the specter that Charles Long, the man who has supported me creatively, inspired me productively, empowered me professionally, and trusted me implicitly will ruin the integrity of our relationship with needless sexual harassment. Should I be more prepared than I was as a young graduate student at Harvard? Should I study the legal definition of sexual harassment? Should I have comments and actions prepared to counteract possible suggestiveness?

No, Charlotte could be mistaken—mere speculation on her part. Or maybe the betrayal would be of an entirely different nature—but what?

Starting my third year at MCD, I conscientiously tried to shed the threatening omen. My first commitment was to continue both teaching and writing, seeking excellence for students' one chance at an education.

27. First Problem

My eighth grade algebra class of all girls giggled as I wrote the equation: $120 + x = 120 + x$. After Daniel's departing no new boy qualified to be grouped with these special girls. Only October, I was already giving them their first lesson in mixture problems, one of the classic problem types. On the board appeared the problem:

How many milliliters of water must be added to 120 ml of 62½% acid solution to dilute it to a 37½% acid solution?

"Why are you laughing?" I asked.

"Your equation is rather obvious," Bethany replied.

I continued. "The 120 represents the original milliliters of solution, and the x stands for the milliliters of water being added. Are you with me so far?"

"Sure," Holly answered. The others nodded affirmatively. Their quizzical expressions told me that they didn't yet see where I was leading them, but they knew to trust me.

"The next step is to insert parentheses, keeping the left-side values distinct and making the right-side values united." I wrote: $(120) + (x) = (120 + x)$. "Separate milliliters plus separate milliliters equals total milliliters. Any problem with that?" I asked.

"Go on," Mimi said in a tone indicating that they still thought I was being silly.

"Now here comes the clever part. By placing the appropriate percentage of acid as a factor in each term, we transform milliliters plus milliliters equals total milliliters into amount of acid plus amount of acid equals total acid. Watch," I stated as I wrote the next equation on the board: $.625\,(120) + 0\,(x) = .375\,(120 + x)$.

"Consider having 10 cups of a 60% water/40% acid solution. The 10 stands for the total number of cups. But as soon as you multiply the 10 by .4, you have the amount of acid, namely 4 cups, rather than the full amount," I reasoned. The girls, who were excellent problem solvers, were comfortable with creating a simpler problem to illustrate a point.

"What's the next equation?" I asked.

Bethany replied correctly: $.625\,(120) = .375\,(120 + x)$.

"Wait," Arielle said hesitantly.

"Arielle, are you uncomfortable with the second term disappearing?" I asked.

"Sure zero times any number is zero, but it seems weird to me here," she answered.

"It actually makes perfect sense. First, we have an equation which says milliliters plus milliliters equals milliliters," I reviewed. "You all laughed, but that is a very important concept in setting up equations. We've talked about this same issue in solving money problems. You may either write number of coins plus number of coins and so on equals total number of coins or value plus value and so on equals total monetary value, but the two cannot be mixed in one equation. That would not make sense."

Just as I was in the middle of the explanation, Charles entered the classroom. The students hardly flinched. Because MCD had an open door policy, they were accustomed to Charles or Catherine walking in and out of classes to observe. Charles nodded at me, quickly seeing that I had the girls engaged. Though he sat in the back, he partook of the exchange, enjoying how MCD students loved learning. I kept on teaching. If he had an important matter, I knew that he would interrupt.

"Then, Arielle, in transforming the equation to stand for acid plus acid equals acid, the second amount of acid is pure water—namely no acid, so it goes away. Okay?" I asked.

"Okay, go on," Arielle said.

"No, all of you finish the algebra. Now—fast. What's the final answer?"

Without calculators, the girls all called out "eighty" in less than half a minute. They were quick, accurate, and insightful. Charles had been smiling at me almost continually throughout the lesson, and he looked at the girls with both a father's tenderness and a headmaster's pride.

"Eighty is correct," I continued. "Why is the answer not eighty milliliters?"

"Because the question asks how many milliliters—the label is already in the problem," Mimi replied.

"And if we label it wrong, the whole answer is wrong—so no labels at math competitions when the label is in the question," Holly added sing-songingly because the girls had heard the warning from me before.

I continued. "We need to formalize one important observation about this particular problem. How did you answer so quickly?"

"We used fractions instead of decimals!" they all shrieked almost simultaneously. They had learned well.

"So what's the correct work?" I asked. I wrote on the blackboard as they called out, though they seemed bored that I insisted on completing the lesson.

$$.625\,(120) = .375\,(120 + x)$$
$$\frac{5}{8}\,(120) = \frac{3}{8}\,(120 + x)$$
$$5(120) = 3(120) + 3x$$
$$3x = 240$$
$$x = 80$$

"Now, you really need to listen to me," I said. "Do you think these percentages are accidental or intentional?"

"Intentional," Mimi answered. "They're both eighths—that's too much of a coincidence."

"Exactly. The students who have a strong background from sixth and seventh grades, who quickly recognize common percentages, have an advantage competing because simplifying fractions is so much faster than multiplying decimals—or even punching all the numbers if the contest permitted calculators," I explained. "But, I'm not done making my point. Even though your textbook is excellent, it shows mixture problems by making a chart as we do for some other problem types. This method I have shown you is better—much faster and more direct. It is known by some math teachers but obviously is not in all books. At a competition the teams that know this method can edge out the others on a mixture problem."

"How did you learn it?" asked Bethany.

"Mimi's grandfather taught it to me," I answered.

"Cool. Let's call it Grandpa's method," she exclaimed. The girls enjoyed having their own private lingo to supplement the language of mathematics.

"Please, make a mental image of this problem—it's very important. We're almost at the end of class, but I have one last question. What would you do if the problem said that liquid evaporated from the original solution?"

"Subtract instead of add," they all called out practically in unison.

"Great. Do all the book problems in this lesson tonight with good work," I said as they packed their book bags and shuffled out the door.

I knew that they didn't listen to the tag phrase. High quality homework was a mutual understanding from our first day together in sixth grade. They indulged me in comments like that as a mother instructing a young child to wear a sweatshirt on a cool day. They were too busy laughing with Bethany as she goaded, "Hey, let's go tell everyone we did acid with Dr. Kelman."

Charles walked to the front of the room. I didn't teach the next period, so I was free for whatever was on his mind. I sat at a student's desk, and he did the same.

"Molly, if I had ever had a math teacher like you, I might have studied math instead of classics. My math teachers never talked to me the way you talk to your students," Charles lamented.

"I'm sorry," I replied. "I guess I was lucky having some great math teachers. It's so variable—pardon the pun."

"So much more heavily weighted on the poor side—look at the national statistics," he remarked.

"I listen to what I say as I teach. If it doesn't make sense to me, then it can't possibly make sense to the students," I explained. "But also, the beauty and the fun of math must always come across."

"I noticed that you did all the writing rather than have the girls come to the board," he commented.

"It depends on the lesson. They're so quick. They would have the problem solved at their desks by the time one student walked to the front," I said. "Even though they can all fit at the board, the chalk slows them down. I trust them to follow what I write, and of course, I pick up any errors when I look at their homework every night."

"You know exactly what they want and how they think," Charles rejoined.

"That's my job," I stated.

"No, it's because you were one of them when you were their age," Charles stated thoughtfully.

"Not that good," I answered. Pausing briefly and hoping to change the subject, I added, "You stayed longer than usual."

Unfortunately, instead of discussing business, Charles answered with exactly what I did not want to hear. "I wasn't only fascinated by the math—I was fascinated by you. You look so great in your peach dress that matches your peach room. Day after day, no matter how hectic things get around here, you always look wonderful."

Was this conversation an indication of the betrayal coming true? While I knotted inside, I vowed not to let the warning cripple me. So, I quickly redirected the meaning of Charles's compliment. "I prefer to influence the girls with my brain than with my clothes," I commented.

"Molly, please don't misunderstand me. You're an outstanding role model for these girls. The authors of those continual articles about boys being better at math than girls should visit your algebra class this year," Charles suggested hypothetically.

I felt better that Charles's remarks returned quickly to academics. "Thanks," I said. "I appreciate your spending so long today. It's important to me that you understand what I'm trying to accomplish."

"But, I do. You've taught me a lot, too," he replied.

"You know, at Blane's former middle school, the teachers' union contract prohibited the principal from visiting a classroom

117

unannounced. The policy is almost an admission that the teachers have something to hide. In fact, the day of the principal's scheduled visit was the only day that the students didn't trade papers, Blane told me. My son was furious. Can you blame him?"

"The kids are wiser than the adults," Charles expounded.

"I'm so glad I got my children out of there. Blane couldn't contain himself any longer, and Mimi would have exploded from the start," I said.

"After seeing this interaction and excitement, I know that I haven't thanked you enough for taking over this class. These eighth grade girls were very unhappy at the start of the year grouped with the ninth graders," Charles stated. "But Molly and her willingness to work overtime came to the rescue. The girls love you."

"You know I would do almost anything for them. I hate to see students unhappy at school. I hope no one thinks I did it just because of Mimi. They're all special to me," I said, seeking approval.

"Don't ever doubt people's opinion of your academic motives," Charles affirmed. "I'm so lucky to have you here."

"I'm lucky to be here. You give me the freedom to do what is necessary to get results," I said, somewhat awkwardly.

Charles laughed as he said, "Remember how Bethany spent the first few weeks turning the inside of her book cover into a stained glass coloring while some students asked questions so obvious to her?"

"Of course, I remember. Once again, we've shown how crucial grouping is," I answered.

"And that's why I started listening to you more and more," he stated.

Feeling uneasy again and thinking about a dormant deception, I ignored the praise and reversed the tone by emphasizing, "Today was just the first problem you observed. I'm predicting an amazing math team season for these girls."

"Believe me, I'm not betting against you or them," Charles said as he stood, tapped the desk, walked toward the door, and waved.

"Wait. Why did you visit?"

"I just wanted to see you," he replied.

28. First Team

The girls—Arielle, Bethany, Holly, Mimi—and I plunged into the Mu Alpha Theta math season with all our energy. Because I used classroom time for new lessons, we needed extra time for team practices. Meeting after school was impossible with the girls so involved in athletics and music. Mimi and I suggested trying Sunday from noon to three at our home—lunch followed by work.

First I served densely chocolate, mini-chip pancakes with fresh fruit rather than syrup on the side—an instant huge success. Then we simulated an actual competition team round for which I prepared all the authentic components.

Team round consisted of twelve questions distributed to each team concurrently, one problem at a time. Students worked as a group or individually, consulting with each other as needed. When a team was ready, typically when the students agreed, the captain wrote the result on a special pad, tore off the top sheet, folded it to cover the answer, and held the slip of paper high. Volunteer runners—teachers, parents, or students—circled the room, collecting the answers and recording the minute—one through four—on the slip as determined by the timer who both announced the current minute and flipped large plastic numbers as a reminder. A correct answer in the first minute was worth sixteen points, in the second minute twelve points, in the third minute eight points, and in the fourth minute four points. An incorrect answer earned no points.

I had prepared a dozen different problems with four copies of each, stapling them in packs so the girls could practice the tearing and distributing of questions without giggling and wasting time. We recreated everything accurately for the full experience. After trying

119

all combinations of working together and alone, they decided that independent problem solving was best, complemented by looking at each other's papers to verify a starting point for a tough problem, to check arithmetic along the way, or to validate a final answer.

When they left, they all eagerly agreed to meet again the next week. "Only if you promise to keep the same menu," insisted Holly.

The following Sunday Bethany entered the front door saying, "I've been looking forward to this all week." I knew then that the girls were a passionate team and the pancakes a supportive ritual.

The opening competition was on the second Saturday in January at Boca Raton Academy. At lunchtime the day before, Emma surprised us with an entire middle school rally, featuring a serenade by her students with the drummer from the school band keeping perfect cha-cha rhythm. Emma had rewritten the words to *It's Raining On Prom Night* from *Grease* for a send-off *extraordinaire*.

It's shi-ning—on math day,
Our sight is just swirls,
It's glow-ing all o-ver our brill-i-ant girls,
It's beam-ing the team-ing in our M-C-D
And al-ge-bra flows right down our brains,
Be-cause of the she.
We don't e-ven have one boy-mate,
Oh, gee,
Ar-i-elle, Beth-a-ny, Hol-ly, and Mi-Mi.
It's shi-ning—on math day,
Oh what can we do?
It's shi-ning—sun from the skies,
It's shi-ning—praise from our tries—over wins.
It's shi-ning—on math day,
Oh what can we do?
It's shi-ning—sun from the skies,
It's shi-ning—praise from our tries—over wins.
Shi-ning, shi-ning, shi-ning on math day, shi-ning.

Spontaneously, Arielle, Bethany, Holly, and Mimi grabbed me and sprung on Emma for a giant, six-way hug. The song, the affection, the effort, the competence—these all make Merritt Country Day special, I thought.

We were all excited when I cautiously drove the girls to Boca. Though they tried to relax by singing silly songs, Arielle interrupted by reciting the quadratic formula. "We know it, Arielle—including if woken up suddenly in the middle of the night and asked to recite it," Bethany pleaded, imitating me.

The individual test for algebra was first, given in seven different classrooms because of the large number of schools attending. The girls caucused to select a lucky room number from among the choices, as if that actually mattered. When they chose a prime number, I smiled at their adorable quirks. They also elected to be in the same room but chose scattered seats according to contest rules.

I made sure that each of my girls had her white plastic, not pink rubber, eraser—a symbol of a Molly Kelman math student—essential for erasing answers easily without smudging. And, of course, several pencils were a must—sharp points for sharp thinking.

"Where will you be?" Mimi asked.

"In the coaches' lounge drinking coffee—tons of coffee," I answered nervously. "But I'll be back."

An hour later I met the girls outside their room. In a frenzy we dashed to the location where the answers had been posted, only slowed by their incessant chatter about the problems. Because the students submitted their answer sheet solely, they kept the actual exam on which they had also recorded their solutions. My girls graded their tests swiftly. Another coach in the lounge had warned me that errors in the answers were somewhat frequent, sometimes due to the typing of the exam. At flying speed we quickly resolved their few questions and decided that, indeed, one official answer was wrong.

Then we dashed to cafeteria—the location of the team round. The girls wanted to get a good table—a shape that allowed them to communicate well and was not too close to a neighboring table.

As they ran around, they decided that a circle was preferable to a square or rectangle. Once settled, I placed more sharpened pencils in the center of their table as well as grapes and granola bars for quick energy.

"Only your Mom," said Bethany to Mimi. I didn't care if they teased me because they welcomed the food. And I certainly didn't care what the other teams thought—I was not going to risk losing an award over a broken pencil point. Then I dashed off to file the one dispute, learning when I got there that another school had already taken care of the matter.

Team round revealed the obvious difference in preparation among the schools. By the time some ripped the four copies from the staple and passed them to the team members, my girls were well into their solution—exactly why I had them practice that routine task at home. Going into the team round, I knew that we were among the top teams based on the girls' own grading of their individual tests. But I didn't know how many other schools also had done well thus far. I knew that we needed a successful team round to maintain a lead because the final team total was the sum of the team round plus the individual scores of the four team members.

Question after question my girls were among the first teams to raise an answer. The distinction was that I knew they had accuracy as well as speed. I called them my ice princesses because they were so cool under pressure. No question rattled them. They could think totally out of context, and they cooperated so beautifully.

The girls had warned me in the car about a particular team strategy that they had developed on their own. After the fourth minute of each question when the proctor announced the answer, most teams naturally cheered if they had submitted a correct solution. But my girls decided to keep poker faces—they did not want the other teams to know how they were doing. They planned that Mimi would sit on her hands to signal to me a correct answer or would fold her hands to signal an error. Halfway through, the proctor announced all team totals to that point. When MCD's girls surprised everyone with the greatest sum, those rascals exploded with laughter and loved their hoax. The next highest score was a team of four boys from a public school in Boca. Fortunately, they were sitting across the room so the two teams couldn't distract each other in the second half. I noticed their coach, an energetic man named Grady Bellows, staring at me. I had met him earlier over coffee.

On the twelfth and final question, my girls raised their answer in the first minute, while the other teams, including Grady's, finished in the fourth. Once all answers had been collected, I dashed to the proctor's table to see the problem. I immediately reconciled the difference in speed—Grandpa's method made the problem so routine. The question was:

A scientist has 15 gallons of a solution that is 11% alcohol. She wishes to create a solution that is 18% alcohol by removing a certain amount of her solution and replacing it with a solution that is 32% alcohol. How much must she replace?

When we arrived back at school in the late afternoon, we were all surprised and thrilled to see Charles outside to greet us. He was discussing some new plantings with Joe.

Seeing my pleased expression, he asked cheerfully, "How was the competition?"

"It was frantically fun," Arielle answered, holding an individual trophy in her hand. Charles put his arm around her.

Then the other girls emerged from my car, each carrying a trophy with Mimi also embracing their four-foot tall, red and silver, first place team trophy.

"Wow—that thing is almost as big as you are," Charles exclaimed.

"Here," Mimi said. "We would like you to keep it in your office for a few weeks. Then we'll move it to our classroom."

"I would be honored," Charles replied.

As the girls dashed off to call their parents, Bethany called back to Charles, "Doing acid with Dr. Kelman really paid off."

On Monday morning, Charles saw me at the mailboxes. "Do you have a minute?" he asked.

"Of course," I replied and characteristically followed him to his office. I assumed that the meeting would be about the math competition.

"Molly, what a victory! I've been thinking all weekend, and I want to discuss your future at MCD," Charles said.

"What about my future?"

"I want you only to teach our mathematically gifted students—both math and computer programming. You are great with all students, but that is where your special talent lies," he commented.

"Oh, thank you," I said. "But I can't. I have too many courses already doing all the middle school computer science as well as sixth and eighth grade advanced math."

"That's exactly what I'm saying. It's time to give up the newspaper and some other classes," he said smiling.

"But who will do them?" I asked, knowing that Emma would be pleased if she were a *mouche* on the wall.

"We'll hire another teacher," Charles answered simplistically.

"You're ready to employ three computer science teachers— Renuka, me, and a new person?"

"We need to meet the curriculum needs. The school is growing," Charles replied.

"I'm so wary after working with D. Dottie," I expressed.

"We just need to hire the right person. You'll advise me the whole way. But when it's done, you'll see all of your students twice a day—once for math and once for programming, so you can really relate the two subjects," Charles said so enthusiastically as if he were a pupil.

"That would be fabulous," I said, though skeptical about an unknown colleague.

"Let's get on it right away," he commanded with his distinctive tap of the desk. I left happy but concerned.

Competitions occurred on alternate weekends across Florida January through April. For far distances, I asked parents to drive. The girls as a team—my first team—consistently took first place along with four of the top individual awards. The victories provided boundless personal joy and unqualified professional satisfaction.

At the May Day middle school assembly, Charles proudly praised the four girls during his announcements. When leaving the auditorium, I overheard a brief exchange between Mimi and Charles.

"You know, Mr. Long, our success was due to my Mom's weekly chocolate chip pancakes," she said pertly.

"Mimi, I always knew I named the right person *Dean of Cuisine*," he replied.

29. First Impression

Pursuing his idea to hire a third computer science teacher, Charles suggested that his old friend Ron Rhinehardt, a professional education personnel director, help find candidates. I had met Ron on campus once previously. He was physically unattractive—painfully thin, with acne-scarred skin and a bald head. His moustache and eyebrows—in exactly the same size, shape, texture, and charcoal gray color—resembled three congruent figures featured in a real-life geometry problem. Capping but not complimenting his visage was a cowboy string tie with a silver and turquoise slide. While I certainly tried to overlook his appearance in forming my first impression, I suspected that Ron was pompous skin-deep.

After a brief chat with Emma at the mailboxes, I passed by Charles's office on the way to the lab. Suddenly Charles bellowed, "Is that Dr. Kelman?" I walked back a few steps to his open door. There sat Charles and Ron.

"Yes," I said as I peeked in, still standing in the hallway.

"We have an unseemly proposal for you," Charles said laughingly.

"No thank you, I'm on my way to class," I replied sternly.

"Ron will find you later," Charles warned. They both chuckled. Hadn't Charles learned not to be chauvinistic with me? No doubt they had a business proposition to discuss but were amused by being offensive. I became resolute to bridle Ron no matter what was on his male-ethnocentric mind.

I was grading papers during a free period when I glimpsed Ron outside staring into the lab. I squinted at his image bordered by the window frame. Suddenly, he decomposed into a Cubist painting almost like a math poster spoof—rectangle forehead, equilateral triangle nose, circle eyes and ears, square neck, ellipse body, kite arms—and, of course, the highly noticeable isosceles trapezoid moustache and eyebrows. I regretted looking up, but he would have entered anyway.

"Mrs. Kelman," Ron said, unaware that my name was Dr. Kelman or Mrs. Melrose. "Charles tells me that you need another computer teacher." He sat comfortably in a chair next to my desk.

"Computer science," I confirmed, agitatedly.

"I have quite a few good candidates," Ron responded.

"How do you know they're good?" I inquired.

"Well, each has several years teaching experience," Ron answered.

"So?" I asked. "Could be years of teaching poorly."

"Here are their résumés," Ron said, handing me papers from his briefcase.

"This first one is a no," I stated. "He is fifteen years older than I am, and my CS education is outdated."

"CS?" Ron asked.

"Computer science," I replied. After a quick glance, I continued. "Negative on this next one. His degree is in EE. I want someone who loves pure math."

"EE?" Ron asked.

"Electrical engineering."

"Well, he uses programming," Ron argued.

"And I use a car. Can I teach auto mechanics? And the third one is also not right—self-taught and teaching at an FN school."

"FN?" Ron asked. "Function?"

"Very good, you know some programming math—but not in this case. A Fluff 'n Nothing school teaches fluff and nothing else," I explained. "So that's done," I added, sliding the résumés on the desk with a firm push until they were before him.

"Oh, I get it—like Fluff 'n Nutter sandwiches," Ron declared proudly.

I stared at him in amazement. He's dumber than I thought.

"Well, I'll be getting more résumés. And to be able to compare them efficiently, I would like you to enter the vitae into a database," he said, almost ordering rather than asking.

"You want me to be the school's office assistant for faculty recruitment—your secretary, in other words, for your work at MCD? Am I hearing correctly?"

"Well, not exactly, but in effect, yes," Ron answered.

"Obviously, I decline, and don't look so shocked," I stated. "Think about your suggestion. First of all, none of the department chairs is going to use the database. Keith, for example, would go to a file drawer of résumés in a minute rather than use a computer system that is neither familiar nor accessible. Second, . . ."

"Well, I," Ron interjected.

"Second," I continued, "I refuse to log in countless hours for nothing—I've done it too many times at MCD. Third, . . ."

"Well, I," Ron interjected again.

"Excuse me, I'm not finished. Third, creating—and then even worse maintaining—a database of garbage makes no sense. I already told you these candidates are out. Why would I want their names cluttering a database?"

"Well, I," Ron interjected a third time, earnestly trying to defend his plan.

"I said I'm not finished. And fourth, if you really want this system, then do it yourself. I don't ask other people to do my work. Now I am finished, and I have papers to grade. Unless, you want to grade them for me." I stared right into the kernels of his spherules.

Ron gathered the résumés, not bothering to place them in his briefcase, and left the lab abruptly. Picturing him running straight to Charles's office, I only hoped that Charles was occupied at a lengthy meeting. Charles, unfortunately, was available all day. So by the late afternoon when I saw Charles at the mailboxes, Ron had already reported to him.

"You made an enemy of Ron," Charles said grimly.

"So I declined his supercilious offer and desecrated his precious idea all in one swift blow. So what?"

Charles frowned at me.

"Oh, come on. Can't he accept a little ribbing? You both started it with your *unseemly proposal* remark. If you guys can't take it in return, then don't dish it out to start," I argued.

"His database suggestion is sound," Charles affirmed. "I'm always looking for new teachers. We should use technology to help."

"Then ask one of your two new office employees. What are they doing with their time anyway, besides drinking coffee and talking to each other?"

"What's bothering you, Molly?" Charles asked.

"What's bothering me is that Ron doesn't have the slightest idea about what kind of teacher I want. Wait, I'm being too specific. I'm not sure that he has a feel for MCD at all," I responded. After a slight pause, I added, "I know! Play matchmaker—introduce Ron and Rhonda. They certainly have similar taste in accessories, and even their names fit like that Paul and Paula Golden Oldie song. Then Ron's presence on campus won't be a total loss."

Charles grimaced severely and looked around the faculty lounge as if worried that someone might have overheard. "Ron stands behind his plan, and I stand behind Ron," Charles insisted in an angry tone.

"And I stand by my reply," I stated. And I stand by my first impression of Ron, I thought.

"We still need another computer teacher, and it's already May," Charles said.

"Computer *science*," I corrected emphatically.

30. First Support

As I was walking down the diagonal path to my car, I heard Charles's voice.

"Molly, wait. I'll walk with you," he called.

"What's doing?" I asked.

"I found a teacher to take the newspaper class next year," Charles explained.

"Oh?" I asked skeptically.

"She's perfect," he said.

"Perfect? Is she a Rhinehardt Special?" I questioned.

"No, as a matter of fact," Charles answered. "She applied on her own. She's relocating."

"Dropped on your doorstep by the stork?" I jested.

"Molly, enough. You're the one who needs help. You should be happy I have someone to take the class," Charles expressed.

"What's her field?" I inquired.

"Well, she's sort of a Renaissance woman," he replied.

"A Renaissance woman?" I asked incredulously.

"Yes, she has experience in many subjects," Charles boasted.

"A dabbler?" I asked.

"No, an expert, I hope," he clarified.

"Has she ever taught desktop publishing?"

"No," Charles stated.

"Computer literacy?"

"No."

"English?"

"No," Charles said again.

"Oh, this is encouraging," I muttered sarcastically. "Do I get to meet her?"

"Tomorrow. She's splitting her day among you, Catherine, Cecily, and Keith. Priscilla will give you a schedule."

"What's her code name—*Wonder Woman*?" I asked.

"Give her a chance," Charles replied, smiling crookedly.

After school the next day I looked for Charles. I found him by the table of cookies in the faculty room. Charles looked around, checking that no one else was present—but not because he was about to partake liberally of the goodies.

"What do you think?" he asked. I knew he was referring to *Wonder Woman*.

"I vote no. Her personality quirks bother me," I answered.

"Such as?"

"Such as she talks incessantly," I complained.

"I think that's because she's been single for so long. She craves company," Charles responded. "Anything else?"

"I haven't seen any writing samples, so I'm not sure if she knows correct grammar and punctuation to help the kids with their articles. And I haven't worked with her one-on-one, so I don't know if she can learn the software. I can't possibly vote yes until I have positive answers to these concerns," I explained.

Charles's look indicated that he thought I was speaking unreasonably. I hated when my needs for thoroughness, carefulness, and logic were labeled obsessive, uncooperative, and difficult. I knew that the students and I would suffer if Charles hired erratically.

"So, the bottom line is that I don't get a vote—right? She's going to save you lots of money—filling in one course here and one course there, in multiple departments," I expressed. "Plus, it's May, and you have no other candidates."

"Yes," Charles affirmed reluctantly.

"I'm going to welcome her and be her first support. Then she's on her own," I stated.

"Good, that's all I ask," Charles said, tapping the table so firmly that the plate of cookies shifted.

31. First Proposition

The misty Friday, May afternoon was peaceful. Mimi had gone home with a friend. As I cleaned the lab, I felt exhausted but gratified. Perhaps I wasn't smiling outwardly as much, but I was smiling inwardly. I had a particular reason to be proud of my work—last night had been another exciting Spring Festival.

"*Bonjour!*" exclaimed Emma suddenly as she entered the lab, invariably with perpetual energy.

"Hi, come in. I could use a break," I said.

"Tell me why we're both still here on Friday afternoon after school," she demanded.

"I don't know about you, but I have to refile all of these disks from my computer show last night, or else I'll never remember what's what," I replied.

"That's why I came to see you. *Magnifique!*" Emma declared. "I thought last year's show was amazing, but you outdid yourself—the entire *Sound of Music* on computers!"

"Not exactly the entire," I said. Emma praised so lavishly.

"I loved the way you had the convent, the Mother Superior, Maria, the Captain, the Baroness, Uncle Max, and all of the seven von Trapp children on the monitors. Oh yes, and also the Austrian and German flags," she enumerated.

"Thanks," I said.

"Tell me, how did you ever get the idea?" Emma asked.

"I don't know—it just came to me. I didn't have time to write my own story this year, and I needed something to generate dozens of separate assignments," I answered.

"Oh, yes, that too," Emma exclaimed. "I loved the printed program where you wrote who had made what. But the animation was the best—the flickering cake candles for *Sixteen Going on Seventeen*, the dancing string puppets for *The Lonely Goatherd*, and the swinging pendulum clock for *So Long, Farewell*."

"Thanks, I really appreciate the compliment. The show was so much work," I replied, trying to settle Emma.

"Tell me," she added. "Who did Gretl's amazing blond braids?"

"That was Noah. He is an incredible programmer," I answered.

"Tell me he used an art package," she said.

"No. None of the kids did. It was all programmed," I stated.

"Like writing line after line in French?"

"Yes, but in computer languages," I affirmed.

"*Incroyable*! The absolute best were all the pictures for *My Favorite Things*," she continued.

"Those were done by the sixth graders in Logo," I explained. "I was worried about running BASIC and Logo on different machines, but it worked okay. Now, I heard your French skits were fantastic. I'm so glad I caught the afternoon rehearsal because I couldn't leave the lab the entire night with the show running continuously."

"Oh, the kids were wonderful. Lorna, in particular, had the audience roaring," Emma said. "And I gave Stephanie Merritt a part even though she's only in fifth grade. The illustrious Parke and striking Charlotte have started their daughter on French early."

"I'm happy for both girls. Are you doing skits again next year?"

"Maybe we'll be lucky, and Spring Festival will die from natural causes," Emma declared. Then she paused and added wistfully, though feigned, "*Au revoir, Printemps Festival*."

"Don't count on it," I warned.

"Then tell me you're doing another show," Emma insisted.

"Oh, I don't know. Two may be enough. Anyway, never fifty minutes and twenty computers again—way too long and too big to get the timing to work without endless worry. But just this morning some of the kids are pushing for a whole new project," I said.

"Tell me, tell me," Emma demanded.

"A humor magazine," I stated.

"A humor magazine?" she asked. "In the remaining three weeks of school?"

"No, next year—as a special ninth grade treat. The eighth graders have been a fabulous newspaper class. They're creative and cooperative—such a welcome change from last year," I explained. "But my big news is that Charles has offered to give the newspaper class to a new teacher."

"Oh, Molly, that's perfect. Then you can just do the magazine with your current students. Their April Fools' Day edition was the ultimate. I loved the spoof portraying the girls' bathroom with cramped measurements versus the boys' bathroom with grandiose square footage," Emma said, waving her arms wide and laughing.

I started laughing as well, recalling other articles. "The feature on the school van was great—saying that after so many breakdowns, it was restricted to trips in the parking lot."

"And the subliminal dialogue, giving Bethany and Arielle's inner thoughts as they went through the entire school day, was hysterical," Emma added.

"Yes, like the new, shortened lunch period: *Sit down. Stand up.*"

"But, Molly, the funniest piece was the one about you. Tell me you didn't mind," Emma said.

"I can laugh at myself," I replied, as we both started giggling.

"There you were—MCD's *Dean of Cuisine* and Master of Computers," Emma began.

"I'm still upset with Charles for leaking my title to the kids—all because of the math team pancakes," I added.

"The pizza delivery man, who was overly late for lunch, feared that Catherine would scream. So, he drove up the diagonal walk and accidentally crashed his truck into the computer lab, spewing tomato sauce and melted cheese all over the keyboards. Suffering a nervous breakdown, you were rushed to the hospital by the pizza driver. Tell me how they imagined these ideas," Emma insisted.

"They're just smart—and observant," I remarked.

"Well, you've taught them to be observant," Emma commented.

"My absolute favorite," I said, laughing even harder, "is the spoof of Charles. It captured all of his quirks—old and new."

"Did Bethany and Arielle write that one, too?" Emma asked.

"They sure did. Nothing stopped them," I answered.

"Tell me they didn't turn Charles into a one-man circus act—twitching his black eye, twirling his tiny glasses, loosening his yellow tie, rubbing his tanned head, bouncing his crossed leg, and tapping his messy desk—all at the same time," Emma described.

"Don't forget the caption about having a bad-hair day," I added.

"Oh, yes—his favorite cliché. He uses it incessantly."

"When they asked Charles for permission to do an April Fools' edition, he said that his one rule was they could poke fun at adults, but not students. They took him at his word," I said.

Emma and I were so engrossed, we hadn't noticed that Charles had just entered the lab.

"What did I miss?" he inquired.

"Oh, nothing. We were just laughing about you," I answered.

Emma gasped, not believing that I dared to taunt Charles. "I'm going home," she said awkwardly. "It's been a long week."

"Thanks for all your effort last night," Charles said to her. "The skits were great."

Emma just nodded as she left. Charles sat down at a table in the middle of the room. He pushed his small chair back and stretched his long legs straight. His body language indicated I would hear more than either praise from last night or complaints from some parent.

Charles smiled at me. "Dr. Kelman, you look especially lovely in your red dress. How was your day after your spectacular event last night?" he asked.

I ignored his comment and answered his question. "A bit of a comedown," I replied. "But the eighth grade girls came in energized. They want to start a humor magazine with me as their sponsor. That's what Emma and I were laughing about—their spoof of you."

Charles smiled at me again. "You've done such a wonderful job with them."

"Charles, I love them. But I can't handle one more special project—even if it's for next year. I'll drop," I expressed.

Charles chuckled as if he were replaying their article in his mind. "We can't quash their enthusiasm. Suggest that they write a proposal to have something to discuss. Maybe we can find another sponsor."

"So what's the reason for your visit?" I asked, purposely changing the subject in an effort to conclude the day.

"I met with the PTO board today," Charles stated. "Afterward, Mrs. Oldfield and Mrs. Kingsley stayed to discuss their idea for a bonfire party. You know how parents seldom keep to the subject. Mrs. Oldfield said, *Dr. Kelman alone is worth the price of tuition.*"

"Wow, I'm touched, I really am," I said. Mrs. Oldfield's son was one of those typical middle school boys with greater math talent than verbal ability. As he became alive in my courses, he found his niche in school. He had participated actively in the *Sound of Music* show.

"Molly, I've never, ever, heard a parent say that about any teacher, anywhere."

Charles smiled warmly at me with his ink eyes and then howled, abruptly breaking the compliment. We both knew that Mrs. Kingsley hated me. She had a very bright son who did poorly in my classes because he didn't pay attention, didn't do assignments, and didn't express remorse. Mrs. Kingsley was a parent who found comfort in blaming her child's problems on the teacher, especially when the other students in the class were successful.

"Okay, you're laughing. So Mrs. Kingsley must have had quite a retort. Speak up—I can take it," I asserted.

"*Well, I guess there is something at this school for everyone*, was her exact comment," Charles imitated.

"Rather polite of her," I remarked.

"Molly, let's run away together," Charles blurted with his head cocked.

Was he serious or kidding? Did he mean romantically or academically? We were living in the real world, not destined for a *Sound of Music* fantasy escape through the Alps. Perhaps he implied we should start our own school away from the Mrs. Kingsleys and craziness that we had endured together for the past three years. I didn't want to know, though.

"Don't be ridiculous. Our work is far from done at MCD," I said. Then, quickly changing the subject, I asked, "Are you going to allow the bonfire?"

Happily, Charles let his offer pass. "Probably, if I can get a Palm Beach County permit. Have a good weekend," he said, tapping his large hand on the table and leaving as spryly as he had entered.

Immediately, I thought about the betrayal warning—the terrible, treacherous caution that haunted me when Charles seemed overly suggestive. But I dismissed Charles's first proposition quickly—I had too much work to do.

32. First Indiscretion

Vernon and I looked forward to Mimi's eighth grade graduation with great pride. Mimi, distinguished in many subjects and with wonderful friends, had experienced three fabulous years at the MCD middle school. Unlike Blane, she decided to stay for MCD's ninth grade. Only disappointing us was that Grace and Brenna were not able to attend commencement.

All of the girls were required to wear white. We were waiting for her in the study when she emerged in her new, polished cotton, white-on-white, cap-sleeved dress with a slight flare at the hem that suited her petite frame perfectly. She had put some small, white silk flowers in her long, thick curls.

"You look fantastic," I said as she and Vernon exchanged huge smiles. "Blane, we're ready. Let's go," I called to him in his room.

When we arrived at school, Arielle, Bethany, and Holly were already there. They rushed at Mimi to join them. The girls twittered about something—their dresses, I assumed. Vernon and Blane went into the auditorium to find seats, and I waited with the faculty in a classroom.

Graduation proceeded as usual. I thought I knew exactly what to expect—after all, this ceremony was my fourth, and the graduation mold had not been recast. Then, out of order, Charles took the microphone and announced that four of the graduates wanted to make an unscheduled, unprecedented presentation to a teacher who was special to them.

Seeing my four math team girls walk to the podium, I knew that this digression involved me. But I could not guess what was next. Bethany was giggling as usual. Holly spoke into the microphone.

"We would like Dr. Kelman to come up here," she said excitedly as she turned to face me. I joined them cautiously.

Holly was bright, vivacious, and of course, great at math. But neither speech planning nor extemporaneous talking was her strength. Though she fumbled her words, people understood that I had been remarkable to these four girls in some way.

Holly stepped aside for Bethany, who only managed to utter something about my supplying abundant pencils, erasers, grapes, and granola. Suddenly, through her garbled discourse, she started crying. Even without the tears, I doubted whether anyone understood her references. The other three girls began crying as well.

Next, Arielle, though hardly composed, took the microphone. Mimi stood back. I imagined she felt that because I was her mother, letting the others speak would be more appropriate. Arielle, between sobs and wipes, spoke about their winning first place in algebra at every competition. I loved them for their ingenuous performance. Hopefully, the guests weren't totally confused.

Then Charles signaled, reminding them of something. I was surprised that he was more than the announcer of this scheme. Holly pulled a bouquet of one dozen, large, red, long-stemmed roses from behind the podium. Hearing the muddled but beautiful words and seeing those magnificent flowers, my eyes filled with tears. We all hugged and sat down. Clapping followed, and graduation proceeded.

As I sat in my seat, stunned, holding my roses for lack of a place to put them, I thought about my students. Such a moment made all the strenuous work of teaching worthwhile, for little is more special than sharing the love of knowledge, the means to acquire knowledge, and the knowledge itself.

Somehow I managed to focus on all the succeeding awards. I even presented the computer science certificates fairly coherently, leaving the flowers on my seat while I spoke. Finally, the time arrived for the concluding recession—the eighth graders followed by the teachers. As I marched down the aisle, I held my roses tightly. The red bouquet covered me, in my cream silk dress, from neck to waist and side to side.

Emma was the first to congratulate me. *"Félicitations!"* she exclaimed. My extraordinary students were gathered in a group outside the auditorium with her. I handed Emma the roses, so that I could give each girl a hug. Vernon snapped pictures.

"Thank you so much, but you shouldn't have done that," I said to the girls.

"Tell me why not," Emma interjected.

"We all planned it together. My mom and I bought the roses on the way to school so they would be fresh. And Mr. Long helped us hide them behind the podium," Arielle declared.

"I had no idea," I added. "This is so special."

"We're happy you're happy," Bethany said.

"But when are you going to forget about the pencils and food?" I pleaded.

"Never!" they all shrieked, almost in unison.

"People are leaving for the luncheon. We better go, too," I said, seeing tears starting again. "Your families must be looking for you."

The graduation luncheon again was at the Chesterfield Hotel Restaurant except instead of a buffet, a plated meal was served. The graduates sat together at one long table in the front of the dining room.

Toward the end of the event, Charles approached our table where I was sitting by myself. Blane had already left with a friend and the friend's parents. Vernon was taking a few more photos of Mimi and the graduates.

The next thing I knew, I sensed Charles's face. He was beyond a comfortable distance apart. He had even passed that critical space just before one person dares to give another an intimate first kiss.

With his midnight blue eyes fixated upon mine, he said, "Molly, I am so happy for you—truly, truly, happy. You've worked incredibly hard for three years. You've given these girls an experience that no other teacher could. What an amazing relationship you've achieved to induce such a spontaneous, public display of affection from them."

His breath smelled of capers from the chicken piccata.

"Thank you," I replied modestly, trying to inch back, though he held the narrow space between us. I was pinned with Charles intractable in mood on one side and chairs impossible to move on the other. Dealing with this improvidence quietly seemed wiser than creating a worse scene. When would he break this hypnosis?

Suddenly, from the corner of one eye, I caught Vernon capturing on film Charles's lips just microspaces away from mine. Charles, so engrossed in his delivery, was oblivious to all other activity.

Then, as if a finger snapped, Charles walked away to say good-bye to the many guests. I felt frozen, physically and emotionally. Hadn't graduation this year been momentous enough with my daughter in the class and the presentation of the roses? I was totally unprepared for Charles's additional improper adulation.

When Charlotte Merritt had warned me of a betrayal, I thought of sexual harassment. Was the prediction coming true? The question drilled to the core of my cerebrum. He has cupped my hands, admired my clothes, and teased my spirit. He has toyed with my feelings and now, literally, been in my face. Vernon saw me numb and puzzled. He put his arm around me and held me a moment before we found Mimi and departed.

The next few days passed with great difficulty. I needed to clean and organize the lab. But, hoping that Charles would leave for vacation, I avoided school. I was reading in the sunroom when Vernon returned from errands.

"I just gave the graduation pictures to Mimi in her room," Vernon said. I panicked. "Don't worry," he added. "I took the indecent shot out of the pack first."

"Oh, thank goodness," I replied.

"Want to see it?" he asked rhetorically, handing it to me.

The actual image was as dreadful as I had remembered. Of course, Vernon had the focus and exposure perfect. Without Charles's academic praise in a caption bubble, the appearance was romantic. "I'm so glad you brought the zoom lens to graduation," I said sarcastically.

"What do you think?" Vernon asked.

"I don't know," I answered. "I always assumed that Charles just enjoyed teasing me. But now I'm upset with him for creating this awkward situation and spoiling an otherwise perfect day. Something must have seized him—he didn't know what he was doing."

"Oh, he knew," Vernon said. "There was no alcohol at a school function."

"No, he probably wouldn't even remember, and I'm certainly not going to show him this picture. This incident must not ruin the job I love." I could see disbelief in Vernon's face—we both knew I was rationalizing.

"Be careful, Molly," Vernon commented.

"I will be. I must be," I said assuredly, remembering that we had spoken these words before.

I thought of contrived television shows where similar, ill-timed photos were used as evidence in some sordid plot. Because I couldn't imagine anything so dramatic happening to me, I tried to forget the event. I just hoped that Charles's first indiscretion would be his only.

33. First Rest

Lying on the sofa in my sunroom, reflecting upon the past nine months, I smiled. To what had I given birth this third year at MCD?

My seventh grade students had scored higher on the math section of the SAT, some breaking 700, due to curriculum refinement. Many planned to attend the Talent Identification Program at Duke, sister program to CTY at Johns Hopkins, where I would be teaching again and visiting Grace. On the morning after the students received their scores, one father called me at school and greeted me with, "Has anyone today told you that you're wonderful?" He was certainly not a candidate for the *Shmuck of the Year* award.

My students loved to program because they loved to think. They had created more computer games, incorporating sophisticated logic, detailed coding, and fabulous graphics. Noah, now at the junior level in the international programming contest, placed third in the world.

Progress writing a programming text was steady, though slow. Still, my drafts worked better in the classroom than any commercial materials, proving my hypothesis: programming books needed daily practice and discrete lessons, similar to math texts. While I wished my teaching left more time to write, I adored my students.

Following the *Shining on Math Day* rendition from *Grease*, dear energetic Emma had written an original musical send-off for each math competition. If her talent for teaching, love of learning, and enthusiasm for education could be bottled and distributed, the problems facing schools would be solved, I thought.

The newspaper class, though eighth grade, won a second tier ranking from Columbia University's School of Journalism in its high school competition. Yet *Wonder Woman* did not plan to enter again. While I wanted MCD to pursue every possible path of achievement for students, I couldn't worry about others' responsibilities. Charles needed to enforce programs for continuity of curriculum.

Charles—was he focused on academic accolades or personal pleasures? I was growing unsure. *Together we will build a great school. Together we will build a great school. Together we will build a great school.* Reciting his distinctive enticement like counting sheep, I fell into a well-deserved deep sleep, perhaps the first rest of real consequence in three years.

34. First Wire

Progress at MCD meant not only new teachers like *Wonder Woman* but also new classrooms. I loved my small, private, peach-colored computer lab used solely by my students. But during the summer I had to move into a new lab in a new building.

I remember dreams when I was a high school student—nightmares of reporting for the SAT without enough sharpened pencils. Prior to my first day at MCD, I had the same type of dream—that I hadn't prepared and everything went wrong. Similarly, now I dreamed that I wouldn't be able to teach in the new lab because it was green—the color chosen by the architect. The walls were that hospital, nauseous, sea foam green and the carpeting that institutional, gloomy, forest green. Given that I never buy green clothes, not by premeditated decree but by natural inclination, my fear seemed grounded. So I bought multi-colored, striped fabric to recover the barbecue-house chairs—green to match the room, but also raspberry and periwinkle to brighten the look.

A few days before the start of school, Charles entered the lab as I was completing finishing touches. He looked all around, clearly delighted, before speaking.

"Molly, this is magnificent," Charles pronounced.

"Yes, I'm very lucky," I replied.

"You've earned every cubic inch of it with all that you've done for the students," Charles affirmed.

Somewhat embarrassed, I replied, "Every *cubic inch*? You're talking like a math teacher."

"I like this piece," Charles said, touching the large, old, heavy, oak table positioned at the front of the room.

"I found it in the same thrift shop where Joe bought my original desk," I replied and smirked. "It's perfect for the teacher's computer. I'm so excited. I've never taught programming like this before—with a demo computer at the front. See—the teacher's program outputs to the LCD panel which then projects onto the screen. The Oldfields bought the screen for me. Wasn't that nice?"

"Who bought the Liquid Crystal Display?" Charles asked.

"I did," I answered.

"How much was it?" Charles inquired.

"Twelve hundred," I replied.

"Submit a receipt, and the school will reimburse you," Charles insisted.

"No, Charles, it's okay," I said.

"But doesn't it make the teaching better?" he asked.

"A million times better. It's like an electronic blackboard," I explained.

"Then MCD should pay for it," he argued.

"No, Vernon and I have discussed it, and it's our donation," I countered.

"Then at least let me help you hide all of these wires," he offered. "Someone could trip on them. I'll be right back."

Within ten minutes Charles returned with supplies. "Joe had exactly what I needed," Charles said.

Charles and I were lying on the floor together under the table—I handing him cables and tacks, and he hammering them into place—when Cecily entered in search of Charles. She quickly surveyed the scene which, though totally innocent, appeared otherwise. Wisely, I had been careful to arrange my skirt discreetly.

"Charles, please come to my room when you two are done," she snapped before exiting abruptly.

"Cecily, wait," Charles called.

"I am so sorry," I said to Charles. "Shall I speak to her?"

"No, I'll go in a minute. She'll understand when I explain. Something else must be bothering her—she normally doesn't come looking for me. Just hand me that first wire again."

35. First Pronoun

Ordinarily, relocation to a new building would be a treat. However, because this lab had two doors, one to the outside and one to an inner hallway leading to other rooms, people could enter from two directions, sometimes disrupting class. While having an office in an inner room initially sounded exciting, keeping belongings in two different locations quickly became cumbersome. And, of course, I had to share the lab with *Wonder Woman*.

Indeed, Charles had assigned *Wonder Woman* the eighth grade newspaper class, but difficulty abounded. Fundamentally, she couldn't even internalize the natural sequence of turning on the computer, booting the software, and loading the files, so to help herself she wrote step-by-step instructions on a card that became a permanent body appendage. She gave me successive drafts of her first newspaper to read, but I returned them looking as if I had spilled blood on each page. And my red-pen eyes were not that critical because so many gross, obvious errors demanded circling.

Wonder Woman never stayed after school to work because she went home to walk her dog. She planned to work evenings or Saturdays at school on the newspaper and asked if she could bring her dog with her for protection. I said no emphatically because I did not want a dog in the new computer lab.

She asked a second time about bringing her dog, and again I replied that the matter was not negotiable. Protection was unnecessary because Joe's cleaning staff was on campus in the evenings. Also, Caroline Jackson, the business manager, worked Saturday mornings, and many of the sports teams practiced during off-hours.

On Saturday, now October, I unexpectedly stopped by school to pick up some papers while doing other errands in the neighborhood. I walked into the lab to find Stephanie Merritt working at a machine, *Wonder Woman* sitting at the teacher's computer, the most frantic dog imaginable running around the computer lab, and a water bowl and feeding dish lying on the floor below the LCD panel.

I screamed at *IT*, ordering her to pack her dog and leave immediately. With this incident I suddenly referred to her as *IT*. I slammed the door behind me because I had no intention of spending another second with the wild animal. I wanted to post a sign: *Beware of the dog. IT bytes.*

I arrived at school early Monday morning to find Charles eager to speak to me. *IT* had written him a note complaining about me as department chair because I had yelled at her in front of not just a student, but the board chairman's daughter.

"Instead of telling you my side of the story, I'm going to show you. Let's go to the computer lab," I suggested. "This situation is much worse than a bad-hair day."

I escorted Charles to the lab where we found at least twenty rips in the new carpet from the dog's feet. Charles shook his head. As I suspected, the destroyed carpet had a much bigger impact on Charles than *IT*'s ridiculous letter.

"Look at the size of these frays," I exclaimed.

"We'll get you new carpeting," Charles offered.

"For what? For her to do it again? No, Charles, you can't put bandages on these tears. You need to fix the source of the problem," I pleaded.

So, Charles and I both proceeded in our own ways to repair the damage. But rather quickly, Charles stopped using the name *Wonder Woman* and simply relied on my chosen pronoun.

To say that the students hated *IT* would not be an accurate description. They ridiculed her, quickly noticing that *IT* chewed her fingers while working at the computer, in a style only slightly more advanced than thumb sucking. The inconvenience of this behavior was the students' asking me continually to sterilize any mouse that she used. They knew whenever *IT* had been at a computer because only she put the mouse and pad on the left side of the keyboard. When the situation became intolerable, I bought boxes of individually sealed alcohol prep pads and told the students that they could wipe the mice whenever they wished, as long as they were discrete.

Suddenly, MCD students created *IT* jokes to rival the largest collection of light-bulb jokes. How long does *IT* take to clean a mouse ball? No one knows—she never tried. How long does *IT* take to format a disk? Forever—she never heard of formatting. Why did *IT*'s computer mouse fail? She fed it cheese. Where does *IT* keep valuables? She uses a data bank. What does *IT* eat at the computer? She dips microchips.

Meanwhile, I spent countless hours, whenever I had a few extra minutes, sewing the carpet's long snags down with green thread and a darning needle, blending the patches into the luckily asymmetrical weave. The flooring was never the same—but at least chair legs and students' feet didn't catch in the large loops, and the rug didn't totally unravel off the mesh backing.

Charles, on the other hand, opted for a quick solution to mending the rift between *IT* and me. He purchased a new computer for the classroom in which she taught her other classes, so that we wouldn't see each other. In typical Charles style, however, he didn't consult with me. Sadly and embarrassingly, I learned about the purchase from students.

On my way home with Mimi on the afternoon of the new computer's arrival, I bumped into Charles on the diagonal path. Seeing him with his innocent expression made me unravel like the knit rug.

"Nice new computer, Charles. Thanks for telling your department chair," I called, bitterly sarcastic.

"I'm sorry, Molly," Charles said timidly.

"I thought you were supposed to consult with me on all new hardware purchases—and for good reason," I asserted, not even looking to see who else was on the walkway.

"You were so upset about the dog that I just wanted to get *IT* out of your lab," Charles explained.

"But you didn't buy enough internal memory to handle the desktop publishing software properly. A card was added to my teacher's computer at the time of the purchase," I blasted.

"I didn't know," he said sheepishly.

"So now who is going to take the machine back to the store? *IT* can't even unplug the cords," I stated.

"I'll have Joe do it," Charles offered.

Just then Mimi put her heavy book bag on the ground, anticipating more than a short conversation.

"Why didn't you check with me initially?" I asked.

"Because I didn't want to bother you," Charles replied.

"Oh, so you're not bothering me now? Do you know how foolish and uninformed you made me look when the kids told me about the new computer?"

"I didn't think about that," Charles mumbled.

"I warned you not to hire her," I argued.

"Molly, let's go inside my office for a minute," Charles begged.

I followed Charles along the diagonal path, and Mimi followed me, lugging her bag on her back. She settled herself on the sofa in the reception area and took out some homework while Charles and I went into his office. He closed the door and immediately started talking while we stood.

"She presented herself as superhuman, capable of teaching so many different subjects, and I wanted to believe her so much," Charles explained. "I always worry about going over budget because I never know how much the Diamond Gala is going to make."

"She was like the little Dutch boy with expandable arms, plugging dike holes here and there and everywhere," I imitated scornfully with my fingers.

"Exactly—in multiple departments—as you once said."

"You know, I tried so hard to like her. I even thought at one time that we might become friends."

"And I needed to get someone else to do the newspaper class. It wasn't the best use of your time. But you made it look so easy that I forgot how hard it is," Charles expressed.

"The problem is that by hiding the purchase, you are wasting my time to have the memory board installed. You conveniently ignore my title when you wish—but not when errands are concerned," I emphasized somewhat agitatedly.

"Please forgive me," Charles said. He was oozing his usual charm.

"Fine. One more time," I answered.

Charles opened the door and walked me to Mimi.

"Your mom is so cute when she's upset," he said.

I cringed but dropped his comment without reply. He had used that line more than once before, but I resented his involving Mimi this time, especially because Mimi was fond of Charles. She was fortunate to have had him as an English teacher, though his field was actually classics. Charles had taught Mimi to love Shakespeare, and they two of them adlibbed Old English that could have been direct from his plays. *Fakespeare*, Mimi called these conversations. I delighted when Mimi matched Charles's wit. However, as a budding feminist, Mimi could have reacted sharply to Charles's teasing me. Fortunately, above all else, we both wanted to go home. Mimi looked at me for direction. But as I motioned my head toward the parking lot, Charles spoke.

"Now is the fall of Maid Molly's discontent,
Made glorious school year by this sudden new machine.
And all the clouds that hovered upon her lab,
In the deep bosom of the hardware buried."

Mimi continued.

"Now are our brows raised for monitor glows,
Our outstretched arms poised for shining trophies,
Our stern warnings changed to merry banter,
Our dreadful arithmetic to delightful computing."

Charles interrupted.

"Grim-visaged *IT* hath smoothed her wrinkled front.
And now, instead of mounting barbed gibes
To fright the souls of fearful students,
She capers nimbly on the MCD campus
To the pleasing tune of an Amiga extraordinaire."

"*Julius Caesar?*" I questioned.

"*Richard, the Third,*" they both responded, almost in unison.

"Where, oh where, is your iron broom when I need it?" I asked Charles disgustedly.

"I gave considerable thought to letting her go immediately but decided that waiting until June would be more comfortable—thus, the new computer," he said.

"I can wait, but can the students?" I asked.

"I hope so," he answered. "I hope they're still learning."

"Well, Maid Molly goeth hometh," I grumbled, grabbing Mimi's arm. After two steps toward the door, I turned back. "Is she the first pronoun as a code name?"

"*IT* is," Charles sighed sadly.

36. First Reputation

"Do you have a minute?"

Charles greeted me at the copy machine with his familiar line early Monday morning. I followed him into his office, and he closed the door as usual. The Diamond Gala, with its theme the Academy Awards, was held this past November weekend at the new Ritz-Carlton hotel.

"Congratulations on your biggest *stone* ever. You know, I think it's cute how you call the grand sum the *stone* as in a diamond stone," I said. "Vernon has an aunt who has a huge diamond ring, and he calls it the *stone* as well."

"Oh, no," Charles replied. "That's not the correct derivation of the term. I have an uncle who taught me how to buy a good, used Lincoln Continental. He always referred to the absolute bottom price as the *stone*—a play on words from rock bottom."

"Oh, sorry, I didn't know. Well, this year you had five hundred extra stones," I added.

"What do you mean?" Charles asked.

"The dessert, of course," I answered.

Charles laughed. "*The Committee* got carried away," he replied.

Desserts, worse than melted ice cream stalagmites, were gold Oscar statues, standing nine inches tall and one inch thick on individual plates in a pool of raspberry sauce garnished with one fanned strawberry and a slice of kiwi. When they arrived at the table, we all gasped at our trophies in disbelief. The waiter said, "Go ahead. They're solid chocolate, and even the gold is edible." Unreal people, namely real movie stars, received this unreal dessert at the real Governors Ball after the real Academy Awards for their unreal salaries, but real people at

153

the unreal Academy Awards, namely the real Diamond Gala, wanted a real dessert for their real money.

For one ridiculous moment I considered taking our chocolate trophies home for Blane and Mimi. However, wrapping them in multiple cloth napkins from the table to prevent a mess and returning the napkins laundered shortly thereafter would have only compounded Vernon's annoyance. His patience for the event had reached its nadir. When we were dressing, he quipped, "I'd pay another hundred dollars to stay home." I wondered what the chef thought when five hundred statues returned to the kitchen, sans fruit.

Suddenly, Charles laughed again bringing me back from my thoughts. "Did you see what Lorna's aunt was wearing? She left little to the imagination."

"I saw. That's not how I would get a man if I wanted one. I would take a job teaching at a university."

I don't know why I said that, but Charles had started the conversation about this woman, sadly a widow looking for a personal adventure. Suddenly, I suspected that I was in a dangerous domain.

"Molly, you're so attractive. I can't imagine you without a man," Charles responded.

How did I get into these situations? Perhaps the problem was Charles's ability to add sexual nuances to any conversation when he wanted. Should I respond that I'm a one-man woman? No, remembering the betrayal warning, I changed the subject quickly.

"What did you want to discuss?" I asked.

Charles became serious. "Mr. Zahn and Mr. Lawton both grabbed me at the Diamond Gala to discuss their sons in your sixth grade advanced math class."

"At the Diamond Gala?" I repeated, incredulously.

"I hate when parents choose social occasions to complain. Cecily and I are becoming hermits just to avoid these encounters," he said.

"Where else does it happen?" I asked.

"Oh, all the time at sports games when I'm trying to watch the kids. The parents don't care that we could have a better conversation in my office with the door closed than in the bleachers surrounded by dozens of people—and in the middle of a soccer play as well. They just want their issues satisfied immediately," Charles explained.

Meanwhile, I had not been listening to Charles very carefully. I was too busy thinking about how I could possibly share my *Shmuck of the Year* title between two fathers. Charles broke my contemplation.

"I've decided to make a bumper sticker for you, Molly: MY CHILD SURVIVED MATH 6 ADVANCED AT MCD." Charles laughed heartily. He was, of course, referring to the proliferation of bumper stickers from various public schools declaring that one's student was on the honor roll.

"Thanks, Charles. I really appreciate that," I commented sarcastically. "So what did you say to Mr. Zahn and Mr. Lawton?"

"I told them to call Catherine to remove their sons from your class if they wished, but we were not changing an award winning curriculum for them," Charles answered. "And beyond that, they would have to speak to me at school."

"And what did they say?" I asked.

"Well, Mr. Zahn said that he couldn't do that because the class was his son's favorite," Charles explained.

"So what's his problem?" I demanded in disgust.

"Molly, it's obvious. Mr. Zahn is reacting on two fronts. For one thing, your half-hour of homework each night is a stress in his chaotic household. The boy is probably so tired and disorganized that the thirty minutes turns into sixty or more. The second issue is that Mr. Zahn feels threatened because he can't do some of the problems," Charles added.

"But they're not his problems," I said incensed. "He is not my student—his son is."

"I know that, but it's a male thing. How can a cute, little woman like you know more math than an imposing, big man like him?"

"This is sad. This is really sad," I replied. "He will ruin his son's education. Let me tell you what happened in class the other day. I gave the students a set of challenge problems and specifically told them that they should get absolutely no help from anyone. They know, anyway, that I like them to do their own work, but I made a really big point of it this time."

"Let me guess what happened—Mr. Zahn did the problems against your orders and pretended he hadn't," Charles interrupted.

"Wait—it's worse," I said. "A few days later the kids presented their solutions on the board. When little Zahn took his turn, he started by saying that his dad had given him the method. Stephanie Merritt nearly fell off her chair. I could see in her eyes that she was going to tell her father that night at home."

"Oh, so now we'll have the board chairman involved in this debacle," Charles interjected.

"And," I continued, "as if that weren't enough, little Zahn presented a solution with incorrect algebra. He had no idea what he was talking about, and he shouldn't. We do some pre-algebra at the end of the year, but not now. It's too early. I was after other methods. Mr. Zahn is going to damage his kid beyond repair."

"And turn the other kids against him, it seems," Charles added.

"On the one hand, he's complaining that I'm doing too much, and on the other, he's attempting to teach his son even more. What does he want?"

"He doesn't know what he wants," Charles stated wisely.

"Well, what about Mr. Lawton?" I asked, bolstering myself.

Charles replied, "He's thinking of removing his son from the class. He enjoys saying that math was never his best subject and that it's not his son's best subject either."

"Good grief—the classic what-not-to-do as a parent," I muttered.

"How is little Lawton?" Charles said with a smirk, enjoying copying my use of the diminutive adjective.

"Talented, but lazy," I responded.

"I'm not surprised," Charles said. "This family is indulged."

"So . . .?" I asked slowly.

"I've set up a meeting this afternoon at four o'clock with you, me, Catherine, and Mr. and Mrs. Lawton—in your lab. Okay?"

"Sure," I replied first and then thought about whether Mimi had an after-school activity.

At four o'clock I was ready with my grade book and supporting papers arranged on one of the barbecue tables. Catherine arrived on time, followed by Charles a few minutes later. I expected Charles to leave temporarily when he saw that the Lawtons were late. Instead, he sat down, slid his chair back, and stretched out his long legs.

"Is this the first chance you've had to relax all day?" Catherine asked Charles.

"It is," replied Charles, looking out the window. "But it's over. Here comes Mr. Lawton up the walk—without his wife."

Catherine went to the door, Charles pushed in his chair, and I took a deep breath.

"Hello, hello, hello," Mr. Lawton said, nodding at each of us.

"Here, have a seat," Charles indicated, as he handled one of the two empty chairs at the table. "We were hoping that Mrs. Lawton would be joining us."

"She's worse at math than I am," Mr. Lawton said.

Catherine, Charles, and I looked at each other in disbelief.

"Let's get right to the point," Mr. Lawton continued. "Math was never my best subject, and it's not my son's either."

"But it's so soon to judge," interrupted Catherine, who generally took control early at parent conferences.

"Yes, that's the point. I should be able to do sixth grade math," Mr. Lawton stated. Then, looking straight at me, he added, "I was on the phone with Mr. Zahn, and together we couldn't do one of your impossible problems."

Charles winked at me.

"Which one was that?" I asked politely.

"I can't remember the exact wording, but it had to do with an average that led to some unsolvable equations," Mr. Lawton replied.

"Dr. Kelman, do you think you could recall the problem for us?" Charles requested.

"I think you mean questions of this type," I suggested, selecting the proper page quickly. I read, "The average of two numbers is 10, and their product is 91. Find the greater of the two numbers."

"Yes, that's it," Lawton answered.

I could sense Catherine's nervousness at the sound of so many numbers and Charles's excitement at the prospect of my quashing this father.

"We set up two equations, but then we were stuck. This isn't normal algebra," Lawton said.

He reached over for Catherine's pad of paper and wrote:

$$\frac{x+y}{2} = 10 \text{ and } xy = 91.$$

Again, I sensed Charles and Catherine's emotions heightening in anticipation of the outcome.

"You're right—it's not a two-variable, two-equation system. But I did not teach the students to write equations in this case. Students attentive in class know exactly what to do. The problem has three main lessons. The first concerns averages. If two numbers average to ten, then before dividing by two, their sum must be twenty. I teach the students the slogan *Get the sum!* because we use it many times later in the course for more difficult average problems. Then, as part of our mental math exercises, we practice, verbally and quickly, similar problems such as: If five numbers average to twelve, what is their sum?"

Mr. Lawton looked as if these explanations were sufficient math instruction for him for the day, but I continued, writing on the pad as I spoke.

"My second important lesson in this problem is the examination of the ones digit as a key to the solution. What two digits would add to zero in the twenty and multiply to one in the ninety-one? The students easily say three and seven. Then, to practice estimating, seventeen times three is too small, while thirteen times seven is correct."

Mr. Lawton was shaking. Catherine was withdrawing. And Charles was beaming.

"What is your third lesson in this problem, Dr. Kelman?" Charles asked.

"The final lesson is in answering the exact question, so the answer is thirteen, not both numbers," I answered.

"Well, this all proves my point. This class is too hard for a sixth grader. I want my boy out—now," Mr. Lawton declared.

"I really think you ought to consider that your son does have math talent," Catherine interjected.

"Mrs. West," Charles said firmly. "I believe in this case, we need to follow Mr. Lawton's wishes. Could you please adjust his son's schedule starting tomorrow?"

"Certainly," Catherine replied.

"Well, that's that," Charles stated, giving the tabletop his signature tap. "Thanks for coming in," he said to Mr. Lawton as they shook hands.

"I'm glad you saw my point," Mr. Lawton said.

"I saw what I needed to see," Charles responded carefully.

Charles stayed after the others left, but I erupted before he could speak. "The man has a severe case of math anxiety and actually takes pride in passing it on to his son," I announced.

"He had already made up his mind, Molly. There was no talking sense to him," Charles said. And then he added, "Get the point?"

I giggled at Charles's imitation of Mr. Lawton, but the levity ended immediately. "If this were my first year at MCD, I could understand complaints. But it's my fourth. I should be known by success, not over-teaching. Think of all the awards my students have won. More importantly, think of how they love math. When are parents going to stop finding fault?"

"Never," Charles stated emphatically.

"Never?" I asked, surprised and scared.

"Never, because it doesn't matter what year you are in. To them, you and your curriculum are a new experience," he commented. "And what you do with their child establishes your first reputation."

I thought about Charles's explanation for a moment. "You are very wise," I replied.

Charles smiled at me warmly, showing he enjoyed the compliment from me. "Don't let today get to you. Think of how many students you have reached. Why don't you find Mimi and go home?"

I considered telling Charles about all the potent candidates for my special award for difficult fathers but decided on maintaining secrecy. "You're right. I'm leaving," I said.

37. First Trip

"Molly, I've given the literary magazine duty to Tom Tufts," Charles said to me one brisk February morning, as we happened to be walking up the diagonal path together. Tom was the new ninth grade English and history teacher.

"I know. He told me. After Alexa's fiasco, I offered to give Tom a lesson on desktop publishing, at least so he would know what was available, even if the students do the layout," I said.

"That was nice," Charles replied.

"Don't get too excited—Tom balked. 'I'd rather use a quill than a computer' were his exact words. Gee, I didn't think that in 1992 a quill was an option in producing a fifty-page magazine," I commented.

"It's too early in the morning for sarcasm. Anyway, the project is his problem, not yours, Molly," Charles stated.

"Believe me. I know," I said assuredly.

Shortly thereafter, Charles decided that experiential education would be valuable for the ninth graders, so he asked Tom to chaperone the students on a trip. Because most of the students liked Tom, he seemed like the perfect choice. Tom, in turn, proposed that a trip to the Rain Forest in Costa Rica would be both exciting and instructional.

To present the idea, Tom and his wife invited all the ninth grade parents to their home one evening. Vernon and I arrived not knowing what to expect, and I was disappointed not seeing Charles present. Curiously, Tom kept discussing the trip as if a definite, positive decision had already been made.

Mrs. Tufts served a wonderful recipe with cooked chicken, brown rice, sweet onions, green chilies, and melted cheese called chicken adobe. Salad and corn bread completed the meal. Unintentionally, I kept referring to the main dish as chicken diablo, as if I had a subconscious feeling of evil or danger.

Running out of conversation topics, I said again without thinking, "This chicken diablo is fantastic."

"Adobe—chicken adobe," Mrs. Tufts replied and smiled courteously.

"The combination of ingredients is fantastic," the mother sitting next to me on the sofa said. Suddenly, she dropped her fork. It crashed on her plastic plate, spattering rice on her skirt. Her eyes had opened terribly wide. My slip-of-the-tongue could not have possibly flustered her to this extent, I thought. Then I looked ahead when her expression turned from shock to fear.

Without warning Tom had withdrawn a machete from a case that was hanging on the living room wall. I panicked when I saw the large, sharp, heavy knife. In another instant he entered into a schizophrenic monologue replete with hallucinations of Vietnam. The woman next to me, still with diablo dribbles in her lap, seized and squeezed my hand, tucking our paired grasp out of sight between the seat cushions.

All I could think was that I was living a mystery novel. The lights would go off, and when they went on again, one parent would be discovered murdered. I'm not sure how much I breathed until Tom put the knife away and reverted back to his teacher persona. After the episode the walnut fudge brownies were very unappealing, and the party ended sooner than expected.

"Another great faculty pick on Charles's part," I commented sarcastically on the ride home. Vernon was noticeably silent.

The next day at school, I found Charles as soon as possible.

"Oh, Molly. How was the get-together at Tom's last evening?" Charles asked.

"I am really sorry that you missed it," I answered.

"Why?" Charles inquired.

"Because I felt as if I were in the opening scene of a sinister script," I explained. "Parent found dead at English teacher's home after pleasant dinner of chicken diablo."

"What on earth are you talking about?"

"Tom actually keeps a machete hanging on the living room wall. Talking about the Rain Forest must have reminded him of Vietnam. He pulled the knife out of its case and brandished it while discoursing unintelligibly about the war," I related.

"I didn't realize he had been there," Charles stated.

"Been there and hasn't gotten over it. Did he leave all that off his résumé along with his quill expertise?"

"Molly, don't get sarcastic," Charles begged.

"Charles, we're talking about whether or not to let my daughter and your students go to a foreign country, into the Rain Forest, with a man who, we suddenly discovered, might not be mentally sound," I said, emphasizing each phrase.

"I think you're exaggerating," Charles expressed.

"I don't think so. Where were you?"

"Home with Cecily—I felt guilty about deserting her so many evenings to have dinner with donors or board members," Charles admitted.

I sighed over his bad timing. "Couldn't you have felt guilty last week and not last night when we needed you?"

"The trip will be fine," Charles affirmed. "When they arrive, a team of local scientists and environmentalists will escort the kids. Tom will be the least important person there. And Mrs. Tufts is very dependable."

"How can she be dependable? She married him," I responded. "Look, the kids are not going out of the country with a madman without your knowing my opinion."

"Molly, you always tell me your opinion about everything. Why should this trip be an exception?"

"That's not fair. I have no opinion on many school issues. And others I don't even know about," I retorted.

"Well, thanks for informing me. But my inclination is to allow the trip," he stated.

"His code name is *Tomahawk*, right?"

Charles grimaced.

I left Charles's office discouraged, anticipating that I would be placed in the classic, awful, parental no-win situation—exercising my right to do what I thought best for my daughter versus making her the outcast of the group. I was angry that I might be forced to compromise my principles regarding my child's safety.

After surprisingly little discussion, Charles as well as the other parents supported the adventure. Because Mimi desired to go and because we trusted her, Vernon persuaded me to agree.

The week of the trip arrived, and each day passed slowly for me. Having a lighter teaching schedule with one entire grade away should have been helpful. In actuality, less work to do meant more time to worry. I was thrilled to finally meet Mimi at the Miami airport, but I could see instantly from her face that something had happened.

"Wait for the car to talk," I told Mimi quietly as I hugged her. Vernon carried Mimi's bag while she walked between us with her arms outstretched on our shoulders.

"We had a great first day in San José—a fun dinner and tour," Mimi explained when we were on I-95 headed north. "But as soon as we got to our cabin in the Rain Forest, Mr. Tufts freaked. He spent the entire week in bed—except for one night when he had a huge fight with Holly. He acted like a big male chauvinist towards her, and she stood up to him. But then in our room she started crying so hard that Bethany and I could hardly comfort her."

Vernon took his eyes off the highway quickly to look at me.

"How were the local guides and scientists?" I asked.

"Fantastic," Mimi replied. "We learned so much. But what do you think happened to Mr. Tufts?"

"As far as his mental breakdown, he had a Vietnam flashback. It's fairly common for men who were there during the war," I said. "Regarding his treatment of Holly, I don't know what to say."

"More happened than this," Mimi said.

"More?" Vernon asked.

"We spent some time in the capital again this afternoon before the plane left. Mr. and Mrs. Tufts took a table at an outdoor café in the center of town and told us that we could wander as long as we stayed in pairs and returned in two hours. Actually, we all stayed together and went shopping. Most of us bought little gifts for our families. Then we went to a different café and ordered drinks—big, fun, fruity ones. But technically, I suppose they contained alcohol. Nobody thought twice, but I guess we were wrong."

"Of course, you were wrong. You're all under twenty-one and on a school trip, no matter where you are," I said.

"I know, but the drinks were the local custom. They were mostly juice and probably so much safer than the water. No one even got tipsy," Mimi explained.

"The problem is that Mr. and Mrs. Tufts should never have let you go off on your own in a foreign country," I said. We continued driving home talking of Blane and his activities. Then Molly asked about her cousin Brenna.

After a restful weekend, thankful that the students were home safely, I spoke to Charles about Mimi's news.

"I am begging you never to let *Tomahawk* take MCD students on a trip again. You are so lucky that nothing worse happened," I argued.

"I'll send an additional teacher to chaperone Tom," Charles replied.

"Why not skip the first chaperone and just send the second?" I asked, bewildered.

I despised these stupid, illogical conversations that were becoming more and more prevalent. I worried that the stress of Charles's job was making common sense leak out of his brain from his every opening—eyes, ears, nose, and mouth—like refrigerator valves losing essential freon.

After Charles had no answer, I said, "So you're telling me that this was Tom's first trip but not his last?"

"I guess I am," Charles replied.

38. First Letter

Charles's irrational behavior appeared again while recruiting a replacement for *IT*. Charles had received a letter from a talented, young, female teacher who wanted to return from teaching abroad, specifically looking for a job near Palm Beach so that her children could know their grandparents. Because she had experience both in math and computer science, Keith and I were very excited about her résumé. Moreover, she had contacted us—she was not a Ron Special.

I was optimistic until Charles happened to tell me at lunch that she was due at MCD that afternoon.

"What?" I shrieked after swallowing in one gulp. "You forgot to tell me? Are you serious?" Then I lowered my voice. "Oh, I'm sorry. I haven't bumped into you at the mailboxes this week, so I guess I don't receive important information."

I shoved my sandwich back into its plastic container and ran off so that I could clear my time for the afternoon.

"Tell me if I can help," Emma called after me, glaring at Charles.

The teacher was wonderful, and I tried not to make her welcome appear too impromptu. I even ran my *Enchanted Amiga Room* show for her, attempting to impress her with the brilliance and creativity of MCD's students. Unfortunately, she decided to stay abroad a few more years for the European excitement and greater pay. Still angry with Charles, I thought that with more time to prepare for her visit, I might have convinced her to accept. But Charles insisted that her visit was just a sham to satisfy her parents.

Nevertheless, Charles and I were in complete agreement that *IT* was going, one way or another. A few weeks later Charles miraculously found a new school for her, passing the trash once again. So the hunt continued for help in the computer science department.

"Don't worry. Ron will find someone for you," Charles offered.

My insides knotted. Charles knew my opinion of Ron. How could he persist with comments like that?

Indeed, Ron found a candidate named Harry Linz. Admittedly, Harry looked good on paper. Because Harry lived outside of D.C. not far from Grace, I asked my sister to interview him first. Already March, she arranged the meeting expediently.

"Molly, I'm not sure about him," she said. "He's afraid of what he's heard from Ron Rhinehardt. Harry's interpretation is that MCD pushes its students too hard, indicating that he has a more lax educational philosophy. That's a serious warning."

I reported Grace's comments to Charles. Regardless, Ron invited Harry to visit MCD, and I approached the interview determined to like the candidate.

I decided to host a Saturday evening, faculty dinner party to offer Harry a grand welcome and to provide an efficient way for Harry and the teachers to meet. I had never officially invited Charles to my home before. As close as we were, I wanted to maintain my privacy. Once, during the literary magazine debacle, he had brought me some papers to save time—almost as a peace offering. At that visit, however, he remained at the front door. Of course, he and Cecily never entertained the faculty at their home—all one large room of it.

For Harry's party I had made brownie ice cream rolls and had stored them in the back of the freezer. At dessert time, the rolls were close to impossible to cut. Charles took charge of the heavy knife, laughing the whole time in typical Charles style. He made all mundane tasks comical—running the knife under hot water, obtaining each slice, and pouring on the chocolate and raspberry sauces. Charles had fun in my spacious, stylish kitchen as if he missed one. He was suspiciously very comfortable at my home.

"What did you think of Harry?" I asked Vernon while cleaning after the guests had gone.

"He seemed a little immature," Vernon replied. "He was awkward mixing—spent most of his time with Tom Tufts."

"I hadn't noticed," I said, distressed.

"No, you were busy serving. What do you think the outcome will be?"

"I don't know. I'll be able to talk to him more tomorrow when I show him Palm Beach. But really, I need to see him teach and interact with the kids."

The phone rang as I was washing the last wineglasses.

"How was your party for Harry?" Grace asked immediately, without even saying hello.

"Oh, the party was great, but I agree with you. I'm not sure about Harry."

"And how was Prince Oddball?"

I described to Grace the story of Charles's continual laughing while slicing the frozen chocolate rolls.

She said simply, "No one is stranger than he is."

At the mailboxes after school on Monday, Charles told me that Harry had confided to him. Harry felt that his visit confirmed his initial opinion—that MCD forced its students too much. Shockingly, he added that he wasn't sure he could work with me because I was too goal-oriented.

"Just make my code name *Pollyanna*," I told Charles. "What a fool I was to host the dinner."

"Your party was beautiful—a treat for the teachers," Charles said appreciatively.

"He told you, quote: *he wasn't sure he could work with me*," I said, ignoring Charles's compliment. "And he isn't even here yet! How significant is this remark? Is he suggesting that I resign so that he can fashion the department in his own image?"

"You are not resigning—ever. You are the school," Charles stated.

"Who would have ever thought that shy Harry was hiding such arrogance? We need to listen to him."

"But there are no other candidates who are better," Charles said.

"That's Ron's problem," I answered.

"You cannot teach all of the courses yourself," Charles argued.

"That's not a reason to employ someone who won't fit," I pleaded. "Harry is sending a clear message, and he will create huge problems. I'm begging you not to hire him."

"As of now, he's the only choice," Charles affirmed.

"You'll have a code name for him by the end of September next year. It's inevitable," I stated angrily and walked away.

Then, I saw Tom.

"Harry's a great guy," Tom announced as he moved past me.

Every breath and pulse resonated in my body like multiple smoke and fire alarms. *Hari-kari*—Charles would certainly think of that option for Harry's code name.

And as for *Tomahawk*—the only insightful comment Tom ever made was that MCD purposely had no faculty room because Charles didn't want the teachers conversing with each other more than necessary. Talking meant bonding, and bonding meant faculty strength against administration. However, Charles always said, and rightfully so, that having another classroom was more important than a faculty lounge. Besides, prior to his conversion to private school, he gloomily recalled these public school rooms as havens for teachers discussing important educational themes such as their new refrigerators.

Because I had no witness to my conversation with Charles, I wrote him a long letter imploring him not to hire Harry, explaining my position with multiple, forceful reasons. I decided to put important exchanges with Charles into writing, suspecting that some day I might need proof. Perhaps foolishly, I didn't hesitate to have this first letter in my personnel file. Yet, what if this correspondence, these strong arguments recorded on paper, fell into the wrong hands some day?

A few weeks later Charles hired Harry despite my protests. *Blind Harry*, I thought, was a good code name. Wasn't he a wandering minstrel in fifteenth century Scottish poetry?

39. First Crown

Another Spring Festival arrived. The *Miss Computer Pageant*, complete with swimsuit, evening gown, talent, and question-answer rounds for Miss Amiga, Miss Mac, Miss IBM, and Miss Apple IIe, was a phenomenal success. My students outdid their previous creativity and programming beyond amateur imagination. The on-screen images of computers dressed in skimpy bathing suits and lavish formal wear had the guests audibly chuckling. Moreover, the students created guest appearances of Miss Eniac and Miss Univac—dingy visions with animated flying moths and crawling spiders. The talent round was perhaps the most clever. Poor Miss Apple IIe could only draw a colored picture in half-inch squares, while Miss Mac and Miss IBM drew in tiny pixels. Of course, Miss Amiga created kaleidoscopic art.

A few days after the May show, my exhaustion maximized, I sat in Charles's office discussing many computer science department related matters. Of course, he mentioned the performance.

"The amount of work was staggering," he expressed. "The playbill alone was impressive—the names of all the students and the various components they designed and programmed." Charles started laughing. "When you electronically crowned Miss Amiga *Miss Computer 1992* while the computers played the Miss America theme song in stereo, you really put it to Mr. Greig."

Then, suddenly, Charles looked at me straight in the eye and spoke haunting words.

"Molly, you know, MCD really does have an Academic Dean. Maybe it's time I crown her," he said coyly.

Marla Weiss

I was shocked. I said nothing. Though Charles spoke in the third person, just as he had done at my initial interview, he was clearly referring to me. If he were teasing, he would laugh. But he didn't. If he were serious, he would continue. But he didn't. He was testing me, trying a transient thought. Because I had never considered being Academic Dean and because his delivery was not a professional way of asking, I reverted to our original conversation after a brief silence. He dropped the topic of the academic deanship as if *Miss Computer* were the first and only crown.

40. First Help

My end-of-fourth-year reflection on the sunroom sofa focused solely on Charles. In essence, to keep my sanity and meet my expectations as well as to satisfy MCD's students and further MCD's development, I had tried assisting Charles in countless ways. But now many of his remarks replayed in my mind. *Molly, you know, MCD really does have an Academic Dean. Maybe it's time I crown her. . . . I need you on my side, Molly. . . . You keep me honest. . . . You're one of my prize teachers and favorite people. . . . Molly, you're so attractive. I can't imagine you without a man. . . . Molly, let's run away together. . . . Molly, you're so cute when you're angry. . . . Molly's cake is better than sex. . . . Day after day, no matter how hectic things get around here, you always look wonderful. . . . Together we will build a great school.*

Did the suggestive comments strongly outweigh the academic ones, or was I not remembering correctly? Most seriously, I wondered if a betrayal loomed, as Charlotte Merritt had predicted.

I tried to comfort myself by thinking of my upcoming teaching at CTY and seeing Grace. However, as I contemplated the first help I had given Charles and the often times dispiriting consequences of later assistance, I realized that my frustrating position of unofficial collaborator without authority, without a crown, was terminal. Together we might not build a great school. Sadly, my annual reflection did not help my apprehension.

41. First Torte

With both my children—Mimi a sophomore and Blane a senior—at the public high school, I worked halftime, just mornings, my fifth year at Merritt Country Day to try writing and teaching concurrently. However, interruptions abounded.

One hindrance was the admission committee's accepting a sixth grader in mid-October. Though he had applied on time, the board scholarship committee couldn't decide about the boy's financial aid. When the student was finally admitted, he was placed into my advanced class due to math talent. After school was his only available time for me to teach him what he had missed during the previous six weeks. I had no choice but staying late every day for a month. Though I tried working on my writing at school during the afternoons, I was not nearly as productive as when at home. My attitude had changed since helping Bethany during my first year. I no longer smiled at every inconvenience, especially those avoidable.

The MCD admission and scholarship committees had little regard for faculty members' prior obligations. Not receiving pay for this extra work was secondary to never volunteering for it. A teacher's time should have been sacrosanct above all extenuating circumstances. This situation and others made me both skeptical and resentful of the Diamond Gala. The annual event was supposed to pay for needy, gifted students. Why couldn't the faculty demand timely admission and contribute valuable insight? Several times Keith and I were expected to produce winning teams while concurrently our best math students had their Diamond Gala scholarships rescinded— without consulting with us. Was I wrong to expect more from the board members? But their approach to scholarships was no different than their approach to computers that I had discovered earlier. The Board claimed that computers were the hallmark of the school but failed to understand their use.

More compelling, my halftime year flopped because Harry Linz's teaching deteriorated steadily, and Charles asked me to help. Predictably, Harry's thinking that MCD overly pushed students made him out of sync with the rest of the faculty. The students had one set of expectations in their other classes and then received entirely different treatment in Harry's. Completing assignments didn't matter—sometimes Harry collected them, sometimes he didn't. He rarely graded papers because he was so overwhelmed by the job.

His school newspaper production was a misadventure—not graphically, as with *IT*'s the previous year, but journalistically. He supported the philosophy that students should just write, letting their words flow, without regard to style, punctuation, spelling, or grammar—that those concerns inhibited the writing process. The theory was certainly a valid one for younger children who didn't have those skills, or possibly as a first draft for middle school students. But then imposing the craft of composition on future drafts was necessary, especially before importing articles through the desktop publishing software for layout in the newspaper. Harry's problem was that the later stages of the writing process never occurred, and the students complained to Charles that they received little instruction or help from Harry.

Charles, trying to treat Harry with professional respect, sent him and his wife on an all-expense-paid trip. Charles instructed Harry to carefully observe a school with an excellent computer science program. The excursion was supposed to be for work, not vacation. Yet, when Harry returned, he conveyed no facts, wrote no report, and instituted no ideas—only submitted restaurant bills. Charles, in one of our frequent conversations about Harry, admitted being furious over the waste of money.

Harry, in his quiet way, also displayed the same arrogance as during his interview. He prepared a written report suggesting that MCD spend a small fortune upgrading computer hardware. Undoubtedly, the hardware would have to be replaced in a few years. However, not only was his report premature, but also more importantly, audacious because his professional performance did not justify spending so much money on him.

Catherine observed his classes many times all fall, and she always found total chaos—both in instruction and discipline. "Without discipline, education is stymied," Charles had told the faculty repeatedly.

To Catherine's dismay, the climax was my discovery that a student had incised *Piss off, Mr. Linz* into one of the computer room wooden barbecue restaurant chairs. This incident was especially significant because Catherine prided herself on MCD's absence of graffiti. And Catherine West did not care if the students called her the *Wicked Witch of the West* as a byproduct of her accomplishment. So Catherine locked all of the middle school students in a room and told them that no one could leave—no matter what—until the perpetrator admitted to the crime.

When a certain girl confessed, I was shocked. Knowing the student, I realized that the carved words were minor to what they symbolized—the student's frustration in dealing with Harry and his classroom attitude.

"Is the iron broom coming out for Harry?" I asked Charles just after this woodcarving incident.

"For whom? *Linzer Torte*?" Charles asked.

"Oh, food—I should have guessed," I proclaimed. "You have other baked goods in your code name collection, but Harry is your first torte."

Charles laughed, very proud of his self-implied cleverness.

"Do you know what a torte is?" I asked.

"Well, I suppose something missing salt and pepper would be appropriate in this case."

"Close. It's missing the rising ingredient."

42. First Remark

I arrived at school on a spectacularly fresh winter day to find Joe and his custodial staff setting up a podium, microphone, and folding chairs on the school's front lawn, adjoining the diagonal walk. Priscilla was working fast, draping wide ribbon across the apron of a portable stage. Some teachers were nearby, trying to keep students away by ushering them into first period class.

"What's going on?" I asked Priscilla.

"The board is holding a press conference later this morning," she replied.

"Why?" I asked, trying to recall if such an occasion had ever happened before.

"To announce its decision to expand Merritt Country Day School to include a full high school, one year at a time beginning with tenth grade next fall," she answered, lifting her eyebrows and holding her breath in anticipation of my response.

"What!" I exclaimed. "The board never asked the faculty."

"Believe it," Priscilla advised, her face resuming its normal look.

"Where's Charles?"

"In his office writing his speech," she stated.

"Figures," I muttered as I walked to my lab.

Concerns rippled through my mind. Even if we weren't questioned about wanting a high school, shouldn't we have been consulted about preparing for one? Perhaps Charles planned to leave the existing faculty in the middle school and hire new teachers for the high school. Still, actual staffing and scheduling would rarely permit a strictly divided arrangement in such a small environment.

Subject offerings seldom come in tidy multiples of five for a full load, especially in the transition years until reaching the twelfth grade. Crossing-over between the high school and middle school would be unavoidable. More importantly, where would new, truly competent teachers be found in six months?

At twelve o'clock Charles's voice boomed in every classroom, asking teachers and students to gather at the outdoor site. However, the event was rather embarrassing because no press attended although invited. Mr. Parke Merritt made several sweeping announcements: MCD would produce a large number of National Merit Scholars and would offer a faculty to rival any high school in the nation. Was I the only one troubled by such speculative, indefensible remarks? One of the students asked about a football team. The answer was thankfully no. Soccer and basketball Snooks seemed plausible, but football players were not exquisite fish.

After the ceremony ended, students went to lunch. Charles waved at me to wait.

"Molly, what do you think?" Charles asked.

"I'm speechless," I answered. Telling him that holding a press conference with no reporters was as sad as hosting a party with no guests would have been cruel.

"The board wanted it and wanted it fast," he said.

"So I see," I replied.

"I'm going to form a faculty committee to oversee the formation of the high school," he explained.

"Isn't that backwards?" I asked.

"Not really," Charles answered. "Things will work fine. I know you're only here mornings this year, but I hope you will stay for the Monday afternoon meetings. I value your input."

"Sure," I said despite that his request, along with helping my late-admit sixth grader and monitoring Harry Linz, was the third interruption to my afternoons supposedly devoted to writing.

I breathed the February air that no longer seemed as invigorating. "By the way, Charles, Mr. Merritt said *National Merit Scholars*, but he should have said *Semifinalists*. As you know, many factors select the scholars or actual winners, whereas the qualifying exam alone determines the first cut—the semifinalists."

"So?" Charles asked.

"So people speaking officially for the high school will need to use proper terminology."

"Why?" Charles questioned.

"Why? Why, obviously—to educate the parents and students regarding the myriad of high school details. Don't you believe in accuracy of the spoken and written word?"

"Molly, a press statement is not a computer program," Charles stated.

"But the school's first remark needs to be correct," I protested.

Charles and I stared at each other, both realizing the divergence of our views.

43. First Committee

At the opening meeting of the high school committee, Rhonda Seddon, right arm decorated in a stack of silver and turquoise bracelets, plunged immediately into one of her favorite topics: socialization. Rhonda, a single mother, wanted forced get-togethers because her daughter, somewhat gawky and immature, would attend the new high school. I wondered why Charles permitted a second grade teacher to participate.

"We can plan the dances and other social events later," said Keith, who served as moderator.

"Don't underestimate the importance of these parties," Rhonda harped, with a dissonant glissade of cascading bangles.

"No one is saying that they're not important," I said in a tone showing my annoyance with her persistence.

"May we please concentrate on education first?" Tom Tufts pleaded.

"Go ahead, Tom," Keith said.

"The finest New England boarding schools allow their students to take only four major subjects," Tom claimed. "In that way the teachers can give the proper amount of assignments for depth and mastery and expect the students to do the work well."

Though initially pleased by Tom's request to discuss academics, I never even considered that he might have his own agenda. But Tom's jealousy of other departments was clear. He must have felt that fewer subjects would bolster the history offerings.

"The problem is that MCD already has a tradition of six majors—mathematics, English, science, history, foreign language and computer science—along with substantial time for the fine arts.

If anything, the high school schedule needs time for seven or eight majors to accommodate all that our best students want to learn. I can easily see some taking two foreign languages or two sciences in one year in addition to music, drama, or journalism," I argued.

"As a new school, we are completely unrecognized by colleges. Therefore, we need to do what the finest prep schools are doing," Tom repeated.

"That logic does not follow. Why are we obliged to duplicate any school? Maybe we have something better here. I would also like to remind all of you that pitting one teacher's program against another in a small school is not healthy—and that is exactly what a restricted schedule would do," I said.

"All students have to make choices—Latin or chorus, for example," Tom declared.

"We are known for keeping those choices to a minimum. And that is one crucial reason why we have happy students," I explained.

"The students need to be well versed in all areas of English and history," Tom stated.

"Yes," I continued, "but not at the exclusion of other subjects. We have the opportunity to establish an extraordinary high school, not a copy. Our eighth and ninth graders are already successfully taking numerous courses. If we change that, we'll have a revolt."

"You would be making a big mistake overloading the kids," Tom insisted.

"I am not talking about overloading anyone. I am talking about keeping what we have already proven can happen with effective classroom time and meaningful assignments," I said with no intention of letting Tom have the final remark.

"Let's not forget the necessity of personal development," Rhonda suddenly commented, followed by annoyingly successive clinks as jewelry slid down her arm.

At that interjection, Keith called an end for the day. I left within seconds with my frustration level peaked. That Charles merely sat quietly did not sit quietly with me.

After another similar meeting the next week, I decided to talk to Charles alone. I found him in his office eating lunch—a scrawny white bread creation that earlier I had noticed wrapped in clear plastic and stuffed into his mailbox.

"Your committee is not working," I stated while closing his door, without asking whether I was welcome.

"Molly, why do you say that?" Charles questioned, taking a bite.

"Are you kidding? We are talking in circles," I answered. "Rhonda and Tom won't relinquish their themes no matter what anyone else wants."

"They are both probably saying the same about you," Charles retorted.

"Very funny," I replied sarcastically. "You should be thinking about firing *Tomahawk* after his escapades in Costa Rica. Instead, you're letting him influence the high school. And Rhonda shouldn't even be there—she hasn't taught above second grade. What's your code name for her—*Rhondola Gondola*?"

"Leave Rhonda out of this matter," Charles demanded.

"I suggest spelling the first syllable of *gondola* G-O-N-E, gone, as in get rid of Rhonda."

"I said leave Rhonda alone," Charles repeated sternly.

"Excuse me," I declared, amazed at Charles's reaction.

"We'll make some progress soon," Charles commented after swallowing another mouthful. "Be patient."

"May I remind you that the Declaration of Independence was written by Thomas Jefferson alone, not by committee?" I asked rhetorically.

As Charles laughed, a drop of yellow mustard oozed from his mouth. He quickly wiped it with a napkin.

"You may remind me of anything you wish," he said. "You do with or without my permission."

I left him to finish eating alone.

Together we will build a great school. Together we will build a great school. Together we were *not* building a great school.

Driving home, I contemplated why Charles didn't realize the folly of his plan. Then, suddenly, his scheme was clear: he intended the high school committee to flounder and stall while giving the illusion of building consensus. We would return in late August to hear Charles declare that he had made decisions himself because no one else was available in the summer.

I grieved, realizing that Charles and I differed greatly on our approach to planning. Charles favored delusive, initial group participation even if the process slowed progress unbearably. Then he followed with autocratic decisions. I preferred intelligent, authoritative designs, followed by genuine communal input for refinement and improvement. The dichotomy was significant.

In addition to a curriculum, a schedule, and a plan, Charles needed many new teachers for the high school debut. Yet, how could he offer these professionals a full job with only ninth and tenth grades next year? For whom was he looking and where would he find them? Did the high school symbolize what was best for the students or what was powerful for the board?

Charles was right on one point: MCD never bothered to have the teachers feel ownership of the high school, so somehow he had to accomplish that. Still, letting people repeatedly and foolishly ramble without his interceding was not a productive method. I shuddered at my experience with Charles's first committee. Quitting was the only other option.

After the next committee meeting was equally self-defeating, I spoke to Charles privately in his office again.

"Charles, do you realize how much must be accomplished before the end of the school year?" I asked. "This committee is never going to decide on anything."

"Molly, I won't have a high school unless people buy into the plan," he replied. I sighed over Charles's obsession with democracy.

"But these meetings are not buying good will. They are buying frustration," I countered. "To me something is clearly wrong when my husband takes it upon himself to have a White Russian ready for me when I arrive home every Monday."

Charles laughed and then remarked, "Only you have expressed disappointment."

"Because I'm the only one who isn't afraid to talk to you honestly—who doesn't fear your iron broom," I said angrily. Seeing the hurt reaction on Charles's face, I realized that I had spoken too daringly. "Look," I continued. "I know that I don't think the way everyone else does. But because I have logic and they don't, I'm not going to reprogram my brain."

"I'm not asking you to," Charles said simply, letting me continue in my blunder.

"Don't you worry that the teachers might resent how much of their time you have wasted by this charade?"

"Molly, the committee is not a charade, but feel free to resign. You're going to voice your opinions to me privately, anyway. You know that," he commented.

"Okay, Charles, I'm off the committee," I stated matter-of-factly, wondering if I would miss my excuse for a drink to start the week. "But your high school is precarious."

"MCD's high school will be superb," he stated confidently.

"We'll see," I lamented as I left his office.

44. First Catalog

With the planning of the MCD high school, Priscilla became overwhelmed. So, in true Long-nepotism style, Charles hired Mrs. Tufts to help Priscilla with office work. Because she seemed organized and capable, Charles assigned her the gargantuan task of preparing the maiden high school catalog. However, weeks went by and nothing happened. As computer science department chair, I never even received an inquiry from her.

Finally, out of caring for Charles, loving the school, hating disorganization, and needing professionalism, I volunteered to produce the booklet. While Charles and Mrs. Tufts both expressed relief, Vernon warned me not to undertake matters that were not my responsibility. The high school could open with tacky, duplicated sheets in lieu of a course catalog, but the image would be wrong. Anyway, I was Dean of Printing, for better or for worse.

I spent countless hours on this project, first releasing a well-designed questionnaire for department chairs to submit their course offerings and descriptions. Some departments, such as math, were so simple. Keith submitted perfectly completed forms. The sequence of his courses was clear, and the descriptions required no editing. Emma's response was also in exact format.

However, some departments, history in particular, generated enormous work for me. That department didn't have a leader like Keith or Emma. Moreover, history as a discipline can be organized in many different ways. I demonstrated to Charles the inconsistency in the submitted proposal: three history courses to graduate, but a scope and sequence with prerequisites requiring four courses in effect. Needing my help, Charles asked me to write a letter to the history teachers explaining the fallacy. While Charles did not like imposing on me, he trusted my writing and was short of time.

After changing what I had already desktop-published, I finally ended the havoc in a meeting with Charles.

"Charles, I'm going to edit the history department only one more time. Stop the arguing among Tom, Cecily, and Alexa. They need to decide on their offerings, or you declare what you want. The deadline is next Tuesday. Whatever you give me then goes in and doesn't get changed for one year," I said angrily.

"Okay, you're right. But the situation is very complicated because . . . ," he began.

"I don't care. I'm not slave labor," I affirmed.

During this disaster, I noticed that in my discussions with Charles, I frequently interrupted him in the middle of his sentences. Had we gotten so close that I knew exactly what he was going to say? Had he used so much educational jargon that his same old lines were no longer inspiring me? Had he started seeming so insincere, that I wanted to converse with him as expediently as possible?

"Molly, I've been having nightmares . . . ," Charles divulged.

"About the catalog?" I asked incredulously.

"No, about you. I've been having nightmares that you are going to leave me in the middle of this high school muddle," he replied.

I didn't know what to say. At least Charles noticed my extreme frustration. While I hadn't thought about leaving MCD, dreams were sometimes the predictor of the future.

"I'm sorry. We have very different approaches to accomplishing goals. I resigned from the committee, but I'm helping you now. You will have a first catalog," I said, ending the conversation.

45. First Hunt

The long, arduous task of finding three high school leaders began—computer science teacher, mathematics teacher, and division head. At the press conference Parke Merritt, MCD's board chairman, had implied that recruiting a fine faculty would be so easy. I hated smooth talk like that. Typically, reality bore out its glibness. When Charles's buddy Ron Rhinehardt registered MCD with private school placement agencies, the résumés, the terrible résumés, started arriving.

Keith, because he had also decided to stay in the middle school, was searching for a high school math teacher. We teased each other over whose collection of papers was worse. We also stayed in touch in case either one of us found a person trained in both fields.

"Keith, I have a great idea. What about Grady Bellows?" I said to him one day. "You know how his teams always place second to our first. Maybe he would like to join us. And he wouldn't have to move from Boca if he doesn't mind the drive."

"He'll never accept. He has a good pension plan in his current public school job."

"You never know unless you ask," I replied encouragingly.

Sure enough, Keith called Grady who was interested enough to accept an interview. Because courting Grady was my idea, I found Charles at the end of Grady's day of guest teaching. Both Keith and Charles had observed him.

"How did he do?" I asked Charles eagerly.

"I'm afraid he talked too much, not letting the kids speak up enough," Charles expressed.

"Maybe he was nervous. MCD is a big step up in math circles," I offered on Grady's behalf.

"His appearance also makes me jittery."

"Why?"

"His haircut—it's sort of like a gangster," Charles complained.

"So he has a jagged cut. Maybe his head is full of cowlicks. You can't be that judgmental—we're talking about hard-to-find math teachers. The record of his math teams speaks for itself."

"Which code name do you like better—*Greedy Grady* or *Mellow Bellow*?" Charles inquired. "Perhaps simply *Scarface*?"

"What about working with him first? Those names are rather divergent in meaning," I protested.

"We'll see," Charles stated indefinitely.

Concerning hiring the high school head, Charles sought faculty input. But the teachers could not agree. I voted for a man whom one of our teachers repudiated by declaring that short men had personal problems—such was the nature of the discussions.

Charles did hire Grady, though, as well as a high school head—a man named Howard Driskell from Boston. Howard had been fired from his previous job for having an affair with one of the teachers. Though Howard divorced his wife and married the teacher, the damage had been done. So, Howard and his bride looked for jobs as far away as possible to start over. I was shocked that Charles hired damaged goods to head his precious new high school, though with Ron in charge of finding candidates, the selection was marginal. Howard, admittedly, was friendly and gregarious, while Charles dismissed the board of the New England school as puritanical.

Finding a computer science educator was more difficult than the other two positions. I eliminated most of the candidates from their papers or after a phone interview. But I used real criteria—not hair or height.

A candidate who passed through Palm Beach guest taught one day at no expense to MCD. I asked him to present a first lesson in Pascal to students who already programmed in other languages. Not only did he totally bore my students, but also he astounded them by his sloppiness. In Pascal the programmer must declare the type of each variable. Integer is one of the standard types. Though the guest declared one of his variables as integer, he repeatedly called it a whole number in his discussion, much to the students' chagrin. They had understood the distinction among the three different sets—natural numbers, whole numbers, and integers—years before.

I sought a candidate with a recent computer science degree from an excellent university—not someone self-declared as a computer programmer. I did find one young man who seemed promising, and MCD paid for his visit.

I invited Charles to have dinner with us because I wanted to make as good as an impression as possible. Charles accepted but arrived forty-five minutes late and drunk—the first time I ever saw Charles inebriated. Tom Tufts had taken the ninth graders on their class trip again, and Charles's way of dealing with my warning was sending Cecily as a chaperone for Tom. I later learned, after we argued and reconciled, that Cecily had arrived home from the trip just as Charles was dressing for the dinner. She was furious that Charles was going out on school business on her first evening home. They had a significant fight, including Charles's having several drinks. I spent most of the evening talking so that Charles—loud, incoherent, and unpleasant—wouldn't. I was mortified by the time I arrived home and, also for the first time ever, scared of Charles.

The candidate met my standards. And though I offered him the position, in the end he declined—a crushing setback because we had no alternatives. Excellent programmers could work in industry for double or triple the starting teaching salary. Regardless of whether Charles's state soured the job, I promised myself never to invite Charles to dinner again with a prospective teacher.

In the middle of this strenuous ordeal, Harry Linz offered to become the high school computer science teacher. He must have suspected that his contract renewal was tenuous and thought that by filling this opening, he might save his job. In this mode of self-survival, Harry categorized me to Charles as MCD's only strict teacher. I became the one toward whom he vented his anger. However, Catherine, by her many classroom visits, both announced and unannounced, of the entire faculty, had established that Harry differed from us all. Sadly, though Harry had great potential in what he could offer MCD, he would not accept advice from Catherine or me. And I knew because Charles, in my presence, was regularly calling Harry by his code name *Linzer Torte*, that Charles was polishing the iron broom for him.

I continued the search interminably. One candidate was superb but had an incompetent husband who was also looking for a new teaching position. One could teach both math and programming but accepted a job that was solely math because it was so much less demanding. One man, who gave a great guest class on how to program a *Choose Your Own Adventure* game, had a pierced earring hole. Charles, who was very conservative about men's appearance and still dressed in the same outfit in which I had first met him, dismissed the candidate for fear that the hole was active.

Yet another candidate seemed likely until he returned with his fiancé to see Palm Beach—and Charles failed to notify me of the second visit. When Charles dropped the news at a faculty meeting, purely by accident about two hours before their plane was to arrive, I became livid. Charles told me not to worry—that he and Cecily were taking the guests to dinner. When the other teachers had left, I sat motionless in my chair and uttered repeatedly, "Why do I bother?" Charles just stared at me—he had no good response. The foursome for dinner never manifested, and the candidate declined the job. In desperation and disgust, I even considered passing the problem on to Parke Merritt.

Ultimately, I hired a wonderful new teacher, Kim Kanter, to help with middle school computer science. She was smart, young, and creative. MCD was her first teaching job right out of college, so she had no bad habits. And I interviewed her very carefully. I taught her the desktop publishing software to see how quickly she could learn. Then I left her alone for a short while to see what kind of images she could create. Following great success, I taught her the Logo software and again gave her time to program. Kim excelled in both areas besides being personally delightful.

Although the first hunt was over, I was left to prepare the high school class, to teach College Board Advanced Placement Computer Science—the job I never wanted.

46. First Choice

The opening of the Merritt Country Day high school gave me an option: assuming upper level courses or keeping my existing work. Most people would not understand my choosing gifted middle school math with its closely related creative programming over advanced placement courses. The decision, though easy for me, was the focus of my fifth, end-of-year sunroom reflection.

If I had needed to make that decision prior to working at MCD, I would have chosen the older students without a second thought. Just married and still a graduate student, I subbed as a math teacher at a well-reputed public high school to earn some grocery money. I walked into class saying, "Okay, I'm not going to tell your teacher. Just tell me honestly what you don't understand, and let's see if we can get these problems cleared up." The approach was amazing, yielding wonderful discussions. As the students left, most of them thanked me individually.

Yet, once I accepted a job at a feeder junior high for this high school, and that day was the worst teaching experience of my life. I spent my time running from window to window, closing and locking them, as the students were right behind me, unlocking and opening them, hanging out, calling to whomever passed by. I swore that I would never teach junior high again.

I certainly did not know that when I became a parent of bright children, I would experience firsthand the travesty of public middle school education. I saw that the years, whether called middle school or junior high, were the gutter of American public education. The philosophy that elementary education was important for fundamental knowledge and that high school education was important for college preparation prevailed. Middle school, however, was relegated to that nebulous ground where students were refreshed on basics, kept off drugs, and gotten through puberty until their brains kicked in for high school, when they finally could learn something significant.

However, my five years at MCD had totally changed—corrected—my thinking. I witnessed how ready to learn children were at that age, and how math talent, in particular the ability to abstract in Piaget's description, started at sixth grade, and sometimes earlier, for many students. Already bored that fifth grade math was a repeat of fourth, they respected teachers who truly taught because children, ultimately, craved learning.

Helping students soar was a treat. And the joy that math brought the children—regardless of the impressive competition scores—was the true measure of success. Yes, gifted middle school education was my first choice even though this summer, the faculty hunt having failed, I needed to study the high school curriculum—just for one year, I thought.

47. First Watch

Day by tiresome day, the faculty and students journeyed through the debut year of Merritt Country Day High School. Now May, I looked back with exasperation over the nine-month long mammoth mess. *Mammoth mess*—wasn't that how Charles had described the Merritt household that fateful evening?

Charles was so preoccupied with starting the high school that he didn't devote the necessary time and energy to other matters. Once he asked Emma to invite some foreign language consultants. But on the day of their visit, Charles never saw them. He dashed here and there or was in conference with his door closed. Emma was mortified. She told me that her guests asked, "What's wrong with your headmaster?" She was very embarrassed but covered for Charles with some excuse, hoping that they wouldn't detect worse.

Another concern was Charles's health. He ate so poorly—cookies and coffee all day long, then a rich restaurant dinner with a board member or prospective donor. Occasionally, Cecily put an anemic looking lunch in his mailbox—not even concealed in a brown paper bag. Moreover, Charles openly declared that he was too busy for regular exercise.

Howard Driskell was so concerned about being popular that he had no discipline. The students bragged that they could get away with anything now sans Catherine. Unfortunately, they were right. Catherine, in fact, was watching, but she was powerless in the school's new division. Because the *Wicked Witch of the West* ruled firmly in the middle school, teachers were able to teach. But Howard's lax attitude in the high school yielded cheating, stealing, and graffiti—uncivil behavior never before seen at MCD.

Meanwhile, Charles brought nepotism to its nadir. Though Charles had promised the faculty that as a condition of Howard's employment, he would not hire Howard's new wife, we returned after the summer to find Mrs. Driskell employed as an English teacher. Despite the fact that Charles's field was classics, he had the worst tropism for poor English teachers.

Sometimes I thought Charles intentionally hired incompetent English teachers. Then when parents or students complained, he could pine about putting the school's money into the high-profile math department as a ploy to get more donations—except that he never spent new money for the English department, so the cycle continued.

Worse than teaching English, however, Mrs. Driskell also took the job of the high school newspaper. In effect, because of the desktop publishing aspect of the course, she became a member of the computer science department. She was assigned to this position without my knowledge or consent. Getting upset over the appointment would have been pointless—the department chair title meant nothing. When Charles wanted something, the titles of others conveniently disappeared.

Mrs. Driskell was a complete failure as the journalism teacher— worse than *IT* and *Linzer Torte* ever were—and she sadly never improved. The newspaper was consistently an embarrassment, both in content and appearance. Moreover, Mrs. Driskell never bothered learning how to use the computer. Had I been informed of her appointment properly, I could have scheduled some lessons last August. Instead, she relied on a few students whose small amount of knowledge was dangerous. I spent considerable time restoring operating systems wiped out by her students, until I finally write-protected the hard drives. No other students in my years at MCD committed such destruction, albeit unintentional.

Furthermore, Howard didn't set a good example for the students with his own behavior—he and his wife were seen smooching on campus many times. The students found their actions amusing. The teachers found their actions immature.

Even with Kim's help in the middle school, demands on me were heavy. Determined that my students would earn the highest possible scores on the AP exam, I had prepared endlessly, sometimes calling on Mimi's expertise.

Opening two new labs with twenty computers each also confounded the year. I spent all fall checking parts, inserting memory cards, installing software on the hard drives, and returning defective equipment. I would typically arrive home at 7:00 P.M. at the same time as Mimi from her swim team practice. Blane was a college freshman. We ate dinner late, and then I would usually collapse after a grueling twelve-hour day. Because I deferred my paper grading, the weekends regularly became just as demanding in an effort to catch up. Vernon worried that I would get sick, that I couldn't possibly sustain the pace. On the worst night I came home at 9:00 P.M.

"Why didn't you just sleep on the office couch and use the gym shower?" Vernon asked.

"Very funny," I replied, although I did appreciate teasing rather than scolding.

In effect I opened a third lab because I moved my previous set of computers to the high school English room for a teacher named Lynn Pelligrini. On a particularly upsetting day Charles told me that his code name for her was *Lynn Tin Tin*—I assumed because her aggressive, incessant talking was like barking. Though Lynn was a highly skilled teacher, comparable to the best of the best anywhere, she gave almost everyone a headache. Vernon had met her at the back-to-school party at Emma's house. Emma loved having parlor games when she entertained, but Lynn monopolized every one. On the ride home Vernon called her one of the most odious women he had ever met. "Is her degree in English or monology?" he asked.

Mimi had helped me set up Lynn's lab. When Mimi realized that we were doing Lynn's labor, cleaning as well as wiring, Mimi said, "Mom, what's going on? Stop doing Miss Pelligrini's work!"

"Look, she's not here," I stated.

"That's right—she's enjoying the beach. And you should be, too," Mimi retorted.

"But if I don't do this, she'll ruin my life with non-stop complaining," I said.

"But, Mom, it's wrong. Let her fall—she deserves it. She's so full of herself. Do you know what she said once? She bragged that she could do anything. So one of the kids asked her what she didn't do. And she thought for a minute and said, *I don't do heels*. Then she laughed at her own joke. What an egotistical fool! And here I am spending my Saturday vacuuming her keyboards," Mimi lamented.

Lynn's actual complaining was severe, regardless of my having connected the lab. She couldn't get the computers to work right—the same computers in the same room my second year at MCD. Though I spent countless hours trying different word processing programs for her, she became hysterical, and the situation became intolerable. When Charles saw that we weren't communicating, he put Caroline Jackson, MCD's computer-literate business manager, in charge of her howling. The solution was yet another regression in dealing with the computer science department's issues.

Despite my quandary about yet another Spring Festival show, I created *Salute to MCD's New High School*. The opening displayed programmed color images of dozens of university insignia in slide show effect to the *Yale Boola*. The middle had numerous scenes depicting, with humorous graphics and music, what various teachers had offered or were planning. The finale was an animation of flying graduation caps. The superb quality of the students' programming comforted me once again.

In many regards the MCD high school was like a ship on its maiden voyage. How would the students behave without Captain Catherine? Who would become queasy during the launch? Could the vessel stay on a straight course with Howard at the bow and Grady at the stern? Would I drown adding the advanced placement curriculum to my schedule? Would Charles be ready to drop an anchor when necessary? Instinctively, I was on first watch.

48. First Fear

Meredith Abbott was both an English and classics teacher whom I had met during a summer at Johns Hopkins. We became close friends and maintained our association over the past several years. Meredith was looking for a new job because she had fallen into the quagmire called academia. She originally came on the job market concurrently with a glut of English Ph.D.s and was a British literature specialist at a time when universities were looking for anything but. Then she earned a second doctorate in classics. By that point universities considered her too middle-aged for a tenured slot, so she bounced around from college to college, assisting professors on sabbatical. Despite her having some rather lofty temporary positions, she was not overly enthralled with college teaching. She fell prey to many pre-meds who wouldn't seize her love for literature and classics.

Because she longed to put down some roots, I had told Charles about her previously. He had conducted a phone interview and had fallen in love with her—professionally. After all, they were both classicists. He was so excited that an English teacher presenting the Greek tragedies could go to the source—to read to the students from the original text. Charles got by, however, this first year of the high school by hiring Mrs. Driskell to cover the missing English classes. *Getting by* was a euphemism for MCD's saving money and students' losing education. Now May, students had reached a boiling point regarding Mrs. Driskell. Instinctively, I suggested that he consider Meredith again.

Thus, at Charles's orders, Howard arranged for Meredith to visit MCD. Shortly thereafter, Meredith arrived in Palm Beach. She stayed at my home, saving on expenses for the school, and purposely traveled on Friday, giving us the weekend together before her teaching on Monday. Saturday evening was a high school dinner dance. Because the faculty was invited, I brought Meredith as a good way to see the campus and meet some people. Howard was very friendly to her, typical to his personality. However, Charles's behavior, cold and aloof, was extremely embarrassing. I kept asking myself over and over again in my head what his problem was. I suspected jealousy.

Meredith had a good interview, but Charles later picked on her every feature—her choice of lessons and her manner of speaking. Lynn also criticized Meredith, probably out of envy as well, though Meredith called Lynn a master during the class when the observation was reversed. Soon, however, because Meredith was in fact an outstanding candidate, Charles agreed that Howard should offer her a job—something that Howard did by phone. She accepted, inquiring about the next step. Howard replied that she should call Charles to discuss the details of the contract including salary. So she phoned Charles—many times, but he neither took her calls nor returned them. Weeks went by. Finally, she asked me to learn what was happening. I was already emotionally exhausted from shuttling between Howard and Charles trying to comprehend the conflicting details.

I seized Charles in his office one day and demanded answers. Charles denied that the job had been officially offered to Meredith. More likely, he had changed his mind and was lying to extricate himself from the situation. A sensation of déjà vu struck.

"Excuse me, Charles, but don't you have the decency to let Meredith know that she has no job at MCD?"

He reiterated his bogus complaints about her. "You know she has this pseudo fancy way of talking, yet she comes from a very modest background."

This comment especially irked me because, in fact, Meredith and Cecily spoke similarly. I didn't make that observation to Charles, however. "Anyone with a doctorate in both English and classics obviously will have an impressive vocabulary and will be above colloquialisms," I replied, imitating formality.

Charles had me so exasperated on this matter that I wanted to grab him and shake him staunchly until he came to his senses. Meredith was exactly what the MCD high school needed. Were competent women, not MCD's high school problems, Charles's first fear?

Charles said nothing, so I continued bluntly. "You gave her your word. And now you won't even call her."

"No, I didn't hear what Howard said to her."

The boldness of Charles's lie portended another reason. *Lynn Tin Tin*, with all her dog-like strength, had quashed Meredith. Nothing else made sense. Did Lynn hold power over Charles? Overwhelmed by futility, I left Charles's office immediately.

Because this incident with Meredith reminded me of my initial interview with Charles—my thinking that he had offered me a job while in his bizarre administrative style, he had not committed—I was very troubled. Of course, in Meredith's case, Howard's specific offer had made the appointment real. But in both situations, Charles intentionally did not return phone calls. I thought about how I would feel if I were Meredith. I had difficulty imagining Charles's reneging on a position with me now, after our long, productive relationship. I asked myself, though, how angry I would be. My answer was *very*.

49. First Resignation

Resigning as Computer Science Department Chairman was a must—as necessary as breathing and sleeping. I wrote a carefully crafted letter explaining my desire to spend my professional, non-teaching time writing. Then, when all seemed quiet at MCD—or as quiet as possible for May both with winding down the current school year and winding up the next—I found Charles in his office seated at his desk. I handed him the letter. He read it and laughed.

"Charles, my letter is not funny," I stated angrily. But, as I spoke, Charles held the letter high and ripped it in half. I stared at him in disbelief and outrage. I dropped into my usual chair, raised my elbow, and slammed the door shut.

"Molly, I'm not laughing at your writing—it's beautiful as always. I'm just remembering a story from your first year at MCD, when the students were still using the larger, flexible, floppy disks, and one of your students stapled the printout of his game to his disk. You were exasperated then, but you got over it. And you will get over whatever is bothering you now," he said as he laughed more.

"Charles, stop. Will you please take this matter seriously? If you don't give in on this department chairmanship, you may lose me permanently," I announced.

"Molly, you know I can't survive without you. I need you. I've told you about my nightmares that you are going to leave me one day. Some nights I'm too worried to sleep," Charles said sensitively.

"Stop exaggerating," I replied.

"I'm hardly exaggerating. You are a key person at this school. But please try to understand. I can't give the department chair title to a first-year teacher—to a stranger. What would I do if I had to sweep away that new person at the end of the year? Firing a teacher is hard enough. Firing a teacher whom I also appointed department chair is a much trickier situation," Charles expressed.

"So, because you can't hire correctly, I have to suffer. Is that what I'm hearing?" I asked.

"You're twisting it around. The department chair job isn't even that much work—you said so yourself," Charles added.

"No, you're the one twisting things around. I said that I don't have the time to do the work it requires, so I don't anymore."

"Your not doing the job is twice as much as anyone else's doing the job, so I'm happy with the situation as is," Charles said.

"Well, I'm not, I'm trying to tell you. And since you are the one who brought up old computer stories, let me review some more for you," I declared.

"You don't need to," Charles maintained.

"No, I insist. How about all the times I found Joe's cleaning staff wiping the computers with water? I wish that I spoke Spanish, but I don't. Both Joe and Mimi have told the workers over and over again not to use water on the computers and monitors. But they can only comprehend the evil of dirt, not water. And when we finally get through to them, they're gone. The school has a new crew. So you know what? I told Joe that they should only clean the boards and carpet. I do everything else. I don't mind—but it takes time."

"The problem seems solvable," Charles stated.

"Oh, as if I haven't tried? While we are talking about cleaning, how about the enormous twice-a-year preventative maintenance—alcoholing disk drives, washing mouse balls, vacuuming keyboards, along with wiping grime on all surfaces with plastic cleaner? Do you think we still have only twenty computers? Guess again—almost one hundred," I informed Charles.

"Could some students help?" Charles inquired.

"Believe me, supervising them takes longer," I explained. "Or how about the times I begged the Lower Division teachers to have the kids keep small objects away from the hardware? Is that instruction so difficult to follow? But whenever I walked through the labs, there were little lead bits from click pencils and loose staples all over the countertops. How about finding an extra mouse in the storage closet crushed by junk? Why do I have to fix what others broke because they won't take the little bit of time to be careful?"

"Molly, I hear you, and I've heard you before," Charles inserted.

"No. I'm the one who drove the computer out-of-town when Greta knowingly inserted a disk with a severely bent plate into a drive. I'm the one who has carefully packaged hardware for shipping for warranty repairs."

"Couldn't Joe help?" Charles asked.

"He is so busy. I hate to give him more work," I said.

"I do treat you twice a year to that repairman you like," Charles emphasized.

"Yes, I appreciate that. He has taught me a lot, thankfully, because we can't have the hardware down for months. But I'm the only one who gives up Saturday to help and learn. Why should the other teachers bother? Expecting me to fix their damage is so much easier," I expressed.

"Well, we need to get them involved," Charles asserted.

"Who—your teachers? Mrs. Driskell still doesn't know the meaning of the little light on the floppy disk drive. She thinks it magically—randomly—goes on and off."

Charles sighed painfully.

"Oh, how about all the times I tried to instruct your teachers in word processing? I scheduled a workshop during the August faculty meetings, but Rhonda told me that she had to set the tables for the luncheon. Where is the PTO when we need it?" I blurted.

"You know how scared she is," Charles said. "That was her excuse."

"Then maybe she shouldn't be a division head. But, for those who did attend, they had to endure painful yelping from *Lynn Tin Tin*," I said. "You talk about help. That kind of help no one needs."

"Okay, tell me what she did, and then that's enough," Charles responded.

"Five words into my lesson, she stood up, seized the floor, and spoke unremittingly about her personal word processing experiences until thankfully she departed for a dental appointment."

"Molly, really. That's sufficient litany about your headaches," Charles pleaded.

"I'm not done," I declared harshly, emphasizing each of the three words. Charles had no choice. He got comfortable for the duration.

"Speaking about Rhonda not being qualified to be an administrator, do you know she is continually after me to talk you into firing Renuka?"

"Yes, I know. And every time you observe Renuka, you report that her classes are fabulous," Charles confirmed. "And Renuka is very appreciative of your suggestions. You work well together."

I nodded, acknowledging Charles's compliment, but did not dare break my rhythm. "You know, I've always felt bad that I don't have more time for software review, curriculum development, and teacher training—public school systems have subject coordinators to do that work. I've found a few, new, great programs for Renuka at the national meetings, but I wish I could do more. But anyway, do you know what I think? I think that Rhonda is petrified of computers, and she is afraid that the children—even the kindergartners—know more than she does," I stated.

"You are probably right," Charles replied.

"No, not probably. I am right. When she walks into Renuka's room, the little ones are using words like *submenu* and *font*. Rhonda quakes. She told me that she thinks Renuka is teaching them too much, that the goal is only to have the kids comfortable around computers. Well, I'll have no part of Rhonda's scheme. Maybe she is the one who should be fired," I said.

Charles looked at me as if I had violated something sacrosanct. Curious, I thought and made a mental note. But I continued.

"How about all the problems in hiring computer science teachers?" I asked.

"We don't have to discuss that again now," Charles pleaded.

"How about all the problems with desktop publishing—such as the literary magazine?"

"We've beaten that to death," Charles stated.

"How about some of the English teachers not listening to me regarding computer-assisted composition? Typing sentences from grammar books and using the menu to underline nouns and italicize verbs is called a waste of time, not writing."

Charles just cringed.

"Did you understand that reference to me in the April Fools' edition of the newspaper—the Screwdriver Lady?"

"No," Charles said simply.

"When the students remove their disks diagonally rather than flat, they throw off the drive alignment. So I have to fix the internal tilt with a broad screwdriver. Do I need that image?"

Charles laughed. "You should be pleased—you always say you're not mechanical."

"Okay, here is my final argument. The parents are trendy, and I'm not. Now that the Internet has gone public, they want their kids using it in computer class. That's not my area of interest. I already fear that we may have a generation of students nationally who can point and click but can't read, write, or think—forget analyze or synthesize. Now they may become even worse at these skills, but they'll be great at surfing. Sure, the Internet will probably prove fabulous for research, but perhaps we should delegate its instruction to the history department and let the computer science department teach real computer science."

"I've always valued your opinion. You've moved us in the right direction so far—and always with substance rather than fad," Charles countered. He smiled crookedly and characteristically leaned across his desk, trying to get closer to win the argument with charm, knowing that I was totally depleted regurgitating my rancid computer room narratives. "I have a solution to ease your work load. Let's put one person in charge of each lab," he proposed.

I knew that his compromise was a farce—*Charlesrhetoric* and nothing more. The burden would still be mine. The teachers, even if forced to accept, would do nothing.

"Does this mean that I'm still department chair?" I asked.

"It does. And Molly, I hope that this first resignation is your last," Charles added.

I sighed, exhausted from my tales. "You probably have a code name for me," I muttered.

Charles tilted his head to one side, smiled, and said, "As a matter of fact, I do."

Horrified and disheartened, I stood abruptly. Shoving the chair to open the door, I said, "I don't want to know it—not ever."

50. First Worry

Somehow, despite the fact that Charles now had a code name for me, I survived the rest of the school year. Once again, as I walked to my car having filed my last report card, the freedom I felt was bewildering. I stared at the silver and yellow snook at the end of the diagonal path. I had at least a half dozen projects to attack during the summer, but not one came to mind. So, I drove straight home, made coffee, and stretched out on the sofa in the sunroom for my sixth annual retrospection. Suddenly, I started worrying.

I realized that I needed to start thinking about myself. Because Charles never approved of any of Ron's candidates, Charles had acted as the high school head the entire year. More frenetic and distracted than ever, he had sapped my energy dry with his crisis-to-crisis management style. What would the second year of the high school bring?

Writing my textbooks would be a rejuvenator, I decided. How could I leave my students though? Hiring a paper grader might free my time. I could discuss the matter with Charles and offer to pay for the person myself. He would approve—he would sanction almost anything to keep me because obviously he knew that my employment was tenuous. Would Charles insist on my posting the job with bothersome Ron?

No, a paper grader was not the solution, I thought. First, such a helper wouldn't fit with the faculty as a matter of comfort. A telling anecdote occurred at one meeting when the teachers discussed the divorce of a student's parents. The teachers praised the father for wanting to forgo his career as a financial consultant to become an economics teacher, while they criticized the mother for installing marble floors at home. Given Vernon's occupation and our home's quality, I perceived possible alienation.

More importantly, Charles's requiring every teacher to grade every assignment was a key part of the MCD education. I needed to see my students' papers with my own eyes and write my own comments. Without doing my own work, I could not be a great teacher. Sadly, other teachers were not as conscientious as required.

Predictably, I was assigned to teach A.P. Computer Science a second time next year because efforts to hire a competent computer science teacher failed again. College Board enlarged the curriculum by adding a case study, increasing preparation time in a new area without a study bank of questions. My A.P. students will be two amazingly precocious eighth graders whom I have taught previously and a brilliant eleventh grader. They will make all the work worthwhile, I thought. And I can count on mutual respect for each other despite the age range. Still, I was tired of the pull in opposite directions—my important middle school work versus the demands of the burgeoning high school. Due to scheduling conflicts these classes must meet during the same period, necessitating my juggling time and attention for the different students.

Charles had once spoken about a de facto Academic Dean and the need to crown her. Now, though, I was sorry that I had toiled so hard and worried so much. To what avail were my efforts directed? To wit, rather than my friend Meredith Abbott, Charles hired an incompetent English teacher who seemed so terrible at her visit that I predicted an early sweeping for her—possibly after only one semester next year.

However, my first worry was most clearly how MCD's new division was damaging my relationship with Charles. The high school, like a volatile chemical solvent, was persistently and painstakingly dissolving our professional bond—eating away at the glue that kept the two of us together in academic sync.

51. First Scrunch

I prepared for my seventh year at Merritt Country Day determined to be free from stress. "You'll be burnt out by Halloween," Vernon told me in August. In my heart I knew he was right. In fact, I feared that I might fizzle sooner.

Driving to and from school during the week of opening faculty meetings, I contemplated all that could go wrong. Charles had made a serious error in hiring Howard Driskell as the head of the high school and a more serious one in not sweeping him away. While Charles was determined to give Howard another chance, the teachers wondered how we would survive a second year with him. At the least the removal of Mrs. Driskell from the high school newspaper course was a consolation for me.

Emma, Kim, and I went through the buffet line at the faculty luncheon filling our plates with grilled chicken Caesar salad, croissants, fresh fruit, and oatmeal cookies. We joined a table for four where a new faculty member was sitting alone. He seemed to be enjoying lunch, though he scrunched his face when he ate.

"May we join you?" Kim asked.

"Certainly," he said, contorting his face equally as much when he spoke.

"I'm Kim Kanter—middle school computer science," she said.

"Eric Fuller—the new college counselor," the thin, youthful man replied.

"*Je m'appelle* Emma Marisienne, and you can guess," Emma added.

"I'm Molly Kelman—math and computer science," I added, noticing that his face resumed normal position when others spoke.

"Marcy, Charles mentioned to me that you prep the seventh graders for the SAT. I think you should consider switching to the ACT," Eric said boldly with his left cheek almost in his left eye.

"It's Molly, but why?" I responded.

"The problems are more straightforward," Eric replied, accidentally flinging a crouton across the table as he tried to spear it with his fork.

"But the students need to know high school math to solve the ACT problems, whereas the SAT problems are middle school math with a twist," I explained.

"Well, there's a trend toward the ACT, Mary," Eric said, this time with his right cheek pressing against his right eye.

"It's Molly, and I don't entirely agree. But anyway, these seventh graders are trained to think creatively—mathematically. They've scored consistently well for several years, so why should I change what has been extremely successful?"

"You'll get more data back—not just math and verbal," he proffered with both eyes narrowed to slits.

"My objective is not more data. The problem solving class that I teach in seventh grade is actually an extension of my sixth grade course. It also complements Keith Clark's curriculum extremely well," I explained.

"Millie, I'm just trying to be helpful," Eric explained with both corners of his mouth pushing against his cheeks.

I glanced at Emma and Kim before speaking. Their heads shook.

"It's Molly, and thanks for the advice," I stated simply.

"Well, I have a meeting with Howard now, so please excuse me. I enjoyed meeting you all," Eric said with one final scrunch.

"Tell me we're supposed to clear his dirty plate," Emma remarked when he was gone.

Without answering, Kim got up briskly, collected Eric's trash, threw it away, and returned to our table saying, "Good riddance."

"Tell me, does all education or just MCD attract such *stupides*?" Emma asked rhetorically.

"It was a two-course lunch, but he managed to call you three different names—none right," Kim said looking at me.

"Tell me that he can remember names of colleges better," Emma insisted.

"So, shall I warn your students to brace themselves for the ACT?" Kim asked teasingly.

"When *one* becomes a prime number," I replied.

"Eric and Howard are going to be quite a team," Kim added. "How could even Charles have missed Eric's first scrunch when he interviewed?"

"Perhaps Charles's sideways head-tilt got stuck, so Eric looked straight to him," I answered and sighed.

52. First Cousin

Charles envisioned building a magnificent library at MCD. And so, in Charles Long style, he formed a library committee very similar in function to his high school committee. Getting people to *buy into* the program took on a literal meaning because Charles hoped that the carefully chosen committee members would, in fact, pay for the new building. Charles included me because the library would house two additional computer labs—one for classes and one for independent work. With the distasteful memory of the high school committee still lingering, I joined this one cautiously.

At the initial meeting in September, I felt sorry for the others. Only I understood the charade—that Charles would do what he wished regardless of discussion or votes.

On the evening of the next meeting, Kim substituted for me because Vernon and I attended a bank dinner. Just as we arrived home, our phone rang. Vernon dashed inside to answer.

"Molly, it's for you," he called.

I took the phone on my desk.

"Molly," Kim said in a panicked voice.

"What's the matter?" I asked.

"You know Garrett Long?"

"Sure—Charles's cousin, Sally's father. He's on the library committee," I said.

"Tonight one topic was library research—CD-ROM databases and on-line technology. But Garrett Long got off subject and attacked the programming curriculum," Kim explained nervously.

"Why? What did he say?" I asked.

"Essentially, he said that programming was worthless," Kim replied.

"He said that? Did he have any justification?"

"That he had studied programming in school, but didn't use it in his career as an engineer."

"What an idiot! Did Charles quiet him down?"

"No, Charles did nothing. He let him talk. He lets everyone talk," Kim responded. Kim had certainly correctly evaluated the process.

"Were you able to say anything?" I inquired.

"I tried, but couldn't," she answered.

"I'll handle this tomorrow. Thanks for calling."

"Good night," Kim said.

"Good night. Sorry this happened to you."

Once again, Vernon fell asleep almost instantly while problems at MCD kept me thrashing. I hated a person's using himself as a single, misguided example of why hundreds of others shouldn't do something wonderful. "I need to sleep, I need to sleep, I need to sleep," I kept telling myself over and over, knowing that I would be facing Charles again in the morning.

Charles, of course, consistent in his practice management of the school, did not contact me about this incident. No doubt, in his overall week of crises, the assault on programming was minor. Still, to me it was important. As always, I would have appreciated a short note in my box. I did find Charles in his office, but he said that something unrelated must have been bothering his cousin—merely a bad-hair day—and that the students' enthusiasm spoke for itself. Did I have a sleepless night for nothing?

Three days later, disaster struck as a consequence of Garrett Long's outbreak. All members of the library committee, myself included, received a memo outlining how and where computers were used at MCD, citing the accomplishments of the computer science department to date. The report was incomplete, inaccurate, and inflammatory.

Temporarily paralyzed, I read the entire piece while standing at the mailboxes and then marched furiously to Charles's office. Fortunately, Catherine opened the door and departed just as I arrived.

"How could you authorize this document without my providing input and without my proofing it—without my even knowing about it?" I demanded, still standing.

"What are you so upset about now?" Charles asked.

"This abomination of a report about my department to the library committee members," I answered, holding it in my hand and waving it at him.

"Oh, that. That's nothing," Charles replied.

"Nothing?" I asked incredulously. "Nothing? It's eight pages of lies or errors—take your pick—about my work," I stated.

"No one is going to read it," Charles offered.

"Well, first of all, I did. And second of all, if no one is going to read it, then why was it written and sent?"

"Because my cousin Garrett is having some middle-aged crisis," Charles replied.

In total disbelief, I dropped into my usual chair, pushed it forward, slammed the door, and focused on the skylight for a few seconds to gather my thoughts. Then I drilled my gaze on Charles with laser precision.

"Let me try to understand this logic. Because your cousin is having a middle-aged crisis about computers, my effort, my plans, my work, and my career get maligned. Don't you think that reasoning is rather convoluted? Shouldn't he, like a typical man, be having a middle-aged crisis about a woman?"

Charles chuckled but then stopped abruptly, realizing the offensiveness of his laughter. "Molly, you really are cute when you're angry about MCD," he said.

"Stop that immediately." I was explosively agitated as I continued. "May I remind you that I tried resigning from the department chairmanship? But since you didn't let me, I continued to take the job seriously. So what does the title mean anyway? Shouldn't I have been consulted before releasing this report?"

"Molly, you know everything around here is an emergency," Charles offered as an excuse.

"No, I don't know. Seems to me emergencies are a child choking or a bomb scare—not a library report that you say no one is going to read. The document could have waited another few days to assure accuracy," I stated.

"No offense was meant," Charles said.

"Oh, I'm not so sure about that. Who is actually responsible for getting it out?"

"Priscilla's new assistant. But don't be angry with her. I hardly pay her anything. And she was just following orders from Garrett," Charles explained.

I could barely tolerate his non-sequiturs. Cringing inside, I fought with every bit of inner strength to prevent a scream—an intense, wild wail like in that old movie when the star waits at a deserted subway station and times her cry with the next passing train. Had I actually screamed in Charles's office, though, he would have labeled me crazy, when, in fact, he was the irrational one. Instead, I continued arguing.

"Did I hear you right? Because you pay her little, that gives her the authority to be libelous. And you allow Garrett, not even an employee of the school, to give orders—and in my department? Charles, take the bread cubes out of your ears and listen to me. We are not at the Diamond Gala."

"How did you know my secret?" Charles asked.

"I notice too much for my own good," I replied. "Remember?"

"Okay, Molly, I'm going to tell you a little story about Garrett that will make you feel better," Charles offered.

"No, I don't want to hear about family skeletons," I insisted.

"Then let me say that Garrett is not just my first cousin. Our fathers are brothers, and we are both only children. So he is very much like my brother. And Garrett is filthy rich, but he hasn't yet embraced philanthropy. This library project would be a perfect start for him with his daughter at MCD," Charles stated.

I stared at him in amazement. Charles was willing to sacrifice my reputation for his cousin's money.

"Don't you see the irony in this fiasco? I begged you to release me from the department chairmanship, but you refused. And now you let over six years of work be discredited. You tell me how important programming is for students' intellectual development—that I am teaching what only the most elite schools in the nation offer—but then you agree with your cousin when he declares programming passé. Is this your new game—telling each person what he or she wants to hear from you? Or is it an old game, but I was too taken by you to realize what you were doing? Does money rule—money over hard work and integrity?"

I put the report in my book bag and stood briskly. I opened the door without saying good-bye.

"Where are you going?" Charles asked. "You've fired questions at me without letting me respond."

"I told you that I don't want to hear any stories about your first cousin—or anyone or anything," I stated firmly and left.

53. First Printing

Charles Long's drive for a new library continued throughout September, into October. At the third committee meeting on a Thursday he announced that invitations had been mailed for the kickoff fundraising cocktail party scheduled for the coming Monday evening at the Four Seasons Hotel. Charles handed us each a copy, as a sneak preview, of the fancy brochure that he would distribute at the party. I tucked the pamphlet into my book bag for evening reading.

When I arrived home, Vernon and Mimi, now a senior, had stories of their days. After dinner, Blane called from college with good news. Procrastinating about starting my paper grading, I remembered the library brochure and decided to look at it first as relaxation. Settling into a comfortable plum leather chair, I started reading. Suddenly, my red-pen eyes went into super high gear. The beautiful, fancy, glossy, multi-paged brochure was full of errors—horrific errors! The *Black Box* theatre was called *Back Box* multiple times. The letter from Parke Merritt had grammatical errors confusing *your* and *you're* as well as *its* and *it's*. The percents on the pie graph summed to one hundred and four. Moreover, singular/plural errors and missing commas were present throughout the text.

Though I rarely called Charles at home, I decided that the matter was serious enough for me to break tradition. After all, the brochures were scheduled for distribution in four days. Curiously, he acted as if the matter were not urgent.

When I arrived at school the next morning, I bumped into Charles in the hallway outside his office, but he didn't speak to me. His discourteous behavior was deeply irritating. As he brushed by, I said, "Hey, wait a minute. I didn't create the errors. I've potentially saved you from major embarrassment by finding them."

"Molly, step inside for a minute," he responded. He closed the door to his office behind me. "I'm not angry with you—I'm just angry. My job is so huge that I have to delegate. And then people I appoint don't do their jobs properly. And I can't even fire the woman who did this brochure because I've already fired her!"

For once I felt that Charles was experiencing the same frustration that I had so often. I was tempted to say that he didn't hire the right people, but the comment would have been cruel. I had noticed the woman to whom he referred come and go, perhaps the fastest yet. I didn't know why she had been dismissed, but gossip established why she had arrived—she was the mistress of an MCD board member who had to remove her quickly as his secretary at work.

"Why don't you just let me proof everything prior to publication? I've offered many times," I replied.

"Because I don't want to bother you. You're so busy. And people have to learn to do the work to which they are assigned," Charles explained.

"But you're not bothering me. I read all school publications anyway. What's the difference when I read them? I would much rather find mistakes before publication than after," I commented. "These incidents are much more of a bother than if you had asked for help initially."

Charles, terribly trodden, just looked at me, so I continued. "Well, what are you going to do about this brochure?" I asked.

"Nothing, it's done," he answered.

"Charles, you can't possibly be serious. You can't distribute the brochure with all these errors," I pleaded.

"But it cost a small fortune," he replied.

"It wouldn't be the first money MCD wasted," I argued.

"No one will read it anyway," he murmured.

"I hate when you say that," I said, cringing.

"You are the only one from yesterday's meeting who has reported the mistakes to me," Charles replied. "Molly, who else but you actually adds the numbers in a pie graph?"

His remark was unwarrantedly harsh, but I let it pass. "Well, if no one is going to read it, then why did you spend all that money on it?" I questioned.

"Because it looks good, and it's expected," Charles said.

I wanted to shake him. "Charles, I'll help you. Let's go to the printer and see if he can redo the brochure," I offered.

"By Monday evening? Not a chance—today is Friday," Charles said negatively.

"It's worth a try. I have next period free, and then it's lunch. Let's go," I said, trying to be encouraging. He reluctantly agreed.

As Charles and I dashed out the office front door, he mumbled something to Priscilla about our running away together—forever. While fastening my seatbelt in his messy, yellow Lincoln Continental, an extension of his studio apartment, I hoped that Charles would not call our jaunt a *scandalle*.

Unfortunately, when we arrived, the printer was at a meeting, but we left the boxes of flawed brochures there. I told Charles I would deal with the matter later, and I did. When the printer called, we arranged to meet Saturday morning. We spent four hours with my sitting next to him at his computer, correcting the errors directly in the computer file. He said that he would bump Monday morning's scheduled job to rerun MCD's brochure. I thanked him profusely.

When I got to school on Monday morning, Charles was standing by Priscilla at her desk.

"The company is reprinting this morning in time for tonight," I said.

"Fine," Charles said.

Fine? Was *fine* a thank-you for all my work—for giving up an entire Saturday morning to fix someone else's mistakes? And why were the errors even undetected? *How are you? Well.* Why didn't his meticulousness with that particular idiom manifest in other matters, including the written word of his colleagues. Then the phone rang.

"It's the printer," Priscilla said, looking at both of us. "He wants to know what to do with the first printing."

"Burn them," I answered before Charles could say a word.

54. First Confidence

Vernon's prediction that I would burn out by Halloween came true. I resigned not just from computer science department chair, but from the entire job—effective in June. I would never leave students mid-year. And this time, not able to face Charles's tearing another letter, I told him in person. Though Charles laughed at my other resignation, he saw that I was serious now. The discussion was brief and direct. We agreed to keep the matter private—after all, October was so early. Interestingly, the betrayal warning that was now four years old hardly shaped my decision, but the exhaustion from MCD's craziness was overwhelming. This issue was my first confidence with Charles of the gravest nature. I knew that he, wanting me to reverse my decision, would keep the secret.

Together we will build a great school. Together we will build a great school. Charles's special words had lost their resonance.

55. First Name

The second edition of the high school course catalog needed discussion, but I decided to wait to hear from Charles on the matter. Though I had resigned from MCD, I wanted to leave all aspects of my work in proper form. Sure enough, at a high school faculty meeting in November, Charles announced that he had given Eric Fuller the job. Emma and I looked at each other, both realizing the absurdity. The entire document, already desktop-published and saved on disk, only demanded relatively simple edits.

Eric spoke after Charles's introduction of the plan. "I would like all of you to complete one of these forms for each of your courses. There's space to enter the course bio as well as its description. Please get them back to me as soon as possible," he explained.

As we left the meeting, Emma looked over her shoulder to see if anyone could hear. "Tell me we're starting this catalog all over," she said.

"Sure sounds that way to me," I replied.

"Why don't we just copy the pages from the catalog that pertain to our department and mark our few changes directly on the copy?" she asked.

"Too logical," I answered.

"Oh, you're right. I forgot—this is MCD," Emma said.

Almost a month passed. Finally, we received the first draft of Eric's new catalog. In short, instead of making simple changes, Eric had mutilated the document. Rather than asking for my disk, he started over in Mac format—except that he only knew how to word process and not desktop publish. His draft was in single-sheet form instead of a booklet.

At the next high school faculty meeting the teachers were clearly disgusted.

"But all the French courses are lumped together as one offering," Emma complained. "I don't understand that."

"I'm sorry to say that in retyping the computer science entries, many errors were introduced because the terminology was not understood," I said, careful not to blame Eric by name in public.

"My corrections were ignored," Grady Bellows expressed.

The discussion continued similarly without resolution until Charles tapped the desk and declared, "Time for class."

During the first week back after December vacation, the teachers endured a similar meeting. Needing to share my opinion with Charles privately, I found him in his office. "He is ruining the catalog—and frustrating the faculty," I stated directly.

"But redoing the catalog is his job, and he needs to learn to do his work," Charles answered. "He's hardly doing much of anything else."

How does one respond to that kind of comment—by banging one's head against the wall?

"Today is Monday, January 9, 1995. Note well—on this day, when Eric called me Margo, at this time, 10:30 A.M., I am telling you that two months from now you still won't have a catalog," I announced.

"I don't need the sarcasm," Charles said.

"He has accomplished nothing in the past several months except destroying the book. The students will be ready to select their courses, except they won't know what the courses are, and neither will you for that matter," I argued.

"Molly, you can't do everything," Charles said.

"I'm not trying to do *everything*. Stop exaggerating and listen. The whole document is on my disk. The few changes could have been made in a week. Instead, the entire faculty is enervated, and you have no catalog."

"That's the point—it is on your disk, and you have resigned."

"What? I own the disk? We are not discussing one of my math books. MCD owns the disk. Plus, I promise you—one way or another, whether by broom-sweeping or trash-passing—Eric won't be here either."

"You don't know that," Charles protested.

"Mark my words," I countered.

"Well, Eric wanted to use the Mac," Charles stated.

"Amiga and Mac are so similar. A middle school student would only need a half-hour lesson."

"You know kids find computers easier than adults," Charles argued.

"Why do you insist on making the easy difficult?"

"Why don't you try talking to Eric directly?" Charles asked in return.

"I have," I replied. "He scrunched his face, called me Myrna, and ignored my edits. I'm trying to remember—was that a repeat of his first name for me?"

Charles sighed and said, "I think we're done for now."

I agreed that the conversation was pointless, and I was grateful, at least, that Charles didn't laugh. But he was in one of his totally illogical moods, defending his poor hiring decision.

"Well, I'm glad you had one catalog because you may not have a second," I snapped as I stood. "By the way, what's Eric's code name—*Fuller Brushman* because of how he whisks away tasks so easily?"

Charles looked relieved, if only temporarily, when he saw me stand to leave.

56. First Puzzle

In February the SAT scores came back from the January testing. For the first time both my seventh graders and the MCD high school students took the exam. The mathematically gifted high school students, who were trained by Keith and me in middle school, scored well above 700 on the math section as expected. However, my current seventh graders scored comparably to them and well above the other high school students. I suspected that these results might cause a stir.

"Molly, do you have a minute?" Charles asked me at the mailboxes one day soon after.

"Sure," I replied as always and followed Charles down the corridor. When we got to his office, I sat down under the tree.

"We have a problem," Charles said as he grabbed the other chair, swung the door shut, dropped the chair next to me, and sat down.

"How so?"

"Mr. French called this morning. He wants to know why his seventh grader scored higher on the math section of the SAT than his tenth grader," Charles explained.

"What did you tell him?" I asked.

"That his older son has normal math ability, that his younger son has exceptional math talent, and our usual story about how math precocity surfaces early yielding a high score at a young age," Charles replied.

"My sitting here now indicates that Mr. French wasn't satisfied," I said.

"He wasn't," Charles responded.

"He shouldn't be. You give your mathematically talented students better math teachers and a much more rigorous curriculum over a period of years. Now you are upset when the others don't score well in high school. Think about the lack of logic."

Charles tilted his head showing he hadn't thought about the problem that way before but then nodded.

I continued. "When you first started the high school, I offered to do SAT math prep. I remember your exact reply: 'You're too busy.' I offered again this past summer. And you ridiculously said that the PTO would schedule test preparation. The PTO? Charles, please. What headmaster lets the PTO make academic decisions?"

"The moms thought . . . ," he said.

"Both times my assistance was refused," I interrupted. "Why do I remember your precise replies? They were irresponsible and absurd. Now I am offering for the third time to help the high school students prepare," I stated.

"Howard has to okay it," Charles expressed feebly, as if he ever needed anyone's approval for something productive for the students.

"That was not only my third offer—it was my last offer," I announced firmly. "Are we through talking about Mr. French?"

"I suppose," Charles replied begrudgingly.

Perplexed, I left Charles's office, wondering whether Grady Bellows was the missing piece of this first unsolvable math department puzzle.

57. First Reversal

A new invitation arrived from a school in Jupiter—a MATHCOUNTS simulation. Feeling that our eighth grade team didn't need another practice, Keith, on a whim, took our top seventh graders to the event without preparation. Amazingly, our students took all of the top individual awards as well as the first place team. They earned their points using the knowledge and insight they had acquired from our daily curriculum for the past year and a half. I had enjoyed these students last year, but now they had truly blossomed into a spectacular MCD cohort.

Suddenly and overwhelmingly, I wanted to be their eighth grade algebra teacher. I felt that I could bring them to remarkable heights. I ran to find Charles immediately.

"What's happening?" Charles asked, sensing something urgent.

"I've changed my mind," I said.

"About what?"

"About resigning, what else? But on one condition—I must have the eighth grade algebra next year," I stated.

"Keith agrees?" he asked.

"Totally," I answered.

"Then it's done. I'm thrilled about your change of heart, Molly," Charles said.

"These seventh graders are amazing. I can't desert them," I expressed.

"That's what's it all about—love for the kids," Charles proffered.

I nodded. "Thanks for understanding," I said.

"I fear this first reversal may not be your last," Charles sighed.

I didn't know exactly what Charles meant. But because I decided to stay at MCD a while longer, I resolved to help Charles correct the shattering of the high school.

58. First Flaw

Spring's arrival was welcome. We all knew that summer was not far away, giving us a break from insanity.

One day after school in the lab, Kim told me that she was thinking of changing jobs. I understood her career uncertainty—she was young and eventually needed to progress. Charles, of course, encouraged her to stay, saying that at MCD she could *carve her own pumpkin*. I felt, based on her tone and the late date, that she would stay one more year, though she enjoyed the game of not committing to Charles and Catherine.

Charles asked Ron to look for a replacement for Kim despite my telling Charles not to bother. Ron found a teacher named Betty Strawnsen and put her application in my box. After reading the papers, I returned them to Ron's box, writing *No* across the top as I customarily did with rejects.

A few days later, I bumped into Charles in the faculty room. Curiously, Betty's papers were back in my box.

"What do you think of Ron's candidate?" he asked.

"Not much," I replied. "Her first and most significant flaw is that she is an archeology major with no computer science courses on her college transcript."

"And second?" Charles asked, as if the previous weren't enough to end consideration completely.

"Second, her current school uses Apple IIe computers. We threw those out with Dottie—unless you want to take a giant, seven-year step backward," I said.

"And third?" Charles asked, now playing some kind of game with me.

"Third, Betty is young and inexperienced. She would need a lot of help from me. I don't know if I have the time, and I don't know if she wants to learn or can learn."

"And fourth?" he asked.

"Fourth, her cover letter to you was identical to her essay written for the placement service. She should have enough common sense to realize that the essay is part of the application, so her cover letter should be different. A person without logic cannot program."

"Any fifth?" Charles asked, clearly amused.

"Fifth, Kim is not leaving. So why waste time recruiting?" And I wondered why I also wasted time with this enumeration.

"Phone for you, Charles," Priscilla said, walking down the hall to us. I waved Betty's résumé at him, but he dashed off. Into Ron's box went the elusive papers again.

The next morning I saw Ron on campus and said, "Betty Strawnsen is not even a consideration. She is the worst of all candidates. Besides Kim isn't leaving this year." In the afternoon Ms. Strawnsen's information was back in my box. This time I placed the cursed collection in Charles's box with a giant *NO* note stapled.

Driving home, resenting having to act as if my code name were *Nancy Drew*, I tried to understand the rationale for the bizarre persistence. Betty offered so little that I couldn't even imagine how she made the first cut. She was no one's relative, I had been assured. In a desperate search for reason, I kept telling myself that stupidity, Ron's in this case, was boundless. Or maybe Ron was not to blame. If not Ron, then who—Charles? Regardless, I had no intention of changing my position. We should have all learned lessons from the failures of Dottie, *IT*, and *Linzer Torte* as well as the success of Kim.

Two days later Ms. Strawnsen's papers were in my mailbox—this time with a note attached from Charles asking me to arrange for her visit. Had I screamed appropriately for the situation, I would have been straightjacketed. I could tolerate the idiocy no further. Charles's door was open, and Ron was with him. I focused on the male-male image. Charles was wearing his gray slacks-white shirt-yellow tie uniform while Ron's bland clothing faded into the background of his turquoise and silver string tie.

Perfect, I thought. Together, they could hear what I had to say. I didn't even bother closing the door. Frankly, I was so livid that I didn't care who heard.

"Would you kindly stop bothering me? I have enormous work to do. I said *No* to Betty Strawnsen. No is no. Her credentials are so minimal that I can give you her code name right now: *Betty Boop*. She has no education, no experience, and no sense. So why are you so fixated on her? No, I don't want to know." I firmly threw her papers on Charles's desk, including his note, and left as quickly as I had arrived, without giving them a chance to respond. The incident reminded me of pitching litter at Lorna.

As I left the office, Priscilla called after me. "What's wrong?"

"The usual—only a million times worse," I bellowed back. Then I went to the lab to tell Kim the whole sordid story.

The next day Catherine told me that Betty Strawnsen was scheduled to visit. As I started to hyperventilate, Catherine said that her interview had nothing to do with me—that Rhonda wanted to look at her for a lower school position.

"Which is she—CS or elementary ed? I can't take this anymore," I said.

"I don't know what's going on either," Catherine answered. "But she's coming."

"Fine, so Ron pestered me for nothing," I said somewhat calmer, generally feeling that Catherine told me the truth. Catherine just shrugged.

The next week *Betty Boop* came and went—I concentrated on my work and never even saw her. However, Kim ran into the lab one day after school when I was working.

"Molly, brace yourself," she said agitatedly. I stared at her, not knowing what to expect. "Charles hired Betty Strawnsen to teach middle school math."

"What?" I shrieked. "No, it can't be. She interviewed for lower school. Catherine wouldn't lie to me."

"Then perhaps Catherine wasn't told the truth either," Kim said.

"But Betty is an archeology major," I protested. "She has no math courses on her transcript."

"Apparently, she wants to be a math teacher," Kim replied.

"Oh, and I want to be a prima ballerina. Wanting and doing are two different things. Who is going to supervise her?"

"Keith."

"He agreed to this farce?"

"He did."

"He's too nice," I muttered. "I predict that Betty will win the prize for the greatest number of parent complaints."

"This place is insane," Kim expressed quietly but assertively. "I'm definitely leaving after one more year."

"I don't blame you," I responded supportively.

While *Betty Boop*'s first flaw was that she was an archeology major, mine was my eternal clinging to the hope that Charles would lead effectively again. What was worse than a leader who didn't lead?

59. First Friend

"Tell me you can meet me for coffee this afternoon after school," Emma pleaded urgently on the first Friday of April.

"Sure," I answered without even thinking about my schedule because Emma seemed so distraught.

"Toojay's in the Square at 4:30. No, let's make it the one in Lake Worth—more private. I'll wait for you if you're late," she said.

When I arrived, Emma seemed more relaxed, although she was already on her second cup of coffee. She had ordered two large black-and-white cookies which were already on the table. After the waitress poured coffee for me, Emma began speaking.

"You know how Charles instructed the teachers to discuss their goals for next year at contract appointments?"

"Yes," I replied.

"Well, I prepared a long list that he allowed me to present in full. And then—after I finished—he told me I had no job."

"He didn't interrupt you?" I asked in amazement.

"No," Emma sighed.

"Did he give you a reason?"

"He declared that I had reached retirement age."

"Oh, and what wonderful, universal number is that?"

"Whatever age Charles thinks I am," Emma stated.

"It's probably a prime number—chop people down in their prime," I said sarcastically.

"Actually, I did tell Charles that I was not even thinking of retirement," Emma stated.

"And he said?"

"All he said was that I was too excitable in the classroom," Emma offered.

"Did you say that you needed more discipline support from Catherine?"

"No. Discussion seemed pointless."

"Did he thank you for your years of tremendous service to the school?"

"Meagerly."

Yes, contract renewal time had arrived—late as always for teachers needing to make other plans. And while I thought Emma's request to meet off-campus on a Friday afternoon was strange, I never suspected her news. Shocked, I slumped back in the padded chair. Charles had used his iron broom on Emma. He had banished her cruelly without warning. The concept was difficult to comprehend. But on whose advice, I pondered—Catherine's most likely. Emma had more energy than most of the younger teachers. She united the faculty with her warmth and humor. But most importantly, her generosity toward students had set the standard for the many years of her tenure. She spent countless hours voluntarily giving private lessons, including during her lunch time, to students who had scheduling conflicts, who were admitted late, who arrived from foreign countries, or who just needed extra help. Wait—Priscilla and Emma were close in age, but Charles had not asked Prsicilla to resign. The situation was clearly unfair.

"Molly?" Emma called, breaking my thoughts.

"Are you going to honor Charles's typical request, telling people that you decided to retire?" I asked incredulously.

"Yes, I think it's best. Tell me you agree," Emma answered.

"I'm not sure. Of course, at MCD there's the party line, and then there's the truth. But people who know you will realize that you would never retire. You have too much talent and drive," I protested.

"Thank you. Thank you so much," Emma said.

"Don't thank me. You were my first friend at MCD," I replied. "Who is going to support me through the MCD insanity?"

"You have Kim, and I'm not leaving Palm Beach. We'll talk and meet."

"For sure—I'm not losing a good friend. But who is going to give the kids French cooking lessons after school? And who is going to write original songs to send off the math teams?"

"MCD will go on without either," Emma replied.

"Yes, but important traditions at MCD have just ended. The school will never be the same without you. But happily, you'll be away from all of this foolishness. And you'll have something better for next fall—I know you will."

"I hope so. Tell me he gave me enough notice."

I marveled at how Charles manipulated teachers into leaving quietly. Dottie, *IT*, *Linzer Torte*, and so many others all departed without an echo. I wondered what kind of power Charles held over people. And I wondered whether I would depart placidly when my time came—though I knew it would be by my decision, not Charles's edict.

60. First Initiative

"Look, we can all tell Eric privately that he's an idiot, but we don't have to do it in public," Grady said at the next high school meeting—the worst one yet, just one day before spring break.

Despite the awfulness of the situation, I felt better knowing I was not the only one completely exasperated over the catalog's mutilation. Still, I left the gathering more agitated and angry than ever. Eric's name for me was Meg. Now he was hopelessly lost. At least his prior names for me appropriately had two syllables.

Although Charles and I walked separately, we saw each other immediately thereafter at the mailboxes. I looked at him, long and hard—I had nothing to say. His usual strategy of building consensus— this time among the faculty for the high school program—was not working.

"Do you have a minute?" he asked.

I was also tired of his pat five-word question—weary of his impromptu way of asking to speak to me. I didn't answer. I just followed him into his office, not knowing what to expect.

Charles closed the door, and we followed the routine—he sat at his desk and I in the chair by the door. Battered from the endless toil of the high school, I continued staring at him. If he couldn't take control, then I really wasn't interested in whatever he wanted to say. However, his midnight blue eyes looked at me warmly.

"Molly, I have never, in my entire twenty-five year career in education, met anyone so skilled and so successful at teaching gifted students as you," he said.

I did not respond. I was also sick of his counterproductive compliments, although the line did come across as especially sincere.

"You aren't going to fall for his sweet talk, are you?" a voice in my gut suddenly pounded.

My body was speaking? Be quiet—I'm listening to Charles, I thought.

"I need to make some changes around here next year for everyone's sake," Charles stated.

"What else is new?" Gut Voice said to me sarcastically.

"You're so good at scheduling multiple courses, evaluating new programs, creating meaningful curriculum, and making academic decisions," Charles elaborated and then paused, tilting his head. "Did you ever consider being an academic dean?"

"Be careful. He's thrown this tease out before," astute Gut Voice warned.

"Charles, I'm too worn out to play games. What are you saying?"

"I guess I'm asking you to be Academic Dean of MCD—a new position," he expressed hesitantly.

"What a wishy-washy commitment. Is this how he proposed to Cecily?" Gut Voice said. "Tell him to stop guessing."

"You *guess* you're asking me?" I questioned.

"I *am* asking you to be MCD's first Academic Dean," Charles said cautiously as he played with his yellow tie. "Your jurisdiction would be both the middle school and the high school at first—maybe the entire school eventually."

"You don't actually believe him?" Gut Voice reinforced.

"How long have you been thinking about this position?" I asked.

"Three years," said Charles, angling his head further and smiling crookedly.

"Well, he confirmed your previous suspicions. Don't trust him," wise Gut Voice said.

"But he finally asked formally. Forgive him."

Who was that? Oh no, a voice in my heart was speaking, I realized.

"Look at how strained he looks. He knows he's been a colossal jerk," Gut Voice said. "He can't stop fidgeting."

"But you have groomed for Academic Dean. It is your job. He may never ask again," Heart Voice argued.

Before Gut Voice could speak again, I said, "I'm glad that Vernon didn't believe in a long engagement. I accept."

"Fool," Gut Voice proclaimed. "And stop being cute."

"Great," Heart Voice countered.

"Wonderful! Molly, we make a great team," Charles replied.

"More like a mixed marriage," Gut Voice muttered.

"We have so much to talk about, but I have class in five minutes," I announced while looking at my watch.

"Discussion can wait," Charles replied. "But one more thing."

"Here it is—here comes the fatal condition," Gut Voice declared.

"Be quiet," Heart Voice begged.

"I've asked Jane Cornelius to be head of the high school. Tell her about our conversation—it may help convince her to accept. I'd like her to come back from vacation with a positive response."

"Why doesn't he tell her himself?" Gut Voice asked.

I nodded at Charles. He stood and walked around his desk, opening the door for me. "Does my new position mean that I have to relinquish being *Dean of Cuisine*?"

"I told you to stop being cute," Gut Voice shrieked.

"And *Dean of Printing*," Charles nodded.

He hugged me, and we both left his office together, though headed in different directions.

As I walked by Priscilla's desk, I was beaming. Priscilla commented, "I haven't seen you so happy in years. Did you get good news?"

"The best," I answered on my way out.

"The worst," Gut Voice contradicted. "He'll frustrate you to tears."

"Bliss, finally," Heart Voice sighed.

As I walked to class, I shook off the mysterious but persistent organ voices. I thought about how two people working together could be more effective than the sum of their separate, individual strengths. *Together we will build a great school.* Now, after seven years of hard work and much success, the time had finally come to seek true excellence in all arenas. We were an official team in Charles's own words. I had visions of furthering MCD's renown in a national realm. Certainly, our regional and state reputation in math would be a good launching point. Ideas spun in my mind.

That afternoon I had a long talk with Jane. I was disappointed to learn that she was not as excited as I was. She had been through an acrimonious divorce a few years before and had sole custody of her son who had learning handicaps. She worried that being head of the high school might place too much strain on her personal responsibility. Besides, she astutely realized that Howard had let the students run so wild that his first successor might face severe battles in returning the proper tone to the school.

When I arrived home, Vernon was in the sunroom reading professional journals. I sat down next to him.

"Charles asked me to be Academic Dean," I stated bluntly.

Vernon put down his journals instantly. "Did he ask or hint?" Vernon questioned.

"He actually asked," I replied.

"And what was your answer?" Vernon questioned.

"I said yes."

"You didn't even say that you needed to think about it?"

"No. You know how things are around there. The offer could be gone in two days," I commented.

"You are being too kind. The offer could have vanished in two minutes," Vernon argued. "And it can still vanish."

"No, Charles was serious. It was a definite offer," I insisted.

"Molly, are you sure that you want to do this?" Vernon asked.

"I know that it's going to be tough—very tough. Not everyone will agree with my positions. But I have no choice. I get so discouraged by all the mania. It must stop if the school is going to improve. I'm at the point of accepting the job or quitting. You know I've already thought about leaving," I reasoned.

"You're assuming that you'll be able to implement your ideas. You'll name a course of action and expect it to prevail. But there will be a lot of give and take," Vernon expressed.

"I know that. Vernon, I do know how to compromise. But I can't stay there and continue being undermined, impeded, and disheartened," I said.

"What about getting the first high school class into college? You might be held accountable," Vernon argued.

"Eric is out, and Charles plans to hire a new college counselor. That area is not my responsibility," I answered.

"But you know Charles's past record of hiring, especially with Ron Rhinehardt involved. Besides, parents would associate the word *academic* in your title with college," Vernon continued, hammering his point.

"I need to balance a certain amount of trust with risk," I replied.

"And you will have to be less blunt and more tactful—both with parents and teachers," Vernon said.

"Yes, and I can learn," I answered.

"That is true. You can learn anything," Vernon said kindly.

"But they will have to meet me halfway and learn to be more logical," I countered.

"Everyone's learning logic is much more difficult than your learning tact," Vernon laughed.

"You know, I have to follow my feelings. The overwhelming sense of frustration and despair I've had for years changed to elation and hope when Charles asked me," I expressed.

"How are you going to handle the new position along with all of your courses? You are so attached to both the math and the programming," Vernon commented.

"Well, I'm already doing some of the work anyway—all of the advice that I give Charles and the memos I write for him. But now Charles will finally have to hire a computer repairman to free up some of my time," I teased.

"Molly, if this is what you want, I support your decision."

That evening my mind kept wandering, contemplating my first initiative as MCD's Academic Dean. For once in countless nights, I fell asleep quickly, completing forgetting the betrayal warning.

61. First Backup

Upon returning to school after spring vacation, I tried speaking to Charles as soon as we were both free. That chance didn't come until late afternoon. I knocked on his open office door and entered.

"Charles, how was your week?" I asked happily.

"Fine," he answered. Yes, a person was *well*, but a week was *fine*. I was accustomed to his idioms.

"I have so many ideas," I bubbled, as I tried to organize my thoughts, not knowing how to begin telling Charles my exciting concepts for improving the academics at the school.

"Molly, close the door," he ordered seriously. Worried, I followed his command. He continued dejectedly. "Jane refused the offer. We spoke early this morning. She said that her son's problems were too important to her at this time to accept such an undertaking."

I was surprised. When Jane and I spoke during the vacation, she was positive. I felt that the other issue had influenced her decision more—not wanting to be the first head following Howard.

"I'm very sorry to hear that," I replied. "How hard did you push her?"

"Pretty hard. She won't budge," Charles indicated.

"What's the next plan?"

Charles named one of the other original candidates, when Howard was chosen, as a viable possibility and then added that he had already turned the matter over to Ron. I swallowed hard. We would never get a good head now, I thought.

Suddenly, I worried that Charles had told Ron about my deanship. But why should I be concerned? Ron was in Charles's inner circle and would hear soon enough anyway. Yet a frightening premonition

236

momentarily shrouded my enthusiasm. Regardless, I continued. "Do you want to hear my suggestions for opening projects as Academic Dean? I have a list," I said as I hunted through my book bag for the certain piece of paper.

Charles looked at me with a strange expression, so I examined him carefully in return. His left eye twitched repeatedly.

"Not now, Molly. I have to finish this letter," he insisted, holding up some piece of paper.

His comment was clearly an invitation to leave. I felt wounded by a mysterious dagger and exited puzzled.

Although I arrived at school the next day still bursting with enthusiasm, Charles ignored me. I knew his mannerisms well—the snub was intentional. The following day was the same. His behavior was childish in its obviousness. On Friday afternoon, I sat in the computer lab alone and exhausted, pondering the situation. Unexpectedly, my body developed a warm sweat. A fierce pain sliced the back of my head. Trembles up and down my arms and legs followed. Reality finally struck—Charles had quashed the offer of Academic Dean but was too gutless to tell me directly to my face.

The betrayal—the warning of a betrayal almost five years ago—had come true! Charles had indeed betrayed me beyond infinite proportions. Though Charles first thought of my appointment three years ago knowing in his heart what was best for the school, he faltered in making the final commitment. And he just faltered again. Charlotte Merritt was right—I should never have gotten so close to him professionally. I was blind to his opportunist character, but she had seen it early.

I was shattered—severely shattered. Sweat turned into chills. I turned off the air conditioning and reached for the sweater draped over my desk chair.

My head pounded. The job had become so important to me. I loved the school. I loved the students. I loved the learning. As Academic Dean I had the opportunity to guarantee that each student would receive a superb education each year. I thought that I could make a huge difference, that I could elevate Merritt Country Day School to the highest quality. I would end inappropriate hirings and painful firings of faculty, balance the wishes of all academic departments, curb the frustrations of teachers, and ensure a comprehensive curriculum. How foolish of me—I should have realized that Charles would never give me the chance.

As I contemplated the deception, I consoled myself by trying to view it as Charles's final blow in a seven-year stretch rather than an isolated attack. Somehow that image seemed easier to endure. After all, Charles had already established so often that he could disturb, disorder, defraud, and debase. Charles had rescinded offers before—including at my first interview. His impulsively changing his mind over crucial matters had been happening for years, making many distraught with each shift. His insensitivity toward teacher morale as well as his mishandling of special interests had surfaced repeatedly.

Had someone gotten to Charles, I wondered, to make him change his mind so suddenly and abruptly? Just one week ago Charles was pleased and confident about his appointing me Academic Dean. Was slimy Ron Rhinehardt responsible? He certainly didn't enjoy my berating him at our various interchanges. Or perhaps garrulous Lynn Pelligrini was the culprit. No doubt she would desire the job herself. At meetings she was consistently obvious in her wanting to control the high school, never thinking that her incessant talking would make us all insane. Or maybe Grady Bellows was the cause. He was becoming less trustworthy. Charles had confided in someone, I surmised—a person with whom I had a dubious relationship.

Suddenly, I felt warm and nauseated. Tossing off the sweater, I took some deep breaths, trying to control the growing emotional outrage. I had enough of Charles's pussyfooting and decided that I needed to confront him or else I would not survive the weekend. I found him in his office and walked in without saying anything. He saw on my face that I had discerned the truth.

"Why, Charles?" was all I said as I closed the door.

"Molly, the Academic Dean offer was only part of a package— you and Jane together. So when Jane declined, your job was off," he alleged.

My Heart Voice, the happy one that loved MCD, expired with that pathetically concocted excuse. Meanwhile, Gut Voice exclaimed,

"What? What? Lie, lie, lie!" But then my anger silenced that voice, and I knew nothing could stop what would come out of my mouth.

"Charles, excuse me, but I never heard that condition at all in our discussions. You never, ever, said anything to me about a mandatory team with Jane. In fact, you said that you and I make a great team."

"Molly, you're too literal," he answered calmly and quietly.

"Taking someone at his word is being *too literal*?"

"But I meant you and Jane make a great team."

"Oh, so now I'm supposed to read your mind instead of listening to your words," I said sarcastically, marveling at this master of distortion.

"Molly, I'm very worried about finding a high school head before sweeping away Howard," he admitted. "Ron is going to bring several candidates through for interviews. You'll have a chance to meet each one. Let me know if you think there's one with whom you can work. But I don't want to tell any of these candidates that you are Academic Dean. I'll get a better person if the job is open-ended, with no strings attached."

"Oh, so now I'm a string," I said even more sarcastically.

"No doubt when they meet you, they will be happy to have you as first backup for academic issues," Charles claimed.

"First backup? Oh, you mean do all of the work and make them look good. You continually amaze me, Charles."

"Let's just let this evolve."

"Evolve? There you go again—never a commitment. When I walked in, the job was off. Now to calm me down, you're talking about evolving. Get the lie straight," I insisted.

"Molly, go home and have a restful weekend," Charles said.

"I'm sure you'll have a restful weekend, but I won't," I said, actually thankful to be leaving. I suddenly worried that Priscilla had already gone home, leaving Charles and me alone.

62. First Reproach

In the next few weeks, several candidates for high school head came and went. I always knew when a visitor was on campus because school gossip was particularly fertile on those days. Charles introduced me to none. He never called, never left a note, never asked to speak to me, never invited me to his office, and never brought a visitor into the computer lab. I marveled at how deceitful Charles had become.

Meanwhile, Catherine West told me that Charles had told her of the predicament and asked for her opinion. Catherine was ecstatic and said so immediately. She was thrilled at the idea of my officially managing course offerings, scheduling, and the proposed middle school course catalog, all of which were only headaches to her. She surreptitiously sought my help on those matters anyway. She also hoped that I would impose some academic discipline on the high school.

After my first conversation with Catherine, Charles must have told her some of Ron's, Lynn's, or Grady's counter-arguments against me, for suddenly Catherine became the great compromiser, suggesting *Academic Registrar* as my title. However, Catherine, not an academic type, didn't understand that no such job existed—that the adjective and noun were contradictory. I told Catherine that registrar work—course registration, grades, and transcripts—was something almost any highly organized, computer literate person could do. I was interested in conceptual problems—in establishing and maintaining high academic standards.

Throughout, Jane was curiously silent. She upheld her decision, but had no comments on Charles's manipulating me. Because the matter was truly and solely between Charles and me, I stopped sharing events with both Catherine and Jane. They were only clutter—and I honestly didn't know if they were friend or foe.

All week, however, I kept Vernon apprised of what was happening. On Saturday, Florida-spring perfect, we settled into lunch in our sunroom. I suspected that we would have a long talk.

"Charles is not a bad person. He just has an overwhelming job and has gotten caught up in it," Vernon commented.

"I can't believe you said that," I replied, placing my fork down. I could no longer eat, feeling as if my ingested salad were foaming.

"I didn't mean to spoil your lunch," he said.

"Well, you did. And you're wrong. The President of the United States has a more overwhelming job but somehow manages to stay in charge and not hurt his cabinet members."

"Try to eat," Vernon said.

"Charles is a bad person—or at least has become one. I remember years ago when he set such a good example for the students. What has happened? I don't understand him. He made the school what it is—from nothing—and I will never take that credit away from him. But now he is ruining it."

"He's not ruining it—he's just not making it as great as it could be," Vernon claimed.

"No, he's ruining it because he destroys the morale of the teachers, who ultimately deliver a quality or non-quality product. And he makes his job more engulfing than it should be because of his disorganization and chaotic management style. Caring so much about the school when he's bent on destruction is really discouraging."

"Molly, this reversal may be for the best. You say you've been banging your head against the wall trying to help the school, but the headaches would be a thousand times worse in the new position," Vernon said.

"I know that, but I've never run from challenges in my work," I responded ardently. "I've given the school the best years of my life. I've missed bank social events with you on school evenings because I had too much work. I've spent dozens of weekends at math meets and dozens more on additional projects. I've skipped having friends for dinner from September through June. I've declined business trips with you so my students wouldn't waste time with a sub. I even have relatives angry with me for not sending birthday cards any more. And for what? To get stabbed in the back? The louse couldn't even stab me in the chest."

"Molly, calm down," Vernon pleaded.

But I continued. "You know what totally irritates me? I'm a wreck, and he's not the slightest bit concerned. I don't know if I can return next year. Charles no longer inspires me—he disgusts me."

"But, you're so excited about teaching and coaching that group of kids," he said.

"I know. I know," I answered, trying and failing to eat a little salad.

The next week at school was no better than the previous. Charles was so desperate in finding a high school head that he even considered offering the job to one of the Palm Beach County public school principals—polite and skilled, but not adequately regarded. Moreover, Charles had the nerve to ask my opinion because the man had been Blane's principal.

All the while, Charles was never stalwart enough just to tell me that the deanship offer was officially reversed. I chose to ignore him because my anger was not in control. So I sent him a letter. I wrote that I was insulted—that after a productive seven-year professional relationship, he didn't have the sensitivity to know that he shouldn't dance around with me. I reminded him that several years ago he teased me about crowning the person who had become de facto Academic Dean. I called his giving me the deanship and voiding the offer the ultimate dance. I recalled his own words that I had stood for academic rigor and excellence more than anyone else at MCD and that I had given him the best advice on staffing, scheduling, and curriculum. I commented that the entire faculty, not only I, was doing a fiery tarantella due to Howard and Eric's incompetence. I wrote that I was dizzy from his dance and that he should be professional enough to tell me if the offer were terminally revoked. I told him that the dance was over—I wanted to think about my future and get on with my work.

On Friday afternoon—now two weeks after the betrayal—I decided to speak to Charles in his office. In typical Long style, he had let the whole week go by without responding to my letter, either in writing or in person.

"Dr. Kelman, come in," he said, as I knocked on his open door. He motioned to me to close the door and sit down. His choice of my formal title was predictable. Well, at least he didn't tell me to go away, I thought.

"You've become the Phantom of the Opera—sending me yet another letter," he jested. When I didn't smile, he tried a compliment. "I always knew you wrote well." Then he waited for me to speak.

I could have been sarcastic, saying that by his lack of response, I wasn't sure he had read the missive. But I didn't.

"So the dance is over?" I questioned, noticing that his long, coarse, curling eyebrows had become hellish.

"It's over," he said resolutely.

"Are you going to have the courtesy to tell me why?" I asked.

"I couldn't count on you, Molly. I never knew if you were going to stay or leave, and I couldn't take a chance on that," he replied.

I was stunned by his bold stupidity. "That's garbage," I said. "Actually, it's a lame excuse as well as character assassination. You know that I talk about leaving only out of frustration—frustration that you create. But if I were given this job, you also know I would make a long-term commitment to the excellence of the school."

"Well, your sarcasm has grown out of control. Sarcasm is the lowest form of humor, you know," Charles stated.

Funny—I thought his sense of humor was the *lowest form*. "I am only sarcastic with you—never with the students. You are the one who made me sarcastic."

"Actually, Molly, the real reason is that you're too emotional," Charles stated.

"That is so unfair," I blurted. "Anyone who knew me before I started working at MCD would tell you that I am, by nature, very calm. Ask any of my programming colleagues in New York."

"I go by what I see."

"I go by what I know—I know that you've affected my personality. And, anyway, when did *emotional* become a swear

243

word? If emotional means caring about the students and being passionate about the school, then, yes, I'm proud to say that I'm emotional," I affirmed.

"I mean volatile," Charles said.

"Excuse me? I'm sorry, Charles, but I cannot accept that. You'll have to give me some examples," I demanded.

"Take your reaction to the library committee memo, when you furiously bolted from my office," he said.

"What? Do you really believe that a good administrator would not respond to such flagrant inaccuracies? You left me no choice but outrage over your idiotic comments that the secretary was paid little, that your cousin was under middle-age stress, and that no one would read the memo anyway," I argued.

"Well, take your response to the hiring of Betty Strawnsen," Charles said.

"What about it?" I asked.

"You were so uncontrollably angry," he claimed.

"Is that all you remember?" I asked.

"Yes," he said.

Every normal, human reaction—screaming, crying, and shaking—would have played right into his argument. "She is totally, totally, totally unqualified—not even within reasonable range—and you and Ron kept throwing her on me," I recalled.

"There are three sides to every issue," Charles posited.

"Perhaps, but in this case they are not equilateral. In fact, they're severely scalene. You'll see—*Betty Boop* will bring you nothing but grief. She can't teach math. Your iron broom will be out for her well before the end of the next school year."

Charles scoffed at my prediction and continued arguing. "Well, I mean inflexible."

Cripple, I thought. I wanted to tell him to find his backbone, but I refrained. "Sarcastic, emotional, volatile, inflexible—you don't know what you mean because you are inventing an excuse as we speak."

"I don't need an excuse to change my mind," he declared.

I cringed at his brash boldness. "I don't deny being emotional at times. But your continually changing your mind caused my reactions. And do you know what else? I resent your use of the word *emotional* as if it were a female malady."

"Okay, Molly, here's the truth." He looked me straight in the eye and fired directly. "You scare me."

His remark was a blinding bullet. I flinched, but rebounded.

"Be honest with me for a change. Yes, I scare you, but not because I'm emotional or volatile or inflexible. I scare you because my standards are too high. You are afraid that some parents and teachers can't meet my high expectations, thus causing problems for you. And you are afraid that you, yourself, cannot live up to my demands for integrity."

Charles half-nodded at me—but clearly affirmatively. Was this gesture a new Long quirk? I was too angry to reflect.

"Do you know what the irony is?" I charged. "My standards are not too high for the students—they rise to my challenges and love every second of the climb. They are happy learning. Just ask any one of them."

"I don't have to. I know the students love you—for the right reasons," he commented. "But Molly and her students do not comprise the school alone. The parents and other teachers add to the mix." His reference to me in the third person reminded me of the first time we met.

I responded agitatedly but earnestly. "I never asked you for the dean job. In fact, years ago, when I crowned Miss Amiga as Miss Computer and you toyed about crowning me, I overlooked the suggestion rather than encouraging it. But quite frankly, you offered the deanship to me because you knew that the right time had come. You knew that everyone at this school would gain—the students, parents, teachers, and even you. Now you concoct reasons to retract it, and in doing so, you denigrate your professionalism."

"I thought the time had come, but reconsidering I think it's premature," he offered. "The *M* in *MCD* does not stand for *Molly*."

His last remark was so grossly outrageous that I could not ignore it. "Nor does it stand for *merit* with one *r* and one *t*. I feel sorry for you, Charles. The bottom line is that you are a hypocrite. You speak publicly about seeking excellence, but you crumble from the pressure of the many special interest groups. You charge above average tuition and offer average education. I have lost my deanship, but I won't lose my principles. I won't let you turn me into a hypocrite. If I surrender my principles, then who am I? You have lost yours, and I no longer know you. You are not the educator I first met."

"I really think you've said enough, Molly."

He let me say as much as I did because he knew that he had brutally wounded one of his best teachers. And he knew that I was right. But I was far from finished lambasting him.

"No, I haven't. Do you know what my children said? Blane said that I was meant to be an academic dean, that it was the perfect job for me, that I knew what was exactly right for students, and that I should become an academic dean at another school. And Mimi said that I am your Cassandra, your prophetess, your predictor of success and failure at MCD, but that you don't realize my role. And if you don't like the comparison, just remember that you are the one who studied *Troilus and Cressida* with her."

Charles said nothing. He looked forlorn.

"Do you know what my sister said? She said that she neither liked you nor trusted you from the first day she met you. No, back that up—from the first day she heard about you."

Charles still said nothing.

I continued. "Do you know what my mistake was? When I first learned that you had a code name for me, I should have realized that our relationship was over. I should have given you four weeks notice then."

"Now you're jesting," Charles remarked, trying to lighten the mood. "Anyway, everyone has a code name."

"No, not the people for whom you care," I said standing. Then I walked out, abruptly and peacefully, by intent.

Two more heart-wrenching weeks passed. I decided to keep my commitment to coach the algebra team next year, so I made an appointment with Charles for my contract discussion.

"Molly, nice to see you," he started.

His first words were immediately offensive to me. I had planned to discuss my contract only, but his two-facedness made my blood boil.

"Must I behave now because I may need you for a future job recommendation, or may I tell you what I really think?" I asked.

"Go ahead," he said remorsefully.

Even his fake penitence angered me. I deserved more than superficial contriteness. So I spoke my mind, revealing an image that tormented me while tossing at night in anticipation of the appointment.

"I have never been so appallingly treated by a colleague. You acted as if I were a doormat—not only wiping your feet on me, but also stomping as well. No, you treated me worse than a floor mat. You handled me like a floor rag—you soaked me, wrung me out with forcible twists, and scrubbed stains with me. And the stains you scrubbed were your mistakes. Then you didn't even have the decency to rinse out the dirt—your dirt. You just hung me on the line to dry in a curled up mess."

The saddest part of my whole speech was that Charles took it all—he didn't answer, and he didn't counter. He knew that I was right. I changed topics immediately because the pain was piercing.

"I'll come back next year only if I can have the eighth grade algebra class. I love those kids. I'll teach for them, not for you," I said.

"Keith still approves?" Charles asked.

"Yes."

"Then it's done," Charles agreed happily, tapping his desktop.

After we settled on my entire course load, Charles offered me a large raise, as if money could buy back my respect and loyalty.

"MCD can't afford that," I commented.

"I know, Molly, but you deserve it," Charles said graciously. "You are an amazing teacher."

"But not an administrator, I guess," I said, stinging Charles more. "I'll accept your standard increase."

"Are you sure?" Charles asked, tilting his head.

"I am positive," I replied. I would never allow Charles to buy me. He stood and offered me his hand, but I left without shaking it. His first reproach was over.

63. First Blinders

Determined to protect myself from further MCD assaults, I conjured up my first blinders. The bilateral head shields were washable and combable—mathematically transparent, but politically opaque. I fastened them securely as I concluded my seventh year working with Charles Long. I even told Vernon about my creation for more reality and permanency.

I was working late in the lab, preparing again for my students' original computer game night but without another multimedia show. Clear blue patches of the May afternoon sky had recast as spidery gray threads of an early evening atmosphere. Surprisingly, Catherine entered the lab.

"Charles expects me to do the scheduling for next year," she announced.

"Well, you are head," I answered.

Suddenly she started crying. "My mother is dying," she said. "I can't cope with the confusion of the schedule now. Molly, will you please do it for me, just one last time?"

I tightened my blinders before responding.

"Catherine, you've been a friend through this entire jumble. But I promised myself that I would never again do any piece of the Academic Dean position without the actual job—no more scheduling for you, no more ghost writing for Charles, no more editing of school documents, no more correcting of matters gone awry. I've resigned from free labor. I've resigned from getting into trouble trying to rescue the school," I proclaimed from my oak table soapbox.

"Please," Catherine begged.

My blinders faltered, and I succumbed.

"Okay," I agreed.

Well, at least the daily routine would be organized for the kids one more year, I thought. By helping Catherine a final time, the day would make sense—no first period study halls, no conflicts with elective subjects, no multiple setting up and tearing down of science labs or art projects, no disappointed parents, students, or teachers. I took pride in having everyone begin the school year happy.

That evening, despite the late hour, I was sitting at my desk examining the schedule—a giant math puzzle to me—when Vernon came into the study. "What are you doing? You've broken your promise already!" he exclaimed.

"Vernon, I actually enjoy the work."

"Molly," he responded sternly.

"You're right. As soon as I finish, I'm becoming tougher," I answered.

I massaged my head right above my ears as if fastening the shields better. Vernon nodded in approval.

64. First Omission

My seventh annual sunroom reflection was brief and pointed. I opened the MCD high school yearbook, now separate from the pre-kindergarten through eighth grade volume, for leisurely browsing. Of course, wanting to see my own photo in the teachers' section, I scanned along the alphabetically ordered pictures—G, H, I, J, K, L. Wait—where was Kelman? My photo was missing from the faculty pages! The reward for my work—chopping myself in half forty-five minutes each day to teach the Programming I and A.P. courses concurrently—was a blatant first omission. The yearbook adviser, yet another one of Charles's annual swept-away fools, had neither inspected the students' layout nor used a checklist of departments. And, clearly, Howard had failed to examine the proofs as well. My frustration over others' incompetence was inconsolable. Can severe dejection be exacerbated by yet more dismay? At least my students' joy was a lasting treasure. On the day of the A.P. exam, the eighth graders joked with me afterwards because the answer form had only four choices to bubble for date of high school graduation—none for them. After all, eighth graders were not supposed to know college freshman material. I was eager for their scores.

But MCD nurtured other omissions as well. In the school library I overheard the most condescending address to women since the acquisition of suffrage. "Girls, now let's be good girls and decide on our Diamond Gala theme for next year," the incoming chairwoman of *The Committee* said. I wanted to run home and bury my head in my writing. Did the Diamond Gala represent omission of respect?

Then, predictably, Charles omitted a calculation of staffing. He had forced Emma to exit expeditiously, while in fact, he was short a French teacher by two courses and needed her part-time. So he sent Ron scrambling, ultimately hiring someone inferior to Emma in French knowledge, teaching expertise, and human kindness.

Next year, I would have blinders toward Charles, blinders toward the high school, blinders toward Ron, blinders toward the Diamond Gala, blinders toward everything but my students. I was determined to stop noticing every little thing—every little thing missing—at MCD. I refused to become *Dean of Omissions*.

65. First Kiss

My eighth year at Merritt Country Day School began with a kiss—a kiss on the cheek from Prince Charles. But this kiss was not part of a fairy-tale romance. No, this kiss was part of a wretched melodrama. I was in the lab one morning, a week prior to the start of school. Seeing me through the window, Charles, holding a piece of paper, came in and gave me the awful kiss as an end-of-summer, welcome-back, and I'm-sorry-that-I-betrayed-you greeting.

"Slap him," Gut Voice said.

"Too kind," declared Heart Voice, suddenly joining forces with its counterpart. "Spit in his eye."

"Oh, good. Kick him in his mouse balls, too," Gut Voice added.

Surprised that the voices had returned, I temporarily shook them off. Did he actually think that one kiss would make everything all better, that I could forgive him? Firstly, one cheek-nibble couldn't heal so much pain and anger. Could one aspirin cure cancer? And secondly, a kiss meant nothing from Charles, a man whose standard greeting was a smooch for any woman who potentially could give money to MCD. I felt sorry for Cecily and was glad that Vernon was not even an air-kisser. Still, for the sake of civility and the entire school year ahead, I ignored the kiss. I hoped that I would not later regret relinquishing a chance to react to such a fraudulent welcome.

"So, you're going to have a good year," Charles said with a slight upward inflection.

"Resign right now," Heart Voice said.

"Yeah, leave him hanging," Gut Voice said.

"Are you asking me or telling me?" I answered.

"Molly, let's not argue. You know that I have the greatest respect for you," Charles stated.

"What's his definition of *respect*?" Heart Voice questioned.

"I dislike being nauseated so early in the day," Gut Voice said.

"No, I don't know that, Charles. Just let me do my work. Just let me care for my students," I replied.

"Well, you finally found the high school teacher of your dreams in Richard Sanders. He seems like a truly fine, caring person, dedicated to becoming an exceptional teacher," Charles offered.

"Yes, he's young, smart, and well educated in math in addition to having a recent masters degree in computer science. Plus, he has worked as a professional programmer. And he accepted the offer because I finally got smart when I gave you and Ron strict orders to stay away from him."

"Let's talk about something nice," Charles said, waving the paper he held. "We'll have three National Merit semi-finalists this year." He was so childish, as if he wanted to say, "I told you so."

"You've missed my point once again," I answered. "I predicted who would make the cut. They could have qualified had they been at a school in hell with the devil as headmaster and his associates for teachers. The question is how many students have you let down—how many just missed? My concern is for those students."

"I never said there wasn't work to do," Charles replied.

"But you're late for them. They only get one chance at high school," I argued.

"Molly, I can't win with you," Charles said.

"Now you're right," I responded.

"So be it," Charles said. He tapped the closest desktop and left.

Despite all of his flirting with me, this peck was his first kiss. I wanted to scrub my face with scalding water. But because my inner emotions had already reached boiling temperature, I needed a fast cool-down. So, I calmed myself by reflecting on the three scores of five that had arrived over the summer, the highest possible scores on last spring's advanced placement exam—and the two eighth graders who perhaps set a national record.

66. First Aid

Two days before the start of school, I received a surprising call at home from Betty Strawnsen who sounded on the verge of a hyperventilation breakdown. Why did she call me? Of course, she had no idea of the strife that her hiring had caused—how Charles had contorted my plea that she was not suitable as a computer science teacher into a vicious attack on my character. Still, we had only just met.

Between gasps, she begged me to allow her to stay at my home until school started—she did not want to be alone. Could this request be any more outlandish? Did I remind her of her mother? But how could I not be nice to her? She was innocent—just inexperienced, young, nervous, and about to embark on a job way beyond her capacities. Because Blane and Mimi had departed for college the previous week, I agreed to allow Betty to move into Mimi's room, despite my huge workload, and more importantly, despite the absurd irony.

That evening I cooked a gourmet version of a classic favorite— chicken, rice, and string beans, the safe trio that Vernon and I, like other newlyweds in the 1970s, served to our initial company. Sadly, my chicken with grapes in white vermouth sauce, arborio pilaf with sautéed diced vegetables, and fresh green beans with toasted pine nuts were lost on Betty. Dinner focused entirely on Betty's continual blathering about her previous small-school job on an island in the Atlantic. She clung to all past experiences as miniature air puffs bolstering a safety raft. Then after eating, she quietly coerced us to look at her pictures from this school.

"You brought your photo albums with you?" I asked, hoping that my disbelief would not sound rude.

"Oh, yes," Betty answered as she settled between us on the sunroom sofa, books in tow.

Vernon, sitting starboard, looked across Betty to me, wedged portside. I knew that somehow I must convince Betty that tomorrow night she needed the comfort of sleeping in her own berth.

In the privacy of our bedroom, Vernon commented, "She's scared."

"She's pathetic," I replied.

On the first day of school I decided that I needed to report Betty's state of respiration to someone in charge. What if Betty drowned in class? Would I be responsible for her expiration by not providing a lifeline? I chose Catherine to be Betty's buoy because I could not bring myself to exhale even one breath to Charles about this creature who bopped into my being. Thus, my eighth year at MCD began with my delivering first aid to the *Boop*.

67. First Religion

In the fall Charles formed yet another committee—a group to discuss religion on campus. Though with great hesitation, I accepted his invitation to join. After all, belonging to one of Charles's committees had become the norm for me, and I tried to make this post-betrayal year as natural as possible.

Charles had invited everyone who had ever complained to him, pro or con, about religion at school. Charles, chairing the opening meeting, acted professionally, strictly as a moderator, without imposing his views. Under the guise of fairness, he sat back and let the members speak, or rather argue, with each other. One woman suggested a sensible, universal, cultural approach to celebrating holidays. However, another woman insisted that decorating the school for Christmas should not be an issue because red and green were American colors. By the end of the session, this religion committee rivaled Charles's high school and library committees in futility.

As I watched this committee in action, I could only think of Charles's typical strategy—encouraging buying into the program. At the conclusion, I waited with Charles as the others left.

"Why do you allow people to voice opinion as fact?" I asked.

"They donate considerable money to the school. I can't afford to alienate them," he answered.

"Gee, I always thought that red, white, and blue were the American colors—not red and green," I said sarcastically.

Charles laughed. "That's what I like about you—you can be funny even when you're upset."

"And what do you tell them about me when they gripe about my opinion?" I questioned.

"I tell them that you're my best teacher, and I can't afford to alienate you," Charles replied.

Charles was no longer just a master of double-talk. He had earned a doctorate in the skill. Had he forgotten how his betrayal *alienated* me?

"What's the final result?" I asked him.

"When they're done meeting, I'll do what I think is right," he replied.

"Of course, as usual."

"I'm not going to die on the hill over this issue," he insisted.

"But you are the commander-in-chief," I stated.

"Molly, you are getting more and more cynical each week this year," Charles observed.

"I'm not sure that you know what the truth is anymore, but yes, that comment is true," I agreed.

Charles frowned at me but did not speak.

"I know!" I exclaimed, feigning excitement. "What you need is a *Dean of Spirituality!*"

"It's been a long day, Molly," Charles said. As he stood, rather than tapping, he pressed both of his large hands strongly on the table.

"I'm not continuing with this committee," I announced simply and directly.

"Fine," he replied in an equivalent manner and tone.

I wanted to ask what the first religion at MCD was—lying, deceiving, or backstabbing. But I departed before having a serious altercation. Frankly, I no longer cared.

68. First Tiring

While walking down the diagonal path on a cool December day and enjoying the fresh breeze, a sad realization struck—I had outgrown Merritt Country Day School. Yes, MCD had become like a prison, a terrible place to live and work, and the warden's management style had caused unbearable anguish. My head was fiercely sore from banging it against the cell bars. Though for years I thought I was a *lifer*, the bars miraculously bent open for my escape.

When I arrived home, I sat down at my desk and immediately composed a passionate resignation. Then, remembering Charles's *Phantom of the Opera* joke about my excessive letter writing, I filed it and started a second.

"What going on? Don't I even get a hello?" Vernon asked when he walked into the study.

"In a second," I answered.

When I finished the two-sentence note, I showed it to Vernon.

"You're sure?" he asked after reading it quickly.

"I'm sure," I replied. "I can't take any more."

"You're going to miss the kids," Vernon stated.

"I know, but Emma has been teaching privately since she left, and she says that one-on-one is very rewarding and a nice change," I explained.

"It's just so inefficient," Vernon commented.

"I can't worry about efficiency now. Sanity comes first," I expressed.

"You look sad. I hate to see you this way."

"I've played out all the options. MCD is over for me. I'll bounce back—I hope." I sighed, then sat quietly for a few seconds and added, "My greatest pain is that Charles lied to me when he broke my appointment, despite his knowing how much I hate lying."

"Maybe in his mind, he didn't lie. He sees all the pieces of the school politics—you only see some. He thought he did what was best for the overall good."

"Don't side with him—not now," I pleaded.

"I'm not siding with him. For sure, the school will take a giant step backwards with you not there. And I can see how much he's hurt you. But you could help yourself if you try to see his point of view."

"You should be a criminal defense attorney—not a banker. You've concocted a plausible but totally untrue argument. He creates the school politics for his own gain," I stated.

"If there were such a thing as an acrimonious divorce between a professional couple, that would be the two of you," Vernon said.

"Yes, so much miscommunication and anger." Then I laughed, perhaps to relieve the tension. "I'm so dumb, thinking I had a sexual harassment problem with Charles because of his flirtatious comments and gestures." I paused before adding, "I was minding his watch when I should have been watching his mind."

I submitted my resignation—effective the following June—to Charles in person the next day.

"Charles, I'm not obligated to tell you so early, but I'm giving you time to find a proper replacement."

"Molly, I'll never replace you," Charles replied.

"You should have thought about that last year before you put me through the wringer," I answered.

"Tell him that you've lost all respect for him," Heart Voice said.

"Tell him you can't work for or with him," Gut Voice demanded.

Charles nodded at me slightly.

"Look, he's nodding," Heart Voice said. "He knows."

"Of course, he knows," Gut Voice declared.

"Molly, you may come back at any time—even in the middle of a year," Charles offered.

"Thanks, but I would never come back in the middle of a year—that wouldn't be fair to the students or the teachers involved," I said.

"But I would create another course, and the students would run to you," Charles responded.

"And he would hurt the other teacher," Heart Voice cried.

"He doesn't care how many people he hurts," Gut Voice explained.

"Thanks, but I've made my decision. It's not sudden. It's been coming for a long time as you know," I told him. "I will offer, though, that we can say I'm taking a leave of absence rather than resigning—if that angle helps you and the school."

"Agreed—a leave of absence," Charles repeated.

Then I became somewhat retrospective. "Do you know when I was happiest here?"

"No," he said earnestly.

"My second and third years, when I had a lab to myself and only my students used the computers. Do you realize that I now teach in three different rooms and fix computers in eight? I'm talking about a tremendous drain on my time and energy."

"You may have your own classroom when you come back. We'll call it *Molly's Place*—Molly's Kingdom of Knowledge and Joy."

"Don't make any more empty promises, Charles. Having my own room is impossible given the physical and operational structure of this school," I argued.

"Well, things can be arranged in special cases," he claimed. "And I'll hire a repairman."

"You could have hired a full-time tech person years ago, but you didn't."

"I know I need to focus more on human resources," he affirmed.

The lack of sense made me momentarily cover my eyes with my hands and shake back and forth. "Where's the logic in my having to resign, leave, and come back to have what makes me productive?"

Charles had no answer to my question.

"So, let's keep this resignation confidential until the spring," I requested. "Revealing it would be demoralizing for many of the teachers and students."

"Yes, I agree. Let's see—this is your third resignation counting the department chair," Charles said jokingly.

"And final," I answered. "Your remembering what you want to remember and forgetting what you want to forget is remarkable."

I left his office quietly and uneventfully after that remark, still thinking about his phony pledge. How could he grant me my own room when he planned to build the library before more classrooms? Happily, I didn't mention that topic—my arguments were wasted.

Together we will build a great school. Together we will build a great school. Together we will build a great school. "Forget the damn sentence right now!" shouted Heart and Gut Voices in unison.

Given that Charles had told me he had recurrent nightmares about my possibly resigning, he took the news rather well. Maybe he thought that I would change my mind—again. No, he had also reached this first tiring. He was as tired of me as I was of him.

69. First Don

In early January Ron Rhinehardt returned to campus. I told him to find one math and one computer science teacher, or one who could teach both subjects. I couldn't trust Charles to remember to deliver the message to Ron, and therein lied one of the numerous fundamental flaws with the school.

"Why?" Ron asked, fidgeting with his ever-present silver and turquoise string tie.

"Because I've resigned," I explained.

"No," Ron said incredulously. "I don't believe you."

"Fine, be stuck this spring, but you won't see me on campus next year," I stated firmly.

Then I told both Kim and Richard of my decision to leave MCD. Though they were my closest colleagues, I told neither the story of the betrayal. I always had marveled at how Charles silenced departing teachers. And now here I was, too, following the mold. Charles was either very lucky or had mastered the preemptive strike to *Kiss and Tell*. He did not try to muffle me, however, in any way. I supposed that he trusted my professionalism, and I saw no point in hurting the school by creating a *scandalle*. Somehow, in the back of my mind, I suspected that I would release the tale in my own way, in my own time. However, I wondered what counter-story Charles would tell if the facts leaked.

I felt terrible deserting Richard after only one year of employment. Kim and Richard both needed to know my plans, though, to prepare for next year and to pester Ron or else they would be without a new teacher.

In February Ron returned to campus again but had not advertised the job.

"Ron, it's getting late," I told him.

"Actually, we're right on time," he replied.

Ron and I were talking outside. While my blinders swayed in the wind, I certainly wasn't going to dispute him. Then Ron showed me the draft of his ad in which he described MCD as having two computer labs—I corrected the number to eight. I knew with his sloppiness, he would never find a quality teacher to meet Richard and Kim's standards. Moreover, Richard had commented to me that Ron wasn't treating the search seriously.

Charles had repeatedly asked his teachers to discuss any concerns about MCD's policies, faculty, or events in the privacy of his office. He did not want teachers' complaints undermining the school in the cocktail party or parking lot circuits. For that very reason I had spent so many hours in Charles's office over the past eight years. I was determined to curtail the habit now that I had resigned, but I let my blinders down for a few minutes. I still cared about the school, and I certainly cared about Kim, Richard, and my students. So, on a quick, intentional visit to Charles's office, I decided to emphasize Ron's incompetence.

"Kim has been so great to work with," I said to Charles after school.

"I know," Charles replied.

"She did not bring any bad habits from a previous job because we hired her right out of college," I continued.

"I know," Charles said again.

"So, based on her success, we agreed that Ron should advertise both math and computer science openings with the placement offices at twenty-five of the top colleges," I said.

"I know," Charles repeated.

"But when I spoke to Ron recently, he said you told him that you don't want a rookie. Surprise, surprise—you're telling me one thing and him another. Which is it?"

"I don't think a rookie can step in for you," Charles responded.

"If that's what you believe, then why didn't you tell me?"

"Because you get on a mission about helping young people get started."

"No, Charles. I get on a mission about helping the school. The distinction is huge. I'm willing to train a bright, young person with the appropriate undergraduate degree as I did with Kim. But otherwise, I'm just walking out the door in June. I'm not willing to undo years of what I consider to be poor teaching, which of course the teacher won't think is poor teaching."

"I know," Charles answered.

"So, just to clarify, you would rather have a non-rookie I won't train than a rookie I will train."

"Yes."

"Good—because I'm under no obligation to find a replacement or to train a teacher. And frankly, the way you and Ron are handling matters, I'm straightening my blinders," I insisted. Charles didn't know about my blinders, but the reference made sense in the context, I felt.

"I know," Charles said.

"Well, I'm glad you *know*. So, you must also *know* that after all the hirings and firings we have endured, acquiring a new teacher is like getting married on the first date. But having *Don Ron* as a matchmaker is no help," I argued.

"*Don Ron?*" Charles asked.

"Ron can be your first Don. If you have Deans, then why not Dons?"

"Because M-C-D is not the M-O-B," Charles said defensively.

"Don't you think that's a good code name for him? Or is he, unlike me, above code names?"

Ignoring my snide questions, Charles continued. "Educational personnel is Ron's profession. I have no time to deal with staffing. I have to trust him."

I liked Charles's *I know* answer better. The non sequitur made me bang my head further against a prison bar. A job title hardly made a person qualified in a field as Ron had frequently proven.

Last month, I had urged Charles to consider a senior at Blane's college—someone who had actually registered with the service Ron accessed. I had also offered for Blane to do an initial screening, but

Charles never gave the word. I pestered Charles persistently about what possible harm could ensue. Finally, when Charles permitted Blane to call the graduating student, he said he had been interested in the MCD listing and had hoped for a contact, but meanwhile had accepted another job. Frustration mounted. I had found two of our best recent teachers, Kim and Richard, but Charles was well past listening to me.

Was Charles so beaten down by endless issues that he no longer appreciated the extreme importance of staffing, that the teachers were the school? Or had Charles gotten so comfortable with firing that he had forgotten he was dealing with people's lives—teachers who were swept away by his iron broom, students who suffered through a year with a poor educator, and parents who paid top tuition regardless? Furthermore, didn't Charles realize that each coldhearted firing eroded the confidence of the survivors?

"Fine, as you wish," I stated.

Why did I persist in having these pointless conversations with Charles? Was I ever going to learn? But then something made me continue.

"Just for your information, the draft of Ron's ad describes the school as having two computer labs instead of eight," I said.

Charles looked annoyed that my red-pen eyes were still at work. He obviously assumed that they had resigned along with the rest of me. He scribbled a reminder that I suspected he would lose.

Sure enough, weeks later, *Don Ron*'s published brochure for MCD's openings described the school with two computer labs. Neither Charles nor Ron had fixed the mistake. I just laughed. What else could I do? My head ached from repeated thrashing. But this error was not merely a missing comma or even a pie graph summing to one hundred four percent. No, false information hurt the school by not attracting the best candidates.

70. First Recipe

"They won again—all eleven of them," I said happily to Charles as he saw my algebra students carrying their trophies. When we got off the bus returning from a meet late Saturday afternoon, Charles happened to be at school to greet us, though he was actually there for another reason. He looked at me without commenting.

Three months earlier in December my eleven algebra students took eleven of the twelve trophies at the first math competition of season. Keith, dear supportive colleague, said that I would have had all twelve if MCD's Russian student, Vladimir, had not gotten stuck in his homeland in August with visa problems. Then, assuming I wouldn't adhere to my resignation, Charles was happy for me. Now, what could he say? His master coach had resigned, and he was the cause.

Of course, considerable time and effort, both by my students and me, went into the success. The students each did about fifty algebra problems every evening, giving me five hundred fifty to grade daily. In the early weeks I pointed out every little error to them—distributing a minus sign incorrectly or adding a number to one side of an equation while subtracting the number from the other. But very quickly we progressed to problems of serious sophistication.

At this competition I had occasion to speak to the coach, a very pleasant man, of the algebra team from a nearby public school. He took a liking to the four boys who comprised my team—Shane, Jim, Ned, and Sam. He watched them carefully during the open-view team rounds and marveled at how quickly they thought and how well they cooperated. His students, by contrast, struggled over most of the twelve problems, though he reportedly had a good reputation as a teacher. In our chatting we discussed questions from the individual exam which had been given earlier in the morning. He mentioned that his students had not yet learned so many of the topics—areas of math that Keith and I had taught our students in sixth and seventh grades.

Again, I marveled at how little parents understood about what their children learned in school. If a curriculum were called gifted, should parents accept that label at face value or examine the content? Would they know what was missing or what actually happened in class? When Blane was at public middle school, both the superintendent of the school system and the coordinator of mathematics told me emphatically that problem solving was an integral part of the curriculum—it wasn't, but trading papers certainly was.

At our next competition, in Tampa, I unexpectedly found that the high school ranked first in the country in mathematics had traveled almost eight hours to participate. These kids were the children of the NASA scientists in Huntsville, Alabama. Though these amazing students won first place in the other four categories, my algebra team beat that school's algebra team by dozens of points. I was gratified beyond my wildest expectations and thrilled with what a proper mix of attitude, talent, preparation, curriculum, teaching, and practice could accomplish.

After returning from that meet, I expected congratulations from Charles. Consistently earning the first place team trophy was something. Repeatedly winning eleven out of the twelve individual trophies was even more rare. But outscoring the school ranked first in the country didn't happen as a normal event. When Charles saw me in the hallway, a large smile appeared on his face. But, to my immediate shock, the greeting was not for me. The new high school chorus piano accompanist was standing behind me. Charles walked right by me, put his arm around this new staff member, and escorted the musician swiftly into his office. Was Charles angry, jealous, threatened, or simply indifferent? I would never know, and the answer didn't matter because the effect was the same. In his mind I was gone although I was still physically present for another several months. Charles had progressed to extolling new people. Though Charles irritated me immensely at that moment, I forced myself into a good mood before entering my classroom. My students did not deserve a poor lesson because Charles had upset me.

A few days later, I told Charles that even if he didn't have the decency to compliment me for a national victory, my students deserved his praise. Forget propriety—certainly Charles understood from a business viewpoint that these students would be earning honors for MCD for four more years. Not surprisingly, Charles came to the algebra class one day and overcompensated with gushiness. When he left, Ned asked, "What the matter with Mr. Long?" And Shane followed with, "What's he on?"

Because we had finished a hugely enriched algebra course by March, my students asked me to start the high school geometry text so that they would have a broader foundation for the upcoming three-day annual state Mu Alpha Theta competition. They already had a solid foundation in geometry from Keith's MATHCOUNTS curriculum. So we plunged into their future geometry text, skipping all proofs but learning any theorem useful for numeric problems. Our preparation paid off—Shane and Sam won state awards in geometry or combined algebra-geometry, still in eighth grade and prior to officially taking geometry, with Jim and Ned close behind.

"Did you save anything for me to teach them next year?" Grady Bellows asked me at the award ceremony.

"Don't worry. There's no limit to what they want to learn," I replied.

The unexpected geometry trophies certainly made the weekend exciting, but we had fun in two other special ways. One was doing math together—eating, breathing, and living math—in a communal environment. In the evenings my students and I worked together on the school-wide exam—the take-home test that permitted unlimited participation and resources. We sprawled our math papers everywhere in the little suite—on the dining table, sofa, and carpet. We debated over which solutions were the best. We also wrote and ran number-crunching programs on Ned's laptop computer for some large, iterative problems. This kind of learning experience was beyond anything that could be accomplished in a traditional school setting.

The other distinctive event of the weekend was my cooking breakfast for all of MCD's students on our last morning before the bus ride home—not just any breakfast, but a revival of the chocolate chip pancakes that I had served to Mimi's algebra team at our weekly Sunday practices. These pancakes were a bittersweet symbol— bittersweet attending this impressive math competition without an original send-off song from Emma, bittersweet surrendering the work I loved without sufficient remorse from Charles, and bittersweet leaving my students without a competent successor. Stephanie Merritt asked for the recipe, which I gladly gave her, for her mother. My first recipe, for both pancakes and teaching, was a winner. Would I have other recipes for success?

MOLLY KELMAN'S (BITTERSWEET) MATH TEAM CHOCOLATE CHIP PANCAKES

3 c. flour
4 tsp. baking powder
2 eggs, beaten
2 ½ c. low-fat milk
6 T. low-fat butter or margarine, melted
12 oz. bag semisweet mini chocolate chips

Combine flour and baking powder in a large bowl. Add liquid ingredients and mini chips. Stir until just moistened. Pour by a ladle onto a hot, lightly greased griddle. Turn once when small bubbles appear on the circumference. Re-grease griddle as needed. Makes about 20 pancakes.

71. First Revelation

Not long after the math convention weekend, word spread through the faculty that I had resigned. Of course, people did not know about my embroilment with Charles. The most typical comment I received from other teachers was, "Good for you. If I didn't have to work, I wouldn't either." I was stunned. What happened to loving education? What happened to adoring students? What happened to teaching as a privilege?

My standard response was, "I'll probably be working harder than ever. Writing is not easy, and it's lonely. But, I'll be in control of my own time and decisions." I was certainly not going to play tennis, eat bonbons, get skin cancer, or worse yet, sell waterfront real estate. If people thought I would attend every fashion show luncheon in Palm Beach, they hardly knew me. With my family, my work was my life.

Parents, too, heard of my departing. While I spent comparatively little time now in Charles's office having private conversations, still, I was teaching a full load, and some issues demanded Charles's information or participation. At the conclusion of one of these recent times, Charles told me that MCD's dedicated PTO president had expressed to him both her sorrow over my leaving because I had greatly influenced her children as well as her concern over whether I was upset about something. Charles told me, with a totally straight face, that he had assured her my sole reason for resigning was my desire to write.

My mouth opened and froze—no words came out. What were the possible options? Charles was either senile or insane—in his mind he had done nothing wrong. Or Charles had told so many circular fibs for so many years to keep the diverse factions at the school happy that he no longer knew the difference between veracity and deception. He glossed over untruths like an electric buffer polishing wax in adjacent swirls on a hardwood floor. However, telling me, the subject of his lie, about the lie, was purely sardonic.

I was shocked that MCD board members never bothered to ask me directly why I had resigned and if anything were wrong. No one requested an exit interview. They let me walk away on Charles's word, without talking to me personally. Their behavior confirmed my opinion that the board members had little understanding of the school's academic issues.

In early May Charles held an all-day, full-faculty meeting to prepare for next fall's Florida Council of Independent Schools reaccredidation—a school-wide evaluation that occurred every five years. Catherine West began the meeting by presenting an overview of the administration. Her chart showed the Headmaster, Business Manager, Academic Dean, Admission Head, and College Counselor. Alexa Smyth quickly asked whether the chart was for the year ending or the next year—a totally sensible question, I thought. I assumed that the concern was aimed at the Academic Dean position. The school certainly didn't have one this year, but adding one next year was plausible—even even if I were not the person. Catherine replied for this current year. The next logical, obvious question should have been asking who the phantom Academic Dean was this past year. However, immediately Grady Bellows changed the subject, commenting about changing a singular to a plural in the written document that Catherine had projected. At that point, I left—I had far better ways to spend my time. If the teachers were so stupid, then why should I bother? I departed right in front of Charles. I thought of the time that I had walked out of the Mousercise, and he ran after me. This time, he saw me and let me go, without a gesture. Our relationship was over.

During the last week of May, Kim, Priscilla, and Charlotte sponsored a simple reception in my honor—an event I didn't want because of its hypocrisy. I was leaving because Charles, my closest professional friend, had double-crossed me, and I couldn't endure working in his duplicitous atmosphere. I hated being fake—the hostesses had no idea, while I had no choice. Still, I chose my outfit carefully—a light pink, cotton gauze dress with a flowing skirt and wide sash, a casual but confident look.

Grace had called asking if she should fly down for the occasion. I replied that the reception was a non-event. I did not want to certify it as important with Grace's presence. Moreover, Blane and Mimi as well as Arielle, Bethany, and Holly were all away at college.

A few of the students, parents, and teachers made speeches about my effect on them. Grady organized the presentations but clearly put no time or thought into the matter. His own comments were superficial. But, Shane, Jim, Ned, Sam, and my other seven algebra students who attended brought me happiness.

Keith's remarks were very gracious about our accomplishments as a team. Keith ironically also resigned that year, at a normal retirement age. Acquiring his work would have been a great joy for me, if isolated from the associated mania of Charles and the school.

Charles's talk was brief and inaccurate. He could have said so much—for example, growing the school from one computer lab to eight and instilling a love of math in hundreds of students. Instead, he said that I came to MCD first as a parent and then later as a teacher. Nothing could have been further from the truth. Errors of omission are unfortunate, while errors of commission are hurtful. But errors of sloppiness—what are they? At first his words irritated me. Then I just viewed him as pathetic—his praise as impromptu as his management of MCD, his comments as inappropriate as his behavior with professionals.

Suddenly, I saw many staring at me. I had been pondering Charles's remarks for too long. I feared that guests saw my pensiveness and might actually realize the truth, so I broke the spell of contemplation with an instant smile.

Which scenario was my first revelation—that hypocrisy was common? That people failed to question why? That illogical reasoning abounded? Or were my revelations more MCD-specific? That Charles was a master of whitewash? That teachers wanted their paychecks above all else? That board members did not place excellence and knowledge foremost?

72. First Good-bye

During the last few days of the school year, I thought about how I should say good-bye to Charles. I refused to go to the maiden high school graduation. MCD was granting Howard Driskell an honorary diploma—a sad, hypocritical gesture in my opinion. Anger swelled again within me for putting mammoth time and energy into the first high school catalog.

Still, I wanted to thank Charles deeply for all of the wonderful professional freedom that he had given me to develop my curriculum and accomplish perhaps unparalleled achievement with my students. Such words of thanks, however, did not seem appropriate after the horrific betrayal. I decided simply to leave—without any conversation. Coincidentally, though, Charles entered the faculty room while I checked my mailbox one last time. He stared at me for a period of time that felt like the closest I would ever come to understanding infinity.

Not tolerating the protracted, boundless silence well, I said one word, "Goodbye."

"Molly, you'll be back," Charles replied.

"I'm not going to say never, but I don't think so," I answered.

"You'll be back. You're too good. You have teaching in your blood. Once you've experienced this kind of success with kids, you'll miss it desperately," Charles said.

"Maybe so. But don't be so provincial, Charles. You know there are other places to teach," I responded. "And several of your parents have already asked me to teach their children privately—both math and programming. I think I'll enjoy one-on-one relationships for a change."

Charles looked worried about an insurgency developing and then nodded as if he were not surprised. He commented, "I know I've disappointed you."

Unmistakably—an indication he knew he had wronged me in the sordid betrayal. He hugged me, and I flinched. Then he released his close grasp but still held me so that we were his long-arms-length apart. Looking into his ink blue eyes, I repelled tears. I would never cry in front of him, over him. With manifest clarity, I passed the *Shmuck of the Year* award to Charles, realizing that he had been the rightful recipient all along, this year and every year. Thus, my secret prize ended.

Suddenly, Charles liberated me and went back into his office. I exited MCD and walked each step deliberately, down the diagonal path. I gazed with blurry eyes at the stone mascot: *Merritt Country Day School, Home of the Shmuck.*

Would I ever come back? If I returned and had another bout with Charles, then this episode would not be my first good-bye. But the thought of more comparable hurt was painfully unbearable. I must never return.

73. First Joke

When I walked out of MCD, happily with another year of major academic success, I did not drive straight home for my annual reflection. No, I stopped randomly at a salon—a setting where typically I had neither time nor patience. Though for years I wore my long, straight hair 1960s Cliffie style, today I had my hair cut short and permed with bouncy curls, now that I could think about myself. Then I went shopping. I no longer wanted to wear any of the clothes that Charles had noticed.

Arriving home after several hours, I left my packages in the foyer and headed straight for the sunroom sofa. I mentally needed to release the odiousness in my life, character by character.

Betty Boop was first. Charles had the insensitivity to mention his dilemma to me—whether or not to fire Betty. She was definitely ineffective. After all, what archeology major would make a fine math teacher, especially in MCD's math department? Given her August hyperventilation breakdown, I was surprised that she had survived an entire school year without a respirator. But Charles rehired Betty Strawnsen because, due to the delayed, inadequate recruiting procedures of *Don Ron*, Charles simply had no other viable candidates.

The *Wicked Witch of the West* was next in my thoughts. Early in the school year I had received a memo from Charles announcing the formation of a middle school curriculum committee, paralleling the high school's, and asking me to serve on it. The memo said that Catherine, as chair, would call the first meeting—except she never did. Was she really either a competent administrator or a friend?

Then I turned my attention to Jane Cornelius. What would Charles have chosen for her code name—a prim Jane Austen character or perhaps, at the other extreme, Tarzan's reckless playmate? The last time she was in the lab, she concentrated on her word processing while I focused on grading my final exams. I remember saying to her, "Jane, you were so smart to turn down the job of high school head. This place is a nuthouse. I'd be here until eight o'clock every evening if I were Academic Dean." Jane just smiled coyly, saying nothing, surprising me by her cool reaction.

Head Howard, *Tomahawk*, and the *Fuller Brushman*—Charles had told me that he had helped them all find new jobs. I held my breath while I thought of passing the trash again.

But Howard's chalk dust needed not only erasing but also washing from my mind. Charles told me that he had asked Howard, before departing, to deal with the issue of SAT preparation by seeking my advice on the matter. After Charles had rebuffed my previous offers as well as ignored my criticism that the English department needed a more consistent program in vocabulary building and critical reading, why now? Howard and I did meet, and, to my surprise, he solely requested tips for his new school regarding my sixth grade math curriculum. I looked at him in amazement and laughed to myself. Howard had fooled Charles, or Charles had fooled me. Either way, the MCD students would continue to lose, and Howard was crazy to think that I would disclose my secrets. I quickly glossed over basic concepts such as introducing math vocabulary early. Predictably, Howard didn't ask any specific questions for fear of showing his math ignorance. And, of course, he pretended that his leaving was his decision.

Worse, though, Howard had informed his faculty that grades were due at noon two days after the last final exams. I arrived at school at nine that morning, only to find grades for my high school students already entered in the master book. I had endured more insanity at MCD than any teacher deserved, but entry of fictitious grades was beyond toleration. When I questioned Howard, he replied that he had accelerated his moving schedule and needed grades earlier. I was tempted to ask, "Did you ever hear of a telephone?" However, *Head Howard*, at that point, did not even warrant sarcasm. His parting gesture was pathetic. I adjusted the phantom grades and silently, miserably, left his office.

Finally, I needed to dismiss Charles. As he addressed the faculty at the closing meeting, I looked at him carefully and objectively, seeing true indications of aging. My staring was only fair. After all, how many times had he looked at my clothes and what else? An old, tired appearance had replaced his handsome, preppy look. I thought of photos of Presidents Kennedy and Lincoln taken in successive years, showing increased wrinkles and signs of stress. I imagined aligning annual photos of Charles and seeing a similar effect.

Of course, Charles didn't help himself aesthetically. While his hair was rapidly receding, he started combing it straight back, making him appear much older than his side part and boyish bangs eight years ago. Moreover, blondes did not gray well, I thought. The color of his intertwining strands resembled cowhide. And why had Cecily not told him that the Richard Nixon hairstyle was not complimentary? For a time he let the sides grow longer to make up for what was missing on top, but he only looked like a clown.

Together we will build a great school. Together we will build a great school. The words still echoed at weighty times. What a fool I had been to believe in Charles Long.

"Wow," Vernon said when he arrived home. I had not seen or heard him enter the sunroom.

"You like it?" I asked hopefully, fluffing both sides of my hair.

"Love it!" he replied. "You just look different."

"I named the cut a *Charlesectomy*."

Vernon did not laugh—not even smile.

"Molly, you need to get over this situation. Someday you are going to see Charles. What are you going to say? How are you going to act? Can you be polite?"

"Of course, I can be polite," I retorted. "Don't you empathize with me at all?"

"Yes, but he did what he thought was best given his high stress level," Vernon commented.

"Sure," I responded, tossing my head deliberately so my curls bobbed as I walked down the hallway to put away my packages. Though Vernon was not pleased with my first joke post-MCD, I was satisfied that I invented a cure for Charles's bad-hair days.

74. First Question

The telephone was ringing as I entered my home. The cross breeze from the open windows on the cheerful October day made me hold the front door tightly as I closed it. I ran into the study.

"Molly, we have to have lunch," Kim said at the opposite end of the line.

"What's going on?" I asked.

"Just be ready to play a game," she said.

"What game?" I asked, very puzzled.

"MCD Roulette," Kim replied.

We arranged to meet on Saturday at a café off Lake Avenue in Lake Worth. Kim, already seated, seemed upbeat as she greeted me.

"Good choice of table," I commented referring to the remoteness of the corner booth.

"Okay, here's the game," she began with a tantalizing grin, pulling a piece of paper from her purse. "I ask you questions that reveal the absurd incongruences happening at MCD since you left. You get four points for a correct answer, minus one for an incorrect answer, and no points for a pass—just like at Mu Alpha Theta."

"Fine," I replied, smiling with anticipation.

Kim read from her list. "First Question: How many meetings of the middle school curriculum committee has Catherine called?"

"Well, let's see. It's been a while since I got the notice to serve, but the committee never met last year. So I'll say one."

"Wrong. Your score is negative one. Catherine still hasn't called a meeting."

"Actually, I'm not surprised. Catherine doesn't like to formalize curriculum because so many courses change each year with teachers coming and going. And after Charles's initial memo, I never inquired about the committee because I needed to be true to my imaginary blinders." I held my hands flat, extending from the sides of my head as I spoke.

We halted the game as the waiter took our order—specialty salads and coffee. Then Kim continued.

"Question Two: Whose computer lab got new hardware?"

I thought for a moment and then replied, "Lynn Pelligrini's."

"Wrong again—Renuka Mohmadd's. That's two wrong," Kim stated factually.

"Well, Renuka needed new computers. I just would have waited another year because she was still managing to deliver a quality program on the old computers. I felt the money needed to be spent other places first. And with each year, the hardware is more powerful at less cost."

"Yes, we know. But stop your detailed analysis of each question if you want to score any points," Kim advised. "Question Three: Whom did Charles ask to be head of the high school?"

"I can't imagine," I responded quite surprised. "I guess he's doing it himself as he said he would."

"Wrong again—negative three. He tried, but both jobs nearly did him in. He recently asked Jane Cornelius to be head of the high school, and she accepted. But I don't think Jane will survive. Lynn Pelligrini is already giving her trouble."

I stared at Kim in amazement and suffered a reminiscent slicing pain of betrayal. We paused while the waiter poured coffee.

"Question Four," Kim said looking at me intently. "Where did groundbreaking for the library occur?"

"That's easy—at the site the committee discussed ad nauseum."

"Wrong again—negative four. Groundbreaking occurred at a new location chosen by Charles himself—as he described it laughingly to us, 'equally inconvenient to all.' Are you ready for Question Five? It's a big one."

"Go."

"Which teacher just got fired?" Kim asked.

I thought and thought. "You're not going to believe this—I don't know. Maybe I actually do have MCD out of my system. I'll guess Alexa Smyth though I can't imagine why."

"No—Betty Strawnsen!"

"After two months of school?"

"That's right," Kim replied. "Her kids told their parents that they weren't learning anything, and the parents put pressure on Charles."

I could not help but recall all the grief that Charles had caused me regarding Betty. "Who's taking her classes?"

"Charles found a retired math teacher. I'm not sure, but I suspect that Grady told Charles not to call you. Anyway, you have five wrong. Question Six: Who was also recently fired?"

I thought for just a second. "Help, I pass."

"Emma's replacement!"

"What a fiasco—and disruption," I grumbled.

"Okay, five wrong and one omit. Let's go on. Question Seven: Who did the scheduling for this year?"

"Cecily," I answered.

"Incorrect—six wrong, one omit. Catherine managed to do the scheduling herself, but half of the seventh graders have first period study hall, and the parents are not happy."

Just then the waiter brought lunch to the table. Again, we stopped speaking for a moment to be sure that he didn't overhear. The salads were bountiful and beautiful.

"Fresh black pepper?" the waiter asked.

"Yes, please, lots," I requested, feeling my mood becoming as irascible as the spice.

"No, thank you," Kim replied.

"Before we go on, I'll give you a little hint," Kim offered, as the server walked away. "You're thinking too logically. What happened to that good old MCD scorn?"

"I'm trying to move on," I said.

"Take a step back—just for this game," Kim requested. She looked at her list. "Okay. Question Eight: Who was hired to replace you in the computer science department?"

"I agree, change in approach—no one," I replied.

"Right! Rhinehardt never found a teacher for us." She marked a check on her paper. "Question Nine: What was Catherine's response to no new computer science teacher?"

"She loaded you and Richard up with overtime," I answered.

"No, come on—scorn. Catherine canceled half of the computer science courses in the middle school, including all in seventh grade."

"How is she getting away with that? I can't imagine that the tuition was lowered."

"She and Charles are pretending that the English teachers are also teaching computer science by saying that it's integrated," Kim explained.

"That's ridiculous. Of course, it's integrated as a tool, but that's not computer science as a subject. Why aren't the parents complaining?"

"How many things can they complain about at once? Betty was more of an issue in seventh grade—plus the first period study halls. Richard was outraged, so he spoke to Catherine. According to Richard her exact comment was, 'We don't have to teach those courses now that Molly's gone.' That flip remark made Richard even more furious."

I sighed.

Kim continued. "He told her he had wonderful classes this year because of your previous work. But with your feeder program gone, his advanced courses would disappear in the future. He asked her if she considered the desires of the students and the reason he was hired, not her convenience."

"Did I not teach Catherine anything about gifted education? Was she just humoring me because she didn't want to cross me? So now, the students are hurting—the courses are gone. But Charles had told me he would ask Richard to incorporate my courses into his workload by giving someone else his less important classes. Apparently that conversation never occurred."

Kim nodded as she ate.

"So I guess the Catherine-Richard relationship is over," I added offhandedly, taking a bite.

"Pretty much. We're on Question Ten."

"There's more?" I asked incredulously.

"Definitely. Who of your wonderful students from sixth grade math last year lost his Diamond Gala scholarship, despite the largest profit ever?"

"Not Nick?"

"Yes, Nick, the future star of the MCD math teams—gone."

"I didn't even know he was on scholarship," I said.

Kim swallowed before saying, "Well, you know now, except he isn't any more. Caroline Jackson was livid—something about Nick's father misrepresenting his financial situation on school forms."

"He'll be so bored," I complained. "Or maybe he won't. Who knows what's happened to the math curriculum?"

Kim shrugged and continued. "Question Eleven: What is Priscilla telling people who call on the phone and ask for you?"

"Well, Charles and I agreed to call my departure a leave of absence, but he obviously fouled that up or else you wouldn't be asking. So he and Priscilla must be saying that I resigned."

"Brace yourself—they are telling people that you retired. They use resignation as a euphemism for firing, so Charles told Priscilla to call your situation a retirement."

I started coughing violently as some black pepper caught in my throat at that instant. I drank almost a full glass of water before I could speak.

"That's absurd. People who really know me understand that I would retire only if I were senile or sick. Oh no—neither rumor is going around, is it? Have you heard anyone say that I'm ill?"

"No, but I guess people are willing to accept that you're now after the good life," Kim replied.

"That's so irritating—yet another one of Charles's moves to endear him to me even less."

I was thinking about whether Charles's violating our agreement by muddling the distinction among leave of absence, resignation, and retirement was intentional or careless when Kim interrupted with another question.

"Question Twelve: Who's mother is still alive?"

"Oh, that's easy because only one person's mother was dying—Catherine's."

"Right! Eight wrong, one omit, and three right. You're doing slightly better. Okay, Question Thirteen: What does Charles say to major donors who want you at school?"

"Kim, this topic is painful. I'm going to pass. I don't even want to speculate."

He tells them unabashedly, "I suspect Molly will be back next year."

I laughed so impulsively that I spit and quickly covered my mouth with my napkin.

"How do you know?"

"Some parents told me because they know we're friends," Kim explained.

"Where does he get this wildness from?"

"He makes it up. He tells people what they want to hear."

"More coffee?" the waiter asked to our surprise. We had not seen him approach, but we both nodded affirmatively and thanked him.

"Let's go on. Question Fourteen: How many National Merit semi-finalists does MCD have this year?"

"I know these kids well. Four would qualify no matter what school they attended, so I'll say four. I'll bet no borderline students made the cutoff."

"Correct. Almost done—Number Fifteen. What is Rhonda Seddon's new title at school?"

"Dean of Dances."

"Sorry, she's Dean of Physical and Emotional Wellness."

"Well, there's a title with trendy buzzwords. Why—to get her daughter through senior year? I am so impressed that she's a Dean," I said sarcastically.

"Last Question: Who has been seen frequently coming and going from Charles's office and has been caught inside with him with the door locked?"

"Are you implying that Charles is having an affair?" I asked, totally shocked.

"Just answer the question," Kim instructed.

"I can't. Teacher or parent?"

"Neither—staff."

"Not Caroline Jackson!"

"Yes, Caroline—MCD's all-business, all-the-time, business manager," Kim stated.

"I'm shocked. Who told you?"

"Joe, and you know he knows everything."

"But Charles is always kissing every woman," I argued.

"Yes, what a clever decoy strategy," Kim remarked.

"But Caroline is so unattractive compared to Cecily," I protested.

"I told you to stop being so logical regarding MCD."

"Well, the only way to settle this matter is to post Joe on the roof next to the skylight," I said playfully.

"We've already thought of that," Kim declared with raised eyebrows.

"Well, their daily 6:00 A.M. breakfast meetings give them plenty of time together, but I'm still skeptical. Charles's office is so small. They certainly don't stretch out on top of his messy desk."

"Yes, but the office has a closet that is always locked—behind the silk tree. No one knows how big it is. No one has ever seen inside. It might even have a couch."

Now I returned the raised eyebrow look to Kim.

"Meanwhile, Charles and Caroline contradict each other continually. You get Charles's permission to purchase something, and then later hear Caroline complain that the budget is overextended. Or you receive one policy message from Charles, and then talk to another faculty member whom Caroline told the opposite. Or you make an appointment to speak to Charles and when you arrive, you discover that he's meeting with Caroline. It's all so frustrating."

I shrugged.

"Time for the final tally—with the last hint, you have five right, nine wrong, and two omitted for a total of eleven points out of a possible sixty-four. At least you're in the positive range, but your algebra team would not be proud of you," Kim teased.

"No, but Vernon would be because I'm losing hold of the MCD gossip," I remarked. "Kim, you've turned MCD's incongruities into a game, but suffering is not a sport. The first question really should be, did Charles ever suffer?"

75. First Dream

Away from school, I tried to avoid social engagements that I suspected MCD parents would attend. They cornered me with distressing disclosures and poignant pleas. A few mothers said that quality control was gone, and, ironically, one of my award-winning fathers even begged me to return.

I did return to Merritt Country Day School—but only in a dream. Charles phoned me—that act alone was enough to identify the scenario as a fantasy. He invited me to be MCD's first *Dean of Wealthy Parents*. By assuring that these parents were happy, he could continue to rely on their donations. And who better to keep them satisfied than Molly?

"But, Charles," I pleaded in my deep-sweat nightmare. "*Dean of Cuisine* and *Dean of Printing* are ethical. *Dean of Wealthy Parents* doesn't seem fair."

"All is fair, my dear, in love, school, and war," Charles replied, tilting his head and smiling crookedly.

I awoke soaked in perspiration, remembering spotty details of the bizarre vision. Probably not even Andrew Lloyd Webber's Joseph in his glorious Technicolor Dreamcoat could interpret the meaning of my first post-MCD dream that I hoped was my last.

76. First Quip

In December I did see Charles at a Grey Parent Eastern Trust holiday event that both he and I were obliged to attend—I, as Vernon's wife, and Charles, representing MCD, as a significant client. Suspecting that this meeting would happen, I had planned to act confident and detached. But I was unprepared for Charles's refashioned appearance—he was wearing a red tie. Was his image solely changed or his disposition as well? Had he also traded in his yellow Lincoln Continental for a red one?

"Dr. Kelman, so nice to see you. You look wonderful in your new haircut," Charles began solicitously, breaking my stare at his daring new outfit. "In fact, everyone who leaves Merritt Country Day seems to look great," he added, followed by his aged laugh.

"Yes, I do believe my brow furrows have lessened and my eye circles have lightened. What a shame one has to leave MCD to lose that frazzled look," I remarked, well rehearsed mentally.

"How is your book?" Charles asked, intentionally changing the ticklish subject that he had started.

"Books," I responded curtly. "Progressing."

"You know, it needn't be this way, Molly."

"What needn't be which way?" I asked, emphasizing the flaws in his spoken grammar.

"Verbal volleying," he answered. "But I detect that you are still critical of me."

"Crisis creation and stress stimulation," I announced, copying his alliteration, "are generally not advocated in leadership programs."

"It seems it is going to be this way," Charles stated. He smiled at me awry and moved on to the next person nearby. Relieved that my forethought had prevailed, I was satisfied with my first quip, post-departure.

Suddenly, Parke Merritt, MCD's never-ending board chairman, appeared. Had he seen me speaking with Charles?

"Congratulations on your new career as a writer," he said.

"Hold the congratulations until I finish something," I suggested, trying quickly to toss the dissident mood into which Charles had submersed me.

"Nevertheless, you are missed. I thank you for the fine reputation you've given MCD. And I am personally grateful for all you have done for Stephanie. She enjoyed you so much."

"Thank you," I replied simply, stunned that he accepted my absence so easily. He's probably brainwashed by Charles, I thought.

"You know, I firmly believe that change is good for all of us," he said. "What are you working on now?"

"Mainly turning my past work into textbooks," I answered, intentionally brief.

Surprisingly, almost flippantly, he asked, "Do you think you have a novel in you?"

I angled my head, smiled crookedly, and only said, "Perhaps."

77. First Career

The day was June first, and I was again reflecting. However, I neither had finished a school year nor had adopted the contemplative position as a ritual engrained. No, when not writing I had spent most of the past three hundred sixty-five days lying on the sunroom sofa, deep in soul-searching thought.

I had surrendered my prize chocolate chip pancake recipe that helped establish me as a master math team coach. Of course, I relinquished my recipe to Charlotte Merritt, a friend, not to Charles Long, the enemy.

Was my recipe a symbol of something greater—a metaphor for my vast curriculum that I had developed? Those volumes, I vowed, I would never yield. The papers belonged to me—they would be the basis of my new career. Besides, Charles would have known equally little what to do with the writing as with the recipe.

Though I offered to adjust my schedule and immediately turn the material into a textbook with a teacher's guide for my replacement, keeping one chapter ahead of her, neither she nor Charles nor Grady ever called. Of course, Charles had never called at all—not after my first interview, not during our entire professional relationship, and not for my friend Meredith. Never calling, I distressingly had learned, was his mode of operation. But what were the reasons for the other two? Did Grady actually want my curriculum gone? Had he only pretended to be part of Keith's and my team? Were Charles and Grady so arrogant that they thought they could create something equally as great with no preparation time? Or were they too disorganized even to understand I had made an offer?

Most likely if Charles tells the story of my career at MCD and of my departure, he will have his version. He will forget most of the sordid details. But if I decide to tell the tale, I will never forget. I only hope that I can create comic relief to the serious examination of the tragic problems of education. The pain tortures less with a little humor, though a child, any child, missing out on the best education possible, is not a laughing matter.

But one serious question remains—is anyone capable of fixing the problems plaguing schools? Is anyone adept at making education all that it should be?

The news circularly reports both ills befalling schools as well as projects targeting reform. One year flows into the next. As a problem partially corrects, more appear. National educational organizations publish their *Plan* one decade, the *Revised Plan* the next, and the *Newly Revised Plan* the following, but little ever changes. Schools are still run by the Howards and Rhondas of the world. Those, like Charles, who have the intelligence and foresight to make a difference, crumble to the incompetence of others. Charles cannot run a school with Molly, Keith, Emma, and Kim alone. Charles must have dozens of Dotties, *IT*s, Harrys, Toms, Lynns, Erics, and Gradys—after all, children must be supervised if not taught.

In 1989 President George Bush and the nation's governors met, declaring that the United States would become first in the world in mathematics by 2000. However, after years of supposed work, an international mathematics exam of eighth graders ranked America twenty-eighth in the world last year in 1996. Had my champion eighth graders represented the United States instead, the placement might have been first. Their framed photograph—a gift to me along with flowers and chocolates when they won their big victory over the highest ranked school in the country—remains on my desk at home as a reminder of what education can accomplish.

True, certain schools shine as lonely stars in a dark gray sky. I helped Merritt Country Day sparkle in mathematics for eight years. However, when I tried to transform the school into the North Star, the school's headmaster, my closest friend, privately rebuked me. How could I tell that story with humor?

I wondered how many other dedicated, expert teachers had been similarly broken. Maybe they should all find each other and build the model school that I wanted to create with Charles.

Governments and institutions will write hollow, meaningless exams declaring educators *master teachers*. The title will be misused and the term misdefined because the people writing the test are not true master teachers themselves. Low quality will self-perpetuate.

Genuine master teachers will continually blossom out of love for a subject and fondness for children, not out of pseudo educational jargon. They, too, because they teach rigorously and seek perfection, will have different parents concurrently say to them, "You ruined my daughter's childhood," and "You were the best influence ever on my daughter," as parents from one class addressed me. These teachers will eventually invent their equivalent of the *Shmuck of the Year* award to keep their sanity. As in my case, when they are frazzled to the last shred, they, too, will depart on a new path.

Immediately, certain parents will beg for their return. But, the memories of incompetent teachers and administrators who think they are masters will prevent the return of the true masters. Recalling their *school scandalles*, they will continue seeking new careers.

My own *scandalle* tormented me relentlessly. At times my anger toward Charles was barely controllable. I guessed that he, in his self-contained MCD world, had no idea of the extent of my fury.

Charles wanted excellence but feared that parents and teachers could not meet my expectations. Thus, he settled for middle ground—mediocrity—and belittled me to justify his position. His unfair attack on my personality was troubling, especially in light of his contradictory remarks. Initially labeling me cute when upset, he recast the descriptor as emotional. Yet he, himself, displayed abundant, extreme inconsistencies. Moreover, his deceitful, disparate manner was the cause of my soul-stirring pleas.

Ultimately, he stole from me the chance to create an ideal school, not only by rescinding the administrative offer but also by devastating our professional relationship that I foolishly thought was built on mutual respect. Can trust be regained once it is lost? Charles's self-inflicted, prolonged butchering of his own honor prohibited any healing of my faith in him.

Asking why he had deceived me on multiple occasions would have implicated him in lying, while he maintained his veracity—therein was my dilemma. Perhaps I am unrealistic, but I believe that people, especially close colleagues, should not be treated the way Charles treated me.

Mimi had called me Charles's Cassandra. True to the character of the prophetess, I could not only predict MCD's future but also was doomed to have people not believe me. The curtailing of computer science courses, the declining of math team members, the failing of some new teachers, and indeed, the dwindling of academic ethos at the school were all in my predictive domain, in reality based more on grounded logic than supernatural power. With these problems surfacing only after a few months according to Kim and others, what would the situation be after a few years?

Charles had no time or energy to be both headmaster and head of the high school. Jane Cornelius had wanted the job all along, and she played the game shrewdly having Charles try and fail first. He had put his sweat into refocusing the budding but troubled division of the school. Of course, neither Charles nor Jane had the courtesy to tell me of Jane's appointment—I was gone. The twisted outcome of Charles's egregious lie, that my position was contingent upon Jane as head, estranged Charles from me even more.

And Rhonda Seddon becoming a Dean? How many new, bogus Deans does Charles need? I thought of the canned public school joke: What happens to incompetent teachers? They become administrators. This time the joke is on MCD. They become deans.

Charles's sweeping away *Betty Boop* shortly into her second contract was tragic. As my mind relived the circumstances of her employment, maintaining composure was near impossible. I had implored Charles not to hire her, only to receive severe chiding. In addition to my suffering, Betty suffered loss of self-esteem, her students suffered loss of education, the faculty suffered loss of morale, and MCD suffered loss of reputation.

Yet, Merritt Country Day might survive. It might survive because of some outstanding teachers, wonderful students, and demanding parents. It might also survive, sadly, because of declining competition from the public schools. However, Merritt Country Day will not reach its full potential. If graveyards were not for death but for unfulfillment, MCD would have an eternal flame at its stone.

While I will always treasure the elation and satisfaction from students, I will also remember the frustration and sadness from Charles. At least my heart and gut voices have perished because I am no longer in his confounding company. Tragically, my first career as a teacher in the trenches has ended. Optimistically, my new career as a writer has begun. I remain passionate about excellence in education, and hopefully, my writing will reflect that passion. Though I will always be an educator, now I will teach primarily through the written word, not the spoken word. If my photo were in the MCD high school yearbook, below it would say: *I, Molly Kelman, leave the fixing of education to society.*

78. First Cheer

Suddenly, Vernon returned from his supposed errands and interrupted my reflection. "Look who I found!" he called. Emma appeared with Vernon in the sunroom.

"I'm going to let the two of you talk," Vernon said. I could tell from Vernon's expression that he wanted Emma to cure me.

"I haven't heard from you in months," Emma said as she sat in a chair next to me.

"I'm sorry," I replied.

"Vernon tells me that you're simply wretched," Emma stated bluntly.

"I guess I am," I murmured.

"Tell me how you are going to improve," Emma demanded.

"I don't know," I answered.

"What do Blane and Mimi say?"

"They say that I should join a gym and workout for hours a day."

"Why don't you?"

"I tried. But after five minutes on a treadmill, I always want to go home."

"Are you exercising at all?"

"Well, I power-walk on the new track at the city park. And with each lap I say to Charles in my mind, *I hate you. I hate you. I hate you. I hate you. I hate you.*"

Emma looked worried. "What does Vernon say?"

"He said that I should call Charles because I belong with the kids. When I shrieked *never*, then he suggested getting some professional help to get over the anger."

"Tell me why you don't."

"Emma, think about my problem. What counselor, psychologist, or therapist would understand my passion for education? Their relating to me is impossible—totally impossible. They probably all send their own children to public school and think it's just fine."

"Tell me you've forgotten that both your children got into top colleges from the public high school," Emma demanded.

"No, I haven't forgotten—I'm very grateful. And yes, they had a few excellent teachers. But the whole ethos is wrong—claiming that the academics are great when the emphasis is on homecoming. What I object to is any school, whether public or private, claiming to be universally stellar when it is not."

Emma sighed in agreement. "Well, somebody should be able to help."

"No. Here's how the conversation would go. I would say, 'My boss offered me a job and then withdrew the offer.' The therapist would say, 'So what?' I would add, 'And my boss also lied to me many times.' And again the therapist would say, 'So what?' I would announce, 'But the person who did it to me was my best professional friend.' Then the therapist would look at me as if I were as naïve as a newborn and say, 'That kind of behavior happens all the time in the corporate world.' I would argue, 'But schools are not the corporate world. Schools are about educating children.' Then the therapist would say, 'No. Schools are business, regardless of the children. Professional jealousy of competent people always exists along with accompanying backstabbing.' Totally disgusted, I would say sarcastically, 'Great, I feel so much better.' And the therapist who, of course, has to have the last word, would say, 'You are the one who resigned. You didn't have to choose that action. If you didn't have such high, uncompromising morals, you would be back at school doing your work, ignoring the others. Why not take up lying and scheming along with the worst of them?' Finally, feeling so horrible that this unknown, uncelebrated person—this stranger in my life—desecrated my core values, I would go home to my misery again."

Emma laughed. "I don't think a therapist would outright tell you to lie and scheme," she commented.

"Which do you think is worse—what Charles did to me or how he did it?"

"Well, your fake therapist would label both comparably insignificant. I would call them equally egregious," she answered.

"Emma, do you think I would have continued working at MCD if I were not financially independent?"

"No. Your principles are too strong."

"I think I agree. At the heart of the matter is integrity or wholeness. Of course, mathematically, integers and whole numbers are different sets. And I remember my students getting so upset when a candidate for the high school programming job used the two terms interchangeably during a Pascal lesson. But my point is that I cannot function effectively unless I have my wholeness. If Charles stabs me in the back on the right side, the left side cannot function either. If part of my work is undermined, then the rest of my work can't be great."

"If you needed a salary, you would have boldly switched to a competing school. And there's your solution—go to another private school!" Emma declared.

"To deal with their versions of the same motley cast of characters? No, thank you. I've had enough."

"How do you know they exist at other schools as well?" Emma questioned.

"Logically, they must," I replied. "Otherwise, great schools would abound."

"But perhaps they're nicer people," Emma argued.

"They may be nicer, but they still wouldn't want excellence—they wouldn't want their routines upset. But what's especially sad is that the headmaster at another school probably wouldn't permit the professional freedom that Charles did. The school would dictate curriculum and textbooks, conflicting with my judgment."

"So you're saying that you left MCD because of Charles's deviousness, but that you can't teach at another school because of Charles's eminence," Emma clarified.

"I guess I am," I brooded. "You can understand that—you worked for him also."

"Yes," Emma agreed.

"Except, do we mean eminence or luck?" I asked.

"Who knows? He was lucky when he defined the curriculum as do what you want—he had an amazingly great faculty at one time," Emma replied.

"He is such a complex person," I said, sighing.

"So are you," Emma expressed. "Fire and water are both forceful, but they don't mix."

"I'll tell you what really bothers me—that all of my hard work for the school is not permanent. Charles actually told me that programs are teachers. When teachers go, programs go. Whatever happened to a school standing for something?"

We sat quietly despondent for a few seconds. Then Emma asked, "Do you remember how Merritt Country Day had no gossip during our early years there?"

"Absolutely. In fact, I recall that only at the end of my first year, when I disagreed with D. Dottie over Spring Festival activities, did I learn—to my complete surprise—that other teachers disliked her."

"Compare that to the constant diet of deceiving, tattling, and snake-biting that existed at MCD during our last years," Emma said, lamenting the change in attitude.

"According to Kim, faculty morale is at an all-time low. Charles is so busy that teachers vie for his attention to show off their accomplishments. Plus, Charles, Rhonda, Grady, and Lynn have gotten very cliquish."

"Such an unhealthy atmosphere," Emma remarked. "Maybe your pretend therapist is right—a school really is similar to a large conglomerate. MCD certainly has no shortage of people who want control."

"You know, some might say the same about me," I commented.

She replied thoughtfully, "No, it's different. You want things to be right—that's different from control. You're happy to have other people in charge as long as they do things correctly. Then you're free for further work. And you certainly are never at a loss for thinking up a new project."

"Yes, but I don't know if people at MCD see the situation that way."

Emma nodded. "It's hard for anyone to see reality the way Charles operates: *à huis clos*.

I looked puzzlingly at Emma.

"Always in secret—always in his office, one person at a time, with the door closed," Emma explained.

"Let me continue the business analogy. Sometimes executives can negotiate so much that all sides lose," I expressed.

"I absolutely understand. Except for the few students coming to your home for private lessons, MCD's students and you have been deprived of each other."

Again we both sat for some seconds. Then I broke the silence.

"I fear that I have given you my terminal suffering rather than you have given me your first cheer," I said.

"Go back to Palm Beach Community College," Emma declared.

"No, I never go backwards," I stated firmly.

"Teach at Florida Atlantic."

"Drive to Boca regularly? No, thank you. I hate driving."

"Then take on more private students," Emma suggested.

"I don't know. I'm concerned that Grady and my replacement are mistreating those who do come here."

"Really?" Emma responded, quite shocked. "Well, then take non-MCD students. You are *la crème de la crème*. Parents would beg to get your math—and programming if you want—without having to pay the full MCD tuition."

"Perhaps, I will."

"At least, you still have your CTY teaching."

"No, I need a break from that, too. I'm a free woman now. I can visit Grace whenever I wish."

"Time has helped me, and it will help you. Remember that I've had one more year away than you," Emma spoke wisely. "Have you told only me?"

"Yes."

"Then you need to talk about it more. I'll call you next week."

"Thanks, thanks for everything," I said, as Emma walked back inside.

I returned to my rumination over my ruination. Though so sad, I was gratified that my values would not allow me to work for a person who had raised duplicity to a fine art. I could not forget the downward succession of Charles's words: *Together we will build a great school. . . . You keep me honest. . . . I know I've disappointed you.* Why didn't we finish building a great school together? Why didn't Charles want to be kept honest? Why didn't he stop disappointing me?

Perhaps the therapist I conjured up for Emma was right—Charles had started running the school like a big business, replete with power struggles and choreographed deceptions. And when that happened, excellence suffered—children didn't have the best possible education. Yet, did Charles fathom his early allure giving way to subsequent alienation? Did he recognize his regressive, repulsive transformation? Did he face some responsibility for MCD's losing a lead teacher? Did he sense any bereavement?

MCD will adjust to a lower standard of math education as new math teachers cover limited material, especially fewer ways of thinking, and parents of the rising students demand less, unaware of past achievements. Maybe this descent is what Grady wants—after all, he is from a public school background.

"Still thinking?" Vernon asked when he returned to the sunroom after walking Emma to the door.

"I was, but I'm done."

"Good," Vernon commented. "Emma is such a true friend."

"And you were so sweet to ask her here."

"Are you're feeling better?"

"I don't know."

"It's time to start being productive again."

"Yes, I'm going to concentrate harder on my writing. I think self-employment fits my personality extremely well. Do you?"

"I do."

79. First Disclosure

The next day I was reading comfortably in a plum leather chair when Vernon walked into the study. He looked serious. "Molly, I've decided to tell you some bank business."

"First, you arranged Emma's visit—which was wonderful. Now you're going to reveal a G-PET secret. You must really love me," I quipped.

"You know how much I love you. I can't stand seeing you so miserable. So here goes." He settled into the matching chair across from me. "Did you know that Cecily is not Charles's first wife?"

"I had heard that, but also that his first marriage lasted a very brief time," I answered.

"Did you know that Parke Merritt is not Charlotte's first husband?"

"Well, everyone knows that Charlotte is not Parke's first wife, but vice versa—no. Wait! Are you implying that Charlotte was Charles's first wife?"

Vernon nodded his head affirmatively but said nothing.

"No," I stated in disbelief.

"Yes," Vernon declared.

I slumped into my chair. I was shocked and bewildered. I couldn't even begin to connect one piece with another.

"This puzzle is very complicated," Vernon said. He knew exactly how I was trying to think. "Let me help you get started. Remember the big scene several years ago when Charles took an inebriated Parke home and stumbled upon Charlotte's bounty?"

"Of course," I said.

"Did you ever think about why no serious repercussion occurred—such as their firing Charles?"

"To Parke and Charlotte the school comes first. They are very much taken by Charles who can charm his way out of any situation. Perhaps they are also afraid of an unknown headmaster."

"But why wouldn't a successful, upstanding man like Parke Merritt not come to his beloved's wife defense more?"

"I guess I didn't think about it—too much other craziness," I replied.

"Exactly. How much of MCD's craziness is intentionally choreographed by Charles so that smart people like you will be distracted from the real problem?"

"I've been saying that for years, but now I'm so confused," I muttered.

"While Charles taught at a private school in D.C., he met Charlotte who is from Alexandria," Vernon explained.

"Wait—so that's why Charles was worried that Grace's field was also education and why he would ask me whom I met when I taught at Hopkins."

"Yes, that fits. He was worried that you or Grace would stumble upon someone who knew the original Mr. and Mrs. Long. During the first year of their marriage, he had a silly one-weekend fling with a visiting teacher. She was interviewing for a job, and Charles was assigned to entertain her—except he took the assignment literally, it seems."

"What a fool to cheat on beautiful Charlotte," I offered.

"Somehow Charlotte learned of the affair which she obviously viewed as a sign of very poor character and judgment. With not much invested in the marriage and with this horrific omen for the future, she decided to cut her losses quickly. They divorced shortly thereafter with a clean financial break. Charlotte kept her money in return for not damaging Charles's professional reputation."

"That also fits because Kim thinks that Charles and Caroline are having an affair now," I added.

"I don't know," Vernon commented.

"And another piece that now makes sense is why Charles hired Howard—damaged goods so to speak—who had an affair with the current Mrs. Driskell at his previous school. But I'm still confused," I repeated.

"Then let me continue. What Charlotte did not know at the time of the divorce was that she was pregnant."

I felt my red-pen eyes ejecting their markers. I wanted to scribble over Charles to the point of obliteration.

"You know the child," Vernon announced.

"Stephanie? Stephanie is Charles's daughter and not Parke's?"

"Correct," Vernon said simply.

I tried to clear my head to do some math. "Stephanie will be a senior, so all of this happened about seventeen years ago."

"That's right," Vernon replied.

"But Charles is indifferent to Stephanie," I protested.

"Probably a defense mechanism," Vernon said. "When Charlotte met Parke at a charity event, she was attracted to his maturity and to their equal financial footing. And Parke adored Stephanie from the start. But there's more."

"More? I still don't have these revelations together."

"The woman, the affairee so to speak, was on vacation in Palm Beach when one evening, totally coincidentally, Charles saw her at a Worth Avenue restaurant while he was dining with Parke. Merritt Country Day had only recently opened."

"Oh, yes, their school tête-à-têtes."

"Charles was mortified that this woman might speak harmfully of him, tarnishing his reputation. Parke, seeing terror on Charles's face, gave him permission to hire her."

"She teaches at MCD!" I shrieked. "Who?"

"Who does Charles protect no matter what she says or does?"

I only had to think for a moment. "Rhonda Seddon—and she's been promoted twice, first a head and now a dean." I pronounced her name as Charles often did in phony French with the accent on the incorrect last syllable. "But Rhonda is so unattractive. I hope she took off her Santa Fe jewelry or else Charles has scars on his body."

Vernon laughed. "He probably has battle scars on his chest anyway."

"So, there's unofficial blackmail going on at MCD. Rhonda keeps quiet about Charles as long as she gets what she wants," I deduced.

"I hope you're starting to feel better about leaving the school."

"I just made one connection," I exclaimed. "I could never understand how Charles used incompetent *Don Ron* to recruit teachers. But because Charles and Ron are old friends, Ron screens all teacher candidates to avoid someone else who might know Charles's past, thus minimizing extortion."

"And Charles may have more that he his hiding—in other cities besides D.C.," Vernon added. "Who knows?"

"What a scary but plausible thought," I agreed. We both sat still for a few moments—I, digesting the incredible news, and Vernon, watching me. Then I asked, "What about Rhonda's daughter? Who is her father?"

Vernon now stared at me, though initially I failed to grasp his meaning. Suddenly, I screamed, "Ron! That's why his string tie matches her jewelry. So their matching names is just a coincidence?"

"Just a coincidence."

"No wonder Charles hated my Paul and Paula, Ron and Rhonda joke. Were they married?"

"Apparently, for a few years," Vernon clarified.

"Did Charles meet Ron through Rhonda?"

"I believe."

"So Ron takes write-offs to visit his daughter by working for Charles. What a sick, twisted mess." After a short silence, I questioned Vernon further. "How did Charles become head of MCD?"

"Back up one. Why did Charlotte and Parke found a school?"

"Okay, start there," I agreed.

"Charlotte's reasons were doing something philanthropic with her family money and creating a model school for Stephanie."

"Most of us think that Parke bankrolls the school's deficits," I interrupted.

"He does, but Charlotte used her money to found MCD. And Parke's reasons were supporting Charlotte and having an interest besides work. They chose Charles as head because Charlotte wanted to create some relationship between father and daughter, although they all agreed no one should know. They also believed in his talents, despite his personality quirks. They chose Palm Beach for the climate, culture, wealth, and distance from D.C. Plus their families had second homes here."

"Now I understand why Charles told me privately that the Merritts are annoying to him—they control him, in effect. But, how do you know this whole story?"

"Charlotte came into the bank to establish a new type of trust for Stephanie. She listed Charles as her natural father and Parke as her adoptive father. She gave me permission to tell you because she misses you and cares about you."

Charlotte is truly supportive, I thought. First came her unusual betrayal warning, and now this information. "Vernon, how long have you known?" I asked.

"Not long," Vernon answered.

"Good, because at times you seem to have sided with Charles."

"No, I was just trying to get you to see the complexities in his job leading to his decisions."

"Oh, I saw the complexities, but I also saw the disconnects. I've learned an important lesson. When actions defy all logic, look beyond the obvious. Just declaring Charles bizarre or stressed was too simplistic an explanation."

"Charlotte told me one more thing," Vernon announced.

"What's that?"

"Elizabeth McFadden was fired because she found out about Charles and Rhonda, not for whatever reason Charles concocted. The fact that Elizabeth is happier near family has eased some of Charlotte's guilt over allowing Elizabeth to be sacrificed."

"I am so naïve," I proclaimed. "But I still don't understand why Charles wasn't fired after that huge matter with Charlotte—after he told virtually the entire city about her possessions."

"Because of one of Charlotte's original reasons—wanting some sort of father-daughter interaction. Remember that Stephanie was still young then. But Charlotte said that Charles has two-and-a-half strikes against him now—one for her incident, one for Elizabeth, and almost one for your departure from MCD."

"My departure?"

"Although she doesn't know why, she blames Charles."

"And why a half?"

"Because she is not certain—she doesn't know what happened. Are you going to tell her?"

I thought for a moment. "No, only Emma knows, and I trust her not to speak. I'm saving the details for the right time and vehicle because my story is not primarily about Charles and me. We are just two chance characters in a vitally important lesson about the future of education."

Vernon looked at me curiously. "Anyway, Molly, in Charlotte's words, Charles will be gone on the third strike. She has no use for him once Stephanie is in college."

"I hope this first disclosure is the last, because I can't deal with any more intrigue," I concluded. I moved from the study chair to the sunroom sofa to think.

80. First Call

One and a half school years have passed since my leaving Merritt Country Day. My precarious anger has subsided, though not to totality. My varied writings have progressed, though not to completion. My publication contacts have expanded, though not to fruition.

The February morning was particularly splendid with cool, crisp air. I walked before working and found the deep breaths and brisk strides invigorating. Then my writing flowed for three hours, page after productive page of pleasing quality. Suddenly, the feeling that my brain needed food broke my rhythm. After a light lunch, I returned to my computer for further work. About a half-hour into my editing, the phone rang.

I answered the phone quickly as usual, after the first sound, because the ringing annoys my thought process. I said hello, not paying attention to who was calling, but rather to what I was typing, again as I normally do.

"Molly?"

With just a single word spoken, I recognized the distinctive voice.

"This is Charles—Charles Long."

Stunned, I immediately detached from my writing and settled comfortably into one of the plum leather chairs so that I could concentrate.

"Hello," was all I said. *The first person to speak loses* was a saying that Vernon had taught me from his business experience.

"Molly, it's nice to hear your voice. I was wondering if you could meet me for lunch one day soon—your choice on Worth Avenue," Charles said awkwardly but very upbeat.

I was offended that he thought he could treat me the way that the Merritts treated him—exerting influence by paying for a nice meal.

"Charles, let's just skip lunch and talk now. What do you want?"

"I heard that you were interested in coming back," Charles said bunglingly.

"No," I replied sharply, feeling Charles's tension.

"Well, ah, oh, I thought I did," he murmured.

"Perhaps someone misspoke," I stated.

"Well, would you consider?" Charles blurted.

"Charles, why are you calling me? You never, ever, called me in all the years we worked together. Why now?"

"Let's just say that all the stars have lined up," he responded with his same laugh, though with a nervous edge.

"The stars have lined up? When did you start following astrology?"

"Molly, look, I want you back," he said boldly.

"Impossible. We won't get along," I said.

"Of course, we will get along. I have tremendous respect for you," Charles said.

"Respect? Don't you remember that you double-crossed me?"

"I remember that you wanted to get somewhat involved in administration, and it didn't work out," he replied.

My entire body shuddered from his manipulated words—his contorted misrepresentation. "Oh, is that what you remember?"

Abruptly changing the topic, he repeated, "Look, Molly, I'm telling you that it will work."

"I don't even know if I still can teach. Maybe I've lost the touch," I stated.

I sensed worry on the phone—but only for a second.

"Don't you have a few of our students coming to your home?" he asked.

"Yes."

"And how is it with them?" he followed.

"Fabulous."

"Then you haven't lost the touch, so forget that idea," Charles insisted.

"This alignment of stars must be quite unusual because you are particularly persistent. So are you going to tell me what actually happened?"

"The parents want you. They are unhappy with the math since you left."

"But why now?" I asked.

"I received a letter—a very persuasive letter from a very articulate parent."

"An attorney parent?" I questioned, enjoying needling him as much as possible.

"What's the difference?"

I felt satisfied that I had received as much truth from Charles as I could expect.

"Charles, I really do appreciate the call, and I don't want to argue with you. So let's just say that the relationship won't work."

"Molly, it's not only going to work, it's going to be great again."

"How do I know that?"

"Trust me."

Suddenly, silence reigned—just silence. I should trust him—the man with no conscience? Was he serious?

"Don't you care about the children?" Charles asked.

"Of course, I care about the children," I replied. "I love the children."

"Then damn it, Molly, come back."

"You don't have to swear at me."

"Come back for whatever you want—a full class, a Saturday morning elective, anything."

"What are you talking about? The kids play soccer on Saturday morning."

"Then a Sunday morning enrichment workshop."

"He's pathetic," Gut Voice suddenly announced. "Shooting from the hip again without a moment of pre-planning."

"Have you ever heard of church on Sunday morning?" I asked sarcastically.

"Then a real course," Charles countered.

"But you already have people teaching my courses. What happens to them?"

"There's room for you and them—I'll make more sections."

"And hurt their feelings," Heart Voice stated.

"Charles, I'm not responding to vagueness. I'll talk to you if you have a specific offer," I said coldly but politely.

"Go back, and he will betray you again—only much worse," Gut Voice proclaimed.

"Okay. I'll call you soon," he stated.

"Good-bye."

"Good-bye."

I hit the off-button on the phone and set it down. I was shaking—trembling from the highest inch of my head to the lowest inches of my limbs. Something was happening at school—Charles was in trouble either over losing me or offering weaker math. I never thought this day would happen, and I was rather relishing it despite my alarm. I missed the smiles of the children. I missed the energy of the classroom. I missed the excitement of the learning. I began doubting my writing. No, I must never doubt my work—it was good, very good. And I could not endure returning to MCD for more pain.

When Vernon came home, I told him about the call—Charles's first call ever. Vernon dismissed it quickly. "See what happens," he said. "Don't commit to anything."

The next morning I decided to enjoy another walk again before writing. Just as I returned, the phone was ringing.

"Molly, it's Charles."

Printed in the United States
24519LVS00006B/124-135